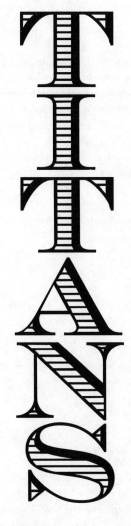

TITANS

BY TIM GREEN

Turner Publishing, Inc.

ATLANTA

Published by Turner Publishing, Inc.
A Subsidiary of Turner Broadcasting System, Inc.
1050 Techwood Drive, N.W.
Atlanta, Georgia 30318

Distributed by Andrews and McMeel
A Universal Press Syndicate Company
4900 Main Street
Kansas City, Missouri 64112

Green, Tim, 1963–
    Titans / by Tim Green. — 1st ed.
    p. cm
    ISBN 1-57036-057-X : $21.95
    1. Football players—New York (N.Y.)—Fiction. 2. Gambling—New York (N.Y.)—Fiction. 3. Organized crime—New York (N.Y.)—Fiction. I. Title
    PS3557.R37562T57 1994
    813'.54—dc20   94-25574
                                                                          CIP

First Edition 10 9 8 7 6 5 4 3 2 1

Printed in the U.S.A.

Dedicated with love to my wife and children,
Illyssa, Thane, Tessa, and Troy
for whom I thank God every day

TITANS

CHAPTER 1

ony Rizzo pulled back the heavy crimson drapes and looked out at the gloomy Manhattan day. Central Park was covered with a blanket of snow, and a gray mist hung in the air. He couldn't even see the Dakota. The barren trees were a dark, inky web against the pale sky. Rizzo smiled and stretched; he had just gotten out of bed and it was already two in the afternoon. It was Sunday, a day to build a fire, sit on the couch in a big soft robe, and watch the game. Then he remembered that he had to work, and he frowned.

But business was business. Rizzo went to his closet, grabbed a T-shirt, and strapped a 9mm Beretta semi-automatic under his arm. He stepped into some ratty jeans and pulled a heavy cardigan sweater on over the T-shirt and the gun. He grabbed a faded army coat from the back of the closet and checked the pockets. In the right was a snub-nose .38. In the left was a silencer—both came from New Orleans and could never be traced. He slipped on a pair of black Reeboks and headed for the door.

"Tony?" called a sleepy voice from the bed.

Rizzo stepped back into the bedroom and gazed appreciatively at the long blonde hair and shapely figure beneath the satin sheets. He loved models. They were like toys, playthings he picked up at the Manhattan clubs that he visited nightly.

"I'll be out for a while," he said. "Stay if you want to. If you leave, just lock the door on your way out."

Rizzo turned his back and let himself out. He knew she'd still be there when he got back. If it was one thing a girl like that couldn't stand it was indifference.

He walked down the hall. Expensive white paper embossed with thin gold columns hung on the walls. Plush red carpet covered the floor. Tony walked past the elevators and headed for the stairs. It was a long haul to the basement, but the old clothes he had picked for today would raise more than a few eyebrows in a building like his, and he wanted to slip out quietly. Only the garage attendant would see him this morning, and Willie was used to his unorthodox comings and goings. Having to sneak about stairwells was enough to make him think seriously about his uncle's repeated requests that he move back to Brooklyn, where the rest of the family lived and where he could come and go as he pleased without having to worry about his privacy.

Mike Cometti and Tommy Keel were parked right next to Willie's booth in an old beat-up maroon Fleetwood. Rizzo gave Willie a wink and climbed into the backseat.

"You wanna coffee, Tony?" Cometti asked as he pulled the steaming cover off a white styrofoam cup and handed it back.

"Thanks, Mikey. Where's Angelo?" Rizzo asked in a displeased voice while absently considering the back of Tommy Keel's head.

"Your Uncle Vinny called him this morning and said he needed him. Ang couldn't think of a reason for saying no to your uncle, since you don't want anybody wise to this . . ."

"Tommy's gotta get his feet wet," Cometti added.

"You up for this, Tommy?" Rizzo said in a harsh tone, looking at Mikey all the while. Mikey shrugged and nodded apologetically.

"Yeah, I'm OK, Tony," Tommy said looking over his shoulder. "Like Mikey said, I gotta get my feet wet sometime."

"OK," Rizzo said flatly. "Let's go."

Tommy Keel put the car in gear and lurched out of the garage into the gloom. He took them straight down Fifth Avenue to Washington Square Park, then wove his way through the narrow streets of Greenwich Village until they found themselves parked in a dirty alley behind a row of buildings just off Bleeker Street. Steam billowed from a grate, and the stench of garbage caught in their throats.

The three men got out and walked around the block to a bar

called Ironside's. The place was only half full, and they were able to find a booth in a dark corner near the back. From there they could observe the other patrons in the bar without really being seen themselves. They ordered three beers from the waitress and settled down to watch the pre-game hype on the big-screen TV.

Before too long the bar was full, but not crowded. Ironside's was not a popular place, but you could always count on the regulars to show up for an event as big as the Super Bowl, this year between the Titans and the 49ers. Mike Cometti spotted an enormous fat man squeezing through the door and taking off his coat. He nudged Rizzo. The Fat Man was wearing a black T-shirt and baggy dark green pants. He was breathing heavily as he made his way to the bar. Two grimy-looking characters vacated their seats to make room. The Fat Man was obviously an important figure at Ironside's.

"There he is," Mikey murmured, his brow darkening.

Rizzo only nodded and took a gulp of his beer. His face turned to stone. The bar got noisier as game time approached.

At the kickoff, everyone except the three in the corner cheered. Tommy glanced nervously at Rizzo, Mikey, and the Fat Man. The longer the game went on, the more Tommy's knee shook under the table. Rizzo counted the empty draft pitchers as they were periodically removed from in front of the Fat Man, who had begun sweating profusely. Both Mike and Tommy ordered another round whenever the waitress happened by. Rizzo nursed his first beer and ordered a second one only at the two-minute warning before the half.

When the half ended, the Titans were trailing the 49ers 17-3. Mikey stood up and turned to Tony, "I gotta piss like a racehorse," he said apologetically.

Tommy slid out of the booth at the same time and mumbled, "Me, too."

Rizzo continued to watch and wait. When his two companions returned, they seemed less uptight. It was well into the third quarter when the Fat Man sent away his fourth empty pitcher.

"OK, Tommy," said Rizzo.

Tommy looked frightened, and Rizzo grabbed Tommy tightly by the arm and shook him a little.

"Go," he said between clenched teeth.

When Tommy had disappeared out the back toward the bathrooms, Rizzo turned his eyes on Mikey.

"You sure about this five-pitcher shit?" he said.

Mikey nodded. "Tony, I told you a thousand times. Every time the Fat Man finishes his fifth pitcher he makes his move on the john. Zeke says he's like clockwork, says the slob would piss his pants if he drank any more without pissing. He says he can't figure how the guy can go that—"

"OK, OK," said Rizzo. "Gimme some snort."

Mikey looked around cautiously, out of habit. Everyone's eyes were on the game. He took a little silver box from his inside pocket and handed it over. Rizzo fished beneath his T-shirt for a tiny gold spoon that hung on a chain around his neck. He took two big snorts, closed up the box, and returned it to Mikey. It was six minutes into the fourth quarter and the Titans were down 20-9 when the Fat Man finished his fifth pitcher.

The Titans were driving and their quarterback, Hunter Logan, ran a bootleg across the fifty-yard line. A cheer went up in the bar. All eyes were fixed on the game. For a moment Mikey was afraid the Fat Man wouldn't leave his seat in the middle of such a crucial drive. Tony would not be happy if he was wrong. Then the Fat Man lurched from the bar and swung his bulk toward the bathrooms.

Logan faded back to pass. All the Fat Man could do was give a fleeting glance before he disappeared into the back. Rizzo and Mikey eased themselves out of the booth and followed the Fat Man as nonchalantly as they could. No one noticed. Tommy Keel was in the back of the hallway. He had checked both bathrooms to see that they were empty, then kept a watch to make sure no one came in from the kitchen. He gave Rizzo a thumbs-up. Rizzo looked back to see that Mikey was standing at the other end of the hallway with his back to the bathrooms. He stuck his hands in his coat pockets and went in.

The Fat Man had somehow wedged himself into the stall. His pants were down to his knees, and his head was bent over in an attempt to see. He relieved himself with an audible sigh. From his pockets Rizzo removed the pistol and silencer. He moved quickly, but appeared to be in no great hurry as he screwed the two pieces together. Finished, he stepped forward, put the barrel of the gun to the back of the Fat Man's skull, and pulled the trigger.

The Fat Man jerked forward but remained nearly upright, wedged in the stall. His feet were crooked and they twitched slightly. His bladder continued to empty into the bowl even after he was dead. Rizzo leaned into the stall and stretched his arm over the Fat Man's enormous back. Carefully he put two more slugs into the Fat Man's brain. He then broke down his weapon and jammed the pieces into his pockets. They would be at the bottom of the East River before the end of the game. Rizzo flipped off the light switch and quickly left the bathroom. He glanced left and gave Mikey a low whistle. Mikey gave a quick final glance around the bar. The crowd erupted in a cheer as Logan connected on a touchdown pass. Everyone's eyes were glued to the TV to catch the instant replay. Mikey turned and followed Rizzo and Tommy out the back door.

With their last drive, the Titans had narrowed the gap, leaving the score 20–16. A touchdown was all that stood between them and the championship. Hunter Logan faded back to pass. He'd missed the blitz and knew none of his receivers were hot. He tucked the ball in tight and prepared for impact. The strong safety hit him at a full sprint. The instant Hunter felt the blow, he spun his body and ducked at the same time. The safety fell uselessly to the ground. Hunter's spin put him outside the pocket, where the rest of the 49er defense was pouring through. His ducking caused the defensive end who had contain to miss him as well.

Now Hunter rolled out to his right, running for his life. Just before he reached the sideline, Hunter leaped in the air, twisted, and launched the ball twenty yards downfield. The tight end, who had seen the predicament, had broken his route to provide him with a safety valve. The tight end caught the ball at the same instant three pursuing 49ers crashed into Hunter, driving him four yards outside the boundary. Yellow flags flew from every direction.

Hunter lay dazed under the pile. He heard cursing and flailing. Above him, his own teammates were violently removing the defenders who lay on top of him. Leading the ruckus was Hunter's best friend, the Titans' nose guard, Bert Meyer. Bert yanked the biggest 49er, Olson Fain, by the face mask and savagely twisted him back to the ground.

"That's our quarterback, you piece of shit!" roared Meyer as he delivered an open-handed whack to the head of the six-foot-six, three-hundred-pound Fain. Another yellow flag was tossed into the melee. Fain would have retaliated with more than a stream of obscenities if he weren't on the Titans' sideline surrounded by the entire team, all of whom were pushing and shoving him. The referees quickly interceded.

"You son of a bitch!" screamed a purple-faced official who had seen Bert's blow to Fain. "That's dirty play, you bastard! Another stunt like that and you're gone!"

Bert paid him no mind. He was too busy helping a disoriented Hunter Logan to his feet.

The trainers and team doctors quickly surrounded Hunter, who was trying to push his way back into the game.

"Hunter!" barked the team physician. "Are you all right?"

"Yeah, I'm OK."

"Hunter," the doctor continued, "what's the score?"

"I don't know. I'm OK."

"Do you know where you are?" the doctor asked.

"I'm OK," replied Hunter as he tried to break free from Bert and the trainers.

"OK, OK," the doctor said, "just tell me how many fingers you see and we'll send you right back in the game."

"Three," Hunter said.

"OK, you guys, get him to the bench," said the doctor as he held up a single finger for them all to see.

Hunter struggled. "Let me go, you assholes! I've got to get in there! I'm gonna win this son of a bitch!"

"Hunter, come on," Bert coaxed, "you'll get back in there. Just get yourself together first."

Time was running out. The Titans sent second-string quarterback Bob Dunham in to replace Hunter. The penalties offset each other, but the Titans still had the ball on the 49er twenty-one-yard line. The Titans ran a sweep that went for twelve yards. The crowd roared. It was first and goal from the nine. With Dunham cold off the bench, the Titans would attempt to run the ball into the end zone.

Dunham fumbled the snap on first down. The Titans recovered, but they were now second and goal from the fourteen. They tried a draw that got them only three yards. It was third down and everyone in the world knew they would have to go to the air.

"What the hell's going on?" Hunter demanded as he tried to peek through the medical staff.

Dunham dropped back and threw a quick and wild ball out of bounds to avoid the blitz. It was now fourth and goal from the four-teen. There were only thirty-seven seconds left in the year's most important football game. A field goal was useless.

Pop Peters, the Titans' head coach, called a time-out and came over to the bench. "Doc!" Pop bellowed. "What's the fucking status? I need Hunter in there, damn it!"

Hunter jumped from the bench. "I'm there, Coach!" he announced.

The trainers and doctors grabbed him by the arms.

"What the hell, Doc?" said Pop.

"I can't let him in there, Pop," the doctor replied. "I don't give a good goddamn if it's the Super Bowl or not. This guy isn't right. He can't even see straight. I won't take that risk. He won't do you any good as he is anyway!"

"Check me, Doc!" Hunter implored. "Check me again!"

Behind them all, Hunter grabbed his friend by the arm. He shot him a quick pleading look. Bert nodded.

"OK," the doctor said, holding up three fingers, "how many?"

Bert gave Hunter three quick pinches on the ass. "Three," Hunter said.

"Wait," the doctor said. "You said that last time. How many now?"

Bert gave Hunter two quick pinches.

"Two."

Everyone looked at the doctor.

"Jesus!" said the doctor. "His pupils are still dilated as hell . . ."

"Time, Coach!" the side judge bellowed at Pop.

". . . OK, go!" said the doctor.

"Roll right ninety-two fade!" screamed Pop as Hunter dashed out onto the field.

When he reached the huddle, Hunter bumped into his center, stumbled, and almost fell.

"Hunter, you OK?" asked Murphy, the center, as Hunter knelt in the middle of the huddle.

"I can throw this bitch in my sleep," Hunter said.

"Get it to me, Hunt," said Matt Brown, Hunter's best wide-out. "I'll make the play."

"No," Hunter said firmly. There was no time to argue. "They're gonna have two men all over you, Matt. I gotta go to Weaver. Weaver, you know what to do. Roll right, ninety-two, fade, on one . . . ready . . ."

"Break!"

The Titans lined up on the ball. Hunter got up to his center. He couldn't really tell what defense the 49ers were in, but he knew they'd send every man on a blitz and go man-to-man coverage on his three receivers. Hunter steadied himself on the center and barked out the cadence.

"Down . . . set . . . hut!"

Hunter dropped four quick steps and rolled three more to his right before he lofted the ball. He was immediately engulfed by defenders. Weaver ran straight to the goal line, then broke for the corner of the end zone. Only when he was two yards from the corner did he look up. The ball was there and Weaver pulled it in, dragging both feet in bounds before he collapsed outside the end zone with the defender on top of him. Touchdown! Weaver jumped up and held the ball overhead for the whole world to see, as the crowd roared its approval.

W hen all the interviews were finally over, Hunter tossed his Farm Aid hat into his locker and took a long, hot shower. Most of the team had showered long ago, and the celebration of their world championship had wound down to the point where most of them had boarded the team buses, which took them back to the Bar Harbor Sheraton in Miami Beach. A single bus remained for the stragglers and their wives, and even they were waiting on Hunter. When he finally left the locker room, two hours after the game, only his wife was left standing there.

"Are you all right?" were the first words out of Rachel's mouth.

"I'm fine, honey," he replied as casually as he could. "Minor concussion. They took pictures of my skull and it's all in one piece, even though they said there's not much in it."

He laughed as they embraced. Rachel had tears in her eyes. Hunter laughed again.

"Now what on earth would you be crying for?" he said to her, kissing her tears.

"I was just so proud of you out there . . . I was scared to death when you didn't go back in the game. I ran down to the railing and they wouldn't let me come over to see you. Then, in you went, and . . . I know how much this means to you. I'm just happy, that's all," she said.

Hunter hugged her tightly.

Someone in the bus blew the horn. When they boarded, Hunter's teammates gave him yet another cheer. Bert Meyer immediately handed him an opened can of cold beer and sat Hunter and Rachel in the empty seats next to him and his wife, Amy. The men talked to each other over the two wives until Rachel finally switched seats. Hunter and Bert went over every single play in the game, laughing over the mistakes they'd made and congratulating each other on their good plays. By the time they reached the hotel, their win and the champagne from the locker room and the beer from the bus had them feeling like they owned the world.

"We do own it," Hunter said.

"To the world," said Bert.

"To the world champions," replied Hunter.

The team party was loud and wild. Most of the players and even some of their wives were drunk. A band played. Everyone danced and sang and hugged and picked one another up off their feet in wild bear hugs. They were all world champions and there was no other feeling like it. It was the dream of every boy who had ever put on a helmet to be where they were right now.

Half an hour after Hunter and Rachel arrived, Mark Sherson, the Titans public relations director, appeared in a black tie and whispered something into Hunter's ear. Rachel watched his face register surprise. He nodded his head and smiled at Sherson, then signaled for Rachel to come close.

"We gotta go," he said to her above the music.

She smiled at him. "What do you mean? We just got here."

"I know, but Mr. Carter is having some private party that he wants us to go to . . . The president is supposed to be there! Can you believe this, Rach, the president!

"Bert," Hunter said, turning to his friend, "I gotta go, buddy. Old man Carter is having some private party and they asked me to show my face, but I'll be back later."

Rachel gave Amy a smile and a wave. She and Hunter quickly left the ballroom. Bert followed them outside and grabbed Hunter by the arm.

"You can't do this, man! Fuck that old geezer and his party! You're our man, not his—" Bert slurred.

"Bert!" said Amy, who had followed her husband.

"Hey, buddy," said Hunter, removing Bert's hand from his arm, "like I said, I'll be back."

"Yeah, but what is this shit, man? You, of all people, you've never jumped when that asshole called. Why are you leaving your boys now to suck up to that money-grubbing asshole? You ain't no brown nose, Hunt . . ."

Hunter tugged Rachel toward the elevator. They stepped in and Hunter gave his friend a light but effective shove as he tried to step on with them. Bert stumbled back.

"You asshole!" were Bert's last words before the doors shut.

"Hunter!" Rachel said as they began to ascend. "I can't believe you did that."

"What?"

"I can't believe you just shoved Bert," she said with a mystified look on her face.

"Aw, he's drunk," Hunter said.

"I know that," Rachel replied, "but why didn't you just tell him that the president was going to be there and that's why you're going? I'm not saying you owe him an explanation, but it would have saved you shoving him . . ."

"Rach," he said, putting his arms around her, "fact is, I'd go to this thing, president or not. I know I'm on top of the world and all that . . . but I'm thirty-four years old. I gotta start planning for the future, and now that I'm on top, I figure it's a good time to start."

"You really did get hit in the head," she said with a serious face.

They both broke out laughing.

"I think it's great, don't get me wrong," said Rachel, seriously this time, "but like Bert said, you of all people . . . You've never done anything they've asked you to do. How many times have you said to me, 'Not me, Rach, I'm my own man. All those big shots can kiss my ass'? Now you're the Super Bowl MVP and we're running right up there as fast as we can."

"I know all that," he said as they reached the top floor, "but I'm serious, Rach . . . I gotta start thinking about life after football. I don't know, maybe it's because I've got it all right now. You know, like how can this last? It can't, and I'd rather have these big shots coming to me offering me a job when I'm done than the other way around. If I snub the old man tonight, I might not get another chance. Not after all the grief I've given them over the past couple of years. And like you've said to me so many times, it can't hurt to at least be sociable."

When the elevator doors opened, they were greeted by two tuxe-doed security guards with walkie-talkies. The guards stared at them from head to toe with looks of surprise. Then they recognized Hunter.

"Oh, Mr. and Mrs. Logan, of course," said one of the guards. "Congratulations on a fine performance, sir. Go right down to the end of the hall, and it's the last door on the right."

They thanked the guards and proceeded down the hall. As Hunter walked, he was suddenly conscious of his clothes. He was wearing cowboy boots, jeans, and a white T-shirt. Only a blue blazer gave him a semblance of formality.

"What about what I'm wearing?" he whispered to Rachel.

"Honey, besides being so handsome that you're every woman's dream, you are the man of the hour," she said, stretching up to kiss him on the nose. "I think you could walk in there with your boxer shorts on, and they'd say it was the latest fashion. You look fine."

Grant Carter III greeted the Logans as if they were old and dear friends. The little man took obvious pride in introducing his quarterback to the various dignitaries from the worlds of business and politics. The men were all in black tie, and the women wore elegant dresses. Hunter did his best to not sound like a country boy from West Virginia. Mark Sherson appeared suddenly and whispered something in Mr. Carter's ear. Carter frowned, then nodded.

"Well, Hunter, I have a bit of disappointing news," he said to Hunter as well as every guest within earshot. "It seems the president will not be joining us tonight. Had something urgent come up back in Washington. He did, however, specifically say he looked forward to meeting you in February at the team dinner."

Hunter nodded. He could think of nothing to say.

"Ah, Camille . . ." Carter said, turning to a beautiful blonde in her late twenties. She was wearing a stunning emerald party dress that was cut low enough to demand a second look. Hunter tried hard to avert his gaze. He knew Rachel would be looking at him for his reaction.

"Hunter Logan," said Carter, "my daughter, Camille. Camille, this is our star quarterback and his wife, Rachel."

"Charmed, I'm sure," said Camille, holding out her hand to Hunter, and then Rachel, but never letting her eyes waver from the quarterback's chiseled face.

"Would you two girls mind excusing the two of us?" Carter said. "I have a few things I wanted to discuss with Hunter, and it will give you two a chance to get acquainted."

Hunter could see that getting acquainted was the last thing on either of their minds, but he gave Rachel a shrug and followed Grant Carter out onto the terrace all the same. After sliding the glass door closed on the rest of the party, Carter leaned out against the railing, snifter in hand, and gazed toward the ocean. "Beautiful, isn't it?" he said.

"Yes," Hunter replied, taking a slug from his beer.

"Hunter, that was an amazing thing you did today . . . Oh, I know everything that happened. You see, today is the reason why I've fought and scraped and battled my way to the top. I've always wanted to be a world champion. And now I have it . . ."

Hunter couldn't help wondering how Carter figured owning the team made him a world champion, but said nothing. In fact, by the time the owner finally stopped talking about all the things he'd done to put the Titans on top of the world, Hunter found he half believed it himself.

"Which brings me to you," Carter said. "I think that you and I have a lot in common, and I think it's time we got to know each other a little better. You have a place out in the Hamptons, don't you?"

"We've got a little beach house just east of Quogue on Dune Road," said Hunter.

"I'm sure you know, then, where our home is in West Hampton?"

"Yeah, we've walked by it plenty, it's huge." Hunter bit his tongue. He knew if Rachel were there, she'd have kicked him for sounding so stupid.

"Of course," Carter said. "Well, if you're not that far, we'll have to get together during the season then—the summer season, that is. Do you play tennis?"

"I . . . yes. I'm not very good, but I have played."

"Well," said the owner, "the worse you are, the better. I have some friends who'd be thrilled to be able to whip the Super Bowl MVP on the tennis court. In fact, I think I'll throw a little party for you at the beginning of the season, just to let you meet everyone."

Hunter knew plenty of people in the Hamptons, but he also knew that they weren't the people the owner was talking about. "That'd be great. I really appreciate it, Mr. Carter. I know I've been kind of . . . well, not exactly sociable since I got traded here from the Vikings, but I'm looking forward to starting to become more involved with things."

"Oh, and another thing before I've got to get back to my guests." Carter seemed not to have heard Hunter's clumsy attempt at humility. "Maybe you and I can work out your contract this summer, just between the two of us. You know how ugly agents and the media can get about these things. Well, I'd like to at least take a shot at you and I sitting down and hashing it out. I promise you, you won't be disappointed."

"Thank you, Mr. Carter, that sounds great," Hunter said, shaking the owner's outstretched hand.

"Good. Now I see that Senator Pilson is waiting to come out here and get my feelings on a few things. Would you mind letting him out on your way in? Thanks, Hunter."

Hunter opened the door and the pudgy senator scurried past him. Before he had shut the door again, Hunter heard the red-faced politician say, "By God, Grant, you really did it!"

Hunter chuckled to himself. He stopped inside the door to slam down the rest of his beer. "What a crock of shit," he said to himself.

Before he could get two steps, a well-dressed man who Hunter guessed to be about fifty-five stepped in front of him.

"Hunter," he said, "I don't want to disturb you, but I'm Senator Ward."

Hunter knew immediately that this was the other senator from New York, who was also the chairman of the Senate Judiciary committee. His face had been all over the *New York Times* in the past few months because of a problem with one of the presidential nominees at the Justice Department.

"Of course, Senator Ward," Hunter said apologetically, "I see you all the time in the paper . . ."

"Well, likewise," the senator said. "In fact, I must confess, unlike my counterpart on the other side of the aisle," he said, nodding his head toward the balcony, "I didn't come here tonight for campaign money. No, the only reason I'm here is to ask for your autograph, for my grandson, you understand."

"Sure, I'd be happy to do that."

"Well," the senator said, reaching into the inside pocket of his jacket, "I have one of your cards here, and it will make his year to have you sign it. I hate to bother you. I know you get this all the time and I don't want to cramp your celebration—"

"Senator, I'm more than happy to do it."

"Well," said the senator, obviously impressed, "I never forget a favor, and a well-received one at that. I hope you'll call on me some-day if there's something I can do."

"Thank you, Senator."

"I mean it, Hunter. A good politician never forgets."

They talked for a few more minutes before the senator had to excuse himself. Hunter looked up to find Rachel. He couldn't wait to tell her.

Rachel and Camille seemed to be talking amicably enough right where he'd left them. As he approached, Camille became silent and excused herself after giving Hunter a final sidelong once-over.

"Bitch," Rachel murmured.

Hunter laughed, "What? You two seemed like you were talking along fine until I pulled up. You're never going to believe who I was just talking to—"

"I just don't like any woman throwing herself at you like that," Rachel said without hearing him. Her face was flushed.

"Rach, all she did was say hello, come on, will you? Talk about antisocial."

"I'm sure you didn't notice the way she looked at you, Hunter," she said with her biting sarcasm.

"Come on, honey," he said calmly, deciding to wait on telling her the news about the Hamptons, "let's get back to the guys."

As the elevator dropped toward the ballroom, Rachel broke the silence. "I didn't mean that. I don't know what came over me."

She stepped close and kissed Hunter on the lips.

CHAPTER

Vincent Mondolffi rubbed his red eyes. It had been a long day. There was a nuclear power plant being built upstate, and one of the union bosses had refused to hire some people on the family's list. The jobs were a good way of returning small favors to thugs who were sometimes necessary to grease the gears of a huge business that operated outside the law. The jobs paid well and the most difficult task for the Mondolffi laborers was collecting their checks. But there had been a misunderstanding and one of the family's soldiers had gotten carried away and grabbed the union boss's twelve-year-old son. Everyone had become excited, and Vincent himself had been asked to intervene.

He didn't like grabbing kids and he told his man to return the kid at once. The problem was one of communication, though. Someone upstate refused to believe it was actually Vincent who was ordering the kid's return. So he'd taken a ride up there to straighten it all out personally. In the end, the union boss begged to be allowed a second chance despite the fact that he already had his kid back, so it all worked out.

Still, the day had been a long one, so when Ears Vantressa told him there was a call on the pay phone, he glared up from his espresso with disgust.

Ears shrugged apologetically and said, "He knew your code."

Vincent Mondolffi nodded and pushed his chair away from the white cloth-covered table There was no one else at any of the other three tables in the small room he occupied. The light was yellow and low, and the room was made even darker by wood-paneled walls and a thick, bloodred carpet. Ears led the way through the kitchen, where the bustle of cooks and waiters quieted as Vincent Mondolffi passed.

In a hallway outside the rest rooms was the phone. Of course, Mondolffi had a phone in his private dining room, but the public phone was necessary to conduct certain special kinds of business.

Dominic Fontane wiped the phone with a clean, white linen hanky before handing it to his boss.

"Yes?" Mondolffi said into the receiver.

"I have some bad news," said the voice on the other end without introduction. "You know about the Fat Man murder?"

"Of course," Mondolffi said.

"You and everyone else. Word is that your nephew Tony had something to do with it—"

"I've heard that."

"Well, when the Fat Man went down, it seems to have gotten the attention of some of the people in D.C. You know as well as I do that the new director is gung-ho after all the families. There's pressure to come up with an indictment of someone who's particularly nasty. You know, to make people feel safe. Well, it seems someone down there thinks this Fat Man thing may be a sign of some instability in the family, especially if Tony had a hand in it. He's been drawing some attention to himself lately. The director himself is sending a supervisor up here to put together a special operation whose only job is to pull a big fish out of your pond. It's unprecedented."

Vincent Mondolffi glanced at Ears and Dominic, then turned his back and hunched over the phone. He didn't want anyone hearing something like this. He'd seen specially assigned task forces become self-fulfilling prophecies. Even when there was no in-fighting, the most stable organizations could boil over when the FBI was snooping around.

"What else?" Mondolffi asked.

"I don't know how this guy is going to handle it. The word is he's to have quite a bit of latitude, but I should be able to keep you up to date."

"Good. I'll be sending you a package."

"Of course," the voice replied.

Mondolffi hung up.

Hunter had done what everyone in America expected him to do after winning the Super Bowl, and when he returned from Disney World he was swamped with cards and phone messages. There were thirty-seven messages on his answering machine, and there probably would have been more if the tape hadn't reached its end. It wasn't until the following week that he was able to meet with Dan Metzler. Metz was Hunter's center and the leader of Pitt's offensive line when he was in school. No one would take Metz for a ball player now, though. He'd gone from a fairly solid two-ninety in his playing days to a sloppy three-sixty in his businessman days. Metz had played five years for the Titans before a bad knee forced him to retire. Like most players, Metz didn't know what to do with his life after football, and he'd gone from job to job relying heavily on his association with the team for opportunities.

When Hunter had first arrived in New York, Metz had been the first person to knock at his door. Like Hunter, Metz was a former farm boy, and Hunter was relieved to have someone like him around to explain the workings of the big city. They had seen each other regularly ever since. Hunter enjoyed his old friend's sense of humor and his lighthearted outlook. Rachel thought Metz was an aimless, drunken slob who was a bad influence. Metz and Hunter talked mostly about the good old days at Pitt, which Rachel couldn't care less about, but Hunter and Metz had been friends before he'd met Rachel and she believed it would be wrong to meddle in such a long-standing friendship. In fact, she was quite nice to Metz, and he thought she was crazy about him. Still, there seemed to be a tacit agreement between Hunter and Rachel that most of his meetings with Metz would take place outside of Rachel's company. This day was no exception.

Hunter drove into the parking lot of the Sherwood Diner and pulled up next to Metz's big old Seville convertible. The car was one of the few things Metz had to show for his five years of service in the NFL. He kept it like new, commuting by train to his job in the city with a big food distributor. The car saw daylight only on the weekends. Metz already had his napkin tucked into his shirt and was working on a platter of eggs and bacon when Hunter sat down.

"How's the market?" Hunter asked as he slid into the red vinyl booth.

Metz looked surprised. "Son of a bitch! I didn't even know it was you, Hunt, with those shades on and that backward hat and the dumpy jacket. Where the hell did you get that? Did you roll some fucking bum in Penn Station?"

Hunter laughed. "It's a good one, huh?"

"Damn good," Metz replied. "No worry about autograph hounds today. I think you kind of like disguising yourself like that, don't you?"

"It's a challenge."

"Well," Metz said, shoveling a forkful of runny eggs into his mouth, "I'm buying today, so order up."

"What's the occasion?" Hunter said, signaling to a waitress.

"What do you mean?" Metz said with a crooked smile as some yolk dribbled down his chin. "You're the guy that won me two hundred bucks on the big game, aren't you?"

"Well, hell, you didn't expect me to say we'd lose, did you?"

"No, but I could've told if you really didn't believe it. You knew you were going to win, and I knew that you knew."

"So why'd you put two hundred down?" Hunter asked, raising his eyebrows and sipping a black coffee the waitress had brought him. "I thought you never went over a hundred."

"I know, I know," Metz replied, "but I felt like I was going at it alone with a hundred, so I called in another Franklin for you."

"For me? I can't bet on my own games, you know that."

"Uh, excuse me, you can't bet on any games, period. You know that, and you don't. I do it for you. I figured if I bet a hundred for you and lost, I could convince you to pay it for me."

"OK," Hunter said, "so I won. Where's my money?"

"Hey, I said I'm buying, didn't I?"

Hunter laughed. "You kill me Metz, you really do."

After Hunter ordered some hash and eggs, Metz said, "You know, I've been keeping track. You're up fourteen hundred on the season."

"Not bad, huh?" Hunter replied. "I guess Hunter knows football."

Metz leaned over the table as far as his gut would allow and spoke in a whisper, "You know, if you ever decided to drop some really big numbers, we could make a killing. For this season you called it right 65.4 percent of the time. Did you know that?"

Hunter thought about it for a minute. "Ahhh, maybe if my contract is super-huge, I'll drop a little more down. Just to keep it exciting."

Although Hunter had been a quarterback in the NFL for many years, this was the first season in which he'd experienced any kind of notoriety. People had known him before, yes, but only the immediate circle of fans of his teams. Now everyone knew him as the world championship quarterback. Part of that newfound fame was an opportunity to make millions of dollars in product endorsements. Bernie Yugotnick, a longtime friend of Rachel's family, also happened to be a powerful figure on Madison Avenue. Bernie had brokered a series of lucrative endorsements beginning the very day after Hunter won the big game. What that meant to Hunter was a series of commerical shoots, photo sessions, and glad-handing with the elite of the advertising world.

For the most part, the whole circus was an annoyance, and Hunter quickly requested that Bernie limit his endorsements to the few highest-paying jobs. The best of these opportunities was with Nike. They put together a five-year, five-million-dollar contract that required Hunter to shoot only one thirty-second commercial each year. That was it. It was a single day's work once a year and the use of his image for five million dollars.

The Nike people wrote a commercial in which Hunter played the role of a sheriff in the Wild West. The horses wore, of course, Nike high-top sneakers. Black Bert and his band of horseshoe thieves were plaguing the town of OK, and it was up to Hunter to shoot it out with the bad guys. Hunter was to appear in a cowboy hat, duster, and a pair of Nike turf shoes to face down Black Bert. Instead of a gun, he was to wear a football on his hip.

The whole thing seemed ludicrous but fun, and Hunter had the leverage to insist that Bert Meyer be allowed to play the role of Black Bert.

"All he has to do is look mean and grunt, and that's what he does best. He doesn't even have to change his name," Hunter said excitedly to Bernie, who pitched the idea to Nike.

Nike agreed. Bernie picked up Hunter in a long black limousine. The big car appeared in the early morning mist, cruising up the

Logans' driveway like a ghost ship. Rachel and Sara were still sleeping. Hunter skipped downstairs like a kid at Christmas. He climbed into the car wearing a foolish grin on his face and shook hands with Bernie. They stopped at Bert's house and then headed to a soundstage in Queens.

Five other members of the Titans team had also been picked to play supporting roles of good and bad sneaker-wearing cowboys. Hunter had chosen his two favorite linemen, Murphy and his left tackle, who everyone knew as "House"; his backup Bob Dunham; and his two favorite receivers, Brown and Weaver, to play the parts. Each of them was thrilled, not only because they had a chance to be in a national commercial, but because each of them would be getting ten thousand dollars to boot.

On the way to the studio, Bernie asked for the copies of the Nike contracts he had sent to Hunter.

"Nothing like waiting until the last moment," Hunter said, taking the contracts from the briefcase he'd brought along. "You got a pen?" Bernie rolled his eyes and took a pen from his inside jacket pocket. "You didn't sign them yet?"

"Nah," Hunter said, taking the pen from Bernie's hand. "I didn't get a chance."

Hunter immediately went to the final page of the first contract and scrawled his signature.

"Aren't you going to at least look them over?" Bernie asked.

Hunter looked up from the papers and said, "Why? I trust you."

"Well, it's not that," Bernie said. "You should be looking at these contracts I've been sending to make sure everything is as you want it to be."

"Is there something wrong?" Hunter asked, raising his eyebrows suspiciously.

"No," Bernie said, "everything's fine. But it's just a good idea . . ."

"OK," Hunter said, and began flipping through the first few pages of the contract he had already signed.

"OK, here's something," he said. "What's this? Morality clause, what's that all about?"

"Read it," Bernie said.

"Come on, Bernie," Hunter said. "Just tell me what the gist of it is. I'm not going through all this junk. All these "whereases" and "wherebys," it'd take me a damn day to figure all this shit out. That's what I've got you for. I trust you, remember?"

Bernie pursed his lips. "Well, the morality clause is nothing really. It just protects Nike's investment in you should you become involved in something that would compromise their image because of their association with you. Say, for instance, that you're picked up on a drunk-driving charge and it winds up on 'Hard Copy.'"

"Yeah, so what happens? Not like that would happen or anything," Hunter added quickly. "I just mean something freaky, like I get caught cheating on my income taxes or something."

"Hunter," Bernie said in a quiet and serious voice, "have you done something crazy?"

"No," Hunter huffed, "I'm squeaky clean when it comes to that stuff, don't worry. I'm just saying what if?"

"Because I have some very good attorneys who can straighten things like that out before they become a problem."

"Bernie! Come on," Hunter said. "I told you. I haven't done anything of the sort. I'm just supposing."

"All right," Bernie said, "you almost gave me a heart attack, but yes, something like that would end your contract. They'd also get remuneration for all monies paid out to you until that time."

Hunter nodded without saying anything, then he looked up. "Well, that's not a problem, so there's no sense even thinking about it. You see? I'm better off just signing these things," he said brightly.

The shoot itself was an all-day affair. Most of the players' time was spent playing cards in a trailer that had been set up for Hunter in the alley behind the studio. There were more than ten different shots for the commercial, and each one had to be set up with meticulous care. There was an actor who had approximately the same build as Hunter who wore a replica of his costume and "stood in" on the set while director and crew got the lighting just right for each shot. Hunter's teammates kidded him about his becoming such a big shot.

During these times the players were expected to keep themselves busy. There was an elaborate buffet and a catering van that changed the fare throughout the day, but the Titans could eat only so much. Bert was the one who broke out the cards, and before they knew it, they were gambling away the ten thousand dollars they were earning for a day of fun.

The shots with the animals took the longest. The crew would get the horses just right, and then one of them would shit on the set and they'd have to clean it and start all over again. It was seven-thirty before they were ready to shoot the final scene. Hunter couldn't believe it took the entire day to shoot a thirty-second commercial, and to cap it off, the last scene took longer than any other. Hunter had to end it by rifling a football at a dummy that looked exactly like Black Bert. The dummy's head would spin wildly in the dust after each direct hit. Hunter missed the first three shots completely. His teammates doubled over with laughter.

"Some quarterback!" they howled.

Hunter eventually got his arm warmed up and was knocking off the dummy's head with every throw. Still, nothing went right and the players had to go through it again and again. It was nine-thirty when the director was finally satisfied and called it a wrap. Bernie had wisely left the set hours earlier. Hunter thanked the director and his teammates, then waved good-bye to everyone else on the set. The limousine was waiting for him and Bert in the now dark alley. Hunter could smell the East River in the night breeze, and the unnatural stillness of the soundstage was replaced with the hum of traffic from the nearby Brooklyn-Queens Expressway.

Hunter and Bert climbed into the limo, ignoring the slurs against their manhood that House was bellowing as he climbed into his own car.

"You pussies!" House cried. "Come drink with us."

"You want to?" Bert asked Hunter as they flopped onto the cushioned seats.

"The hell with those guys," Hunter replied, pulling the door shut. "In the first place, they're crazy. In the second place, they're single."

Bert nodded and said to the driver, "Let's go . . . to Hewlett Harbor."

The two friends said very little during the ride back to Hunter's home. They were both tired. The excitement that had carried them through the day left them drained. Hunter's shoulder was sore from throwing the ball so hard without properly warming up, and his body was stiff from all the standing around on the concrete surface of the studio floor. Finally the car pulled into the drive and up to Hunter's front steps.

"Hey," Bert said, extending his hand before his friend could open the door, "thanks."

"For what?"

"Just for including us."

"Aw, what the hell," Hunter said, trying unsuccessfully to stifle a yawn.

"No," Bert said, "I mean it. You're big time, Hunt. It was nice of you to bring us along with you. Bernie told me about how you made them put me in as Black Bert. It was nice. It really was."

"No problem, buddy," Hunter said, clasping his friend's hand.

"It was fun, wasn't it?" Bert said.

"Yeah, it was fun," Hunter replied, opening the door, "but I'm glad to be back home. I couldn't do that shit every day."

"No . . ." Bert said. "Golf tomorrow after lifting?"

"I can play a quick nine if we're in and out of there," Hunter said.

"You got it, Hunt," Bert said with a broad smile. Hunter watched as the car drove away. He climbed the steps in his costume, smiling at the silly sound of the spurs against the stone and at the amount of money he had made for a day of fun.

Tony Rizzo hated mass. He tuned out the priest and thought about last night. He felt himself getting hard as he remembered the way the girl had moaned and writhed on top of him, the way his hands felt as they stroked her belly and breasts and then wrapped neatly around her smooth, thin neck. He had choked her, not to really hurt her, but to scare her, and watch her eyes bulge and feel her pussy tighten with fear. She had writhed and clawed at his hands and tried to scream.

Tony shifted uneasily in the pew. He glanced right and left at his aunt and his teenage cousin Maria. They would surely see the bulge that protruded from his crotch. He quickly unbuttoned his jacket and folded it on his lap.

It was only to please his uncle that Tony was at church at all. He would have much rather just rolled out of bed around noon like every other Sunday, and shown up for dinner later in the day. But this was Easter Sunday, and just dinner with the family would not do.

Tony looked forward to the day when they would be all out to please him. There'd be no mass then. A dinner maybe, at some place like Gino's on Lexington, something with a little class. He could have the place all to himself for the afternoon. No kids running around. No wives gossiping and bitching. Only the men would sit around, eating and drinking wine and having espresso. This way they could talk about business and pussy. Boy, would that piss off the old-timers.

Tony bowed his head and smiled as the priest said the benediction. He took Maria on his arm and followed his aunt and uncle to the parking lot. Maria rode the four blocks back to the house with him.

"I love riding in a Mercedes," the young girl said as they pulled out onto Lincoln Avenue. "A lot of my friends' dads have Mercedes. My dad says we have to buy American, though. That's why he drives a Cadillac. How come you don't buy American, cousin Tony?"

Tony gave her a big smile. His teeth were perfect and their whiteness contrasted nicely against his tan skin and long dark hair. After that smile he could say anything and it would be gospel to a young girl, especially his cousin Maria, who had adored him for years. Like most of the women who crossed Tony Rizzo's path, she was drawn to his sculptured features and his half-lidded, indolent eyes.

"Sometimes, my angel, things have to change," he said. "But as long as it's for the better, it's OK."

Maria blushed and nodded as if she understood.

Uncle Vinny's house was in the middle of Bensonhurst. It was similar to every other house on the block, modest, painted white, and well kept. There was nothing unusual about the block except that maybe it was a little quieter and a little cleaner than those in other neighborhoods. Out back on a large fenced-in lawn, children ran about in Sunday clothes. There were five picnic tables laid out in the April sunshine. They were spread with fine linen and china. Women bustled about the kitchen talking and cooking. The men stood in clusters around the back patio. Uncle Vinny was already busy in his apron turning sausages and steaks on the grill, just beyond the patio.

As always, Dominic Fontane and Ears Vantressa stood like two over-size statues on either side of the grill. They both wore Ray-Bans, and would have looked silly if Tony wasn't used to seeing them with Uncle Vinny wherever he went. Uncle Vinny seemed to be concentrating hard on the meat, but one at a time the men would break off from the group and approach him. Some of them would talk for a few minutes, others appeared to say no more than two words. Occasionally Vinny would put down his fork and embrace the man he was about to talk to. This is what he did when it was Tony's turn. Then Uncle Vinny kissed Tony on either cheek.

"Tony, Tony," the older man said in a heavy accent, "how's my sister's son?"

"Fine, Uncle Vinny, thank you," Tony said.

"Good, good. We need to talk, Tony, come on . . . here," said his uncle, pointing at two lawn chairs on the grass, "let's sit down."

Tony looked toward the patio. All the men were watching but quickly averted their eyes. It was not often that Uncle Vinny would have someone sit with him on a Sunday afternoon before dinner. Tony tried to appear confident. He casually shook the gold Cartier Panther down on his wrist.

"Now, Tony," Vinny began, leaning forward in his chair and speaking as much with his hands as his voice, "I know what you got in mind . . ."

There was a long silence. Tony was glad it was a bright day and that he wore sunglasses so that his uncle would not notice his furtive glances at Dominic and Ears. Dominic remained motionless, and Ears only stepped forward to turn the meat.

"You want to please me," said his uncle finally. "You want to impress me, and I must say, I'm impressed. You're enthusiastic, Tony, just like your father was, and that's good. But Tony, you're too important to dirty your hands with something like the Fat Man. We have people for things like that."

"Uncle Vinny, I—"

Uncle Vinny held up his index finger. Tony was quiet.

"Now I know, Tony, that I told you someone needed to have a talk with the Fat Man, and I know he was making his own business arrangements on the side, but if I wanted you to get ugly with him, I would have told you, and I certainly wouldn't have expected that you would involve yourself personally, Tony. The Fat Man was an employee, and although he was a disgraceful thief and was cheating the family, I am the only one who decides when a person is no longer useful. When someone is eliminated in today's world, there must first be careful consideration. In this case, there was none, and now the entire family may have to pay the price."

Vincent Mondolffi's eyes turned cold.

"When you killed the Fat Man, you raised eyebrows, here and in Washington. Now there will be a special FBI task force whose sole purpose is to bring down this family. They will be looking at you, Tony, because they know you are a hothead. They figure if you've fucked up once, you'll fuck up again. You're a liability to us now."

Vincent Mondolffi looked off into the sky before he said, "If you were not my sister's son, Tony, I would have to make some kind of example of you."

There was a long pause. Tony tried to swallow, but his mouth was dry.

"But that I will not do," his uncle finally said, turning his gaze back on Tony. "However, this must be the last time we have a talk like this. You understand that, don't you, Tony?"

Tony nodded. "Uncle, may I say something?" he said quietly.

Uncle Vinny nodded.

"I meant no disrespect, none at all. But when I looked into the Fat Man's books and checked around, I found out that he was cheating a little during the regular seasons, but it was during the series and the championship and the Super Bowl that he was taking his big bite. A lot of people, it turned out, knew what he was up to. So, I figured the best way to send a message to everyone on the street was to do him, and do him during the game that he was raping us on."

Vinny nodded. Then he said, "And why did you not tell me this until now?"

"Uncle Vinny, I want to please you. You're good to me, you always have been. I want to do things the way you did when you were my age. I want to work my way up. I'm not afraid to get my hands dirty. I want people to respect me, like they do you—"

"Tony, Tony, Tony . . . respect comes with time, not killing."

"But Uncle Vinny, I always remember you and my father talking about the old days, about how you used to make examples of people and how you'd never ask someone to do something that you would not do yourself. That's what I want. That's what I want to be."

"Times have changed, Tony," said his uncle with a tired sigh. "What we did then, we had to do. We've moved away from that now. We have businesses now that require tact and knowledge and finesse. That's why your cousin Vinny is at Wharton. The family is changing. I don't want you boys to have to do the things your father and I did when we were your age. Drugs and killing and violence, that's for the chinks and niggers and Colombians. I want you boys to have what your father and I could never have—respectability. I want you boys to be able to enjoy the fruits of life. I know you want that too. Look at the car you drive, and that Jew palace you live in. You can't live like that and go around killing people. We have to focus on the businesses. The gambling will be there, of course, that's our lifeblood, but no one cares about that, that's not even considered dishonest anymore. We've got to get the feds and the IRS off our ass. We've got to begin to act respectably, then you and your cousin Vinny can live like kings. That's what I want for the future of this family, respect."

There was silence for a long while. Tony listened to the fat drip from the meat and hiss on the grill. He needed to please his uncle.

"Uncle Vinny," he said, "it's funny you should mention the gambling, because I've been working on an idea that I think could be very good for the family."

Tony waited.

"Go on," his uncle said.

"Well, I met this girl at one of the clubs. Her father is the owner of the Titans. I've been thinking it might be a good idea to get close to this girl's family. Maybe I could get to know the old man a little better. See what kind of guy he is . . . maybe I could even get something on this guy. It's just an idea, but I wanted you to know about it." He concluded as the women started to bring the food out onto the patio and a soft breeze carried the smoke from the grill across the yard. Tony was suddenly hungry.

His uncle considered his proposal.

"I think it certainly can't hurt to keep an open mind," he said. "That's the kind of thing I'm talking about. Those are the types of things that we can do and no one gets hurt. That's how you get respectability."

The two of them sat for a few more minutes. Tony was glad he'd said what he did. The idea had come to him at that moment. He had met that Carter bitch two months ago. And now he'd have to see if he couldn't look her up again.

"Tony," his uncle finally said in a soft voice, "your father and I did what we had to do. You may find times in your life when you'll have to do things that get your hands dirty, but do them because you have to, not because you want to. I'm not unhappy with you, Tony. You're a good boy. Now go and get something to eat. Your cousin Maria is bringing out the salad."

"Thank you, Uncle Vinny," said Tony as he stood, and then stooped to kiss his uncle on both cheeks before walking off toward the tables.

Vinny went back to the grill and took his fork from Ears.

"Dominic," Vinny said, his eyes intent on the meat as he wiped his brow with a handkerchief, "I want you to have someone keep an eye on Tony, and I don't want anyone to know about it. That kid worries me."

If the in-crowd was there, so was Tony Rizzo. In his own mind, he was a celebrity. If the debutantes and stars were likely to be at the Palladium on a Friday night, then Tony Rizzo belonged there, too. With the warm spring weather, the nightclubs of New York came to life as they did at no other time of the year. As usual, Tony arrived in a chauffeur-driven limousine. Angelo Quatrini and Mike Cometti got out first and talked with the bouncers at the door. Tony had done some business with the owner of the club, and the employees knew they were to accord special treatment to whoever was friends with the boss.

Immediately they made a path for Tony. No one could see through the tinted windows, and everyone craned their necks to catch a glimpse of him as he stepped from the car. Without a glance to his left or right, Tony walked into the nightclub.

There was a table overlooking the main dance floor reserved for Tony, and the three friends sat down and ordered drinks. Tony liked to look out over the dance floor because it gave him a perfect opportunity to scan the crowd and select the lucky woman who would be his prey for the evening. This was a Friday night tradition. Angelo and Mikey would sit around getting stoned, watching Tony and laughing at whatever he said or did that was supposed to be funny. Sometimes they would get lucky with a friend of the girl that Tony was hitting on.

At forty-one, Angelo was the oldest of the three. He was also the largest; a big barrel-chested man, with arms as big as most men's legs. He had short dark hair that was only just beginning to gray, and the face of a large, mean dog. He made people nervous.

Mike Cometti was trying to look as much like Tony as possible. He had the same long hair pulled back in a ponytail, the same style Armani suit, the same dark complexion, and even a handkerchief in his breast pocket, just like Tony. The difference was, Tony drew looks from even the most reserved women. Mikey looked like a cheap imitation and never drew a second glance. At five-eight he was four inches shorter than Tony, and the effect was comical, although no one was about to laugh at a friend of Tony Rizzo's.

The three sat for quite a while before Tony said, "That's the one."

Immediately Angelo and Mikey followed Tony's gaze toward the bar and saw a beautiful girl with long jet-black hair. She was petite, but there was no mistaking that beneath the floral summer dress she had a wonderful body.

"I'm gonna tear that up," Tony said loudly so he could be heard above the music. "Mikey, go bring her over here. Tell her I'm gonna buy her a drink."

Mikey got up to go, but there was no need. A young sandy-headed blonde in jeans and a polo shirt turned from the bar, handed the girl a drink, and brought her over to the table without Mikey's help.

"Tommy," Tony said in a loud, friendly manner that made Tommy Keel burst with pride, "how the hell are you, buddy?"

"Good, Tony. Hi, Mikey, hi, Ang." Tommy then turned red. "Guys, this is Sonya . . . She and I went to school together."

"Sonya, it is so nice to meet you," said Tony as he stood up to take hold of the girl's hand. "We never see Tommy with any girls. You sit right down here with us. Here, sit here. Tommy, Ang and I will keep her company while you and Mikey go check on Frank Stern. Mikey just saw him come in and said, 'That guy owes us some money.' I guess you and Mikey worked out some credit for the guy or something, and I know you won't want him to get out of here tonight without reminding him. So you two go ahead and we'll be right here when you get back."

Tommy looked unsure, but when Mikey got up and tugged his arm, he followed. Together they wandered about the labyrinth of people. They covered every inch of the club, but no Frank Stern. Finally Mikey went into the men's room, but instead of looking for

Stern, he took a leak, and then began fussing with his handkerchief in the mirror.

"Mikey," said Tommy after standing idly for several minutes, "don't you think we oughta be looking for Stern?"

"Ah, Stern ain't here, Tommy," said Mikey, who was now patting his hair.

"Whadaya mean? Tony said he saw him and we gotta get that money from him."

"Tommy, don't be so damn thick. What did you learn in college anyway? Seems like you were smarter before you went than since you got back."

"Never mind that, what are we supposed to be doing?"

"All we're doing is giving Tony a chance to get acquainted with your little treat."

"What the hell's that supposed to mean, Mikey?" Tommy said, his face flushed with anger. "Sonya's my girl! Tony ain't gonna be getting to know her, Mikey!"

Tommy turned to rush out, but Mikey grabbed the back of his collar and spun him around.

"Listen, Tommy," Mikey said, putting his face up close, "you ain't been around for a while, I know, but you gotta wise up. If Tony's got his mind set on that bimbo, you just go back downstairs and find yourself another one."

"She's not a bimbo, Mikey! That's my girl!"

"Since when you got a girl? Huh? You ain't said nothing about no girl, Tommy! You'd be a damn fool to make a stink over some bitch just 'cause you got the hots for her."

"You son of a bitch!" Tommy screamed, and shoved Mikey into the sinks.

"Hey!" the attendant said. "You boys gotta take that outside, before I call the bouncers in here to clean your asses up!"

Tommy glared and stomped out back toward the table. No one was there. Tommy turned and shoved Mikey who was right behind him, then raced to the stairs with Mikey in hot pursuit.

The long black limousine was just pulling up as Tommy broke through the entrance. The bouncers and the line of people waiting to get in all turned their attention to the huffing, disheveled man as he warily approached the three figures at the curb.

"No, Tony!" Tommy said in a loud voice that surprised even himself.

Tony and Sonya turned, along with Angelo, who was opening the back door of the car.

"Tommy?" Sonya said with a puzzled and frightened look on her face. "I thought you were already in the car."

"Sonya, come here." Tommy said, returning Tony's hateful glare.

Sonya took a step away from the car. Tony grabbed her arm tightly and she let out a gasp.

"Nooo!" Tommy lurched forward, but was dropped in his tracks when Mike Cometti slugged him in the back of the head with a set of brass knuckles. Sonya started to scream. Tony flung her into the car. Angelo Quatrini glowered at the crowd of people.

A bouncer who was new and didn't know better broke away from the doorway. "Hey! Hey, you assholes! Let her go!"

Angelo walked straight at the bouncer, and then with amazing speed for a man his size he threw a chop to the bouncer's throat. The man fell instantly and lay writhing in pain on the sidewalk. Angelo looked questioningly at the crowd. The only response he got was a shriek from his boss behind him.

While Mikey admired Angelo's work, Tommy pulled himself up and grabbed Rizzo's ponytail as he slid into the car. Tommy gave Rizzo a forceful yank that brought him back out onto the pavement. He grabbed Rizzo by the throat and was actually able to slam his head against the curb before Mikey hit him again from behind. Angelo and Mikey pulled the dazed assailant off Rizzo and tossed him onto the sidewalk. Angelo gave him a quick insurance kick to the groin. Tommy lay in a crumpled heap.

A dazed Rizzo gave a shriek of rage as he got up, and began to kick Tommy violently again and again. Mikey slammed the car door shut as Sonya tried to spring free. The door hit her head and she fell back onto the floor of the car. Rizzo continued to kick the helpless and now bloody Tommy Keel. Sirens could be heard in the distance. Angelo grabbed Rizzo, who was still kicking and screaming that he would kill Tommy, and carried him to the car. When Angelo finally got Tony into the car, he turned to give one final, challenging look at the crowd. No one had moved, not even to help the writhing bouncer. Angelo flashed them all a demonic grin before he too disappeared into the car, which sped into the night.

The city cops were keeping people back and asking if anyone could describe what had happened. Ellis Cook, a handsome but sad-looking man, stepped from the crowd. The cop who was kneeling over the bloody, motionless form of Tommy Keel looked up questioningly at him. Was this tall, sharply dressed black man the only one who would come forward? The cop stood. The black man peered down at his badge.

"Officer Tremont, I'm Ellis Cook, FBI," Cook said, showing the cop his ID.

"So?" Tremont's face turned hostile as he jotted down Cook's name on his pad.

"So, I'd like to ask you a few questions," Cook said, pocketing his badge.

"Listen, I don't care if you're with the CIA. I'll ask the questions. Did you see what happened?"

"Yes."

"Good, then I can get a statement from a professional," said Tremont.

"No, I can't give you a statement, Officer, but I can tell you what happened. And I can save you from wasting a lot of time."

"How's that?"

"Because the man who did this was Tony Rizzo. Heard of him?"

Tremont's expression softened a bit. "Not anything to do with the Mondolffi family, is he?"

"Absolutely, and since you know about the Mondolffis, you also know that you probably won't be getting any statements from anyone, and you probably won't have a victim who'll want to press any charges. And since I've saved you the trouble of finding that out on your own, I assume that you will be a little more inclined to help me. Who is that man?"

Two paramedics had arrived and were loading Tommy Keel onto a stretcher. Tremont pulled a pad out of his back pocket.

"Name's Thomas Keel, age twenty-two. Lives at 1900 South Street, Apartment 7E, Brooklyn." The cop shut his pad dramatically and looked up. Cook was gone.

"Fucking fibbies," he said under his breath before following the stretcher into the ambulance.

Ellis Cook rolled over and hit the alarm clock, knocking it off the nightstand and sending it spinning across the floor, where it continued to buzz. It was six o'clock and Cook wondered why in hell he'd set his alarm so early. Then he remembered the previous night. It was almost too good to be true. He'd spent the past few months studying the Mondolffi family, looking for some way to penetrate their defenses. Without ever seeing him in person, Cook had come to know Tony Rizzo well.

Cook's surveillance work at the Palladium had really been just preliminary. The real investigation wouldn't take place until he had his team set up in an old warehouse he'd found on the west side, just below Canal Street. Once he had his agents together and his plan drawn up, the real work would begin. Cook knew from the FBI profile on Rizzo that the man favored the Palladium. And since the club was not far from Cook's new apartment, he figured he'd try for a firsthand look at one of the most powerful capos of the Mondolffi crime organization. Cook had walked in and spotted Rizzo right away. Then, as if it were scripted, Rizzo and his cronies had whacked out and pummeled one of their own men.

Cook knew he shouldn't have asked the cop who Keel was. He should have gone through channels. But Cook had been in the field long enough to know that sometimes you just had to act on instinct.

He climbed out from under the covers and told himself to stop worrying. That cop wouldn't give him a second thought, and if he did, Cook was certain that the bag of wind wouldn't even be able to remember the name Ellis Cook.

He showered and, drying himself, walked into the kitchen to put on a pot of coffee and pour himself some orange juice. He moved quietly, taking care not to wake his Aunt Esther or his daughter, Natasha. Esther had been with them in Atlanta, even before his wife's death, and Cook considered himself fortunate to have her in New York. Naomi had been in the middle of her residence at Grady Hospital when Natasha was born, and Esther had moved in to care for the child during what they all knew would be a difficult period.

Cook could remember arguing with Naomi about having a child at such an inappropriate time. They were up to their eyeballs in debt. He worked constantly, so did she. He wanted kids but not then, not until she was established in a practice and he was settled in the Atlanta regional office with no need to worry about jumping around the country to fish for promotions. Naomi's practice and his steady government job would have given them all the security they needed. They would pay off all their loans and eventually move into a house in Buckhead, and then they could have kids.

Of course that wasn't how it turned out. Naomi had won out, as she almost always did. Natasha was born. Aunt Esther came to live with them, and they worked at making the best of those trying times. Cook felt his throat tighten. Tears welled up in his eyes. He could think of nothing he wouldn't give to go back and relive those times.

He silently thanked Naomi for her stubbornness. It was painful to think of life without Natasha. He saw more of his wife in her every day, and she was the only thing that kept him going when things got tough. He poured some milk into a glass of ice and then filled it with coffee before placing it in the refrigerator. It was one of the ways he showed his thanks to Esther. Whenever he was up early, he'd fix her an iced coffee, which he knew she loved to drink first thing in the morning. There was no way he could have kept Natasha with him and still worked if it weren't for Esther. Of course, he never told Esther that.

The two of them rarely had anything pleasant to say to each other, and the move north of the Mason-Dixon was something Cook suspected his aunt would never forgive him for. But New York offered the chance that he needed. Organized crime was the number one priority under the new director, and everyone knew that only the best were chosen for New York, the center of worldwide mob activities.

Cook was hopeful that by the time Natasha was a teenager, he would have a position behind a big desk in Washington, and they would have a modest but nice home in one of the better D.C. suburbs in Virginia. Cook had seen more than enough to know the dangers and risks of the urban environment, particularly for a teenage girl. He was determined to at least partly fulfill the dreams he and Naomi had had together. The place they lived in now was small: two bedrooms, a kitchen that was big enough to hold a small table, a living room that was just big enough to hold a couch, and one bathroom. Esther and Natasha slept together. But Cook had opted for tighter quarters that enabled them to live in a relatively safe neighborhood in Greenwich Village near NYU. Also, Cook was a saver. He forced himself to put money away every month. It was money he would use as a down payment on that house in the suburbs.

Cook sipped his coffee.

"Daddy?"

He turned to see a sleepy-eyed eight-year-old in pigtails trying to stifle a yawn.

"Did you kiss me last night, Daddy?" she asked.

"Of course I did, princess," he told her.

"How come you didn't wake me? We're going to the zoo this morning, aren't we?" she said.

Cook tightened the towel around his waist and moved toward her, putting his hand on top of her head.

"We're going, princess. Just a little change of plans is all. I've got just a little more work to do this morning, then I have to see a man in the hospital. Then I'll be back here by lunch to take you, OK?"

He led her to his room and tucked her into his sheets, which were still warm.

"Is the man sick?" she asked quietly.

"Yes, darling, this man is not well at all," he said, bending down to kiss her. "Now you go back to sleep until Aunt Esther gets up. You can tell her I'll be back before lunch, OK?"

"OK, Daddy . . . "

Cook took some clothes from his closet and made his way out of the bedroom.

"Daddy."

He stopped and turned to her.

"It's nice that you're going to see the man who's sick. I don't mind waiting until later."

Cook smiled at her and said, "I know you don't, princess. I love you."

Cook went to the office and pored through the Rizzo files for anything on Thomas Keel. He was only vaguely aware of Keel as a relatively new and junior figure in the family, more like a pledge than a full member. By nine o'clock Cook knew a lot more.

It seemed Keel had originally become involved with Mike Cometti in high school. Cometti was two years older, and the two of them had been busted for grand theft auto in '83. Keel was sixteen at the time, and was released with probation and some community service. Cometti, however, had actually done a couple of months in the Nassau County jail.

Cometti was Keel's link to the Rizzos. Mike Cometti and Tony Rizzo were third cousins. They had always been close, but when Cometti got out of jail, he and Tony had become inseparable. Cook figured Rizzo had somehow made things easier for his cousin during his time in jail and created a fervent disciple in the process.

Cometti was arrested a number of times subsequently, mostly for aggravated assault. Nothing had stuck. Keel, on the other hand, stayed out of trouble after the car theft. He'd gone on to college at Albany State and earned a degree in marketing. But Cook was able to spot Keel in a 1986 photo with Tony Rizzo and Cometti. The shot was taken at a Manhattan nightclub during a birthday party for Rizzo. It seemed that although Keel had kept clean, he had stayed in touch with the Rizzo family through the last six years. Cook suspected that Keel, like so many others fresh out of school, had found that a college degree was no longer a guarantee of good times and prosperity. In fact, it no longer even meant a job. Cook figured that Keel had fallen back in with his old crowd as a last resort.

After what he had seen last night, and after what he now knew, Cook figured Keel was a perfect contact to help him get some dirt on Tony. The bad news was that Keel was so obscure and so far from the inner workings of the Mondolffi family that he probably had almost no information of any value. Still, Cook knew that there were long shots out there. And even though Keel himself would probably prove useless, he might provide Cook with some ideas about another member of the family who might have what he needed.

Cook had just put all his files back in order when Duncan Fellows appeared in the doorway wearing a golf sweater and slacks. Fellows was an assistant special agent in charge, or ASAC, of the FBI's Manhattan office. All the supervisors in Manhattan reported to him. In New York only the special agent in charge and the assistant director were senior to him. Fellows was tall and handsome with a full head of silver hair and just enough of a potbelly to let you know he was used to the good life. He looked every bit the part of the successful Princeton graduate he was.

"Cook!" said Fellows in a surprised voice, pointing at him with the stem of his pipe. Cook and his boss were about the same age, but Fellows's pipe and demeanor made him look ten years older. The difference made it easier for Cook to call him sir.

"What brings you here on a Saturday morning?" Fellows asked. "I thought you people from the South liked to rest on the weekends."

"Well sir," said Cook with a pleasant smile, "I figured if I was going to teach you Yankees anything, I'd have to work overtime."

"Ha! Well put," Fellows said, stabbing the air with his pipe.

"And what about you, sir?" Cook said, despite being uncomfortable with small talk.

"Oh, just brushing up on a few files of my own before I hit the links, ahh . . ." Fellows frowned, "the golf course . . . I'm playing with some of the director's top people from Washington."

"Oh," Cook said, doing his best to make some small talk. "Where are you taking them?"

"Uh, to my club, the Montclair Country Club . . . We'll have to go there sometime."

Cook knew his boss didn't mean it. He sat silently for a few moments, wanting to talk about his possible breakthrough, but not wanting to mention last night until he'd had a chance to talk to Tommy Keel to see if he would be willing to cooperate in any way. The ventilation system for the building was off for the weekend and Cook was hot and uncomfortable as he waited for Fellows to leave his office.

Finally, Fellows said, "Well, I'm off, Cook, good talking with you. I'm looking forward to reviewing your plan on the Mondolffi family. Two more weeks?"

Cook nodded. "Yes, sir. I'll have the team assembled by then. I've already signed a year lease on our offices."

"Good," Fellows said and disappeared.

Cook took a cab to New York Hospital, where he learned they had taken Keel the night before. He checked with information to get Keel's room number, but when he found it, the room was empty. The nurses at the station were surprised when Cook asked them where Keel had gone.

"He shouldn't have gone anywhere," said a nurse. "He wasn't supposed to be released until tomorrow." Cook thanked them. He looked at his watch. It was ten o'clock and he probably had enough time to make at least an initial contact with Keel and still make it back by noon, so he flagged a cab and headed for Brooklyn. The cabbie knew where South Street was, and together they located the address the cop had given him. It was a typical brick mid-rise. Cook walked up to the Indian doorman, who was sitting on a chair in the lobby, and asked for Tommy Keel.

"That's seven E," the doorman said in a heavy accent, without looking up from his newspaper.

"No," Cook said, holding up his hand as the man reached for the phone on the nearby desk.

"Sorry, I got to call before you can go up. I lose my job."

Cook cursed to himself, then looked around. No one was there, and he had found that the best way to get things done quickly and quietly was to let people know that he was one of the good guys. He flipped his badge out.

"OK?" Cook said. "You make sure you don't call."

The doorman glanced at the wallet that was now closed, then seemed to consider Cook's hard brown eyes before he dropped his head again and nodded yes.

Cook stepped from the elevator on the seventh floor and rang the bell after locating Keel's apartment at the end of the hall. After several more rings, a voice from behind the door said, "Who is it?"

Cook had already figured that with a nice boy like Keel, the way to play it was straight up. "My name is Ellis Cook, I'm with the FBI. I think it would be in your best interest to open the door and let me in to talk."

There was silence for almost a minute before the door opened. Cook's face remained impassive as he assessed Keel. One eye was reddish purple and swollen shut. There was a gauze pad taped to his forehead that was stained with blood. One cheek was discolored, and his lower lip was stiched together. A tiny end of thread protruded near the corner of his mouth. He seemed stooped and Cook suspected there were some broken ribs as well.

"Who are you?" Keel demanded again.

"Like I said, I'm Ellis Cook, and I'm with the FBI."

Cook held out his ID, and Keel peered at it suspiciously through his one good eye.

"What do you want from me?" Keel sounded angry, but Cook detected some fear in the young man's voice as well.

"May I come in and sit down? I want to talk with you about Tony Rizzo."

"Why should I talk to you? Am I under arrest? I don't have to talk to you."

"You don't have to talk to me, that's right," Cook said harshly, realizing just how green this kid was, "but you better take a look in the mirror and think about it 'cause in case you hadn't noticed, you got yourself some problems."

Then in an easier tone he added, "I might be able to help you, and if I can't, well then, I'll just go and you'll be no worse off than you were before I came. Besides, if I really wanted to talk to you, I could just take you in for something."

Keel thought about it. "OK," he said finally, and led Cook into the kitchen to sit down at a small table. Cook decided to press him a little. He felt lucky.

"I'm with a special office within the Bureau that investigates organized crime. We know about you and Rizzo, and we know about your recent activities. I'm here to give you a chance to help yourself."

"Tommy?" came a soft voice from the hallway outside the kitchen.

Both men glanced up. Cook quickly returned his gaze to Keel, not wanting to stare. It didn't take more than a glance for Cook to know that the girl had been beaten and choked. Both eyes were black and there were discolored finger marks on her neck.

"Go in the bedroom, Sonya," said Keel firmly, but not meanly. Keel eyed Cook and wondered if he'd seen the shape his girlfriend was in.

"I know about last night," Cook said, changing tactics. After what he'd seen, he figured there was little need to try to scare the boy into helping him. He figured the kid was scared shitless, like a man in a lion's cage. But take that same man out of the cage and he'd be the first one to shoot that cat through the bars. After the way he'd reacted to the girl, Cook suspected that given any safe opportunity, Keel would do anything he could to hurt Tony Rizzo. Cook stared intently at Tommy. The boy was clearly shaken and scared.

Tommy tried to hold Cook's stare, but his battered lip begin to quiver. Tears fell down his face as he slammed his fist on the table with rage.

"The son of a bitch! I'm going to kill him!" sobbed Keel. "I'll kill him!"

Cook remained impassive until Keel composed himself. "Like I said, I think I can help. Now, both you and I know that you're not going to kill Tony Rizzo. But you can do worse than kill him. You can help to ruin him. There are things you can do to help me take him down, and believe me, if Rizzo goes to jail, it'll hurt him worse than death."

"Even if I could help you . . . they'd kill me," Keel said, wiping his face on the sleeve of his jean shirt.

"If you help me," Cook said, "I can get you and your girl out of here and into the witness protection program. For years the federal government has been protecting witnesses from organized crime. I can put you someplace where the Rizzos can never find you, where you and your girl can have a new life. You're finished here, whether you help me or not."

Keel put his elbows on the table and ran his hands through his hair. Cook let some time pass. Finally Keel said, "If I was to help you, what would I have to do?"

"I want Tony Rizzo. The way I see it, he's positioning himself to take over the family. There's no sense going after the old man. By the time I got him, Tony'd be in charge anyway. I'm going to want you to tell me everything you know about the family, no matter how insignificant. You may not think so, but there may be something you know that will help me put Rizzo away."

"Huh! That's not even hard. I can fry his ass for you easy." Keel raised his eyes and looked directly at Ellis Cook. "He's the one who hit the Fat Man."

Cook's heart pounded.

"The Fat Man . . ." Cook said.

The Fat Man murder had been a front-page story for a week after the Super Bowl. No one had guessed that someone connected with the Mondolffi family had been responsible. The Fat Man had been a lucrative source of income for the family.

Murder one would put Rizzo away for life. How could Keel have that kind of information? Maybe the kid was jerking him around.

"How could you know about something like that?" Cook asked.

"I was there," Keel said flatly.

Cook felt a rush of adrenaline. Something like this came along once in a lifetime. It was almost too good to be true. It was luck that he had seen the blowout between Rizzo and Keel last night. His investigation hadn't even officially begun. Now, less than twenty-four hours later, he held the key to possibly one of the biggest organized crime busts of the decade. Tony Rizzo was more than the future head of the Mondolffi crime family. He was a symbol who glamorized crime. If Cook brought him down, his career opportunities would be boundless. There had never been a black director . . .

"You were there?" Cook said, wanting to be sure.

"Yeah, me and Mike Cometti and Tony went to Ironside's. When the Fat Man went to take a leak, Tony went in and whacked him. Cometti watched the front, and I covered the back."

"The gun?" Cook asked, knowing it was far-fetched, but so was this whole thing.

"In the East River."

"Tommy," Cook said, snapping out of his daze and rising to his feet, "you have to stay here. I mean, don't leave this apartment, not for anything. I want you to lock the door and don't answer it for anyone. Don't answer the phone either. It sounds crazy, but it won't be for long. After last night Rizzo might be keeping an eye on you, especially with what you know about the Fat Man."

"Do you think?" Keel said nervously.

"Probably not. Rizzo has no reason to suspect that someone from the FBI was standing outside the Palladium last night, but I'm kind of . . . overly cautious, you might say. But on the million-to-one odds that they've got someone keeping an eye on you, I just want you to lay low until I can get a team in here to bring you out. I'm going to try to get back to you by tonight, tomorrow at the latest."

"I don't know about this . . ." Tommy said, standing and pushing his hands through his hair rapidly.

"Tommy, there's nothing for you to know," Cook said, taking Keel by the shoulders. "You're in it now. But I can promise you that this is the best way out for you. Especially if you want to have any kind of life with that girl.

"Now," Cook said, moving to the door, "is there a way out the back through the stairs?"

"You're leaving? Just like that? I gotta think about this. I gotta be sure."

"Tommy, every minute I stay here is a chance that Cometti, or Angelo Quatrini, or even Rizzo could stop by here to smooth things over with you, or to keep an eye on you. I hate to put it to you like this, but you've got nothing to think about. If you back out now," Cook thought for a second, "I'd be forced to subpoena you, and the Rizzos would have your ass. You just do what I say, and before you know it you and your girl will be safe."

Cook pulled a card out of his inside breast pocket and handed it to Keel. "This is my card. If anything at all happens that makes you nervous, you just call me. My home number is on the back. You probably won't need it, but like I said, I'm overly cautious. You sit tight now. I won't ring, I'll knock, like this, three . . . two . . . and one, so you know it's me. Anything else and you just sit tight. I'm on your side, Tommy. Everything will be all right. OK?"

Keel closed his eyes shaking his head. Then he said, "OK," and nodded.

"OK, call me Cook."

"OK, Cook."

"Good. Now, how can I get out of this building without anyone seeing me?"

"If you go down the stairs to the basement, you can head to the back of the building and get out a fire door, but there's an alarm on it."

Cook patted him on the shoulder. "I'll handle the alarm. You just sit tight and I'll be back before you know it."

"Tomorrow, right? You'll be back by then?" said Keel.

"No problem," Cook said, and left.

Cook took a cab back to Manhattan. Natasha was dressed and ready to go when he walked in at twelve-fifteen.

"Daddy!" She ran to him and hugged him. "Aunt Esther said you wouldn't be home by one, but I told her all morning that you were coming! Now she's wrong and she has to buy me an ice cream!"

Esther was dressed in a housecoat which, like her hair, was almost white. Her wiry frame shook violently. She was washing something in the sink, and she didn't even look up to greet Cook. Her dark hatchet face was intent on scrubbing some vegetables that would no doubt end up on Cook's dinner plate.

He held his little girl's face in his hands. His heart sank.

"Princess," he said, "I'm going to give you and Aunt Esther money so you can both have ice cream, two if you want. But I've got to go back to work. I don't want to, but something very, very important has happened and I have to go."

Her eyes wrenched his heart, so did her words. Both were sad but resigned.

"That's OK, Daddy," she said. "I know it's important. You go ahead. I can do my homework. Then if you get home tonight, we can watch a movie."

Cook stared at her. He saw Naomi. He heard Naomi. He had to leave. He kissed his daughter, then allowed Esther the brief privilege of meeting his eyes with her reproachful glare before he walked out onto the street.

Cook went to the FBI garage and signed out an old olive green LTD. He drove uptown and headed to New Jersey through the Lincoln Tunnel. He had never been to Montclair, but had gotten directions at the garage. Soon he was twelve miles west of the city, winding his way through tree-shaded streets lined with beautifully maintained Victorian homes. These warm and welcoming houses distracted Cook. They were what he would love to be able to afford for Natasha. He envisioned her wheeling up one of those long driveways on a bright yellow bicycle.

Although he had no problem finding the country club, Cook was confused as to just how he was supposed to enter. He ended up entering the club's circular drive the wrong way, and found himself face-to-face with a sour-looking old man sitting behind the wheel of a new Mercedes. The old man sat staring bitterly at him until Cook backed out of the drive and onto the street. Feeling foolish, he circled again and followed a big white Town Car through the club's front gate.

He had never been to a country club. Cook didn't golf, and his social life had never extended beyond a friendly poker game or a neighborhood barbeque. He felt self-conscious in his toned-down government car. When he pulled up to the porte cochere, three attendants dressed entirely in white and wearing caps bearing the club's crest looked at him curiously. Cook rolled down his window and said, "Hello, I'm looking for a club member, Duncan Fellows. Do you know where I can find him?"

The attendants looked confused.

"Look," Cook explained, "I work with Mr. Fellows, and it's important that I talk with him right away."

The tallest and skinniest of the kids evidently knew just who Duncan Fellows was and put two and two together.

"You with the FBI?" he asked.

"Yes," Cook nodded, relieved that he was getting somewhere.

"I saw Mr. Fellows and his party on their way to the tenth tee not too long ago. You should be able to find him on eleven or twelve by now."

When the kid saw the confusion on Cook's face, he pointed to a wide asphalt path that wound past the putting green and curved around a stand of large oak trees and out of sight.

"You just get on that path and keep going past those trees until you see him," the kid said. "One of his foursome is wearing a pair of bright green pants, so you should be able to pick them out OK."

"Thanks," Cook said, then rolled up his window and set out down the path in his old LTD.

He was so intent on finding the eleventh tee and not missing the green pants that he didn't notice the kids yelling at him to stop. When he rounded the bend he chugged past a foursome who were teeing off at the tenth hole. They stared mutely and pointed at him. Cook wondered if the club was restricted. He fumbled in his jacket pocket for a piece of gum, not once taking his eyes off the course that stretched out ahead of him. Cook passed another foursome on the green, then another on the eleventh tee. They all gaped. He rounded a bend right before the green on number eleven. Someone had left a golf cart squarely in the middle of the path. Cook swerved frantically to avoid it, and his car ripped through some soft turf before he was able to get it back on the path.

He was relieved when just past another group of trees he saw the bright green pair of pants. Then he saw Duncan Fellows, who was about to tee off. Cook eased to a stop behind his boss's golf cart. He waited for his boss to finish his swing before he got out. He heard the yelling before he was out of the car.

"Hey!" came a shout from the direction in which he'd just come. "Hold it right there!"

Cook turned to see a middle-aged man striding importantly toward him. The man wore a tweed cap and knickers. He was nothing more than a club member that took himself too seriously, Cook thought. His face was flushed and his angry blue eyes scowled at Cook from behind round rimless glasses.

"You get your ass out of here, mister!" the stuffy club member commanded, stabbing his finger at Cook's chest. "The police are already on their way!"

Three other men appeared behind the bespectacled man, one of whom was talking into a cellular phone, evidently to the Montclair police. Cook had to smile. He was about to tell the cranky son of a bitch that he was the police when he heard his boss's voice.

"Cook!" roared Duncan Fellows as he stepped down off the tee. "Cook, are you mad? What in God's name are you doing here?"

"You know this man, Duncan?" the man said incredulously. "This maniac just went racing by us on eleven. It's a good thing we were on the green, or one of us would have been killed!"

"I . . . are you all OK, Don? Did anyone get hurt?" Fellows was red from embarrassment. The man and his party all shook their heads.

"But he drove right out onto the fairway!" Don bellowed.

"Don, gentleman . . . please, I'm sorry. Go back to your game. I'll take care of this." Before the men were even out of earshot, Fellows turned his fury on Cook. "What are you doing here like this?"

"I needed to see you," Cook explained. "The boys at the clubhouse said to just come down this path and I'd find you. I need to talk to you! I have something that you're going to want to hear about."

"Cook goddamn it! You're drunk or something! No one drives a car out onto a golf course, and there isn't a kid that works at this place who'd even think of telling you to do it!"

"Christ, sir," Cook said, "I didn't mean to embarrass you. I didn't know I couldn't drive on that path. But listen to me," he continued forcefully, "I've got something that's vital to our operation!"

"Cook, goddamn you, you're not even in the field yet! How in hell can you have anything that would cause you to do this!"

"Sir, please, listen to me! You've got to hear me out! I saw something last night by chance. It was one in a million, but it led me to someone within the Mondolffi family who can pin the Fat Man murder on Tony Rizzo. He was there! He says Tony pulled the trigger! Tommy Keel, you wouldn't know him, he's nothing, but he was there, and he's ready to sing. I've got Tony Rizzo! We can hamstring the entire Mondolffi operation! Now do you see why I'm here?"

Fellows turned to see if his guests had heard all this. But they had politely remained on the tee and were talking animatedly among themselves.

Fellows turned back to Cook and in a low voice between clenched teeth said, "You get yourself home, Cook. You sleep it off! I want you out of here!"

"But, sir! I need a team to get Keel and his girl to a safe house. Rizzo may be watching him!"

"Cook," Fellows hissed, "if you could hear yourself talk you'd know how absurd you sound. You don't need a team, but you may need a job! You have your ass in my office first thing Monday morning, and you better have a written apology to the members of this club! Now take that damn car and get the hell off this course, Cook! And I don't want to even hear your name until Monday morning!"

Fellows turned and ascended the grassy slope that led to the tee. Cook couldn't remember the last time he had been so humiliated. He cursed to himself and as gently as he could he turned his car around before easing back down the cart path amid the stares of outraged club members.

Fellows returned to his party.

"I'm sorry, gentlemen," he said, "just a little confusion with one of my supervisors of all things. Damned embarrassing I must say."

"What was the problem?" asked Miles Zulaff, the director's first assistant.

"Seems Ellis Cook, the new supervisor for the special task force on organized crime, needed to tell me something that couldn't wait. Then it seems one of the club attendants told him where to find me. Why on God's green earth he drove out here in his car I really don't know."

"What was so important?" Zulaff asked, pointedly ignoring the comment.

"Nothing really," Fellows replied. "He's not even in the field yet, it was just some crazy idea he had . . . wanted my opinion on it."

"What did you tell him?"

"I said it could wait and I'd talk to him first thing Monday morning," Fellows replied as he stepped up to the tee.

W

ell," Hunter said, turning the radio off after hearing the big announcement in the sports world, "all the waiting is finally over."

Pop Peters had retired a few weeks after the Super Bowl. The Titans had taken their time in naming a new guy. Since the player personnel department was separate from the coaching staff, Grant Carter didn't feel the urgency that some other clubs might have felt with the draft only a few days away.

Pop's replacement was a man named Martin Price. After a highly successful tenure at Notre Dame, where Price had brought the Irish back to their days of bygone glory, he was awarded the plum of an NFL job. Some sports pundits argued that the New York Titans job was a no-win situation. If the team won the Super Bowl again, well, they were supposed to. They were, after all, the defending champions. If, however, they did anything but repeat their prior championship season, then Martin Price just wasn't the coach that Pop Peters was. Still, all in all, it was better to come in to a program that was already on the winning track. Hunter believed in a saying that Pop Peters had often repeated: "Nothing helps you win like winning."

"I still can't get over Pop Peters retiring," Rachel said. She knew Pop had been Hunter's favorite coach in all his years of playing in the NFL.

"I know, me too," Hunter said. They were cruising down a rural highway, and the terrain was beginning to look familiar. "But like I said all along," Hunter continued, "the guy sure went out on top. I mean, really, that's the way to do it. He'll always be considered a winner leaving the way he did. That's the thing players never do. You never see a player going out on top. These guys always beat it into the ground."

"Would you ever retire now?" Rachel asked, with a thinly veiled note of hope in her voice. "You're on top, too."

Hunter chuckled. "I've got a lot more years in me, honey. I'm just finally getting started."

Even she knew that was part bluff. He was one of the oldest players on the Titans, and getting to be one of the older guys in the entire league.

"Besides," he added, "I can't exactly afford to quit. Especially now with my contract up. We'll be looking at some big money this year. We need it, too."

"You don't have to play, Hunter. We could live with less. We don't need both houses. We don't have to live in the Harbor either."

"I know, I know that's how you feel. But I like that house. I like the place in the Hamptons. I like our lifestyle, too, and so do you, honey."

"I know I like it. I'm just saying that if you decide you want to quit playing and give your body a rest, I could do without all that. I'd rather have you healthy."

He pulled off the road and guided the big car up a narrow gravel drive. As they climbed the hill that led to the house, a wonderful view of the surrounding mountains unfolded. Trees everywhere were exploding in a full bloom of bright, lime green leaves. May was the prettiest month in West Virginia, and Sunday had always been the best day on this farm where Hunter had grown up. He tried to return every year. He had a break right now for a few days from the off-season training schedule before the team had to report for its annual mini-camp.

Most of their sprawling farm was gone now, sold to developers. The earth had been stripped of its coal and the scars had never healed. But his childhood home still looked the same and the barns were still standing, though they had faded and sagged in the years since Hunter's father had them painted a brilliant red. The colonial homestead had been built atop the hill in 1758. The dozen or so trees that surrounded it, enormous oaks and maples, were centuries old. Hunter couldn't help the feeling that every year he returned, the place looked smaller. Still, he felt good.

"Home," he murmured.

"What's that, honey?" Rachel asked.

Hunter smiled at her. If no one heard her accent, they'd think she was born in these hills. She wore cowboy boots and one of his plain white T-shirts tucked into her faded jeans. Her glossy black hair was pulled back in a blue bandana. She had removed all her jewelry except for her wedding band. One thing about Rachel was that she could fit in anywhere. Before Hunter knew it, she'd be in the kitchen with his sisters and his mom and they'd all be clucking away like hens.

"I was just thinking that it feels good to come back here," Hunter said.

"Even though things have changed?"

"Yeah, I was thinking about that too. It would be nice if the whole farm was still together, but . . . well, things change, you know. I was thinking that it's good that the house is still here."

"Thanks to you," Rachel said.

"Honey . . ."

"I didn't mean it badly, you know that. I just meant that you should feel good about what you've done for your family. In a way, you really kept them together."

"Thanks, Rach, it's nice to hear you say that."

"Well, someone's got to," she replied as they pulled up to the house.

Hunter turned off the engine. Sara jumped out and headed for the barn, where she knew she would find her cousins and their new kittens. Hunter remained still.

"Let's just not get anything started, OK?" he said. "We're only going to be here for two days, so let's make it smooth."

"Hunter, I won't start anything. I never do. But I won't let your brother lay a guilt trip on you either."

"Honey, admit it, you just don't like Henry."

"That's not true. I do like him, but he makes me feel strange. It's more than being your twin," she said.

No matter how much Rachel prepared herself, she could never get used to the odd feeling it gave her to look at Hunter's brother. Besides his clothes and full, thick mountain beard, the two of them were indistinguishable. Even Henry's build was the same. Working around the house and barn whenever he had a free moment had kept him in just as good shape as Hunter's weight lifting and running for football. In fact, part of Rachel's uneasiness with Henry came from the last time they had visited. She'd come up from behind him and wrapped her arms around his waist, thinking he was Hunter.

Henry had been born three minutes before Hunter, and for that he had always been the older brother. In a family whose English ancestors had been among the first white men to settle this region, being the older brother meant a lot. It was Henry who had inherited the farm, as other Logans had for over two hundred years.

"Sometimes I feel bad for him," Hunter said. "I know it's hard for him, seeing how different our lives are."

"My gripe is this," she said. "You were the one who saved this place. Your hard work. Your money. Everyone, even your mother, fails to recognize that."

"Honey, it's different. My family is different. I know you don't understand, just like I don't understand a lot of things that go on in your family. But it's just that what I did isn't something you talk about. It's what was expected. It's what any of us would have done for the others, especially with my dad gone."

"I know that," Rachel returned, "and I don't expect them to fall down and worship you. I don't even expect them to thank you anymore. But I can't let your brother lay everything bad that's happened to this family on you when he's the one, if there's anyone, who's to blame, and when you were the one to save this house where he lives."

"OK, OK, look," Hunter said, throwing his hands up and bringing them down hard on the steering wheel. "We can't get into all this again right now. I'm not going to start arguing with you just because you're looking out for me. But, Rach, I'm a big boy. I can look out for myself on this one. Please. Please, just don't say anything. For me?"

They sat looking at each other. Hunter smiled. Then Rachel smiled. "OK. Let's go in," she said.

Sunday was Vincent Mondolffi's favorite day as well. It was the one day when things were quiet and relaxed in the city. He rarely conducted business. Everyone knew that whatever had to be done could wait until Monday. Sunday was a day to talk and eat and laugh and be with the family. So when Ears told him the phone call was urgent, he looked surprised. Family members up and down the table were suddenly silent. He pulled the white linen napkin out from his collar and dabbed a bit of red sauce from the corner of his lip as he rose from his place with a frown.

"Mr. Mondolffi" came a voice over the phone that Mondolffi recognized as one of his many sources for valuable information. "I have some important news for you."

"Yes . . ."

"Yes. It may require some action today, otherwise, of course I wouldn't have bothered you at your home on a Sunday."

"Go on."

"Your nephew Anthony, he has a friend by the name of Tommy Keel?"

Mondolffi thought for a moment. "Yes, Tony has a friend by that name."

"Yes, well, it seems that your nephew is a little careless in choosing his friends. This one seems to be quite willing to talk to people who are not what you'd call sympathetic to the family. In fact, he had a visitor yesterday from a certain federal agency. This visitor's not tough to spot. He's black."

"What kind of things could Keel have to say? He is nothing."

"Wasn't he with Anthony when a final call was paid to the Fat Man?"

"The Fat Man! Was he?"

"That's how I understand it. And Keel is ready to take a long vacation—maybe to someplace safe, where you might not be able to find him."

"I realize the importance of this information," Mondolffi said in an uncharacteristically thankful tone. "It will not go unrewarded."

"It hasn't so far, Mr. Mondolffi."

"Would you also like to take care of this problem?"

"Now, Mr. Mondolffi, you know I don't involve myself with those types of things."

"Of course not," said Mondolffi with a jovial laugh, "but I like to ask you just to be polite. I thought you might like some extra work."

"Mr. Mondolffi, our current arrangement is more than satisfactory. I thank you. Good-bye, Mr. Mondolffi."

Mondolffi hung up and right away dialed another number.

"Angelo?"

"Yes . . ." said a heavy voice that immediately came to life. "Yes, Mr. Mondolffi!"

"Angelo, I have something I need you to do . . ."

When Cook finally awoke, he cursed himself. Sunlight had filled his bedroom long enough to make him sweat under the covers. His tongue felt swollen and hairy. His mouth was dry and his head pounded. An empty bottle of Jim Beam lay on the floor. Cook felt sick. He stumbled to the bathroom and retched. Nothing came up. Natasha and Aunt Esther were gone. He assumed they had gone to church, and he returned to bed.

Cook had gotten home the day before in time to take Natasha out to dinner. Afterward they rented *The Little Mermaid*, her favorite movie. He botched the night, though. He was completely distracted throughout dinner and during the movie. His mind just would not let go of the humiliating scene on the golf course, and the danger he sensed Keel and his girlfriend were now in. Natasha was perceptive enough to sense his withdrawal, and when the movie was over, she kissed him quickly and ran into her room. Instead of making up for leaving her during the day by being attentive, Cook's remoteness increased the distance between them. He was too upset to go after her and try to explain. Instead he got a bottle from the cupboard and sat with it on the couch, staring blankly at the wall.

He had to do something. Getting out of bed, Cook shuffled to the kitchen and phoned the office. "Swanson? This is Cook. Look, I need Fellows's home phone. I've got an emergency—"

"No can do, Cook," said Swanson.

"What the hell does that mean? I've got an emergency and I need to talk to the boss! You're on the desk, so give it to me, damn it!"

"Sorry, Cook. I already got the word that you'd be calling. Boss said you don't get his number."

"Shit!" Cook slammed down the phone.

In the shower he cursed Fellows and the entire Montclair Country Club. He would have to wait until Monday to talk with the son of a bitch. Cook dried himself off and washed down four Advils with a big glass of juice. Relief was now only twenty minutes away, but they were always the longest twenty minutes of his hangover.

He needed to do something, but he had to be careful. The less contact he had with Keel, the better. But he also needed to let Keel know that it would be another day before he could get him out of that apartment. He considered moving them himself, and possibly even bringing them back to his own small place until he could talk some sense into Fellows. He imagined Aunt Esther's face.

If something went wrong, though, he'd look like a real ass. He didn't exactly blend in down there on South Street. If he was seen, he could get them killed. If he'd known how explosive Keel's information was, he'd have taken care of the details instead of going there yesterday.

Cook dialed Keel's number and let it ring twenty times on the odd chance that Keel hadn't listened to him and would pick up. No answer. Cook told himself that that was a good sign. As the day wore on and Cook didn't arrive with the cavalry, Keel was sure to get nervous and call. He hung up the phone and made himself some eggs. As he ate, he thought of how he was going to break it to Natasha that they were going to have to spend the day inside when it was so sunny out. He didn't want to tell her it had to do with work again, even though it was true. He needed to be there in case Keel called. He put his plate in the sink and, waiting for his little girl to come home, sat down on the couch with a Walter Mosely novel. He loved the mysteries about the tough, black, private detective, Easy Rawlins, and reading the book, Cook felt sure a solution to the problem of making a good home for Natasha would be possible if he could just nail Tony Rizzo. Tommy Keel's testimony would be key.

That evening, on the Brooklyn side of the East River, the doorman from India looked up suddenly from his book as a gust of cold spring air swept through the lobby. It was dark outside and he watched Angelo Quatrini's evil smile as the man stomped through the door. The smile was on a cold face. The kind of face that belonged to a man who could hurt you. The doorman smiled.

"You here yesterday?" Angelo asked in a dull, flat voice.

The doorman nodded. He couldn't find his tongue to speak.

"Anyone come here asking for apartment 7E?"

The doorman nodded again.

"Was he from the FBI or something?"

The doorman hesitated. Something flickered in Angelo's eye, and he quickly nodded.

"You tell someone else as much about me as you just did about him, and I'll come find you."

Angelo pulled a pistol from his coat and pushed the fat silencer against the doorman's nose. He grabbed the man's hand and yanked it up toward his face. He fingered the doorman's worn silver wedding band.

"You got a wife, huh?" Angelo said. "I could find her, too. Maybe you got some kids . . ."

Angelo's eyes flickered when he saw the terror on the doorman's face. He let the man's hand drop and made his way to the stairs.

"Why aren't they here, Tommy?" pleaded Sonya. "Didn't he tell you that they'd be here today? Maybe we should just go."

"Where we gonna go?"

"I don't know," she said, touching the swollen purple flesh around her eye. Sonya wanted to understand what was going on. All she knew was fear. She had never been beaten before. She had never been raped. She was afraid both would happen again.

"When are they coming?" she asked again.

"I don't know. I don't know! Stop asking," said Tommy. He ran his fingers through his hair, only more slowly than the day before. Now he pulled it nervously. The two of them sat on the sofa. The blinds were drawn and there were no lights on. Only the silent Mets–Dodgers game on the television cut into the gloom. It was still light in L.A., where the game was being played. Tommy wished he was there.

"I'll call him," Tommy said finally, picking up the phone.

Cook knocked over half the pieces on the Monopoly board when he scrambled to answer on the first ring.

"Tommy?" Cook asked as he picked up the phone.

"Yeah, where the hell are you guys? You told me today, Cook. Today was the latest."

Cook snaked the phone cord across his apartment and went into his room, closing the door on Natasha and Aunt Esther, who had returned from church and spent the afternoon in the cramped apartment playing board games.

"Listen, Tommy, I know. I tried to call you."

"You're the one that told me not to answer the phone, man," Keel yelled. Spittle flew angrily from his mouth and landed on the glass coffee table.

"Tommy, listen to me," said Cook. "I know. I'm glad you didn't answer. I just didn't want to show up over there again in case someone was watching. Believe me, I've been sweating you all day. I've just been sitting here waiting for your call. I've got a small problem. It's no big thing. I just need until tomorrow to get everything worked out the right way."

"A small fucking problem. That's just great! Why can't we just leave? All that talk about us being watched. I don't like it. If Tony's got someone watching me, I figure the best thing I can do is run. If no one's watching, then running is still the best thing. I gotta get out of here, man. I don't see any reason why we can't just go out the same way you did, and have you meet us in the back alley with a car. We don't need no team, we can just head upstate and—"

"Listen, Tommy," Cook said, trying to sound confident. "I know you're scared, and that's OK. I'd rather have you scared and cautious than relaxed and careless. But you've got to listen to me. I've got to do things by the book. I can't just take off upstate someplace with you and your girl, and Tony Rizzo on our tail. I need to arrange a safe house to keep you protected until we can get this thing ready for trial. I'm doing this for you. You have to be totally safe, not just for tonight, but for the rest of your life. The best way for me to do that is to follow procedure. You understand that, don't you? It'll only be another day. I promise."

Keel was silent, thinking.

"Listen," said Cook, "if I don't get all this worked out by tomorrow at noon, then I'll get a car and pick you up out back myself. I promise you. Just give me until noon."

"I don't even know you, man," Keel whined. "The only way I know you aren't working for Tony is 'cause you're black. But just 'cause you're not with him . . . I don't know."

"Hey, Tommy . . . I hate to put it like this," Cook said, his voice firm, "but like I told you yesterday, I'm all you got. You just sit tight. I'll be here all night if you need to talk."

Keel paused for almost a minute. Sonya was staring at him, biting her bruised lower lip. "OK, Cook. OK."

"Good," Cook said. "Now remember, I'm right here until seven-thirty in the morning. Then I'm going in to the office to get this all worked out, so if you need me anytime after that, you call me there. If I'm not there, then I'm on my way. Don't worry. You're probably the last thing on Tony Rizzo's mind anyway. Like I said, I'm known for being a little overly cautious."

When Tommy hung up the phone, he felt a little better. He talked to Sonya until she felt better, too.

"Look," Tommy said, "we'll call for a pizza and have a few beers, get some sleep and tomorrow we'll be outta here." They kissed each other lightly and Tommy called for the pizza. Then the two of them settled down on the couch to watch the rest of the game.

When the door to the apartment burst open with a loud crack, Sonya jumped in her seat. The noise itself was enough to make her heart race. Her only thought was that the pizza came incredibly fast. She saw a large figure enter the apartment and carefully close the door he had just kicked in, as if he had done it by accident. The figure turned and she saw Angelo Quatrini's leering face. Sonya felt her stomach sink and twist. She was sick. The big man called Angelo seemed to move in slow motion. She was frozen, as in a dream.

Tommy sprang from the couch and met the big man halfway across the living room floor. Angelo quickly spun Tommy about, then deftly kicked the back of his legs, bringing him to his knees, facing her. She remained frozen on the couch in a silent scream. Angelo had a fistful of Tommy's hair twisted in one hand and a large pistol in the other. The gun was jammed into Tommy's ear.

"I'm gonna ask you something, bitch," Angelo said in a low, guttural voice, "and I ain't asking twice. Did some nigger cop come here to talk to you yesterday?"

Sonya couldn't speak. She only nodded slightly. It was enough. Tommy's head exploded, spraying scarlet bits across the room with a quiet pop. She drew a breath to scream, but another bullet from

Angelo's gun hit just to one side of her nose. The explosion tore through her nasal cavity and left her face a mass of pulp that whistled as her lungs emptied one final time.

The next morning, Cook didn't know whether it was a good or bad sign that he hadn't heard from Keel during the night. He had never been in a situation like this before. There were other times during his tenure with the Bureau that he'd felt helpless, but never because a superior had hamstrung him. He stepped into the shower and was dressed in twenty minutes. He took a cab to the office. Even though he knew Fellows wouldn't be there until eight, he was too impatient to take his usual walk.

To his surprise, Fellows was in and waiting for him. Cook kept his head high as he passed Fellows's secretary and through the solid oak door into his boss's spacious and finely decorated office. He wasn't going to get uptight about a silly mistake, and even if Fellows wanted to blow off some steam about it, Cook would just take it and then move on to the business at hand. He knew something was really wrong even before Fellows spun around in his leather chair.

"Sit down, Cook," Fellows said quietly.

Cook sat and held a direct gaze with his boss.

"You told me that you found a witness yesterday who could tie Tony Rizzo to the Fat Man murder."

Cook nodded and wondered if Fellows might be working up to an apology.

"During the time of your investigation," Fellows continued in an unnaturally subdued voice, "did you identify yourself to anyone?"

Cook thought for a moment, then said, "Yes. I showed my badge to an NYPD cop at the scene of Keel's assault, the nurse at the hospital, the doorman to Keel's building, and then of course, to Keel himself."

Fellows leaned back in his chair and formed a steeple with his fingertips.

"We have procedures in this office. The Bureau has procedures," he said in a calm monotone. "You have violated some of the most basic ones. You jeopardized a potential witness. That witness is now dead."

The word hung in the room like pipe smoke. Cook blinked but kept his eye contact with Fellows. His Adam's apple bobbed. His mind whirled with a hundred possibilities, all the things he might have done differently.

"They were found late last night by a pizza kid. The place was a mess; both of them got .357 dum-dum slugs in the head. Besides your embarrassing behavior at my club this weekend, your record before you came here speaks for itself. I'm not the type of person who likes to see a man with as much experience as you have get tossed out because of one mistake, even if it is a huge one.

"I want you to finish up your research and begin working on the Mondolffi family, only this time, the right way. I expect from now on that if you so much as decide to sneeze, you'll notify me first. I'm saving your ass, Cook, not because I like you—what you did at my club was stupid and ignorant, and if anything like it ever happens again I won't be so forgiving. I'm saving your ass because you owe me, Cook, and I like things that way."

Cook stepped out into the street, numb with shock. He wanted to pull his brains out of his head and smash them down on the pavement. He began to walk. He should have known better! He did know better!

His mind jumped to Tony Rizzo. Rizzo had killed Keel and the girl. The girl was young, as his own wife had been. There was no reason for that girl to have died. It was senseless. Keel, yes. Cook didn't like it, but he could understand it. It was the girl, though, that bothered Cook most of all. His thoughts spun. He knew it would be easy. Easy for him. He knew where Rizzo lived. Even if Rizzo had six of his goons, Cook could do him. He already knew what the hunger to kill a man for revenge was like. Cook thought about that man. He could still see the white fungus that hung between his twisted teeth. He could hear the man's depraved ravings as he leveled the shotgun at his head. He could still see Naomi too—her body had been cold when they pulled open the freezer door and asked him to identify it.

She had disappeared for three days. He had known that she was dead. Some psycho, a mental outpatient at Atlanta's Grady Hospital, where she'd been a resident, had waited for her in the back of her car. He had brutally beaten and raped her. Then, while she was still alive, with her hands and feet bound by duct tape and her mouth stuffed with her own underwear, he had tossed her off a bridge and into the Chattahoochee River.

A friend of Cook's, a sergeant with the Atlanta police, had come to him three weeks later. He had found the man who'd killed Naomi, and he offered his whereabouts to Cook, giving him the opportunity to seek personal revenge.

Cook hadn't done it. He remembered struggling with the idea that it was for the law to serve justice. No one man could ever supersede the law. That idea was what had led him to the Bureau in the first place. It was that idea that had gotten him out of the ghetto. But no matter how hard he clung to it, it hadn't kept him from spending countless sleepless nights wondering and praying that he had done the right thing. Because late at night, when no one else was there, a voice in the back of Cook's mind would tell him that he should have killed the man. The voice told him that if Naomi meant anything to him at all, he would have snuffed the man who'd killed her with his own hands.

Cook struggled to control himself. He grasped for order. Order, the way things were supposed to be . . . he wasn't sure he knew what that was anymore, or if he ever would again.

In a waterfront warehouse, under the shadow of the Whitestone Bridge, Tony Rizzo closed a case of money and smiled. He was clearing two hundred and fifty thousand dollars in this transaction. It made so much sense. He controlled the docks. The customs officers came cheap. He had ready buyers and eager suppliers. The money came easier than plucking it from a tree. The Colombians were just getting into their car when a black limousine roared into the warehouse and screeched to a stop. They trained their pistols on the car.

"No!" Rizzo shouted, holding up his hands. "It's my uncle. Just go. Just go!"

The Colombian leader shrugged and climbed into his car. The three others followed, and their long white car with dark windows drove away slowly. When it finally disappeared from sight, Ears Vantressa and Dominic Fontane emerged from their car, followed by Tony's uncle.

"Uncle Vinny!" said Tony with a smile.

Vincent Mondolffi was not smiling. Mike Cometti and two other thugs crowded behind Tony, as if to hide.

"Tony," the uncle said, ignoring the other men, "we need to talk."

The older man slipped his arm through Tony's, and they began to walk toward the back of the warehouse. Ears and Dominic followed about twenty paces back.

"I told you, Tony," said Vincent Mondolffi. "I told you no niggers and no Colombians, and here I find you dealing drugs with those animals."

Tony knew better than to lie, so he kept quiet.

"I can't let you go on like this, Tony. Last night I had to have Angelo get rid of your friend Tommy Keel and his girl."

Tony couldn't help his look of surprise.

"Yeah," said the uncle, nodding with approval at the younger man's shock. "I am still further ahead of you in this game of life, Tony. Your friend Keel was going to talk to the feds. You took him with you to kill the Fat Man. I had to make a mess before the feds got him out of town. I had to risk losing Angelo, had to have him walk in there and kill those kids like a common criminal. Why, Tony? Why do you do things like that, careless things? That Keel was nothing in this family. You take him to a hit that you carry out yourself, without my authority, then you rape this same man's girlfriend?"

Vincent Mondolffi slapped the back of his nephew's head hard, causing him to stumble. Tony kept his eyes down. He said nothing. He knew if he retaliated in any way, he would be dead.

"You act like a goddamned animal! No wonder you're selling drugs like the niggers and the chinks!"

The older man stopped short and lifted Tony's chin. Tony met his uncle's ice-blue eyes.

"I'm putting you on notice, Tony. This is the last time I'm going to let you slide. This is the last time blood gets in the way of my business. I'm the head of this family, and I won't have it going into the sewer. I already told you the heat is going to be on us all because of the Fat Man. People are watching! I told you that, and you haven't listened to me, Tony. That's a sign to everyone around that you don't respect me. The next time you get messed up with this kind of shit you'll be *gone.*"

The word hung in the air. Tony said nothing. His heart had jumped in his chest when his uncle said "gone." He knew just what his uncle meant. Vincent Mondolffi turned abruptly and walked back to his car. His men followed him inside and the door slammed shut. The long black car pulled slowly away.

Tony Rizzo stood by himself, cursing. He wondered if he might not be able to kill his uncle. No, the time was not right, not yet. This would set him back. He knew that to take over the family he needed power, and power was money. There was plenty of easy money in drug trafficking. He turned and made his way back toward his men, who were still pale behind their dark glasses. If there was a way to make some big money without pissing off his uncle, he was going to find it. He thought again about Camille and the Titans.

The night was pure, the air fresh and cool. Stars and a crescent moon glowed through wispy clouds. The soft light from the sky was enough to illuminate the gently rolling shapes of the timeworn Appalachian mountains that surrounded the Logan homestead. Hunter could almost imagine what it would have been like to sit on this very same porch, in this very same rocking chair, two hundred years ago. This was the only place he'd been in his life where there wasn't the sound of traffic somewhere. He loved the quiet and peacefulness of these West Virginia hills.

Then Henry spoke. It surprised Hunter because Henry was a man of few words, and he seldom spoke to Hunter. He was happy that Henry had come out on the porch with him to sit at all. Hunter laughed to himself, thinking about all the bullshit that people said about twins being so close.

"I said it's late, why don't you stay the night. Why'd you laugh?" Henry said.

"No, thanks. I wasn't laughing at that. I was just thinking about you and me," Hunter replied.

"Not much to think about there," said Henry. "You and I are opposites—besides the way we look."

"That's about what I was thinking," Hunter said.

"So, why don't you stay the night? Sara's already asleep in the girls' room. You and Rachel could sleep in the front room downstairs. Ma always keeps that room nice in case you decide you might stay; dusts it every week. Like maybe you'll just pop in unexpectedly. Why don't you just stay for once and make her happy?"

Hunter lifted his beer to his mouth and finished it off. He set down the empty bottle and reached into the cooler positioned between them, opening another before he spoke. He chose his words carefully. "Henry, this is your house. You live in it with your family. I know no matter what Ma wants, you don't want me here . . . so, I stay down at the inn to keep out of your hair as much as I can."

"Don't feed me that shit, brother," Henry said, his voice suddenly angry. "This fucking place belongs to you and we all know it."

Hunter stiffened in his chair. His insides felt cold. It was happening again, and there was nothing he could do but watch, like a third-party observer, as the scene played itself out. He knew just how it would go, no matter what he tried to say or do.

"You know I don't mean it like that. I've told you that for ten years now, Henry. What I did is what Dad would have wanted. This place belongs to you; I never had a problem with that growing up. You know that. So I made my own way. I did what any of us would have done."

"Like hell you did," Henry said flatly.

Hunter knew they were both drunk, and the alcohol-induced venom in his brother's voice made him think maybe this time they would fight. That was something he would have welcomed, anything to help extract the poison that had infected their relationship.

"You did what was good for you, Hunter," Henry continued. "You always did. When it was good for you to throw that fucking ball through the tire, that's what you did. When it was good for you to go to college, that's what you did. And when this family really needed what you had, you did what was good for you. You played Mr. All-American at school and didn't want to put yourself out for your family. Then, when it was good for you to buy the home you could have saved in the first place just by staying here, that's what you did. No, brother, you didn't do what any of us would've done. You never did what we did. You never did your share. You did what you had to do to leave here, because you couldn't take being second. You couldn't take being the younger one. And when you saw it all being taken from me, from Dad, from Mom . . . you just played your games, and went to your parties, and looked the other way."

"You got no right talking to me like that! You got no right!" Hunter said, standing and glowering over his brother, his fists clenched and shaking.

"Sit down," Henry said. "Sit down. I ain't gonna fight you. I ain't gonna give you the satisfaction of thinking you can settle something like this by having me kick your ass. You think you're such a hot-shot athlete. I'm just as strong as you are. I might not lift weights, but I work, and I'm a lot meaner than you'll ever be. No, I'm not fighting you. You gotta live with what you did. I won't help you."

Henry looked off into the distance and took a slug from his bottle like Hunter wasn't there. Hunter stood for several minutes, wishing, just hoping that his brother would stand and fight. But he knew Henry believed what he was saying, and that he'd never fight. Hunter took his seat and picked up his beer.

"All you had to do," Henry continued as he stared out into the night, "was use some of that influence, that recognition that you loved so much. What did it ever do for you? Sure, you're rich, but that's 'cause you can throw. But the influence? You never used that, did you? What in hell were you saving it for, Hunter? What? Everyone between here and Pittsburgh knew Hunter Logan. They loved Hunter Logan. They had Hunter Logan days and Hunter Logan parades. You met them all, the politicians, the news people, and the millionaires. You knew them all, and all you had to do was go to bat for us. All you had to do was use some of that influence to save this farm, but you wouldn't. Not couldn't . . . you could have done it, but you wouldn't . . .

". . . and then you let this family go broke and you stepped in at the last minute and bought us from the bank. Not the farm, though, that was gone. They'd stripped that bare. They raped our land and they raped us.

". . . So you think you saved us by buying this house? Shit! Living here is just a reminder of what we've lost. It killed Dad. And now it's hell on Mom, and it's hell on me. Julia and Marjorie, they got husbands to take them away and give them new lives. But me? I got nothing. I put everything I had into this place, and now I work at a fucking gas station."

Hunter was silent. His insides wrenched, partly from anger, partly from sadness. He'd said it before, and he wondered how many times he would say it again. "I was a junior at Pitt, Henry. A fucking junior in college. Yeah, I was a star! But that didn't mean I could change the world. I was a college football player. I didn't have any money. All I had was my arm, and those big shots liked to have me around, yeah. But sure as hell no one was going to stop what had to be done for me! You don't know what it was like. You never knew anything about what was going on in my life. You just figured because everyone knew who I was that I could do something about it. I didn't have that power then. Hell, Henry, I don't even have it now."

"Don't you understand what happened?" Hunter asked. "There was an oil shortage. People needed coal. They had the leases to take that coal. They stripped the land to get it, yeah. It was wrong. They ruined us. They ruined everyone like us. They didn't care, Henry. They didn't care about this farm, or this family, or you and your inheritance, or even me, Hunter Logan, the All-American. You're not living in reality.

"You don't think I didn't try?" Hunter pleaded. "I told you. I tried. I talked to people. You think they listened? You think a kid that plays football can change things like that? Just because I didn't come back here and lay myself in front of a 'dozer to make the national news doesn't mean I didn't try. I did . . . I did what I could, but it wasn't any better than what you could do. Face it, Henry. Face it, man. It's gone. It's not my fault. I didn't sign those mineral leases. I did all I could."

Henry rose abruptly and walked into the house, slamming the door as he went. Hunter continued to sit and rock. It happened every time. But every time Hunter would try. He didn't know why. Maybe it was because part of what his brother said was true. Hunter didn't think so, but maybe.

The front door squeaked as Rachel came out onto the porch. Hunter stood, but continued to stare out at the mountains and the sky.

"Let's go," he said, pulling the keys from his front pocket. "Sara's OK. We'll get her in the morning before we go."

"Don't you want to just—" Rachel stopped. Hunter had turned to her. She saw the tears and the pain on his face. She wouldn't ask. She understood.

"I'll drive," she said, taking the keys gently from his hand. Together they got into the car. It rolled down the hill, crunching the gravel beneath its big, thick wheels.

In a dark window on the second floor of the old house, a tall figure watched them go. His hands and forehead were pressed against the glass, and he stood there, watching the taillights from Hunter's car weave through the valley and up the opposite side. He remained until the tiny red dots disappeared over the other ridge.

Two days later Hunter showed up at the Titans facility at eight-thirty in the morning. It was much earlier than he was used to, but the Titans players were required to report for a three-day mini-camp just like every other team in the league. To the players, mini-camp was an exercise in control, coaches and management flexing their might, reminding the players just who was in control of whose life. The real work would begin in training camp in July, but this was a good warm-up, a harbinger of the evils to come.

The players would attend meetings and go out onto the practice field twice a day to run through agility drills and plays that the coaches had concocted in the confines of their offices. The team wore none of their normal equipment except for their helmets. The reason for wearing helmets was supposedly to protect the player from breaking his nose or jaw. There wasn't supposed to be any contact. This was one of the longest-running jokes in the NFL. Coaches inevitably got out of hand and started instructing individual players to turn up the intensity a few notches if they wanted even to be invited back to training camp. These tactics worked best on the rookie linemen who, to a veteran, were wide-eyed with bewilderment. Each of them was on the verge of making their childhood dream come true, and there was nothing short of suicide that any of them would not do if ordered by a real-life NFL coach.

The older vets had no use for this nonsense, but even they would rise violently to the occasion because inevitably some rookie, wet behind the ears, would ram into one of them at full speed and tear their jersey or bruise their body in some way. By the end of the three days, practice was a melee. Players would drop like flies because they were going at it without the protective gear that normally kept them safe. Coaches would snicker among themselves because they knew their men had a good eight weeks to heal before training camp began.

Amid all this tumult and expression of anger and resentment, Hunter Logan's position as the Titans quarterback was being challenged by a rookie, at least as much as a rookie could challenge an established quarterback of the Super Bowl champions. The Titans' personnel department had taken it upon themselves to draft for the future. While Hunter was in West Virginia, the team had chosen a young quarterback out of Stanford University in the first round of the draft. Everyone on the team knew that Hunter's position was safe, everyone except the young rookie.

Blake Stevens had a mouth that befitted a quarterback. He loved to talk, and the thing he loved to talk most about was himself. In fact, since Hunter's return, the only thing he had heard or read about concerning the New York Titans had something to do with the team's new young quarterback. He was calling himself "Broadway Blake," and making one outrageous statement after another. Stevens was actually telling the press and anyone else who would listen that he was brought to New York to replace "the aging Hunter Logan."

Of course Hunter was being asked to respond.

"We'll just have to see how it goes," was all he would say to the press.

In private he was incensed. "Broadway Blake" had struck a nerve. Hunter knew that he was old and didn't have too many more years to play. That a rookie was calling him out and reminding him of it was pissing him off. He was angry with the Titans organization for picking a guy like Stevens. If they were going to bring in a protégé, the least they could have done was bring one in who had sense enough to keep his mouth shut.

When Hunter walked into the facility, he was glad to see that the rookie's locker was nowhere near his own. Bert came up to him immediately, already taped and dressed for practice.

"Did you catch a load of that punk yet?" Bert asked, pulling up a free stool and planting himself next to Hunter, who was stripping off his street clothes.

"Nope," Hunter said.

"You read about him, though, didn't you?" Bert asked.

"Yup."

"Well . . . aren't you going to say anything, like what an asshole this little fucker is?" Bert said.

"Nope."

"You know," Bert huffed, "you're really starting to annoy me, Hunt."

"I just don't want to talk about it," Hunter said, sitting down and pulling on his practice socks. "The best thing I can do to shut that kid up is go out there today and show him what it means to be a QB in the NFL. It's got nothing to do with talking."

"Yeah! That's what I'm talking about!" Bert whispered fiercely. "Ha, ha! I love it! You're just laying low. Now when you get out there today, you'll just . . . you'll . . . What are you gonna do?"

Hunter shrugged. "Just show him what a real arm can do. Show him what timing really means. Show him that when a blitz is on, you better know which receiver is hot or else you end up wearing your ass for a hat."

"Oh, yeah!" Bert said. "That's good thinking. I mean, he's not gonna know what the hell is going on. He's gonna look like a damn fool! That oughta shut him up for a while."

"Especially if you guys on defense turn up the intensity . . . just a little," Hunter said with a small smile, "as kind of a welcoming to the NFL. Who knows? Someone might even call a few blitzes by mistake."

Hunter could see the light in Bert's eyes, it was sheer delight.

"Why didn't you tell me that in the first place?" Bert said. "I love this idea!"

"I'm telling you now," Hunter said simply, and flipped his helmet off the hook just as the whistle called them to the practice field.

One thing that surprised Hunter was the size of Broadway Blake. He was enormous, standing almost six and a half feet tall and probably weighing as much as a good-sized linebacker. His hair was long and blonde. His chiseled features were accented by diamond studs in each ear. Hunter thought he looked like a biker prince. He was holding court among a group of rookies who were out on the field early. Hunter jogged right by the rookie, planted himself next to the bag of balls, and began warming up with Bob Dunham.

Other players were broken down by position. Linemen were crashing into padded bars of steel that were dressed up like opposing players. Linebackers and tight ends were busy with ball drills. Running backs were high-stepping their way through an obstacle course of tires. Wide receivers and defensive backs were doing one-on-one pass coverages. Coaches watched, barking, slobbering, and blowing whistles. Amid the flurry of activity, Broadway Blake ambled over to the ball bag and pulled out a ball. He stood next to Hunter, looked his way, then hurled a football down the length of the football field as far as he could. The ball landed in the opposite end zone, a good hundred yards away, and Blake hadn't even gotten a running start. It was an amazing throw.

"I'm Blake Stevens," the rookie said in a low smooth voice.

Broadway Blake then planted his feet shoulder width apart and stared intently at Hunter Logan, waiting for his response. Hunter smiled, looking straight ahead, and continued to throw warm-up passes to Dunham as if the rookie didn't exist. The rookie snorted in disdain, then walked away from Hunter and began tossing a ball with another free-agent QB from Tampa Bay. In a few minutes, the whistle blew and the team lined up for stretching exercises.

"I saw that shit!" Bert exclaimed, taking the time to jog over to Hunter's place in the line.

"Hell of a throw, wasn't it?" Hunter said calmly.

Bert grumbled and made his way back to the ranks of the linemen. Martin Price took the opportunity to introduce himself to his new team and give them some rah-rah college bull about how everybody would be starting from scratch with him and how he didn't care if they were world champions, that this was a new season coming up and they'd have to do it all over again if they wanted real respect. Most of the veterans secretly rolled their eyes at one another.

After stretching, the team broke down again into groups to work on positional skills. Price attached himself to the quarterbacks and the receivers, who worked on the timing of their pass routes. Hunter went first and he put on a display of accuracy that made even Price smile. When Dunham stepped up to take his turn, however, Price spoke out.

"I want Blake running the second team," he said.

Dunham stared at Price in momentary disbelief. He had been Hunter's backup for three seasons now. A rookie didn't just step in and take that kind of thing away without ever throwing a pass. It was not the way things were done, or at least it hadn't been. The move miffed Hunter as well. It made him feel as if the rookie had just crawled onto his back. Broadway Blake rose to the occasion, throwing his balls with incredible accuracy.

Hunter's stomach began to knot up. He had been looking forward to a nice relaxing summer, the first time in his career when he wasn't going to have to worry about his position with the team. He was returning as a champion and an All-Pro. There shouldn't be anything at all for him to think about. But he knew he would spend a lot of time on the beach in the Hamptons thinking about how this young rookie was right behind him, and how easily people could forget what you did for them only the season before. He'd seen it happen to quarterbacks time and time again. Jeff Hostetler, Doug Williams, and Mark Rypien all came immediately to mind. They were all Super Bowl champions who had come back the very next season only to be criticized and challenged for their jobs. Just when Hunter was looking forward to enjoying his last few years as king of the hill, the Titans had to go ahead and bring this guy in. Worst of all, it looked like the kid was good.

It might turn out that the rookie couldn't hold up under pressure, but that wasn't likely in mini-camp, and that would do nothing for Hunter's peace of mind. There would be a big difference in training camp. The crashing of heads and the violent fury of the pocket as a quarterback tried to seek out his receivers was a distraction that some quarterbacks could never overcome once they got to the NFL. The defensive players were bigger, faster, and much meaner than they were in college, and up here they thrived on punishing quarterbacks. The more punishment a defensive player could dish out to the opposition's quarterback, the more likely it was he would be signing one of those multimillion-dollar deals in the off-season. Blake Stevens would get some heat in mini-camp, but it would be all bark and no bite. The bite would come when the pads went on.

After almost a half hour of drills, the team came together to work as offensive and defensive units. There was supposedly no contact, although the linemen would butt, grab, kick, and punch each other as though they were in a bar fight. Rookie running backs would get butted down to the ground when some veteran defender jammed his shoulder in the rookie's gut, but veteran running backs were simply tagged with two hands. Receivers and defensive backs rarely hit one another during practice, with or without pads. Quarterbacks, too, were never hit during practices of any kind. They were too valuable and would even wear special red jerseys to insure that no one made any mistakes.

Hunter stepped into the huddle of the first-team players and got the unofficial scrimmage started. The offensive starters were up against the defensive second team. Hunter was perfect in everything he did. The season hadn't really ended all that long ago, and his timing on everything from taking snaps to handing the ball off to throwing passes was right on the money. On the sixth play, however, House mixed up the pass protection and let a rookie defensive end come barreling through the line. The rookie, completely surprised to find himself in the backfield, and confused after all the pounding he'd taken in his first hour as a pro player, lost all sense of where he was and plowed into Hunter's back. Hunter went down like a white-tail deer shot through the heart.

Murphy was on the rookie immediately and began pummeling him as if he would kill the young player if left to his own devices. Hunter popped up and got into the fray himself, trying with his teammates to pull the two battling bulls apart before someone got seriously hurt. When Murphy was finally subdued, and the defensive line coach had the rookie off to the side and was giving him a rabid verbal lashing, Hunter realized that something was running into his mouth. He put his fingertips to his lips, and they came away bright red with blood. The impact had crammed his helmet down onto the bridge of his nose, and he was bleeding like a stuck pig.

Hunter had the trainers jam some cotton up his nostrils and immediately stepped back into the huddle so he could continue to run the offense. After four more plays, the teams switched and the backup offense huddled up to take their turn against the first-team defense.

The defenders, more violent by nature than their offensive counterparts, were lathered up with excitement at the sight of blood. They couldn't help themselves. They were like sharks, or a pack of wild dogs. When they saw blood, it made them hungry for more. Broadway Blake stepped up to the line and checked the defensive formation.

"Gonna get you, rookie!" Bert bellowed from directly across the line. "Gonna get your blood, too!"

Players began barking out calls all up and down the line on the defensive side of the ball.

"Get you, rookie!"

"Gonna bust your ass, rook!"

"Rookie's got that long, pretty hair! He must be a punk!"

Hunter was almost blushing on the sideline at the obviousness of Bert's and his teammates' intimidation ploy. The ball was snapped and the rookie fumbled. Bert pushed past the center and bumped into Blake hard, like they were on a crowded elevator.

"Come on, rookie," Bert said, pushing his face mask into the quarterback's until the two rang and clanged like armor. "You can't throw it if you can't hang on to it."

The next nine plays went downhill for Broadway Blake. As the defense growled and snorted and bumped and bruised him in what Hunter would consider very innocuous ways, Blake lost his cool. When they threw a blitz at him on the fifth play, the young QB did not even know it was coming. He tossed the ball pathetically into the air and cringed at the same instant like some little sissy on the playground. The ball went up and the defensive backs were actually fighting among themselves over who was going to get the interception. It was bad.

"No wonder you got them earrings," Bert said loudly in disgust after the play. "Shit, we didn't even hit you, punk. I can't wait until camp comes and we can get a shot on your big sissy ass in a live scrimmage!"

The rookie mumbled something under his breath and started back to his huddle.

"Don't you mumble shit at me!" Bert bellowed, not giving the young player an inch. "You got something to say to me, you say it, punk! You come in here shooting your mouth off, you better be ready to back it up!"

Bert jogged after the rookie and grabbed for his face mask. Again the rookie cringed. Bert got him anyway and turned his head toward where Hunter was standing silently behind the huddle with the other offensive players who were watching.

"You see that man there?" Bert said. "What? I said, 'Do you see him?'"

"Yes," Broadway Blake said.

"Yeah, well, he's the man around here. You got that?" Bert demanded amid grunts of approval from players on each side of the ball. "He's our man. He took us to the show last year, boy. You ain't shit until he says so. So you better start to fly straight and shut your fucking mouth, 'cause everyone here can see that you're just a big-mouthed pussy!"

Bert shoved the rookie back toward his own huddle and returned to the other side of the ball.

"All right, Meyer," Price said, "that's enough."

Only Broadway Blake's original arrogance kept Hunter from feeling truly sorry for him. Besides, Hunter figured Bert's rough treatment was probably the only thing that would keep the rookie quiet long enough to let Hunter enjoy a peaceful summer with his family.

CHAPTER

||||||||||||||||||||||||||||||||||||||||||||||||||||||||||||

A week later Hunter and his family were at their home in the Hamptons. Hunter was feeling good about the prospect of spending the summer at the beach. With the challenge from the young draft pick behind him and the hurtful encounter with Henry a fading memory, Hunter was ready to relax before training camp cut the summer short a few days after the Fourth of July. He got dressed in the sunny master bedroom suite that overlooked the grassy dunes and the sparkling surf and was feeling a little nervous and self-conscious about the party he and Rachel were preparing to attend at Grant Carter's home that afternoon.

"So how do I look?" Hunter asked.

"Fine, honey," said Rachel. Then she saw his frown. "You look sensational. Hunter, how can you even worry? A man as handsome as you next to all those old geezers with their knobby knees sticking out of their shorts like hairy beanpoles . . ."

"I don't mean me, I mean what I'm wearing. Does it look OK?"

"Hunter, it's a pool party. You've got on a nice pair of shorts and a polo shirt. You look fine, really. You don't have anything to worry about."

"I know. You keep saying that. I'm just not used to this kind of thing."

"Having second thoughts about all this?" she asked.

"No, not really."

"Well, remember, you've always looked nice, even when you haven't given a shit. You've got me for a wife, don't you?"

"I want to make sure I don't dress like I just popped out of the hills of West Virginia," he said, looking awkwardly over his shoulder into the mirror, "even though that's exactly what I've done."

"I told you," Rachel reminded him, "just drink your beer from a glass, look bored, and frown at everything anyone says. Oh, and don't forget, don't rave about the food, even if you love it. Remember, you've had better. They'll think you've summered here since you were born," she chuckled.

Rachel's parents had a modest home in nearby Quogue near the center of town. They dropped Sara off there for the afternoon, then headed back toward the beach. They turned west on Dune Road and drove down the wide street lined with old, wind-tortured pine trees until they spotted the enormous gables of the Carter mansion. The house could only be truly appreciated from the beach, and Hunter and Rachel had walked past it many times from the ocean side. It was a little over three miles from their own house, and they had admired it many times on their early-morning walks. Being able to take long strolls on the beach was one of the reasons they'd purchased property in the Hamptons.

Hunter drove the Town Car up under a large portico in front of the house. A valet took the car, and a butler guided them through a maze of beautifully furnished rooms and out to a fantastic redwood deck with an unmatched view of shoreline that stretched for miles. At the center of the deck was a diamond-shaped pool that mirrored the azure blue of the cloudless sky. Tables with umbrellas scattered around the deck were half filled with West Hampton's social elite. It was Memorial Day, the beginning of the summer season, and even the large, accommodating deck was crowded.

Before long Hunter was actually having a good time. He found that most of the people there were friendly and excited about meeting the New York Titans quarterback. Grant Carter was a gracious host, introducing his guest of honor with effusive compliments.

Hunter tried hard to remember as many names as he could. He received invitations to countless tennis games, dinners, and barbeques. He gave out his phone number liberally.

"Hunter," Rachel whispered to him during a break between introductions, "I guess they like what you're wearing. It would take us all summer to do all the things you've been invited to."

"I feel like I'm making up for seven years of social seclusion in one afternoon," he said.

"You're doing a pretty good job at it, that's for sure," she replied.

After about an hour, Hunter excused himself and went inside to look for a bathroom. A caterer carrying a silver tray of freshly shucked oysters pointed down a long hall. Hunter took in the grand scale of Carter's home as he passed a vaulted room filled with antiques. Large windows looked out over the ocean. The bathroom was equally impressive. The floor was covered with a plush Oriental rug, and an ornate divan was set against a wall that faced a full-length mirror and an expansive marble sink. Hunter pulled the solid mahogany door shut behind him and found the toilet. Afterwards, he stared at his face in the mirror as he washed his hands. He thought about the rural farm boy he had been. He could still see signs of that boy in his face, but they were growing fainter every year.

A figure appeared behind him suddenly and made him jump. He quickly turned around.

"I didn't mean to scare you," murmured Camille. "I followed you."

She was dressed in an electric blue one-piece bathing suit covered by a long, silk beach shirt. Her golden hair hung wildly about her shoulders.

Hunter was surprised to see her and could not keep his eyes from traveling down the length of her long and supple body.

"They say fear illicits the same neurochemical reactions as sex," she said in a husky voice.

Before Hunter could respond, Camille closed the gap between them and pressed her body to his, finding his lips with her own and separating them with her tongue. Hunter felt her large, firm breasts and the soft mound between her hips as she ground against him. He lifted her arm from around his neck and turned his head away slowly as he gently pushed her away. Even as they separated he felt himself stiffen with excitement. He could smell the liquor on her breath. His pulse pounded in his chest from the stirring of blood, and he actually found himself gasping for a breath.

"I can't do that," he said.

She looked at him in a puzzled and hurt way. She was drunk, he knew.

"You want me," she said with certainty.

Hunter felt his head nod almost involuntarily. "I can't imagine anyone who wouldn't want you. But wanting and having are two different things with me."

"How, different?" she said in an almost bored tone of voice.

Hunter shrugged. He felt embarrassed. He started to move toward the door.

"I admire it, though," Camille said abruptly as Hunter stepped past her into the hallway. He entered the great room and looked nervously about. No one was around. He glanced back down the hall. Camille was leaning against the wall, staring after him hungrily.

He found Rachel among a group that included Grant Carter. Hunter was only able to exchange perfunctory smiles with his wife before the owner asked if he might speak to Hunter alone. Hunter was relieved. He'd done nothing wrong, but he was afraid Rachel's sixth sense would detect what had just happened and that she'd make a scene. He wondered what had made him rush back to her side. He needed to cool down.

"Of course, you two go ahead," Rachel said pleasantly. The rest of the group nodded, and Carter led Hunter by the arm away from the pool. They ambled along the private boardwalk that passed over the dunes to the beach. Carter nodded to other guests along the way and occasionally stopped to introduce Hunter. When they reached the stairs to the beach, they were alone.

"Mind if we take a walk?" Carter asked.

"Not at all," Hunter said. He couldn't shake the nervous feeling that he had done something wrong, that Carter knew what had just gone on with Camille. That, of course, was impossible.

When they reached the firm sand just above the tide line and turned, Carter put his arm around Hunter's shoulder, "I wanted to talk with you about your contract, Hunter," he began. "That's not why I asked you here today. I want you to know that. But I didn't want to miss an opportunity to reiterate what I said to you in January after the Super Bowl. I'm serious about us hashing out this deal between ourselves. Your bargaining position is fantastic, I know that. You led my team to the top, and I want you to be compensated. There's no need to let some agent get between us and muck things up for next season. Hell, I'd like to see us do it again."

Carter released Hunter and looked at him for a reaction. Hunter only nodded, listening. Rachel had told him to say as little as possible when Carter brought up his contract. She'd warned him when they got the invitation to the party that just such a discussion was going to happen. Hunter marveled to himself now that she had known what Carter was up to.

"Once you say something in a negotiation you can't undo it," Rachel had said when he told her he was determined to settle this contract on his own. "Let him do the talking. Take everything in, and then you can take time to think about what he's said to you. You can ask other people what they think. The less you say, the more Carter will respect you. The more he respects you, the more fair he'll be with you."

They walked almost another hundred yards before Carter finally accepted Hunter's silence and continued. "Now, Hunter, I'm not trying to demean what you've done, but I want you to know how I'm figuring this. I look at Dan Marino and Joe Montana. They're the two top-paid players in the league. They've both led their teams to the play-offs year after year. They've also both been perennial Pro Bowl quarterbacks. Now, what I've got in mind is this: I'm going to put you in their category, but you'll have to prove yourself again this next season to make their kind of money. I want to tie part of your contract to your performance. If we do well again, or if you have another Pro Bowl year, no one will make more money than you."

Again Carter looked at Hunter for some sign. Again Hunter remained impassive.

"If you agree with what I'm saying in principle," Carter continued, "we'll sit down, you and I, and look at their contracts. Then we'll tailor it to what you want within the bounds of what I'm talking about. I think it makes sense for us both. If you have the kind of year you had this past season, you deserve to make that kind of money. But if there's some kind of unforeseen problem, which we both know there won't be, then I won't feel cheated for having paid you a king's ransom. But . . . if I do this, I don't want you running to the press talking about how you should be paid more than anyone no matter what. I want to be fair. I want us to work this out. You'll make a lot of money either way, at least a three-million-dollar base. I'm just talking about the big, big money being tied to your performance."

Now Carter stopped and began walking back toward his home. Hunter was having a hard time containing himself. He wanted to jump in the air when he heard the words three million. But he'd promised Rachel he'd hold his tongue, so he waited.

Finally Carter said in an exasperated voice, "So what do you think, Hunter? Have you heard anything I've said to you?"

Hunter couldn't help breaking into a small smile, even though he kept his eyes trained ahead. "I'm going to go home and think about everything you've said to me, Mr. Carter. I'm sure between us we can work something out. I just need to think about it a little more."

That was it. Hunter had repeated it to Rachel a hundred times. That was all he would say. And as Rachel had predicted, it was enough. Carter smiled and patted him on the back.

"You're right, son," he said jovially. "This is no way to enjoy a party. You think about what I've said, and I'll call you some time next week. Maybe we can play some tennis out here next weekend and talk a little more. . . . Let's get back to the party."

Camille was not a woman to take rejection lightly, even if the man was married. She thought of herself as a magnet that pulled men to her like helpless bits of steel. No one was immune, or so she thought. So when she awoke on Sunday morning, she was feeling low. She wanted to get away from her father's house and away from Hunter Logan. He was a trophy that had gotten away, and she needed no reminders of it. By noon she was in her Mercedes convertible, headed west on the Long Island Expressway, back to the city. There was little traffic, and an hour and a half later, she was home.

Her apartment looked out over the East River, and on a clear day like this she could see for miles. She pulled the blinds. The bright light did nothing good for her headache. She flipped on her answering machine and poured a screwdriver while she listened. The messages were dull, a party next Friday, two requests for dinner during the week, and an old friend from school calling to say hello. Then she heard an unusual voice from the past. She hadn't expected to hear it ever again; he didn't seem like that type. The voice brought back the image of a wonderful and dangerous night she had spent in the company of Tony Rizzo, several months before.

She'd met him at a party. It was a big party, not the kind with the same old crowd—it had been something different. It had been in the winter, and it had been cold out. She spotted him the moment he walked in the door. He slung off his long black leather coat like a cape. He was dark and exotic-looking. She suspected he was a for-eigner, so when she heard him speak with a silky Brooklyn accent she was surprised. The way the other women in the room followed his movements made her determined to have him much the same way she had been determined to have Hunter Logan just the night before.

The attraction was mutual, and before midnight they were both high and his limousine had delivered them back to his apartment overlooking the park. Soon they were naked on his bed. Camille remembered his voice, soft but threatening. He talked dirty to her and fucked her violently. She remembered being frightened. She remembered liking it. She wrote down the number he left on the answering machine, thinking she could use a little excitement in her life.

CHAPTER 10

Ellis Cook strode purposefully down the sidewalk. The sun was bright. He took off his jacket and dabbed his forehead with his shirt sleeve, leaving it soaked to the skin from his elbow to his wrist. He had walked home to meet Natasha and Esther for lunch. He cursed himself for not taking one of his team's air-conditioned Crown Vics. He had assumed a summer as far north as New York would be a relief from the heat of the deep South. He was wrong. The city held a special heat of its own. It drove those who could escape far out to the cool beaches on the end of Long Island and blistered those who remained behind.

A stench wafted up into his nostrils, and Cook instinctively searched for the source. A bum lay stretched out on the sidewalk, clad in a tattered gray overcoat and a ratty wool cap. The bum pulled a bagged bottle of whiskey to his lips and tipped it up. Cook wondered what could bring someone to such depravity. He hadn't seen bums like this growing up; poor people, yes, but not like these. At first he had given change or singles to every bum who asked for money. Now, after only a few months, he was like most New Yorkers, overwhelmed and immune to their suffering.

New York City was not friendly to anyone, including Cook. He had finally come to grips with what had happened to Tommy Keel and his girl. He had fucked up. It had been ludicrous to think he could bring down Tony Rizzo single-handedly. He was sent to New York to do a difficult job, and thinking he could just ride into town and collar the bad guys on a lucky break was ridiculous. He had always been calculating and methodical in his investigations—that's why he was here now.

The big boys in the Bureau wanted to sting organized crime in New York. Of late, the indictments had been sparse and the big fish still swam free. The director felt that maybe a fresh approach was needed. Cook was being sent in to run a special operation against a particularly large crime family with a particularly rotten fish in its midst. It was a costly operation to devote an entire team to indicting one mob member. Immediate results were expected. But if Cook was successful, it could very well change the way the entire Bureau assailed organized crime. It could also easily turn into an assistant directorship for Cook. He might even get shipped back to D.C. to administrate a nationwide operation from behind a desk. More than once, he had imagined himself returning to a lavish suburban Virginia home every night to help Natasha with her homework.

But that was all far away. It wouldn't happen unless he brought down Tony Rizzo, or Rizzo's uncle. Tony would be Cook's focus. Not just because Cook owed him one for the Keel killing, but because Tony Rizzo was arrogant and greedy and hungry for power. All those things, Cook knew, made a criminal vulnerable. Cook crossed Twelfth Avenue and looked up at a four-story brick warehouse that had seen better days. He used a heavy key to let himself in through the only opening on the first floor that was accessible from the street, a steel door in the south wall of the building.

He peeked his head into the tap room. Amid the sophisticated electrical and recording equipment sat a balding man in his mid-forties.

"How's it coming, Duffy?" Cook asked.

"Nothing really," Conrad Duffy replied. "Guy made a few appointments. Told a dirty story to Cometti about the bimbo he was with last night, then went out for lunch."

Duffy was their communications expert. He had set up and monitored the phone taps they placed on Tony Rizzo and Vincent Mondolffi. They had been tapping their phones for only a few days, and it was still a novelty for Cook. He couldn't help but hope that something big would turn up on the tapes. Cook had his own surveillance team as well, made up of nine men who ran three shifts of three and followed Tony Rizzo every minute of the day. The rest of his team was hard at work investigating bank and tax records, looking for some dissatisfied associate of the organization who they might turn, and following up leads from information gathered by surveillance.

When Cook got to his office, John Marrow, his second in command, was waiting for him.

"You're gonna like this, sir," Marrow said.

"What have you got?" Cook said anxiously.

"Nothing too big"—Marrow saw the fire in his boss's eyes fade—"but it is interesting. It seems our ladies' man landed him some real class. Since we've been tailing him, he's only seen one girl more than once. This one he's seen three times. Well, we checked her out and the interesting thing is, she's the daughter of Grant Carter."

Marrow could see Cook's puzzlement. "Carter is a big developer in this area, a Donald Trump type of guy . . . He also owns the New York Titans."

Cook raised his eyebrows. "Does the old man know she's seeing Rizzo?"

"We don't really know since we just started following Rizzo two weeks ago, but I've got Tom Snyder looking into it. Could be nothing. This Carter girl, Camille's her name, she's kind of a wild one. Could just be a quirk."

"Let's keep a close eye on what goes on between them, John. I've got a feeling. Tony Rizzo doesn't strike me as the kind of guy who does much of anything without a purpose."

Out on the Island, Hunter was teeing off in the fourteenth Annual Leukemia Society Celebrity Golf Tournament. Colorful flags adorned the clubhouse, and thousands of people milled about, craning for a glimpse of their sports heroes. Hunter smacked the ball and it lifted off down the fairway, straight and long. The crowd burst into applause. Hunter grinned from ear to ear and waved his cap to the crowd.

"A ringer," Patrick Ewing murmured as he passed Hunter on his way to the tee, shaking his head woefully.

"Couldn't do it again in a million years," Hunter said under his breath to the giant basketball player. Ewing's clubs were almost as tall as Hunter, and he marveled as the big man gently swung his club. The sound was like a shot. Ewing's ball hit the turf ten yards past Hunter's, then rolled another forty. The crowd went wild.

The two shots turned out to be the only bright moments on the course for New York's two favorite athletes. Their games went steadily downhill from there, until finally Hunter and Patrick decided to bet a case of beer on the guy who lost the fewest balls. At the halfway mark Hunter had lost five to Patrick's four.

Hunter was sharing a cart with the president of Mitsubishi's American division while Patrick played with one of the younger Rockefeller heirs. Each man had paid $10,000 to play with the celebrities. The idea of paying that much money for a round of golf with them got Hunter and Patrick laughing together throughout the afternoon.

"At least I've got an excuse," Patrick said as they crossed over into the opposite fairway to play their hooked tee shots.

"What's that?" Hunter said. "Your clubs are too short?"

Ewing looked as him sideways, then laughed when he realized Hunter was ribbing him about his enormous sticks.

"Nah," he said, looking around to see that no one else was within earshot. "I got a damn bad ankle that kills me when I pivot around."

"I've heard it all now," Hunter chuckled.

"Don't believe me if you don't want to." Ewing shrugged.

Hunter swung, topping the ball but getting it back into legitimate play.

"Man," Hunter said as they approached Patrick's ball, "if you were hurt it'd be the talk of the town. Especially with the Bulls coming in here Friday night."

"I know that," Ewing said, hitting the ball through some trees and into a trap near the green. "That's why I ain't the talk of the town. I don't want no one finding out about this. The damn reporters would make my life more miserable than they already do."

Hunter changed the subject to the upcoming play-off series with Chicago, and soon they were back in their respective carts with the paying guests. Hunter, however, carefully watched the way Patrick moved for the rest of the afternoon. It was very slight, but Hunter did detect a slight wince in Ewing's face whenever he really tried to clobber the ball.

After the tournament there was a brief awards ceremony inside the clubhouse. Patrick and Hunter gave out the prizes. When the day ended, but before Hunter's car had left the parking lot, he was on his phone to Metz.

"Metz, it's me, Hunter," he said when his friend answered the phone.

"Hunt, what's up? I just walked in from work," Metz said.

"Can you meet me at Rafters?"

"Now?"

"Yeah, now. Can you meet me?"

"It's a little early to start drinking. Don't you want to eat first?"

"I can't hang out. I've got to be home for dinner by seven. I spent all day at that Leukemia golf tournament and Rachel will kill me if I don't get back, but I need to talk to you quick."

"So talk."

"Metz, will you meet me or not?"

"It ain't like you to be so mysterious. Of course I'll meet you. I'll be there in ten minutes."

Rafters was a bar and grill close to Hunter's home, and although it smelled strongly of stale beer, they kept the AC up high and it was nice and cool inside. Hunter got a beer at the bar and waited only about five minutes before Metz walked through the door. Hunter felt the warm air rush in from the street. Metz sat down in the booth and ordered a beer for himself. He was still wearing a dress shirt and a tie that was loosened to accommodate a collar that wouldn't button around the enormous rolls of fat that supported his head. The shirt was rumpled, almost like he'd slept in it. Beads of sweat rolled down Metz's jowls as he tipped his head back to slurp down half his mug of beer.

"Ahh," Metz exclaimed, slamming down the mug and smacking his lips. "Hot as the devil's dick out there."

Hunter smiled at his friend. There was something so comical about the enormity of him that Hunter tended to forget he was a slob.

"So what's up?" Metz said. "You gonna sit there grinning at me, or are you gonna tell me what all this James Bond shit is about?"

Hunter looked around and leaned forward before he said in a low voice, "You can't talk on those car phones. Anyone can listen. Can you bet basketball through that bookie you know?"

"Sure," Metz said, "but I told you you know your shit when it comes to football. What makes you think you know dick about hoops?"

"I don't know," Hunter said, "but I got a scoop on Friday night's game against the Bulls that can't miss!"

Metz looked around too before dropping his own voice. "You know something?"

"Yeah," Hunter said, talking still lower. "Ewing was at that golf thing today and we played together in the same foursome. So one time we're going over into the other fairway to hit our shots, and he tells me his ankle is killing him. I tell him that I didn't see anything about it in the papers, and you know what he says?"

Metz shook his head no. His eyes were wide with excitement.

"He tells me he doesn't want anyone to know about it. Even the team's doctors. He says that he doesn't want to listen to any bullshit about it with Chicago coming to town. Metz, I watched the man. I watched him close after he told me that. When he turns that ankle just so, his face twists all up in pain. The man is hurt and no one knows it but you and me!"

Metz's face was red with excitement. Then it seemed to fade.

"What if he gets better?" he said.

"Metz, believe me, I know about this kind of thing. The man is hurt and he's not getting better by Friday night."

Metz sat for a while, then drained his beer and signaled the waitress to bring him a second one.

After the beer arrived, Metz said, "So what are you gonna do about it?"

"I want you to put some money on the Bulls for me."

"Man, that's not like you. This thing smells bad even to me."

"I know," Hunter said quickly, "it's crazy, but I was thinking about it. What the hell? It's no big deal. It's a little edge I got from being at the right place at the right time. It's too crazy, it's like this roll I've been on lately, like nothing can go wrong for me."

Metz nodded, "You got that right."

"So, you'll put the bet down?" Hunter said.

"OK," Metz said with a shrug. "You know I will. How much?"

Hunter leaned in again.

"Ten large."

"You don't mean ten large," Metz said. "Ten large isn't ten hundred dollar bills. Large means a thousand."

"I mean ten large," Hunter said.

"Ten thousand?"

"Ten thousand."

Metz let out a low whistle between his teeth. "Jesus, Hunter, Rachel will kill you if you lose ten thousand dollars. Then she'll kill me! Where do you come off betting that much?"

It was Hunter's turn to take a long drink. "First of all . . . I know I'm gonna win. Second, my contract this year is so damn big that ten grand is looking like pocket change to me."

"So they're gonna come through and pay you, huh?" Metz asked.

"Carter already offered me over three million a year," Hunter said quietly.

"Holy shit! That's twice as much as I made in five years together! No wonder you don't give a shit how much you bet."

Metz gulped down half of the new mug.

"Now you got no problems getting the cash, right? In case you lose, I don't want these guys coming to break my legs or something, you know. They like cash. They don't want no checks."

"No problem," Hunter said. "Just make sure you place the bet tonight, just in case someone else finds out and the line changes." Hunter got up and tossed a ten on the table. "I gotta get home. Thanks, Metz. Let me know if you have any problems."

"Hey, no problem, buddy. These guys love me. I just hope you know what the hell you're doing."

"Don't worry about me, buddy," said Hunter, "I know exactly what I'm doing."

Vincent Mondolffi spent much of his time away from home in the private upstairs dining room of a small Italian restaurant in Brooklyn called Romans. Mondolffi owned the building but not the restaurant itself. Martino owned the place. He catered to all of Mondolffi's needs and fed him for nothing. This meant staying open as long as Mondolffi needed, and making available a private room with its own phone. In return, Martino got a good deal on the rent and he never had any problems with the liquor authority or with lawsuits from any customers who slipped on the floor.

Mondolffi was finishing up dinner with an old banker friend and a builder who put up houses in Brooklyn when Ears stepped into the room and announced that there was an urgent call downstairs. Mondolffi frowned, then rose from his chair, excused himself, and made his way down some back stairs, then through the kitchen to the pay phones. He was tired of all this shit, walking through kitchens, talking on pay phones. If he could just throw his nephew over to the feds and have them go away, he'd do it in a heartbeat. If it was only that simple. The minute Tony started going down, he'd drag everyone with him he possibly could. He knew Tony well enough to know that. He cursed himself. It was his own doing that Tony was as powerful as he now was. It was a weakness not to have had him killed. His brother-in-law would have killed Vincent, Jr., if the roles had been reversed. But viciousness killed his brother-in-law at an early age, that and greed.

Vincent Mondolffi stopped momentarily to watch a lobster reddening in a large boiling pot. He left the kitchen and picked up the pay phone.

"Hello."

"Are you ready for the vehicle descriptions?"

"Go."

The voice read through a series of vehicles, giving the license number of each one. Some were old, some new. Three were vans with commercial markings on them. Vincent Mondolffi listened carefully and committed the information to memory. He wondered why he bothered when Tony would simply write it down anyway. But it was one of the habits he knew had enabled him to survive so long, so he never broke it.

"Also," the voice continued, "your home and Tony's home are being tapped."

"When did this happen?" Vincent Mondolffi snapped.

"They got them on a couple of days."

"Why wasn't I informed?"

"I wasn't able to get you. I can no longer call you at home, and I was unable to reach you at the restaurant. The heat is getting rather intense, Mr. Mondolffi, and I do think some additional token of your appreciation for my allegiance through bad times as well as good would be nice. Do you think that would be all right?"

Mondolffi was silent for a moment. It never failed.

"How would you feel if I doubled our present arrangement?" he said finally.

"I think that's very generous, Mr. Mondolffi. I'll look for the package."

"I'm sure you will. And something else . . . I want to know the minute my nephew is compromised in any way. If he's going to take a fall, I want to know about it before it happens. Can that be done?"

Vincent Mondolffi would tell this to no one, but in his mind he had made plans to have Tony eliminated the moment he compromised the family. Tony was a survivor, not a romantic. Loyalty and honor were lost ideas on a man like that.

"How could I refuse in the face of your generosity?" came the response over the phone.

"Good."

Vincent Mondolffi hung up the phone and turned to Ears.

"Get Tony over here," he said, "but don't call him. Go get him. I'm going back to finish with those two upstairs, then I'll have a drink. Tell him I expect him to be here by the time I have my coffee."

I

t's M-17. He says he won't place a bet with anyone but you, Jimmy."

Jimmy the Squid took the phone from Carl, one of his thick-necked underlings.

"Whadya want?" he said rudely. He didn't have time to talk personally with small fries, especially small fries who were up on him. Jimmy was bound to a wheelchair. His pallid skin and clammy hands had earned him his name even before the "accident," as he called it. He was a surly man in his mid-thirties who had taken a bullet in the back in a shoot-out between the Mondolffis and the Capozzas back in 1979. Like anyone who had fallen in the service of the family, he was well taken care of. He was made and eventually given the responsibility of handling all of the Mondolffis' action in the "Five Towns" just east of Queens. He got a thirty percent take on everything. This enabled him to have a retinue of five or six thugs to do his constant bidding. Carl was his favorite, and despite being dim-witted at times, he showed promise. Jimmy had hopes for Carl.

"Jimmy, this is M-17."

"Yeah, I know who you are, Metz. Cut the shit and tell me what the hell you want that you couldn't say to no one but me."

"I want to put some money on Friday night's Bulls game."

"OK, the line's New York by one. I got heavy action on the Knicks this week, so I can only give you one."

"I'll take Chicago."

"I'm happy for you, Metz. Now tell me what your fucking bet is so I can get back to picking my ass."

"Can I bet ten thousand, Jimmy? On Chicago?" came Metz's voice tentatively.

Jimmy hesitated. He was thinking. He raised his eyebrows to his men, who were all watching him closely. Then he said, "Of course, Metz! You can bet ten thousand if you want to. I know you're good for it. You've been a good customer, and I want to get even with you after what you did to us during the football season."

Jimmy winked at his men.

"That's great, Jimmy!" Metz said. "I hope you don't mind losing ten large."

Jimmy hung up and immediately dialed Mike Cometti.

"Mikey, what's up? This is Jimmy. I got a live one for you."

"Yeah?" Cometti said.

"Yeah, get this . . . this guy's been nickel and diming me all football season, right? Never bets over five hundred, tops. Ever. No, once he bet a grand on a Titans game, come to think of it. Anyway, I figure you might want to let someone up high know what I got here."

"I'm glad you called, Jimmy," Cometti said. "Tony likes to know about stuff like that."

"Yeah, well, let me know what you want me to do, Mikey. If you need some muscle on this, I got a good guy here who knows the area . . . And say hello to Tony for me, will ya?"

"Yeah, sure, Jimmy."

Jimmy held out the phone in Carl's general direction. Carl took it before he asked, "Hey, Jimmy, how come you called Mike Cometti to tell him about fat Metz's bet? I mean, we want guys to bet a lot of money, don't we? But you seem like something's bothering you."

Jimmy the Squid gave his other cronies a bewildered look as if to ask if Carl was for real.

"We do want them to bet, you dumb ass. But this guy ain't betting for himself. He's betting for somebody else. Somebody big."

"Yeah, so what?"

"So what? Do I gotta tell you everything? Al, you tell this dumb-ass why."

Al looked at Jimmy with his good eye while his bad one meandered about the room.

"Well," he said, "I figure it this way. This guy Metz only bets a couple hundred most times. But now all of a sudden he calls in ten large on a basketball game. So I guess you're thinking that this Metz guy's got a lot of money from someplace, and we want to find out how 'cause if it's something good, we want to get in on it."

Al smiled broadly and nodded his head in agreement with himself.

"Minkya!" Jimmy said, throwing his hands in the air and looking at the ceiling. "All over people are out of work. They say there's college kids who can't get jobs, and I've got a pack of fucking dummies working for me!

"Now, watch and learn something. If you fucking idiots ever want to be made members of this family"—Jimmy looked at Carl specifically—"you gotta show you got at least some small fucking ability to think and to know what the fuck is gonna happen. It's called preception. You gotta have pre-ception to be made. Like this . . . Mike Cometti is calling Tony right now. In a few minutes Mikey's gonna call me back and tell me if this guy Metz wins to pay him and then follow his fat ass. If he loses, then they'll tell me to follow his fat ass after the game to see who gives him the money to pay us. Either way we find out who the mystery man is, and then Tony can decide what to do with him. Get it? This stuff happens from time to time, it's standard procedure. Now, you fucking idiots just sit here with me and wait, 'cause like I said, it's all about pre-ception and what I just said is what's gonna be."

Jimmy the Squid got his call in five minutes.

Hunter worked out with the rest of the Titans at the team's training facility four days a week. He would usually go in the morning and do his lifting and running, then throw some balls to his receivers for about an hour before lunch. After lunch he would take care of the deluge of personal business that besieged a world champion quarterback. This meant dividing his time between charity fund-raisers like the Leukemia golf tournament, endorsement opportunities like shooting a commercial for Scott's Turf Plus, or schmoozing with people on the golf course who he thought would be valuable contacts when his career ended.

He'd actually signed on with Stern and Lipsky, a public relations agency, to handle his schedule for charity appearances. He also consulted closely with Mark Lipsky on just who were the right people to schmooze to best help himself in life after football. One thing the people at Stern and Lipsky understood about scheduling him for anything was that Friday afternoons were out. Hunter wouldn't even throw to his receivers on Fridays. He'd finish his workout by ten and be on the road with Rachel and Sara by eleven, heading for the Hamptons and trying to beat the mobs of traffic that flooded the Long Island Expressway until well past midnight every Friday of the summer. Hunter's other trick was to leave Monday mornings and miss the inbound rush as well. As it was, they were able to enjoy the tranquillity of their modest ocean house without packing the weekend between two stress-filled drives with all the other New Yorkers who were insane with their desire to get to the beaches.

Hunter and Rachel's house was set on one hundred feet of oceanfront. Fortunately, the neighbors on either side each owned four hundred feet, so the Logans were able to enjoy a sense of privacy that was paid for by their neighbors. Their house sat atop a dune and was surrounded by clusters of scraggly pines that had been crippled and stunted by the harsh ocean winds. The house itself was contemporary with vertical wooden siding that was painted white and accented with groupings of glass cubes to let light in as well as give some life to the outside structure, which was otherwise as bland as a stack of sugar cubes. Neither Hunter nor Rachel particularly liked contemporary homes, but this one had what they wanted on the inside and was perfectly located as well. Hunter had insisted they be on the ocean. Rachel wanted a place that had a casual layout with one large living area and some bedrooms.

They had spent this particular Friday out on the beach. They'd stopped in town for lunch, then brought blankets, umbrellas, and toys out to the beach to swim, play, and nap in the warm summer afternoon. Around five, Rachel picked up and headed to the house to get dinner ready. Hunter took Sara for one last romp in the waves before he too headed back to the house to shower. After they ate, Hunter helped clear the table, then pulled a beer from the refrigerator and flopped down on the couch.

"Want to see a movie tonight?" Rachel asked. "We could drop Sara at my folks' house for the night."

"Yeah! Nana and Poppa!" Sara screamed with delight.

"Am I that bad to be with?" Hunter said in mock pain.

"You're silly, Daddy," she said with a giggle.

Hunter looked at his watch and picked up the TV remote.

"You know, honey. Let's just hang out tonight. I want to watch the NBA play-offs. We can see a movie tomorrow night."

"I can't remember you ever wanting to watch a basketball game on a Friday night," Rachel said without looking up from the sink where she was scrubbing out a pan.

Hunter was slouched on the couch now with his arm around Sara. The game was just getting under way. His feet were crossed and resting on the coffee table. His bottle of beer sat on the end table, and he felt for it without looking. He took a swig and said, "I just figured I'd watch Patrick Ewing to see how he does. Hell, it's not every day you play golf with a guy who's going up against Michael Jordan in the NBA play-offs."

Rachel peered up from her work to see if Hunter was playing with her. She knew damn well he didn't care about the NBA play-offs. He continued to stare at the screen. She shrugged and got back to her pan. She was loading the dirty dishes into the washer when she looked up suddenly and glared at her husband on the couch.

"So," she said abruptly, "how much did you bet on the game?"

Hunter pretended not to have heard her.

"What'd you say, honey?" he asked, trying to decide how to handle the situation.

"You heard me, Hunter. You've got a bet on this game, don't you," she demanded.

He looked up sheepishly and shrugged.

"Well, Patrick gave me a scoop on Wednesday that I couldn't ignore. It's not a big thing, honey. Don't go giving me the evil eye."

"You do what you want, Hunter," she said in a huff. "I'm not going to be your mother. You made all this money. If you want to squander it away gambling, I guess it's your business. But don't say I didn't warn you."

Hunter gave a halfhearted laugh and said, "Oh, come on, honey. Don't get so damn sour about one little bet on a basketball game. Besides, Ewing is hurt. The Knicks don't stand a chance."

"I know you think you know what you're doing," she replied, "but just remember I told you that it's not a good idea."

"OK, honey," Hunter said, his eyes already reglued to the set, "I'll remember."

CHAPTER 12

That will be all, gentlemen," Duncan Fellows said to the group of supervisors that was gathered around the large conference table. They had each reported their progress and the status of their individual groups. One at a time they had stood and reported in a way that reminded Cook of grade school. The idea was that each man could get original management ideas from his contemporaries. Cook thought it was absurd.

"Ah, Cook. I still need to see you. You can sit back down."

The other men looked at Cook and smirked.

Fellows was fucking with him. Ever since the Keel incident, Fellows had been condescending toward Cook. Cook knew this was his boss's way of reminding him that he had one up on him, but Cook didn't like Fellows and he didn't like what was happening. Unfortunately for him, Fellows was his immediate superior, and if he wanted his grand plan to be fulfilled, part of the equation was keeping Fellows happy. Not to mention the problems the whole Keel incident could create for Cook if Fellows ever wrote it up.

Cook looked at his watch. It was Saturday and the meeting had already run over. It was quarter past noon, and Cook had promised to meet Natasha and Aunt Esther at the Plaza Hotel for lunch in the Palm Court at twelve. It was Natasha's birthday and Cook wanted to do something special. He had promised her a carriage ride through the park after lunch and then a trip to FAO Schwartz across the street. He had also promised Esther that he wouldn't be late.

When the room was finally empty, Fellows spoke.

"Everything here in New York to your satisfaction, Cook?"

"Yes, sir," Cook said, "just fine."

"Good, Cook, that's good. Everything moving along as planned?"

Cook shifted impatiently in his chair.

"Just like I said in my report a few minutes ago, sir. Everything is still the same."

"Oh, I know about your report, Cook. I just wanted to know if you had anything going on the side again, you know, some interesting leads that maybe you thought you might keep to yourself."

"I get your point, sir. I don't think it's really necessary to constantly remind me about the mix-up with Tommy Keel."

"Mix-up?" Fellows interjected. "Don't you mean fuck-up? Isn't that what it's called when you show up at the home of a potential witness and flash your badge around before you even have a clue as to what you're going to do with him and what kind of compromised state he's already in? Then, to top it off, the guy gets killed? Don't you think that might have something to do with the fact that you and your men can't get Rizzo on a parking violation? Every snitch on the East Coast knows what happened to Tommy Keel, and they know why. Word on the street is that a black agent shows up at Keel's house the day after he's been beaten up by Tony Rizzo. The word is the agent stayed for fucking tea! Then Keel winds up with his head blown off! You couldn't get someone in that organization to help you if you stuck a cattle prod up their ass. You did more to protect the Mondolffi family since Tony Rizzo, Sr., put a piece of piano wire around Luca Mirrolo's neck! Mix-up, my ass."

"I know what I did was technically wrong. I know you know it. I know you didn't make out a report on it. I know you're holding that over my head. But why don't you just give me some slack and let me get out of here and do my job. I know I'm infringing on your territory. But it's Washington that makes these types of policy decisions. So why don't you just let me do what I've got to do and get on back to Washington?"

Fellows smiled and leaned back in his chair at the head of the long table.

"I'm sure that's just what you want, too, isn't it, Cook? To get on back to Washington, where you can be a real big shot. I know that if this comes off, you'll be in a position to manage the teams they send around the entire country, and that's fine with me. But I want you to know one thing. While you're here, you'll report to me. I want to know everything that's going on before you do it. Any more surprises and you'll be back in Washington all right. You'll be a traffic cop on M Street."

"Is that all, Mr. Fellows?" Cook said in a pleasant voice, despite being unable to hide the contempt in his face.

"Go on, Cook," Fellows said with the wave of his hand, "you look like you're late for something."

Cook got up slowly and left the room, determined not to let Fellows know that he'd probably ruined his day by making him late. But when Cook reached the street he sprinted after a cab going uptown. Five minutes later, he was racing up the steps of the Plaza. He picked Esther and Natasha out of the crowded room easily. They were the only black faces in the place. He rushed to the table and Esther looked up at him with a smile.

Cook looked around. "Is everything all right?" he asked, fearing Esther might have had a small stroke.

"Of course," Esther said. She was dressed up in a floral sundress similar to Natasha's.

"Well," Cook said, bending down to kiss his daughter, who reached up to hug his neck, "Esther, I thought all hell was going to break loose with me showing up late."

"Did you think I would ruin this child's birthday because you're late like you always are? Why, you old fool, Ellis, I'm glad your mama isn't around. Big man in the FBI, but sometimes you haven't got the sense of an ass."

Natasha giggled.

"Now that sounds more like the Aunt Esther I know," said Cook as he sat down with a smile and signaled to a waiter.

Jimmy the Squid wheeled himself out into the middle of his living room. He lived in a modest home in a row of similar homes on a suburban street in North Woodmere. The only thing at all unusual besides the wheelchair ramps was the constant flow of traffic in and out, day and night. When people won a lot of money, they had to come to Jimmy to get it. This was the first time Metz had been invited to pick up his money at Jimmy's.

Metz put one large fat hand on Jimmy's shoulder and with the other grasped a thick stack of hundred-dollar bills that was bound with two rubber bands. The flash exploded and left Metz with a spot in his vision.

"That OK, Lonny?" Jimmy asked one of his thugs with unusual deference.

The man named Lonny, who was wiry and older than anyone else in the room, only nodded.

"Yeah, that's great," said Jimmy. "Thanks, Metz. I always like to get a picture with the big winners."

Metz nodded and shifted nervously. He didn't like being around people in wheelchairs. A wheelchair was the nightmare of any football player, past or present. It was weird that Jimmy wanted a picture, but Metz was so uncomfortable about being there at all that he didn't give it a second thought. He was happy, however, with the feel of the thick stack of money. And he liked being a big bettor. These thugs were treating him with respect. Usually Carl or someone would meet him at a bar and shove a couple of hundreds into his hand, dismissing him with a grunt. But here he was now, at the center of it all. He knew Jimmy was in the Mafia. Carl had told him repeatedly. And although Jimmy made him nervous, he was tantalized by the mystique. He thought it might be nice if Hunter bet this kind of cash every week. He could see himself being something of a fixture at Jimmy's, someone they expected to see, someone they treated as an equal.

"So who are you taking in Sunday's game?" the Squid asked, looking up from his chair and showing Metz a crooked set of teeth that were black around the edges.

"I'll have to let you know," Metz said with as much authority as he could muster.

"Oh, come on, Metz," said Jimmy. "Don't tell me you're gonna sting me like that and stop the action?"

Metz got nervous again. He looked around to read the expressions of Jimmy's cronies. They grinned oafishly. Metz smiled and gave Jimmy's shoulder a final squeeze before he moved toward the door.

"I'll have to let you know, Jimmy. I gotta check my source with the Knicks to find out what's up," Metz said, intending to have a little fun himself.

"Oh?" Jimmy raised his eyebrows with mock deference. "And who's your source?"

"Patrick Ewing, who else?" Metz said.

The whole crew laughed at that one, even Jimmy.

"Thanks, Jimmy," Metz said as he stepped through the door with a grin and a wave as if they were all old and dear friends.

Metz was glad to be away from the wheelchair, and he was glad to have Hunter's money. He congratulated himself on how smooth he'd been, joking like that with his bookie and his thugs. If they only knew about Ewing! The day was sunny but not too warm. It was Sunday. Metz couldn't wait to see Hunter after work tomorrow. He couldn't wait to see his friend's face. They had actually done it! They'd bet ten thousand dollars and won. Metz felt like a little kid. He never noticed Lonny and Carl jump into a blue van that was parked in the street in front of Jimmy's house and follow him down the road. When Metz pulled into his own driveway and went into his house, the van pulled up across the street and parked. No one got out. The people inside were waiting for Monday, too.

Tony had seen Camille Carter three times since she returned his call. The first night he'd taken her to the Four Seasons, where the waiters and even the owner bowed deferentially to Tony, then to the Palladium, where they were also treated like royalty. Camille seemed bored with the whole thing and that had frustrated Tony. He was trying to be a gentleman, and she could barely hide her yawns.

Things changed when he invited her to his place. She eagerly accepted, and, like their first encounter, they began by snorting some coke. It was then that Camille surprised Tony. Instead of being frightened by him, she was excited. He could see the thrill in her eyes as he thrust himself inside her. This enthusiasm goaded him. He got rough with her, flipping her body over and taking her from behind. She moaned in ecstasy. He wrapped his hands in her soft blond hair and twisted her face toward him. He knew it had to hurt, but pleasure lit her face.

Tony was torn between his desire to hurt her, to see real fear in her eyes, and fulfilling his plan to somehow get on the inside of her father's professional football team. If he beat her the way he wanted, it would be over, he knew. This girl wanted excitement, even a little pain, but a black eye or a broken rib would mean the end of any entree to the Titans organization. So Tony had to control himself, and oddly enough, he found himself drawn to her even more. Instead of waiting a week to call her, he called her after three days.

The next date went much the same way. He tried to treat her nicely by taking her to dinner at Palio and then a small jazz club. It soon became obvious that she wanted to skip the formalities and be taken back to his apartment and fucked.

"What do you think?" she asked at the jazz club, "that you're some kind of Romeo? Why don't we go home?"

Then she laughed out loud at his gallant efforts. He could see that she wasn't afraid of him. He let his rage loose on her when they got back to his place. Again she seemed to thrive on it.

And now, tonight, he was to see her again. He dressed himself carefully in the mirror, thinking that she would mock him with her eyes if she knew. He would have stuck with her though, even if he wasn't attracted to her. He wanted to meet the old man and get acquainted and search for a key to the Titans. Maybe he'd suggest dinner with her parents, he wasn't sure. He knew one thing, though. If he kept seeing her, he'd get a chance.

Tony had a vague plan to grease a trainer, or a doctor, or even a player or an equipment man if he couldn't get to anyone better. He knew it had been done before with other teams. It happened all the time. Of course, a trainer would be his best bet. He would know the most about which player was really hurt or who was having family problems at home during the week. Tony had been around gambling long enough to know that it was these seemingly minor details that affected the line on a game.

If Tony could get an inside line on the team, he could adjust his own line to take a little more money on one side or the other, depending on the quality of the information. Even if it was only ten or twenty thousand dollars that he allowed the books to be off, it would be like his own personal bet, and information like that would pay off throughout the course of a season. That's what gambling was all about, information. His uncle would be placated on two counts. First, Tony would appear to have taken his advice to focus on gambling. Second, to be seen around town with Grant Carter's daughter on his arm would make a real show of trying to forge new paths into legitimacy.

Tony checked his face in the mirror and bared his white teeth to admire their perfection. The best part about the whole thing was that he wanted to be with her. He wanted to see her toss her head at him in public, and then cringe and moan in pain and supplication later in the same night. She was beautiful and she was wild, and Tony Rizzo was determined to possess her whether she led him to a pay-off or not.

When he arrived at her apartment building, the doorman said she wasn't ready. He cursed her. He hated when people weren't ready. Then he realized that his hang-up with promptness had come up in one of their conversations on their last date, and he wondered if she wasn't taking her time on purpose.

Tony was told by the doorman that she left instructions for him to wait in the lobby. The affluent of Manhattan flowed in and out. Tony watched them all, stripping the women with his eyes and assessing the wealth of the men by their clothes, their jewelry, and the kind of car that was waiting for them. There were other young lovers there like himself, waiting for rich and haughty young women. Camille made him wait for fifteen minutes, and he was livid until he saw her. She moved across the lobby like an empress. Her head was high and her splendor drew stares from everyone who saw her.

He stood and she kissed him. He forgot that he was mad. When they separated, she examined his face to see whether or not she had been worth the wait.

"Where are we going?" she asked.

"Are you afraid to go into a bad area?" he asked politely.

She huffed in response.

"There's a little Italian place in Far Rockaway that has the best food in the city. Not many people know about it, and it's in a neighborhood that most people in this building wouldn't be caught dead in—garbage, bums, and criminals everywhere. If they were caught, they probably would be killed."

Her eyes lit up and she smiled. "Let's go," she said without hesitation.

Tony smiled at her and nodded OK.

"There it is," he said as the car rolled down a dirty street near Far Rockaway Beach. Camille looked at the row of rundown shops that lined the darkened street. Most had boarded-up windows, and those that didn't were black on the inside. A small neon shamrock flickered from one window, and Camille assumed it was a kind of bar when she saw two grimy men stagger out of the door. The only other sign of commerce was a neon pizza sign that cut through a dirty window. Above the storefront was another sign that Camille could not read since it wasn't lit up. The closest streetlight was almost a block away. There was no place to park on the street. It was littered with old, rusted cars, some of which were up on blocks. They had to park down by the beach and walk back. Tony could have called ahead and had someone waiting to park the car for them, or even had a wrecker haul someone else's car from the street in front of the restaurant, but he imagined Camille would like the walk in the dark.

When they got out of the car, the surf was crashing loudly at high tide. The dark water licked at the beach below. Each bench that lined the boardwalk bore a tattered bum, some flopping lethargically, but most still as stones. Garbage was strewn everywhere, and they had to step carefully over a fetid puddle to continue on the sidewalk. As they reached the row of buildings, a rat scrambled across the street and disappeared into a crack in the curb.

Tony laughed. "I warned you."

"I don't mind," she said casually, as he opened the door to a small restaurant.

They were seated at the biggest corner table by a fawning owner as soon as they walked in.

"The way I grew up," Tony said, "you have to be ready for the unexpected."

"Just how did you grow up, Tony?" Camille asked, leaning forward, obviously interested.

This attention made Tony happy. He had obviously impressed her. He was glad she was interested in him. This was the first time he had cared about that from a woman. But Camille was no ordinary woman. She broke all the rules.

He paused, frowning before he spoke.

"When I was ten I woke up to the sound of my mother screaming. When I got to the hall, I saw three men dragging my father out of his bedroom by his pajamas. I ran to help him. One of the men hit me with the butt of a pistol. See . . ."

Camille leaned forward in the candlelight to examine the faint white scar above his eye.

"I woke up in the hospital. My mother was dressed in black. We never saw my father again. There was no funeral or anything. They never found him."

"Jesus," Camille said. "I'm sorry. . ."

"My father was the treasurer of a mason's union. He was a mason himself and he worked hard. Everyone respected my father, but he crossed the wrong people. I guess there were some crooked people in that business at the time; he didn't want to get mixed up with them. That's how that stuff goes. You either play or you pay."

Tony stared at a candle that burned in a bottle on their table. He seemed lost in the story. Much of it was true.

"After that," he said, "I grew up hard. You know, a kid without a father. I had an uncle who looked after me some, but mostly I looked after myself. I got into a bad crowd for a while, and fighting in the streets was part of our daily lives. After high school I started in business for myself. I was able to get a pretty successful construction company going. I straightened out and obviously stayed off the street, but I keep in tune by training in the martial arts."

Camille nodded. "Thank God. This neighborhood scares me."

"Not you," Tony said. "I can't believe there's anything that could scare you."

She laughed. "Something new every day with you, I guess."

"Good. I'm glad that I'm different."

"Yes," she said, "you are that."

L

et's go, Carl," Lonny said in a tone that reflected how tired he was of his muscle-bound companion.

"OK," Carl said through a mouthful of Big Mac, his dinner for the day. "Just a second. Lemme finish this last bite."

Carl held up the remaining quarter of the sandwich. Lonny slapped Carl's hand, sending hamburger all over the dashboard.

"Hey, what the fuck did you do that for?" Carl demanded, his face turning red with anger.

Lonny slapped Carl's face, leaving a welt. Carl looked stunned. Lonny was half his size but almost twice his age and obviously mean as hell. Carl knew better than to hit Lonny. Lonny was in the family. That gave him power.

"You lose Metz and I'll personally watch Tony Rizzo cut your balls off," Lonny said with a nasty sneer. "Now move it."

Carl started the van and jerked away from the curb. Metz's Cadillac was already halfway down the street. They stayed three cars back and followed him down Peninsula Boulevard to the Sherwood Diner. The diner was a remnant from the fifties, complete with stainless steel siding and multicolored neon lights that wrapped around its exterior. Carl was able to park the van close to the window of the booth where Metz sat.

Lonny picked up his camera and fitted on a zoom lens. It was almost seven o'clock, but there was still plenty of light for him to get a shot if he needed to.

"How come you're getting the camera ready?" Carl asked, too dumb to be miffed at the slap he'd just received.

Lonny looked at him briefly, then directed his gaze back at the diner window.

"He's meeting someone, that's why," Lonny said flatly.

Carl furrowed his brow and thought for a minute. "How do you know?"

"He sat down and the waitress gave him a menu, right?" Lonny said.

Carl nodded. He guessed that was right.

"But the guy's just sitting there right? He hasn't even looked at it. So, he's waiting for someone."

Carl was impressed and he grinned to prove it.

Hunter Logan walked into the restaurant wearing thick prescription glasses, a gray sweatshirt, and a Yankees cap. Not even the hostess who seated him recognized who he was. When he sat down, Lonny shot off a few frames. Hunter's face looked familiar, but he couldn't place it. Metz pulled out the wad of hundred-dollar bills and held it up high. Hunter reached for it then shoved it into the front pocket of the hooded sweatshirt he wore.

"Perfect," Lonny murmured as the camera clicked and whirred. "You'd think Metz was working for us."

Lonny chuckled and clicked as Hunter peeled two of the bills off the stack and held them out to Metz. Metz's hand gobbled up the bills like a hungry dog under the table. Lonny wondered if his camera had been fast enough to capture such a brisk transaction.

Lonny and Carl sat through Metz's enormous meal, wishing he'd eat rather than stop every minute or so to gesticulate wildly at his companion. For his part, Hunter was obviously happy, but not as excited as his enormous friend. It was almost nine o'clock before Metz finally finished his second plate of pie and pushed the bill over to Hunter. They could see Hunter chuckle good-naturedly and pull some money from his wallet, leaving it on the table before they stood to leave. By the time Hunter stepped out of the diner it was dusk outside, and the red furnace sky in the west was being slowly cooled by a wave of purple darkness that left scattered twinkling stars in its wake.

"All we gotta do now is find out who this guy is," Lonny said to himself.

Carl nodded, not knowing that the comment wasn't meant for him.

"How we gonna do that?" Carl asked quietly.

Lonny looked at Carl to make sure he was serious. When he saw that Carl was really wondering, he snorted through his nose.

"We're gonna follow him. How else could you find out who the guy is?" Lonny said in disgust.

Carl twisted his head around and backed the van out. They followed the path of Hunter's Town Car as it made its way out of the parking lot.

"I know this guy," Lonny murmured to himself for the fifth time as they trailed Hunter through the winding back streets of Hewlett. Carl pulled up slowly to the driveway that Hunter had pulled into. Lonny gave a low whistle. From the road they could see one end of the large Tudor home. The dark shadows of its roofs were visible in enough places through the trees to give them an idea of where the other end of the house finally stopped. It was enormous.

"This guy's some kind of big shot," Lonny said as the Town Car disappeared into the garage. "What's the number on that box?" he asked, squinting through the gloom at a cobblestone column that marked the end of the driveway.

"I think it's seven ninety-three," Carl said.

"You sure?"

Carl nodded.

"OK," Lonny said as he wrote on a pad, "you can take me back to Jimmy's to get my car. I'll meet you back here at nine tomorrow morning. We'll come back here and drive around these streets until we see the mailman. When he puts the mail in the box, we'll just take a peek. It's a little bit more of a pain in the ass, but it's quicker than going through Motor Vehicles."

Lonny raised his head to see that Carl was listening.

"In case you don't know it already," he said, "if you do something for Tony Rizzo, you do it fast."

Lonny paused to look back at the elegant home and said, "By tomorrow afternoon Tony will know exactly who this guy is."

Rachel Logan glanced at her watch. She decided to finish one more chapter of her book before getting up. She tried to allow herself some quiet time every day, and these were her few moments for today as well as yesterday. The trees swayed overhead in the warm summer breeze, and she hung her foot over the edge of her chair, dipping the tip of her toe into the pool. Several minutes later, Rachel looked up from her book and scrambled out of her chair, pulling a soft robe around her. She'd lost track of time. It was three o'clock and Sara would be done with her tennis lesson. It was just down the road, but Rachel hated for her to have to wait. Inside, she pulled a pair of shorts and a T-shirt over her suit and then climbed into her dark green Jeep Cherokee. She backed out of the garage and started down the driveway.

Rachel jerked to a stop when she saw the man. He was enormous. The first thing she thought was that Hunter had brought home a new teammate. But Hunter was golfing this afternoon and wouldn't be home until dinner. When the man looked up and saw Rachel, he froze. He had a dark tan and wore red spandex shorts and a white, cutoff sweatshirt. A flat-top haircut made his thick neck look thicker than it actually was. Around his neck hung heavy gold chains. There was something not right with this man being in this neighborhood. He was out of place. He looked more like a comic book character, or someone you might see at Jones Beach, but not in Hewlett Harbor. Something was wrong. The man grinned foolishly at Rachel and stuffed something back into the mailbox. Then he held his hands up in the air. She couldn't see his eyes. They were hidden behind a pair of Terminator sunglasses. Rachel remained halfway up the drive, but rolled down her window.

"What do you want!" she said with a forcefulness she didn't feel. "Who are you?"

"Sorry," the man yelled back as he began to move sideways like a bloated ghost crab caught out of its hole. "I thought this was my friend's house, but I wasn't sure. I just thought I'd look at the mail to be sure, so that I didn't bother you. Sorry."

The man turned and began to walk, then disappeared down the street behind Rachel's hedgerow. She eased her car out slowly and peered down the street in the direction the man had gone. A blue van was disappearing around the bend. It gave her the creeps, but then again, as Hunter always said, she was a big chicken anyway. She couldn't help it, though. Growing up close to New York City had supplied her with more than enough horror stories to feed her fright of strange things and strange people. She made a mental note to discuss it with Hunter when he got home. Then, seeing that she was now truly late, she raced down the street in the opposite direction.

"Did you get it?" Lonny said again, impatient for Carl to stop his blathering and give him the name.

Carl had almost pulled the van door off its hinges as he jumped in, fired the engine, and raced off down the street, careening around corners in a way that thumped Lonny against his door. When they were three blocks away and nearly lost, Carl began excitedly to tell his story, none of which made sense to Lonny, and little of which he could understand.

"Did you get it?"

Carl stopped jabbering and looked at Lonny as if he were from Mars.

"Didn't you listen to me?" Carl said. "I told you she saw me. She saw me. She came out and caught me! I didn't know what the hell to do. You didn't say nothing to me about if she came out."

"Who? The wife?"

"I guess. It sounded like it. She started yelling at me, asking me what I was doing."

"You should have just killed her," Lonny said matter-of-factly.

Carl glared at Lonny. "That's what I was thinking I shoulda done. I was thinking I should just try to get her out of her car and strangle her or break her neck or something."

Lonny was miffed. "You fucking lug-head," he said. "I was kidding. You don't kill someone because they catch you looking in their mail. It's no big deal. It was a mistake is all. That's all you had to say to her. If you didn't look like such a muscle-headed goof with those fucking clothes from outer space, she wouldn't have thought nothing of it."

"I did say that," Carl protested. "That's just what I said. I told her I was looking for a friend's place and I put the mail right back in the box."

"So, for the tenth fucking time, Carl. What's the guy's name?"

Carl pursed his lips and scowled. "I didn't get it," he finally said.

"Jesus Christ," Lonny muttered. "Take me back there, you fucking idiot. I'll get it myself."

This time they didn't bother being careful. Lonny figured if they were going to draw attention to themselves, Carl had already done it in a banner way. He directed Carl to pull up alongside the mailbox. There was a gardener working on the lawn across the street and a Lexus sedan rolled by, but Lonny hopped out and pulled the mail from the box anyway. He fished through a couple of advertisement fliers that were addressed to "Resident" before he found a business letter.

"Son of a bitch," Lonny said to himself, replacing the mail and jumping back into the van. "I knew I knew him. Son of a bitch."

Carl looked at him quizzically.

"Just take me back," Lonny said in a tone that Carl took to mean that there would be no questions and no answers. He had blown his assignment, and somewhere through his thick skull filtered the notion that he had squandered a good opportunity to make himself more valuable to the family. He cursed himself under his breath.

Carl had guessed right; Lonny had no intention of talking. He needed to think. His mind whirled with the possibilities that could arise from the information he alone now had. He wanted to give it to Tony on a silver platter. Tony would be more than pleased. Lonny had done this job right. He had photos of everything. He'd gotten Jimmy's records on all Metz's betting. He'd put it all together in a nice neat package. Tony would love it. Even with his limited knowledge of sports, Lonny knew that Hunter Logan was now a compromised man.

Lonny smiled to himself. Tony never forgot to reward the bearer of good tidings. It turned out to be a good thing that Carl had fucked up after all. If Carl knew the name, Lonny had no doubt that Jimmy the Squid would jump the gun and deliver the news to Tony himself.

Lonny sat silently for a while, then chuckled out loud. Carl looked over at him, but only Lonny knew what was making him laugh: the image of an idol named Hunter Logan whose life was about to be shattered to pieces.

Sara talked on about how her instructor had told her that if she dedicated herself, she had the talent to be a professional by the age of thirteen. Rachel was barely listening. She couldn't get the man at the mailbox out of her mind. It was strange. The feeling that something was wrong wouldn't leave her.

". . . So, can I go to the camp, Mom? Mom?" Sara said.

"Huh? What, honey?"

"Can I go to the camp? Sharon says that's where all the tennis stars start out. Can I go?"

"Sara, honey, you're five years old. I don't think you need to start worrying about being a tennis star quite yet. You have plenty of time for that. I just want you to have fun."

"But Sharon says five is when you have to start dedicating yourself," Sara said with a little huff and a shake of her head to imply that her mother couldn't very well understand the intricacies of tennis like her teenage instructor, Sharon.

"You know what, honey, we'll talk to Daddy about it," Rachel said, peering nervously up her driveway and moving slowly to make sure there wasn't anyone strange lurking about. She stopped the car halfway up the drive.

"What are you doing, Mommy?" Sara asked.

"Nothing," Rachel replied, picking up her car phone and dialing. Julie, Rachel's housekeeper, answered on the third ring.

"Julie? Is everything all right?" Rachel asked, laughing nervously at her own silly behavior.

"Yes, Mrs. Logan. Everything is OK," Julie answered.

"Did anyone stop . . . at the house?"

"Mrs. Logan? I no understand . . ." Julie said apologetically.

"Has there been anyone, a man, to visit the house since I've left, Julie?"

"No, no one here since you leave . . ."

"Thank you, Julie. I—I'll be right in."

Rachel hung up the phone and pulled into the garage.

"That was weird," Sara said, getting out of the Jeep and shaking her head as if she never would understand her mother.

Rachel gathered her thoughts. She hit the garage door button to close the garage.

Where was her Mace? She fished through the glove box of the Jeep. Hunter had put a canister in each of the glove boxes of their cars. She pulled everything out, papers, hairbrushes, gum, candy, tapes, but no Mace. It was a crazy notion, she knew, but she wanted it. She wanted to have it with her, at least until Hunter got home. Half of her felt silly, but half of her felt unsafe.

She crammed the junk back into the glove box and crossed the garage to Hunter's car. Bert Meyer had picked him up for golf, and she imagined that Hunter's glove box would have its Mace in it. She got in the driver's side and reached across to open the box. It was locked. She looked for Hunter's keys under the seat. They weren't there. She sighed and headed into the house. Sara was already watching Barney on TV, and Julie only gave her an understanding smile as she looked up from the dinner she was preparing. Rachel climbed the broad spiral staircase two steps at a time. It was beyond ridiculous now, her running through the house like this, but she would have that Mace. Rachel was the type of person who, once she made up her mind about something, even a small thing, was almost impossible to deter.

She fished through Hunter's drawer in the bathroom. She scoured the top of his dresser. She looked in the pockets of his jeans. His keys were nowhere to be found. He must have taken them, another strange thing, but she gave it no more thought. Rachel went into her closet and began digging through her file cabinet.

"Aha!" she said, pulling the master set from a file that held the Town Car's title and insurance documents.

Down the stairs she went, through the kitchen, past the playroom, and into the garage. When she opened Hunter's glove box she was more upset than before. The Mace was there, but so was something else. It was money, a lot of money, a neatly bound wad of hundred-dollar bills. Rachel flipped through it. She figured there were several thousand dollars there. Her mind began to whirl.

Why would Hunter have this kind of cash in his car? It was obvious he was hiding it from her. Why else would the glove box have been locked and his keys nowhere to be found? She'd heard stories of husbands in the NFL who would keep large sums of cash to spend on drugs and whores. Their wives were usually the last ones to know. She cursed under her breath. Her father had warned her when she'd first brought Hunter home. Football players, he'd told her, were no good. She tried to brush bad thoughts from her mind. She knew Hunter was a good man. He wouldn't do anything like that to her. Would he? She shut the box and was halfway across the garage before she realized she'd forgotten the Mace. She stopped, then decided to forget it after all. She had more to worry about than strange men rummaging through her mailbox. She gripped the money tightly and looked at her watch as she walked into the house. Hunter would be home within an hour and he'd have some serious explaining to do.

J esus!" Tony bellowed as he slammed down the phone.

Mike Cometti looked sideways at his boss with his face still bent toward the *Post*. He knew better than to speak before being spoken to, especially when Tony was mad about something, and now he was mad. The two men were sitting in the office of a warehouse where the family's construction company stored its heavy equipment. In back of their desks was a wall of one-way glass that looked out over the busy warehouse where yellow and orange payloaders, bulldozers, and backhoes were constantly coming or going. Besides being owned by the Mondolffis and being all union, the company was like every other big construction firm in the metropolitan area. Like his father before him, Tony was ultimately responsible for this part of the family's business, as well as for his many other enterprises. In practice, Tony did little more for the construction business than keep an office on the premises. Also like his father before him, he had a man named John Mann run the entire operation for him. John was almost seventy now, but he was still tough and capable, and his efficiency allowed Tony the luxury of involving himself in other ventures.

"Mikey, you believe this shit?" Tony complained.

Cometti's paper went down like a finish flag.

"Believe what, Tony?"

"Between these fucking FBI boners and my fucking uncle, I can't do squat. Now I got those fucking Colombians pissed as hell at me because I can't deliver to them. So now when we do get to start up with those fucking animals again, I'm gonna have to start from square one again. Fuck. Sometimes I half think Uncle Vinny's got a point about dealing with those assholes. But the fucking money! Then I think of that, and I know Uncle Vinny ain't got no sense."

The intercom buzzed and Tony hit the button.

"Yeah?" he said.

"Tony, Lonny's here. Says he's got something for you" came a voice over the box.

"OK," Tony replied, "send him in."

"This," Tony said to Cometti, "oughta be interesting."

Lonny appeared through the door and stood before Tony's desk with his head hung slightly. Mike Cometti liked to see people, especially people like Lonny Watts, prostrate themselves in front of Tony. Mikey knew that outside Tony's presence, Lonny was a mean and dangerous man. But here he stood, docile as a lamb, and dressed ridiculously in a suit that must have been fifteen years old, and a wide tie that reached only halfway down the front of his shirt. His hair was slicked back in a way that only further accentuated his hatchet-shaped face.

"Lonny," Tony said in a friendly way, holding out his hand to shake, "what have you got for me? I bet it's something good. Whadya got?"

Lonny looked around the room as if to make sure that no one else was there. He handed a large envelope over the desk to Tony before he spoke.

"I think you're gonna like this, Tony," Lonny began. "I got pictures and everything in there. I got the records of how this guy's been betting for the past year. You're not gonna believe it. It's Hunter Logan. Hunter Logan is the guy behind this fat Metz character."

Tony and Mike Cometti stared at each other, their mouths hung wide open.

"You talking about the Hunter Logan? The quarterback for the Titans?"

"Yeah," Lonny said, nodding his head. "Look there. See that. That's him taking that wad of cash Jimmy paid off to that Metz guy. I know it don't look like him much with those glasses and that hat and all, but it's him. I followed him home. I figure he does that so no one in public will bother him for autographs and shit. There's a shot of Metz with Jimmy. Here's the betting records from football season. Hunter Logan and Metz did real good."

"Why, that dumb bastard," Tony murmured, gazing at the photos as he laid them out on the desk in front of him. "I guess he must've turned into some kind of big shot, betting ten grand all of a sudden. Did this fucking guy think no one would notice that? Could the great Hunter Logan be a big fucking idiot football player after all?"

Tony was quiet for a few moments, thinking. Then he began to chuckle at his own idea. "Oh," he said between breaths, "Oh, this is perfect. This is just . . . perfect."

Once he settled down, Tony looked seriously at Lonny and said, "Lonny, I want you to stick to Logan like glue. I want you watching him all the time. Get to know what he does, what his routine is. I'm gonna try to talk with him and once I do, I want to know the minute he takes a piss in a place he doesn't normally piss in. Got that? I want to make sure this guy doesn't go queer on me the minute I break the bad news to him. You're gonna get to know everything that goes on in this guy's life, Lonny. Hunter Logan just got himself a new shadow."

Tony picked up Camille at seven and took her to Sixth Street in the East Village. The block was lined with Indian restaurants, and Tony told Camille to choose the one she liked the looks of best.

"Word is, they all got the same kitchen anyway," he said.

They were there because Camille mentioned her appetite for hot food and Tony told her there was no hot like the Indian food on Sixth Street. As he drove from his warehouse in Brooklyn to Camille's building in Manhattan, Tony had contemplated just what would be the best way to get himself introduced to Hunter Logan without making it obvious that that was what he was trying to do. Camille was sharp, and she'd pick up on anything that didn't seem natural. So, during his drive he mentally rehearsed different conversations that would lead to Hunter Logan. He imagined if he just hung on to Camille, he would meet Logan eventually, but Tony had a plan, and he wanted to implement that plan now. There was no telling how long it might take to run into Logan unless Tony took some initiative, and he wanted to strike while the iron was hot. He wanted that ten-thousand-dollar bet fresh in Logan's mind when he spoke to him.

After they ordered, Tony said, "So, how do you like owning a professional football team?"

Camille rolled her eyes.

"First of all, I don't own them, my father does," she said. "Second, I'm not real big on sports. I go to the games because it's my father's pride and joy, that team. But for me it's no big deal."

After a pause she said, "I don't imagine you're much of a sports fan, are you?"

"Why do you say that?" he asked as their waiter spread appetizers out in front of them.

"I just don't see you as a fan. You're more of a participant. Am I right?"

Tony smiled. He took that as a compliment.

"You're right," he said, "but there is one guy that I must admit I'd like to meet sometime . . . Hunter Logan." Something flashed across Camille's eyes, but Tony didn't notice. He saw only the bland expression on her face.

"Yes, well . . . I guess a lot of people want to meet him right now," she said. "It's really amazing when you think about it. He came here from some other team, what, six or seven years ago? I think the team that he came from, Minnesota or Green Bay, someplace cold . . . I think they didn't even want him. The New York fans actually booed him the first time he ever went in to replace the old quarterback, that Dan Farber guy. Now the Titans win the Super Bowl and Hunter Logan is the most sought-after man in the city, probably in the entire country, if you think about it."

"Well, I admire anyone who's the best at what they do, and at the risk of being like everyone else, I'd still like to meet him."

"OK," Camille said, "I can make that happen. My father is having a July Fourth party in the Hamptons. He'll be there. If you want to go, we can. I'm sure you'll bump into him. But I want something from you, too."

"Oh," he said, raising one eyebrow, "what's that?"

"When we went to that Italian restaurant in the Rockaways, you told me about a place that you go to be alone sometimes, a place in the mountains that almost no one knows about."

Tony's face flushed slightly. It was more than the food. It embarrassed him to have talked like that to someone, like he was some kind of romantic. That stuff was bullshit, and for some reason he'd slipped into it on their last date. Maybe it had been the wine. Maybe it had been her. Either way, it annoyed him, and he reminded himself not to be so soft in the head. He was doing just fine with Camille without turning into some kind of Mr. Sensitivity.

"I want you to take me there," she said. "If I'm going to drag myself out to the Hamptons just so you can meet some muscle-headed jock, I want you to take me someplace special."

"You make it sound like it's the last thing on earth you'd want to do," he said, annoyed at her demand.

"The Hamptons is all right, but it's so damn conventional. Polo shirts and golf pants . . . people in sailor outfits who don't even own boats . . . I just don't see it as the place for you and me.

"So, is it a deal?" she said. "You take me up to that cabin and I'll take you out to the Hamptons."

He didn't like her saying what she thought was right for "you and me," as she'd put it. That kind of talk didn't float with Tony Rizzo.

"I'm not used to people making demands," he said menacingly.

"You're not used to me," she replied arrogantly, even though in the back of her mind she had the sensation of being a child playing with fire.

Hunter and Rachel were sitting in the great room. The twelve-foot ceiling was spanned by heavy timber beams. The wood floors were covered with richly colored Oriental rugs. Rachel sat across from him on the opposite couch, her arms crossed. A coffee table was between them. Hunter felt as though he were being interrogated from the moment he sat down.

He had not wanted Rachel to find out about the bet. He knew from the start that she would be upset, and now, thinking back, he realized that the thought of making her unhappy had almost prevented him from placing the bet in the first place. He told himself it was a lesson he should have learned long before now, the lesson of listening to that inner voice. But he had rationalized that he would not get caught, and that if he did get caught, Rachel wouldn't be that mad if he had some productive plans for the money he'd made.

But he knew then, and he certainly knew now, that no excuse

would deflect Rachel's anger. He could say, "Hey, I make enough that I can afford to lose a little." But he wouldn't. He didn't even like to remind himself of how much money he'd already made and lost over his years as an NFL player. He hadn't been the best at maintaining his finances.

He knew what she would say: "What if you lost?" And she was right. He'd been irresponsible with their money before, when he got hooked up with Dick Madigan. But this bet hadn't been a risk. He'd known that, and that's what he was trying to explain.

At first Rachel was close to tears with anger and pain, and although she was visibly relieved when he promised not to gamble any more of their money, the anger at what she was calling his foolish and dangerous attitude remained.

"Don't you think you're overreacting?" Hunter exclaimed passionately, willing her to see his side of it. "I mean dangerous, how could it be dangerous?"

"It's dangerous, Hunter, because when people start throwing money around like that they can lose control. I saw it happen to a lot of people in my neighborhood while growing up. I had friends whose fathers were successful men, rich men. Some of them got into gambling. Next thing you knew, they were broke, or going to jail because of some embezzlement scheme that they'd pulled to pay off their debts. There's no way to lose money as quickly as gambling, and I'm not just going to sit around and nod my head when I see you doing something like this!

"How?" she began for the tenth time. "How on earth could you think of gambling ten thousand dollars? I know you've got this big new contract, but ten thousand dollars on one game. What will it be next? Will you bet the title to your car? To the house? If you start getting into that, Hunter, you can never stop. I've seen it."

"Rachel, honey . . . just relax."

Rachel raised her voice and said, "I'm not relaxing, Hunter, so stop saying it."

"Well, you'd better relax," Hunter said, beginning to tire of her attitude. "I knew it was a lock. Win or lose, it's not like I bet like that all the time. It was a one-shot deal. Don't you think maybe you're just reacting like this because you thought I was whoring around or something crazy like that?"

Rachel stopped as if to consider. "Maybe. Maybe you're right. But it's always just one time, Hunter. That's how that starts. You started with those hundred-dollar bets and now this. I just want it to stop, Hunter. I don't want you betting on anything anymore."

"Aw, Rachel, Metz and I just have a little fun. That stuff is no big deal. It's nothing like this. Look, I don't bet like that, and I'm not about to start. Come on. I love you."

A small smile started to form on Rachel's face.

"Come over here, will you? I don't like not being able to get my hands on you."

She skirted the table and sat down next to him. Hunter kissed her on the lips. "By the way, not that you don't have every right to look in my glove box, but what were you doing there anyway? You never told me that. You weren't just snooping around, were you?"

"I don't snoop around, Hunter," she said testily. "I was looking for a can of Mace. I couldn't find mine and I wanted it."

"Why?"

"It's silly," she said. "It really is. But there was some weird guy out at our mailbox today when I went to pick up Sara from tennis. He looked almost like a player, like one of those guys on steroids."

"What?" Hunter said with concern. "What was he doing?"

"He said he was looking for a friend and that he was checking the mail in the box. He said he made a mistake, but then I drove to the end of the drive and he just seemed to disappear. I saw a van driving away. I don't know. It was just weird."

"Did he say anything more to you? Did he threaten you or something, or make some kind of comment?"

"No," Rachel said. "He didn't say anything. He looked more scared than anything else."

"Well," Hunter said, relieved, "it was probably like the guy said. Maybe he just had the wrong place, or maybe he was trying to find out if we lived here so he could jump me for an autograph or pitch some business deal at me. He probably felt embarrassed as hell. Who knows? I'll talk to the team's security guard tomorrow and see what he thinks, but I wouldn't worry about it."

"I know," she said. "He probably was just some fan looking for you, but the guy gave me the creeps. In a lot of ways I liked it when you weren't such a superstar."

"I've got an idea," Hunter said in a low voice as he pulled her close. "How about working on that new baby you've been talking about?"

"Really!" Rachel said, her eyes incandescent.

"We'd better, before I get into training camp."

Rachel led him up the stairs, her face aglow, already completely forgetting about the Mace, the gambling, and the strange man.

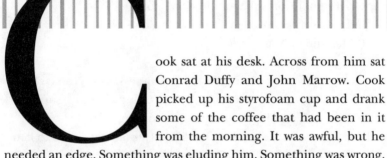

CHAPTER 15

Cook sat at his desk. Across from him sat Conrad Duffy and John Marrow. Cook picked up his styrofoam cup and drank some of the coffee that had been in it from the morning. It was awful, but he needed an edge. Something was eluding him. Something was wrong, and he couldn't place it. It was there, just beyond his reach. He could sense it, but he just couldn't see it.

"Play it again," Cook said.

Duffy leaned forward in his chair and rewound the tape in the player on Cook's desk for what seemed like the tenth time. The three of them sat silently while the tape spun. Marrow shifted restlessly in his seat as if there were better things he could be doing. The tape clicked to a stop, and Duffy leaned forward again to play it.

Tony Rizzo's voice came alive in the room.

"Fast-forward through that beginning stuff about his damn dentist appointment," Cook said.

Duffy punched the fast-forward button and Rizzo's voice became a high-pitched squeal, buzzing intermittently with his dentist's about what Cook knew to be some enamel bonding he'd had done. The tape held every conversation that Rizzo had on his phone from the entire day before. Duffy stopped the tape and played it at normal speed as a new voice began to intermingle with Rizzo's.

It was Angelo Quatrini.

"How's it going?" said Angelo's voice.

"Good," Tony replied. "Did you get my message?"

"From Mikey?"

"Yeah. Can you do it?"

"Yeah, I can do it if you want."

"I do."

"Don't you think it might make the roosters crow?"

"Maybe. I'm not worried about it. You just set it up."

"OK. You sure you want her to see it?"

"What?"

"You know, where you're going."

"Oh, I'm not worried about it. Don't you."

"OK, but you know we got a policy."

"I'll handle it, Ang."

"OK, talk to you soon."

Cook leaned forward himself this time and shut off the tape.

"It's that part that gets me. I've got a feeling about it that I can't shake," he said, looking at Duffy for an answer.

Duffy shrugged. "Like I said, sir, there's absolutely no way to know what they're talking about. They haven't given us enough to reference with. For all we know, they could be talking about Rizzo's dry cleaning. We just don't have enough references to decode it."

"I think . . ."—Cook let the word hang and studied Marrow who was looking at the tape player—". . . that they know they're bugged."

John Marrow's head shot up and his gaze met Cook's. The two men looked into each other's eyes. The office was silent for several moments.

"Why?" Duffy finally said, breaking both men's concentration.

"Because Rizzo talks like there's nothing up when he has conversations with his dentist, or his mother, or his new little girlfriend. But as soon as Quatrini, or Cometti, or any other one of his thugs calls, they start talking in a way that we can't understand. What do you think, John?"

Marrow looked up again and met Cook's eyes.

"I think that this is the way these guys talk to each other. I've listened to these kind of conversations before. Most of these wiseguys won't talk business over the phone."

"I know they won't normally say anything of value, but to talk in code? Isn't that what that was, that bit about the roosters crowing and the policy? And what is 'it' that they don't want 'her' to see?

That's not normal, is it? I mean, to not say anything is one thing, but to start talking in code words that seem to have come out of the blue suggests to me a level of caution that could only come from knowing that someone's listening."

Duffy shook his head and said, "I just can't see it, sir. We're tapping from the box under the street. We waited to set it up until Rizzo and all his cronies were gone from the area. We used all the NYNEX equipment from trucks to uniforms to the damn cones we put out on the street. That stuff goes on all the time in the city. It's not like it would have raised any suspicions. We've got trace sensors on the line, and they haven't picked up a thing. I just don't see how he could know. It's not really possible."

"OK," Cook said cheerfully, breaking the somber mood of the meeting. "I've been wrong before, but I want both of you to think about it and keep your eyes open for any other signs that confirm what I'm saying. You can get back to it, Duffy. John, stay a minute. I want to talk with you about Rizzo's bank records in St. Martin."

Cook spent the rest of the day going over various aspects of the Rizzo case. So far all their searches had led to nothing. There was some hope that one of their agents would be able to infiltrate the family through one of their bookies on the upper East Side, but besides that long shot, everything else was a bust. Cook was beginning to get frustrated. He had vast resources at his disposal, and he knew that Washington was expecting quick results. At the very least, he knew he needed to show some progress.

Cook worked until seven, then left the building and made his way home on foot. The sun was getting low, but the heat still wafted up from the pavement. The city smelled ripe with stale air from the subway, and exhaust vented to the streets from restaurants cooking food whose origins came from every corner of the earth. Cook shouldered his way through the throngs of people until finally he turned off Seventh Avenue and onto his own street, which was relatively quiet by comparison. There was little crosstown traffic this far downtown at this late an hour, and Cook enjoyed a reprieve from the taxi and bus fumes. He eyed a lean, well-shaped woman jogging on the other side of the street in tight black spandex pants and a cut-off T-shirt.

Cook realized how long it had been since he'd had a woman. He briefly wondered if there wasn't something wrong with him, then stretched for a final glimpse and ended up bumping into a surly-looking doorman who was sweeping the sidewalk directly in front of his building. The man snarled in disgust and glared. Cook wondered if it was his suit or the color of his skin that alienated the man—the bump itself had been mild. The doorman muttered something that sounded like "nigger" under his breath. Cook involuntarily clenched his fists. Then he decided he didn't care, shrugged, and walked off.

Natasha jumped on him the minute he got home. Cook laughed and kissed her face, holding her light form tight to his chest. She giggled.

"Can you eat fast so we can go to the park before it gets dark and throw my new Frisbee?" she said in one gasp.

Cook peered into the kitchen. Esther glared at him, turning her gaze to the clock, then to his dinner plate, which sat alone on the table, carefully covered with tin foil.

"Couldn't hold dinner I see, Aunt Esther," Cook said mildly.

"You got that right," said the wiry woman with fire in her eyes. "When I tell you the child needs to eat her supper by six-thirty, that don't mean for you to show up here an hour late making smart comments. Now sit your bottom down and eat so you can take that little girl to the park. Lord help me if I ever saw such a selfish man as you, Ellis Cook. Lord help me. My own husband, the heathen good-for-nothing, was a sight better man than you when it came to being on time."

"Well, Aunt Esther, any man that coulda been married to you is a damn sight better man than me. That goes without saying," Cook replied mischievously.

Esther pursed her lips, blew past him, and slammed the bedroom door behind her.

"Well," Cook said cheerfully to Natasha, "now that's over with, why don't you sit with me, and I'll get this food down as fast as I can so we can go to the park?"

Natasha tried to frown at her father and said, "Daddy, you're going to have to treat Aunt Esther better than that. That's just bad manners."

Cook sat down and gazed across the kitchen fondly at his daughter.

More and more she reminded him of Naomi, even in the things she was beginning to say. Tears misted in his eyes.

Natasha crossed the floor and hugged him gently.

"I didn't mean it, Daddy," she said. "Don't be sad."

"Oh, I'm not sad, sweetheart," he replied, brushing his hand roughly across his face. "I'm happy, happy to have you for my little girl."

Cook hugged his daughter hard, then fell into his dinner.

By the time they got to the park, the shadows were long and a breeze that somehow found its way through the streets from the Hudson River made the evening pleasant. It brought relief, but at the same time, the balmy air seemed to draw the city's miscreants out like roaches after dark. Countless bums staggered about the park tipping bottles of cheap wine, and young putrid-smelling men offered drugs for sale without looking Cook in the eye. He looked down occasionally to see how Natasha reacted to the human slag. She observed everything, but it didn't seem to faze her.

They found a spot of dusty ground spiked with an occasional swatch of crab grass that refused to die and began to throw the Frisbee back and forth. Natasha squealed with delight whenever she caught the lime green disk. Cook smiled back but his eyes furtively scouted the riffraff that surrounded them. Natasha, in her simple white cotton dress and with her smooth dark skin, looked frightfully innocent and out of place surrounded by dirty concrete and shabby derelicts.

A blue-and-white squad car rolled past. The cops' heads swiveled slowly from side to side, as they coolly looked out of their rolled-down windows from behind dark Ray-Bans. A scuffle broke out suddenly between a leather-booted skinhead and a black homeless man. The squad car moaned and flashed its lights as it advanced on the melee. The skinhead got the bum down on the ground and began to kick him brutally. Before the cops could get out of their car, the skinhead bent down over the bum to work on him with his hands. The bum lashed out suddenly and the skinhead pulled away, bleeding wildly from his face. Bright blood splashed about on the sidewalk as the skinhead danced maniacally, trying to plug the gash that opened his face.

The bum tried to scurry away, his bloody razor in hand, but one of the cops dropped him in his tracks with a blow from his blackjack across the back of the neck. The other cop clubbed the skinhead in the abdomen, doubling him over before putting him to the ground with another swing that thumped off his head like a soft melon. Each cop bent over his victim with a knee in his back and clapped on their respective cuffs, two trophy hunters bagging their game.

"Come on, honey," Cook said nonchalantly to his daughter, "it's getting late. Let's you and me go get some ice cream and then head home before your Aunt Esther gets riled."

"Did you see that, Daddy?" Natasha said, turning to him, her eyes wide and her eyebrows climbing up her forehead. "Did you see the blood? Wow! That raggy man cut that big bald guy up good! And then those policemen, did you see them?"

Cook nodded and took Natasha by the hand. "Yes, I saw," he said.

"Do you ever do that to people?" she asked.

"No, that's not the kind of policeman I am," he said. "Come on, honey. Let's go."

Cook led her away. Natasha looked back over her shoulder occasionally until they crossed the street and began their walk up Fifth Avenue to the ice cream store. Cook ordered a double mint-chocolate-chip for himself and a strawberry for Natasha. The sky above them was dark as they turned off the avenue onto their lantern-lit street. Mint green ice cream rolled down Cook's hand. He swabbed it with a napkin and licked furiously around the edges of his cone. Natasha broke into a long tale about her friend Rina's cat that had been hit by a car on Sixth Avenue. She seemed to have already forgotten the bloody outburst at the park. As Cook listened to Natasha, his mind fought to come up with a way to get to Tony Rizzo and get his family out of this mean and dirty city.

Cook rode along slowly in the Manhattan traffic. This was one of the most boring parts of the job and one he wasn't required to do as a supervisor. This was what he had agents for. But Cook had decided on a back-to-basics approach to his mission. He had called on his men to focus their attention on the details. To emphasize his message, he and Marrow had begun to spread themselves among the different areas of investigation to make each man feel that his role had a great importance to the overall effort of quelling the Mondolffi family. That was why Cook was now riding along in an unmarked van with a two-man observation team.

He suddenly sat up straight when Tony Rizzo's Mercedes veered toward the entrance to the Lincoln Tunnel. They had all assumed that he was taking the Carter girl out to dinner in Little Italy. There was another agent in a Crown Vic who roamed the streets adjacent to the van as a backup chase car that could move in and take over the tail if the van lost Rizzo or if Rizzo stopped suddenly, forcing the van to continue on in traffic.

The backup was about a block ahead of them on Tenth Avenue, and Dan Mott, the agent in the back of the van, immediately radioed Ira Stone in the Crown Vic to double back because it appeared Rizzo was headed into the tunnel.

"Not usual for Tony to head into Jersey on a Friday night, is it?" Cook said.

Peter Meara, the driver of the van, nodded in agreement. It was eight o'clock, late enough that the congestion at the tunnel wasn't bad. Still, traffic had slowed enough that Ira could catch up and see the van before it entered the tunnel about ten cars behind Tony Rizzo. Cook could make out the back of Camille Carter's blonde head. There were two lanes going under the river to New Jersey, and once inside the tunnel, traffic sped up to about thirty-five miles an hour. Cook gazed out at the yellowing tile walls of the tunnel. It made him think of a public rest room.

Suddenly, about four cars in front of the van, an old Fleetwood Cadillac and a beat-up Impala began to slow down dramatically. The two cars swerved back and forth in unison. Then, at about ten miles an hour they bumped and came to a complete stop. Rizzo's Mercedes, along with the rest of the forward traffic, continued quickly through the tunnel until they were out of sight.

"Shit," Cook said.

He opened the door of the van and leaned out. "Hey!" he yelled at two burly thugs who had gotten out of the collided cars. "Hey! Get one of those cars over to the side!"

"Fuck you!" one of them bellowed.

"Yeah, fuck you," said the other loudly.

Other cars in the jam began to honk their horns. The two men appeared to assess the damage to their vehicles, which looked to be minimal, oblivious to the sound of the blaring horns. Cook reached the two men in an instant and flashed his badge at them.

"FBI," Cook said angrily, "now get one of these cars over to the side."

The two men were apparently unfazed by Cook. They continued to inspect their cars as if he weren't there. A Tunnel Authority officer walked up along the catwalk and jumped down to see what was happening. Cook showed the officer his badge.

"Get one of these cars out of the way," Cook demanded. "This is official business."

The tunnel officer looked at him and smiled.

"Oh," he said sarcastically, "well, in that case . . . OK, come on, you two. I'll ride up to the end of the tunnel with you and fill out a report. You can tell me all about it when we get out of here."

"No problem," the one with the Cadillac said pleasantly.

"See?" said the tunnel officer to Cook with his same smile. "All you gotta do is ask sometimes."

"Shit," Cook said under his breath, and sprinted back to the van.

By the time he was seated, the two cars were moving. When they reached the other side of the river, Rizzo's Mercedes was nowhere to be seen. "Which way?" Peter asked as they looped up and around the long ramp to the interstate.

Cook thought only for an instant. "South," he said. "I'm thinking maybe they're headed to Atlantic City. We'll take the turnpike."

Cook turned to Dan Mott and said, "Call Ira and tell him to keep going west on Route 3. Tell him to go to the goddamn Meadowlands, maybe they're going to the races. Those are our two best bets."

"He's missed most of the races. You don't think he's going north?" Dan asked.

"If he was going north, why would he have gone downtown to the tunnel? He'd take the G.W.," Cook replied. "Why the hell don't we have a tracking device on his car?"

"We've got three cars on him," Dan Mott said apologetically.

"That's the kind of detail I've been talking about," Cook said, then cursed under his breath.

The van raced down the highway at a hundred miles an hour. An hour and a half later, they were in Atlantic City. They went to the Star Casino, where Rizzo liked to stay. He wasn't there and soon they were heading back to New York. Ira had waited for them at the toll station on the New Jersey side of the tunnel. "It took you guys long enough," he muttered as they regrouped, the irritation and frustration at having lost Tony coming through in his voice.

Cook and Meara found the tunnel officer who had handled the accident report. Cook wanted to check out the two men who'd stopped the traffic. He had a feeling the accident was not an accident at all. The tunnel officer was in a break room having a coffee and cigarette with a fellow worker. A twisted tin ashtray filled with wasted butts sat between them on the yellow formica table. Cook asked to see the report. The tunnel officer looked up at him smugly and blew smoke out his nose.

"Funny thing," he said, smirking at Cook, "when we got out of the tunnel, those two were like a couple of old pals. Neither one of them wanted to fill out a report. Good thing for me, just more paperwork. Whadya wanna do? Bring federal charges for having a fender bender and making you late?"

Cook stared blankly at the man, his protruding gut, his rumpled brown uniform, his cigarette with its limp tail of gray, smoking ash.

"Did you ever wonder why you're just a tunnel cop?" Cook said, then turned and left.

Tony was cranking a CD of the Red Hot Chili Peppers. Camille never even noticed the commotion behind them in the tunnel. Tony did and he laughed to himself. They headed west on Route 3, then turned onto Route 17, and wound their way slowly north through the stop-and-go traffic of north Jersey's suburbs. They were soon in Rockland County, and shortly after that, the Catskill Mountains rose around them. It was cool out now and Tony rolled down his window. A crescent moon hung orange in the late June sky just over the mountaintops.

"Huh," Camille snorted when she realized what they'd done. "You only wasted about an hour going that way. We could have taken the Thruway or even the G.W. and gotten here a hell of a lot faster."

"I know," Tony said, "but then we wouldn't have gotten to go through the Lincoln Tunnel."

Camille looked over at him.

"So what?"

"So, I love the tunnel," Tony said with a smirk. "It's so romantic . . . like the tunnel of love."

"Jesus, Tony," Camille said, shaking her head and looking back out into the summer night, "sometimes I wonder if you're not completely crazy."

G rant Carter's long gray limousine slowed in front of the First Bank Building in midtown Manhattan. Carter got out. The early morning traffic droned thickly about him as he strode purposefully, cutting a path through the throng of pedestrians on their way to work. There was an executive entrance, and a doorman in gold and white livery opened the large brass-trimmed glass door and wished him a good morning. Carter took the express car to the fiftieth floor and walked out into a spacious hall of cavernous proportions. Marble and mahogany bordered Oriental rugs and European tapestries. This was where the true power of the city lay. First Bank was first, and the money that went through its tills could finance the operation of almost any country that wasn't one of the G-7.

At the end of the hall was a large reception desk, set amid several comfortable chairs and smaller tables. Other well-dressed men sat about waiting to be summoned to the inner offices, or talking business among themselves or with First Bank executives. Carter announced himself and was immediately shown to the spacious office of Morgan Lloyd. Carter sat alone in the office overlooking the Plaza and Central Park for almost twenty minutes before Lloyd himself entered. Carter was incensed.

"Keeping bankers' hours, Morgan," he said tersely.

Lloyd seemed unfazed. "Good morning, Grant," he said, sitting down at his desk, not bothering to shake hands. "You've got some problems."

This threw Carter off balance. To be summoned to the bank was insult enough without making him wait and then throwing this curt language at him.

"You're the one who'll have the problem, Lloyd, if you think you can talk to me like I just got off the farm," Carter said indignantly. "I was doing business on the fiftieth floor when you were in diapers, and I'll still be doing business here after your usefulness has outlived your manners."

"There's really no sense in going on like this, Grant," Lloyd said, folding his hands in front of his chin. "The fact is that I'm bringing you down. I'm closing up shop for you, and if you want to do any business at all with First Bank in the future, you'd better get used to the idea of doing as I say, and being damn grateful that I'm even bothering to say it to you."

"I don't have to listen to this," Carter said, rising from his chair. "I'll see Felix about this, and you'll be lucky if you're not out on the street by noon."

"Unfortunately, Grant," Lloyd moaned in a dramatically bored tone, "Felix will not see you. In fact, no one will see you besides me. I've been given the tasteless job of dealing with you, and if you walk out of here now, I get to wash my hands of you and you won't even be able to get on the elevator, let alone past the reception desk. Felix is through with you, Grant. First Bank is almost through with you, too."

Carter was flushed and angry. He picked up a phone on a small round conference table beside Lloyd's desk.

"Yes?"

"Get me Felix LaMonte," he said roughly into the phone.

"Mr. LaMonte's office," said the secretary.

"This is Grant Carter. Tell Felix I need to speak with him right away. Tell him it's important."

Carter waited and smiled grimly at Lloyd.

"Mr. Carter, Mr. LaMonte is busy right now, but he said that you could talk to Mr. Lloyd."

Carter's face turned red, then purple.

"You tell him I need to speak with him now!" Carter roared at the secretary.

Lloyd leaned back in his high-back leather desk chair and smirked.

"Mr. Carter, Mr. LaMonte said any business you have to discuss with First Bank should be discussed with Mr. Lloyd," the secretary said, and then promptly disconnected him.

Carter set the phone down gently and took a deep breath. He had known he was in trouble when he was called for this appointment. He hadn't counted on this, though.

"All right, Morgan," he said, finally gaining control and sitting back down. "Let's talk."

Morgan Lloyd smiled at Grant Carter. He was enjoying himself. Carter was one of those big-shot developers who had thrived during the economic boom of the eighties. He was rich, and because of the New York Titans, he was famous. Those two things had given Grant Carter the notion that he was invincible. Morgan and the executives at First Bank had kowtowed to Carter and his kind for almost a decade. But now the tables had turned. Real estate prices had plummeted, and banks like First Bank could call in loans and literally bankrupt the men who had made vast fortunes in the eighties.

"The way I see it, Grant," Lloyd began, "the only thing that separates you from a hundred other developers in this city is the fact that you own the Titans. That is really the only thing of yours that First Bank doesn't own."

"First Bank doesn't own anything of mine!"

Lloyd held up his hand for silence. "Grant, if I make the recommendation, the board is prepared to call in every outstanding loan you have to First Bank. If that happens, then indeed First Bank will own everything, and I mean everything, that you possess. Your harbor project, your high-rises on the upper East Side, your shopping centers on the Island, your warehouses in New Jersey, even your house in the Hamptons. All of it is over-leveraged. Like I said, the only thing that separates you from a hundred others is the team."

"What about Trump?" Carter demanded. "You people have bailed him out! He's overextended like the rest of us! Why should I be any different than him?"

Lloyd chuckled. "Do you think that we aren't calling the shots with him? He doesn't roll over in bed before he checks with us. And the only reason we're carrying him through this is because he's a symbol. He represents capitalism and we feel it's in everyone's best interest to keep him afloat.

"You, on the other hand, are not a symbol of anything beyond greed. You are looked upon as an elitist, one of the NFL owners, the richest of the rich who make money hand over fist without lifting a finger. It's everyone's dream to own an NFL team, and quite naturally, every other person in this country is extremely jealous of you. They don't like you. Ironically, the very thing that makes your image unworthy of preservation makes your portfolio worthy of preservation.

"So, I've come up with a plan," Lloyd continued with a smile. "I'm prepared to extend your credit on all projects outstanding, except your holdings in New Jersey. I want those liquidated. We'll hold fifty-one percent equity in all other developments. In exchange, you will sell the Titans for a fair-market price to a party that will be determined by me. The proceeds from that sale will be used to capitalize existing projects underway, of which we'll also hold a fifty-one percent interest."

Carter looked evilly at Lloyd. He started to talk but couldn't. His heart was in his throat. Everything he'd worked to create was being stripped from him. And the team, his team, the thing that had made him a household name, this miserable prick wanted his team. Carter knew what he was up to. Lloyd would command enormous power if he could control the assignment of an NFL franchise, not to mention that the bank would be able to continue to finance him almost risk-free and enjoy most of the benefits when the economy finally did turn around. Carter was sick. He'd have to stall. He needed time. Maybe there was another way. He wasn't going to lose his team.

"Can I think about what you've said?" Carter said quietly, with as much humility as his enormous ego could muster.

"Of course you can, Grant," Lloyd said amiably. "I want you to think about the alternatives. Once you do, I think you'll thank me."

Carter got up to leave.

"Let's get together after the Fourth," Lloyd said. "Say . . . the eighth, at ten o'clock, bankers' hours, you know."

Carter nodded and walked through the door, closing it quietly behind him.

It was Saturday, but Grant Carter had been up since six. He'd taken a walk on the beach before the crowds and gone to town for a *New York Times*. Then he played tennis with Matt Schiller, one of his many guests for the weekend. It was his typical weekend routine in the Hamptons, and usually gave him the most peaceful moments of the week. Today, however, he was withdrawn and irritable. Even sneaking an infrequent victory from Schiller in a three-set match couldn't pull him out of his gloom.

After a shower Carter ambled out onto the covered terrace adjacent to the east wing of the house. There were close to twenty people sitting around linen-covered tables, eating brunch or just talking. Everyone he passed greeted him deferentially. He was, after all, their host. He enjoyed surrounding himself with business peers and sycophants every weekend, but the Fourth was his biggest gathering by far. There were at least fifty guests staying with him this weekend, and there would easily be another three hundred attending his party tomorrow. But for the first time since he'd begun the annual celebration almost ten years ago, he wished the house was empty. He had no desire for guests and fireworks and champagne.

There was a long buffet table set out with a maid and a carver in attendance. Carter loaded up a plate with eggs, melon, and roast beef.

"Can I bring you some juice and coffee, Mr. Carter?" the maid asked quietly.

"Yes," Carter said gruffly, looking around at where he would sit.

At the far corner of the terrace, nearest the beach, sat his daughter Camille with some ponytailed buck he'd never seen before. Of course, it wasn't often he'd see Camille with the same man more than once or twice anyway. She was dressed in a blue-and-white-striped top and her hair was piled on top of her head. The young man had on white shorts and a beige, hand-knit cotton sweater. The two of them looked like a picture out of the pages of a magazine. Carter was struck by the young man's intense eyes as he stood to be introduced. The handsome appearance was status quo, but this was the first man Camille had brought around in a while who didn't remind Carter of some Ivy League air-head.

"Daddy, this is Tony. Tony is president of his own construction company," Camille said, watching the two of them shake hands from behind her dark sunglasses.

"It's nice to meet you, Mr. Carter," Tony said with a deference he usually reserved for his uncle.

"Hmm, yes, nice to meet you, Tony. Mind if I sit with the two of you?" he said to Camille. "Won't cramp your style, will I?"

"Sit down, Daddy, please," Camille sighed.

"Would you like to sit next to Camille, Mr. Carter?" Tony said, offering his seat.

This seemed to amuse Camille. Carter raised one eyebrow and looked intently at Tony, searching for the jest. "No," he said, sitting down across the table from his daughter. "No, thank you."

"What do you find so amusing, young lady?" Carter said tensely, even though they both knew from years of experience that she was the one person from whom he would tolerate almost anything.

"Oh, Daddy," she complained, "you're so damn grumpy."

Carter cut himself a piece of beef and began to chew. He looked out at the beach. People were already setting up their umbrellas and spreading their towels. A heavy middle-aged woman in a floppy white sun hat ambled along the water's edge with a wet golden retriever.

Carter swallowed and said enigmatically, "Camille, if you were me right now, you'd be grumpy, too."

He shifted his gaze to his daughter's guest.

"Tony, let me give you some advice. Camille said you're in construction, right?"

Tony nodded.

"Be ruthless," Carter said. "If you want to succeed in business today, you have to be ruthless. You can't let people run all over you. If someone looks like they're going to be trouble for you down the line, take them out now. Don't wait. If you let your enemies get strong today, they'll bring you down tomorrow."

Tony smiled wickedly and nodded. "I agree with you, Mr. Carter."

"Daddy," Camille huffed, "I'm sure Tony doesn't want to talk business philosophy. He owns a construction company."

"It doesn't matter what kind of business you're in. Business is war, like the Japanese say. Tony probably has to deal with banks all the time. Banks are the worst. They're scum. When times are good, they want in. When times are bad, they're ready to take everything you've got and fault you for being an entrepreneur."

Carter could see that Tony agreed with him. He shifted his gaze back out at the ocean. "I have a man right now who is trying to bring down everything I've made. I have a man in my life right now who's making me miserable, and it's my own fault. Do you know why?" he said, looking back at Tony.

Tony shrugged, and leaned forward.

"It's my fault because I could have taken him out years ago. Years ago, when I knew he was no good, I let him stay. I could have taken him out. He was nothing back then, and I had a feeling about him. I even complained about him, that was worse. I complained, but I didn't pull out all the stops to eliminate him. So he continued to climb and now he's standing over me with his foot on my throat. Now it's too late. I wasn't ruthless enough."

"This guy sounds pretty bad," Tony said. "Maybe I could help you."

Carter looked at Tony carefully. It was the second time he wondered if the young man was joking.

"Unless you've got an uncle on the board of First Bank, I don't think there's much that can be done. Morgan Lloyd is a powerful man now. I don't even know if an uncle on the board could help me."

"I don't know, I know a lot of people. Maybe I could talk to this Lloyd."

Carter saw that Tony was serious. He sighed. He must have been wrong. This guy was just another dope, same as the others.

He said, "OK, Tony, you do that."

Tony nodded his head and smiled as though they had just struck a bargain.

Carter was sorry that he'd ever gotten started. It wasn't like him to talk about his problems, but being around Camille always did something to him. He let his guard down around her. He supposed it was normal. She was really the only person in the world he had. Not that Camille didn't have her faults. He knew she did. She was a little wild and a little spoiled, both probably his fault.

Carter grew silent and continued to eat. Camille seemed to realize the change that had come over her father and she rose, excusing herself and Tony, saying that they'd see him later in the day. They were going out on the beach. Carter watched them go. They were aloof from the other guests, Camille merely nodding in acknowledgment to the people who greeted her. Carter crammed a piece of

cantaloupe into his mouth and huffed. What had Tony said? Maybe
he could talk to Lloyd? What an idiot.

The sky was beginning to turn dark. A few stars winked above. A
boardwalk extended from the decks and terraces of the Carter mansion out over the dunes that protected the narrow strip of land
between the inland waterway and the pounding ocean. At the end of
the private walk was an observation deck that looked out over the
beach. Hunter and Rachel leaned together against the deck's railing
and gazed out at the thundering surf. A stiff breeze wrapped the two
of them in the smell of salt and seaweed.

It was the first peaceful moment they'd had since arriving at
Carter's party that afternoon. Since then, Hunter had answered
question after question about football. He had the feeling that he
was more of an attraction than a guest. So when the tables of food
finally drew the crowd toward the house, he and Rachel retreated to
the beach. As they stood looking out at the Atlantic, groups of
Carter's wealthy friends climbed the stairs to the boardwalk and
came in from the beach. Two couples passed quietly, stopping only
to look back and whisper that it really was Hunter Logan.

"Beautiful, isn't it?" Rachel said above the breeze. They were used
to people stopping to stare and seemed not to notice.

Hunter nodded, "Mmm. I'm beginning to think we should have
stayed home and had a nice quiet Fourth with your parents and Sara."

Rachel turned to him. "I want you to know that I think what you're
doing is good," she said. "I know you aren't really comfortable social-
izing with these people. I know you're not having a good time, and I
know you're doing it for Sara and me. As bad as it seems sometimes,
people groping at you, not giving you a minute to breathe, it is a
good idea to make these kind of contacts now. I know you, Hunter,
you'll want to stay in the thick of things long after football, and the
people you meet now can help you do that. Look at your friend Metz.
He was a big name around New York one time, wasn't he?"

"He went to the Pro Bowl," Hunter said. "That's big."

"Right," said Rachel, "and look at him now, working a job he
doesn't really like, scratching to make ends meet."

"It seems like that's what happens to most players when they're
done," Rachel continued. "I know it won't happen to you, honey,

but I just want to make sure. Not for me. I don't care if we're rich or poor, you know that, but I know you, Hunter. You like to be on top, and you should, even after football. I mean, you have so many opportunities right now."

"You don't have to apologize, Rach," he said. "I'm here tonight because I want to be. I think you're right about taking advantage. I realize that in a couple of years no one will care about Hunter Logan. I'm glad you got on me about it. As much as I like Metz, I'd hate to have that kind of life, where the only thing you've got is something that's already gone.

"The only thing I think is," he continued, "that after the money I make this year, I won't have to worry about working after football anyway."

Rachel opened her mouth to speak.

"I know, I know," Hunter said, raising his hand to cut her off, "the more you make the more you spend, I know."

Rachel smiled at him. "Do I say that?"

Hunter pulled her close and hugged her.

"If you weren't so right all the time, you'd be hard to live with," he said, kissing her soft dark hair.

After a few more minutes, Hunter's hunger overcame his aversion to the crowd, so they headed back to the house, hand in hand. Hunter loaded his plate and half of Rachel's with steamed clams, corn on the cob, and three fresh lobster tails. They found two unoccupied seats together at one of the tables on the breakfast terrace. Hunter got a sweating bottle of Amstel Light out of a silver tub for himself and asked one of the bartenders to mix up a sea breeze for Rachel.

"Can you imagine what all this must cost?" Hunter said between mouthfuls of lobster.

"This is a nice party," Rachel replied. "But he can afford it with a team like the Titans."

"Someone told me Carter has his own fireworks display after dinner. They said it's bigger than the show they put on in town. I guess people come from all over and line the beach to watch his show. Can you imagine that? Your own damn fireworks?"

Rachel nodded and said, "If they're going to start soon, I'm going to go in and use the ladies room, OK?"

"Sure," Hunter said, "I'll wait right here."

Hunter watched Rachel make her way through the guests and disappear into the house. He thought of the time he had gone in to use the bathroom at his first party here. Blood surged involuntarily to his face. Despite himself, he began to look around, just to see if Camille Carter wasn't there. Hunter didn't think it would hurt to take a discreet look at her as long as Rachel didn't see him doing it.

"Mister Logan?"

Hunter turned toward the heavy Spanish accent that had come from behind his chair. One of Grant Carter's servants was standing there shifting nervously on her feet. A small, dark-skinned boy with jet black hair peered out from behind the woman's black-and-white uniform. Hunter guessed the boy was about eight years old.

"Yes?" he said politely.

"I'm so sorry, Mr. Logan. I do not wish to bother you. I wait until you and you wife finish eating. I no mean to bother you, but I promise Jesus I try to get him to meet you. Jesus is very good boy. He work hard in school and he get good grades. He know you come to this house sometimes because I talk to him about it after you here last time, and Jesus, it was his birthday last week. All he want is to meet you, Mr. Logan, and get you autograph. I'm sorry, Mr. Logan. I no mean to bother you. I wait until you finish eating and you wife leave you."

Hunter held his hand up. "Please," he said, "I'm happy to give Jesus an autograph. Come out here, Jesus, and let me shake your hand, buddy."

Jesus's mother beamed from ear to ear. "I told Jesus you are a very nice man, Mr. Logan. This mean so much to him. He have your card and here is pen to sign with."

Hunter held out his hand and gripped the young boy's hand firmly but gently.

"So you're good in school, huh?" Hunter said.

Jesus nodded, wide-eyed with awe.

Hunter smiled at him. "Well, it sure is nice to meet a boy who does good in school," he said. "You keep working hard, OK?"

Jesus nodded so hard it looked like he might snap his own neck. Hunter chuckled and whipped his signature off on the card.

"Maria!"

The caustic voice made all three of them turn and stare. It was

Grant Carter himself. He was dressed in a white sports shirt and a blue blazer. His face was beet red from either too much sun or too much drink.

"You know damn well better than to be out here with your boy!" Carter said. "I don't pay you to socialize with my guests. I've had this talk with you before about your boy. If you insist on bringing him to my house when you come to work, he stays in the kitchen with you, and I mean it!"

"Mr. Carter," Hunter said calmly, rising from his seat, "this really is my fault, sir. I saw Jesus in the kitchen and I told him if he had a football card of mine to bring it out after dinner and I'd sign it for him. It really is my fault. I feel terrible."

This seemed to confuse Carter. It wasn't normal for someone to intercede on behalf of one of his servants. He stuttered between continuing his remonstrance of Maria and telling his quarterback to mind his own damn business.

"What a nice thing to do," said Camille, who appeared beside her father from nowhere. "I think that is so nice. Don't you think that's nice, Daddy, that Hunter would ask the little boy to come out here to give him his autograph?"

With that, Camille put her arm through her father's and led him away, saying, "I'm sure Maria was just coming to get him. Oh, not that you don't have reason to be angry, Daddy . . ."

Maria gathered her son and hurried him off, giving Hunter a smile so grateful that it made him sad. Hunter shook his head and wondered whether Carter was drunk or if he was really that big an ass. He turned back to his table and grabbed for his beer. He was surprised to see that a sharply dressed man with long, sleek hair pulled back into a ponytail had sat next to him during all the commotion.

"Tony Rizzo," the young man said, holding out his bronzed, carefully manicured hand to Hunter.

"Hi, I'm Hunter Logan," Hunter said, shaking his hand and instantly getting a bad feeling about this guy.

"Of course," Tony said in a heavy Brooklyn accent, "everyone knows who you are. That was really nice, Hunter, what you did for that wetback. You must be a really nice guy."

Hunter scowled. He didn't like to hear that kind of talk. First it was wetback, then nigger, then dirty Jew. He didn't go for that shit.

"Yeah," he said coldly, hoping his tone would get the message across, "I guess so."

"So," Tony said, not affected in the slightest, "who do you like in tonight's game? The Yankees or the Red Sox?"

Hunter could only figure this guy was on drugs. He shook his head and looked around for Rachel, hoping she'd return and get him away from this loud-mouthed jerk.

"I don't know," Hunter said. "I don't follow baseball much."

"No? But you follow basketball, don't you?" Rizzo said with his eyebrows raised in mock surprise.

"Not really," Hunter said.

"No? Gosh, I happen to know that you did real good on the play-off game between the Knicks and the Bulls. Made yourself an easy ten, didn't you?"

Hunter felt sick. This guy was giving him the creeps. He simply stared at Rizzo, not knowing what to say.

"Yeah," Rizzo chuckled, "you like basketball, but your real thing is football, huh? You been kicking my ass during the football season."

"I never, I don't—" Hunter stammered.

"Forget it, Logan," Tony said, rudely dismissing Hunter's denial with a wave of his hand.

Rizzo leaned forward. He motioned for Hunter to do the same. Hunter hesitated, looked around, and then did as he was told.

"I got you by the balls, motherfucker!" Rizzo hissed. "I got the whole deal on you and your fat buddy Metz. I got records of your bets, and I got pictures of your fat friend paying you off, so don't you try to fuck with me!

"You got guts, too," Tony continued malevolently. "I give you that. I checked the records real careful, and I see that you bet a grand on one of your own games last year late in the season. That took some balls, betting on your own game like that, against your own team!"

Hunter saw hatred in Tony Rizzo's eyes. It scared him. He didn't even know this guy, but here he was staring at Hunter with hatred and contempt. He was crazy, too. Hunter had never bet his own game. His mouth was dry. He swallowed. Tony sat back and smiled.

"Yeah, but that's nobody's business but yours and mine, right?" Tony said. "Sure, if that was to get out, that you were betting on NFL games, and then bumping up the stakes against your own team when you personally have your worst day of the season? Let's see . . . they'd boot your ass from the league forever. Well, I don't want to see that happen. No, especially with you owing so much money on those two nice houses you got, as well as the family farm back in fucking Podunk, West Virginia."

Tony savored the shock on Hunter Logan's face before he said, "Oh, yeah, I know all about you, big shot. I know about your little girl and your cute wife. See, I like to know everything about a guy before I go into business with him. But you got nothing to worry about with me. I'm just gonna ask you a little favor some time, maybe ask you to come my way, and when I do, you're gonna fucking do it without giving me any shit, 'cause if you don't make me happy, motherfucker, I'll drop the fucking curtain on you. I'll end your fucking show, Mr. Big Shot."

Rizzo got up and put his hand on Hunter's shoulder.

"Enjoy the fireworks," Rizzo said pleasantly.

A bsolutely not" was Fellows's reply.

"I don't see why not," Cook said. "Maybe we can get some help from him. Maybe he knows something."

"Cook, I wish you could hear yourself," said Fellows. "This is an important man, and you want to shake up his life because his daughter is sleeping with Tony Rizzo? How many other women has Tony Rizzo slept with in the past six months? Do you want to contact their fathers, too?"

"But this man owns a professional football team! Rizzo spent the damn weekend at his beach home. There may be some connection," Cook said.

Fellows stared malignantly at his underling. They were seated in the large conference room where Fellows always held his Saturday meetings. The rest of the supervisors had gone home to play with their kids or golf or do whatever it was that senior-level FBI agents did in their spare time. Cook had remained. He didn't want to have to go through this with his colleagues looking on. He had known how Fellows would react.

Actually, it was how most FBI higher-ups would have reacted. If you wanted to get some help from a small-fry businessman, go ahead, threaten to shut him down or sic the IRS on him. Remind him that his daughter in Seattle grows pot in her backyard. You do what you have to in order to get people to cooperate. No one wanted to help law enforcement these days. No one wanted to get involved, so it was standard procedure to lean on the little people.

But you just try to talk to some big shot like Carter, and you had someone from the attorney general's office on the phone telling you to back off, police harassment and all that shit. Cook didn't think for a minute Fellows would go for it, especially since he didn't really have a good reason to do it. He just had a feeling. Unfortunately, since the Keel incident, Cook's intuition wouldn't count for much with Fellows.

"Cook," Fellows said finally, "if you want to inform Grant Carter of Tony Rizzo's involvement with organized crime, OK. You can even politely ask him if he has any information that might help us in our effort for an indictment, but I know what you've got in mind and I'm not going to let you harass a man like Grant Carter into helping you do your job. In fact, if you do decide to contact Carter, I'll go with you. I don't trust you, Cook, and I don't trust your instincts."

Fellows rose, signaling an end to the meeting.

"You let me know if you want to talk with Carter," he said on his way out of the room without looking back. "Then call my secretary and I'll see if I can set up a meeting. I don't want any calls from Washington telling me to back off of a guy like Grant Carter, so you make sure you do exactly as I've said."

"Fucking pompous ass!" Cook said when the heavy door had slammed shut.

Metz had taken the Fourth and made a vacation out of it. An old Titans teammate that he'd kept in touch with was now a U.S. Tobacco rep up in Watertown, New York, near the Canadian border. His buddy had a house on an island in the middle of the St. Lawrence River, and the two of them, along with some of his friend's other cohorts, spent a full week on the island, fishing, drinking, and playing cards. It had been a dream vacation for Metz and already he was planning on going back for Labor Day. When he pulled up to his town house, cramped tightly on a street of town houses that looked just the same as his, he was depressed. He missed the wide-open river and the air and the trees. The way he saw it, his life was pretty much a shit pile.

As he pulled his gear from the trunk of his old Cadillac, he remembered the words of his buddy: "Come up here," he'd said. "I can get you a job as the rep for Syracuse. We could fish every fucking weekend."

The only thing bad about that was Syracuse. Metz had grown up in a small town, and when he arrived in New York years ago, he'd sworn he would never go back to one. It was something to think about, though. He would be able to afford a house of his own upstate, a house with some trees and a lawn.

Instead of making two small trips to get his stuff inside, Metz bogged himself down with all his gear. When he got to the door he ended up dropping half of it to get his key in the lock. There was no welcome inside besides the familiar smell of himself and the bowl of potpourri he kept on top of his TV. The answering machine was blinking, twenty-seven messages. That was more than he'd ever had before. It was strange. He rewound the tape. The first message was Hunter.

"Metz," said a disturbed voice, "it's me, Hunt. I'm out at the Hamptons. It's the Fourth at night. Call me whenever you get in. I don't care how late."

The next message was from Hunter as well. And the next, and the next. By the fifth message, Hunter was audibly angry.

"You fucking son of a bitch! Why aren't you calling me back? Call me, Metz. I need to talk to you!"

Metz waited no longer. He clicked off the machine and dialed Hunter's home at the beach. Rachel answered.

"Is everything OK?" Metz asked Rachel.

"As far as I know," Rachel said, her voice turning wary.

"Oh . . . good. Well, is Hunter there?"

"Yes, he's in the back, throwing," Rachel said, and then Metz heard her call to her husband.

"Hi, Metz," Hunter said in a cheerful voice. Then to Rachel, Metz heard him say, "Honey, will you go keep an eye on Sara? She and her friend are out on the dune, and I don't want her disappearing on us."

Metz could hear Hunter waiting for his wife to leave.

"Metz, tell me the fucking truth," Hunter said in a low, angry voice. "Did you put money on a Titans game last season?"

"No," Metz said reflexively.

"Metz," Hunter said in a pained way, "don't lie to me, man. It's so fucking important. Did you bet a Titans game?"

Metz thought for a moment. He wished he was back on the river, sitting on the front porch and watching the sun go down over Canada.

"Metz!"

Hunter's voice startled him.

"Well, just once," Metz said meekly. "It was that one game at the end of the year, Hunter. I didn't mean nothing by it. You were sick, remember? You had the flu and you guys were playing out in L.A. I had the money from all I'd won during the year. The game didn't mean nothing to you guys. You were already in the play-offs. I just figured I'd take a chance with all my winnings in one shot. You were pretty sick." Metz gave a nervous laugh and then said, "Why?"

"I told you never to bet the Titans, man. How could you do it? How the fuck could you do it, Metz? You fucking promised, you son of a bitch. You were supposed to be my friend, Metz."

"Hey, Hunt, I am your friend, buddy. Don't get so down. I didn't think it was any big deal. It's not like you did anything wrong—"

"Metz, don't call me anymore," Hunter said. "You fucked me, man. Just stay the hell away from me."

The phone went dead. Metz's lip quivered. This was bad. He wondered what could have happened. He sat down in his chair and dialed his buddy in Watertown. Something was really bad.

Carl sat rigidly in the leather seat of the new-smelling Cadillac Seville. The car shot down the Cross Island Expressway through the dark, thumping and bumping over potholes and random gaps in the road. Even at this late hour, traffic was not thin. Carl was nervous but excited. He had the feeling that this was a big opportunity for him. He had been begging Jimmy to give him some big work, some real work, for a long time now. He'd worked for Jimmy since he graduated from high school four years ago. It was his dream to be made a member of a family. He'd always been in and out of trouble as a kid and had never thought of aspiring to be anything other than a gangster in the Mafia.

Now, here he was, not just sitting next to a man everyone knew as "The Ax," but out on a job with him. Carl had been afraid that he'd blown his chance to do something big. Lonny had had nothing but complaints for him the entire time they had been together, and Carl thought Lonny would do him in. Not so. Jimmy said it was the results that Tony Rizzo remembered, not how Lonny felt about Carl's IQ.

Carl had done some rough work for Jimmy before. That's why he was here now. He had always been able to inflict fear and pain without the slightest bit of remorse or pity. Until now, that had been limited to roughing up stiffs who didn't pay on time, or breaking the fingers or noses of guys who looked like they weren't going to be able to pay at all. Tonight was different. Jimmy had told him so. Tonight would be his chance to make an impression not just with Jimmy, but with the higher-ups. Carl knew that a man could spend his whole life working for a guy like Jimmy and never even be considered for membership in the family. Membership was something special. Membership made you more than just a tough guy or a petty criminal. Membership put you above everyone else.

It was a dream for Carl. Angelo Quatrini was known throughout the underworld. He was known and he was feared. Carl wanted that for himself, and he knew that the best way to accomplish that was to do a few jobs with The Ax and maybe have him take Carl under his wing. Carl rode quietly, imagining that. He stole a glance at Angelo. He had to start thinking of him as Angelo. He knew that's what everyone in the family called him. No one would call Angelo The Ax to his face. It was an unpleasant reminder of what had earned him the nickname.

The story went that Angelo had only been sixteen when his sister, three years his junior, had been molested by some guy who was supposed to have been teaching her gymnastics. It was said that the guy had been sodomizing his young students for quite a while until Angelo caught word of what happened to his sister. The only part of the guy they ever found was his left hand. It floated up on a Staten Island beach, and the cops determined that it had been severed with an ax. They found the ax in Angelo's basement. He was arrested, but since the D.A. was never able to find the rest of the body, all they could charge him with was assault. A good argument was made for the possibility that the guy had simply skipped town after Angelo disposed of his mitt. Angelo was sentenced as a minor and did a couple of years in a juvenile detention center. When he got out, Vincent Mondolffi had a kind of holiday celebration for Angelo in Brooklyn. It seemed that one of Mondolffi's nieces had at some time been bothered by the teacher as well. Thus began the career of The Ax.

Carl thought about it. How lucky could a guy get? He would glad-
ly hack some pervert to pieces if it would get him in the good graces
of Vincent Mondolffi. Hell, he'd do it for Tony, or Angelo, or even
Jimmy. He'd do anything to get in, and he knew tonight might further his chances.

Angelo got off at the Port Washington exit and wound the big
black car through the old streets of one of the wealthiest suburbs of
New York. Soon they were going past large homes set back and up
from the street level like mini-castles. They slowed down and rolled
by a large Georgian mansion that was surrounded by a black iron
fence and trees that had seen the better part of the last century. Carl
glanced at Angelo. He was concentrating on the house. Carl tried to
concentrate, too.

They pulled around the corner and parked the car a good three
blocks away in an area where the homes were not as large and a
Seville on the street was nothing to look twice at.

"C'mon," Angelo murmured, shutting off the car and getting out
without so much as a glance at his sidekick.

Angelo took a six-foot ladder from the trunk and slung it under
his arm. It was painted black, and as Carl hurried after Angelo, he
couldn't even make it out under the shadows of the sidewalk.
Together they walked back up the street until they reached the
fence that Carl knew belonged to the Georgian mansion. Carl felt
almost invisible. They were both dressed in black from head to toe.
Angelo glanced around quickly before bracing the ladder against
the fence and scaling it like a man half his size.

"Hurry up," he grunted.

Carl scrambled up and jumped down to the other side as he had
seen Angelo do. Angelo slid the ladder through the fence and laid
it gently over the top of some bushes. He pulled a pair of dark sunglasses from the pocket of his jacket and put them on. Then he
pulled a long, heavy-looking BB air pistol from under his arm.

"Don't worry about the lights," Angelo said. "You just stay right
here in these bushes until I get back. Don't move. You'll hear the
alarm go off, but stay here. Got it?"

Carl started to wonder if The Ax wasn't insane, standing there
staring at him in the dark through black-lensed glasses, telling him
not to worry about the alarms. But he knew better. He knew that

part of being in the family was unquestioning obedience. That was one thing he knew for sure he could do—that and hurt people.

"Get in there good," Angelo said, pulling a branch over his head, "and keep down. I'll be back."

Carl sat, shifting nervously and watching Angelo make his way carefully up the side lawn through the trees and carefully manicured shrubbery. Suddenly two floodlights streamed light down on Angelo and lit him up bright as day, a prowler in black. Carl shrunk instinctively back into the shrubs but kept his eye on his partner. Angelo raised the pistol. One light popped, then the other. Everything was dark. Everything was quiet.

Time seemed to stand still for Carl. His heart raced in his chest. He waited for the sound of alarms and sirens, wondering if he could remain where he was in the face of wailing sirens. More lights went on, this time on the side of the house. Again Angelo raised his gun and again the lights popped out. The next time Carl could make out his mentor, he was at the service entrance, working methodically on the door like the Maytag repairman. The area was completely illuminated. After a good ten minutes of fussing and fidgeting, the alarm screamed from above. Lights all over the house went on. Angelo scrambled away from the house and was soon beside Carl, wriggling into the shrubbery and sitting down right next to him with his legs crossed like an Indian.

Within three minutes a squad car came racing up the street with its lights flashing but without sirens. There was no need. The noise from the house alarm would have drowned out anything for two blocks.

The cops made their way, cautious as cats, up to the house and in the front door. After ten minutes they came back out and walked around, testing doors and windows and looking for signs of a forced entry with their flashlights. When they were satisfied that all was well, Morgan Lloyd came out onto the front steps in his robe and slippers and stood between the towering front columns talking with the police. An hour after the alarm went off, things were quiet once again. The shrubs rustled gently as Angelo eased himself out.

"I'll be back," he said and disappeared again into the darkness toward the house.

It was only a few moments this time before the alarm was

screaming, and again Angelo returned to take his place next to Carl amid the bushes. Carl smiled when the car that had just left pulled casually up the drive again and the same two cops ambled up to the front door. This time they went with Morgan Lloyd directly to the door that Angelo had jimmied open. The cops tested it to show Lloyd that all was well. Carl wasn't sure what was happening, but he was close to peeing his pants, he was having so much fun. Twenty minutes later, Angelo repeated the process. Again the police came. This time Lloyd was waiting for them in the drive and they didn't even bother to get out of their car.

"That oughta do it," Angelo mumbled as the squad car pulled out into the street.

This time Angelo returned without any alarms. Again he sat down—waiting for what, Carl didn't know.

"Come on," Angelo said finally. "They oughta be settled down by now."

"Wait one minute," Carl whispered loudly. "I gotta piss."

Angelo looked on with disgust while Carl relieved himself in the bushes that had been their hideout for the past two hours.

"OK," Carl said in a whisper, zipping his fly and falling in behind Angelo. "I know what you told me I'm supposed to do, but just tell me again so I make sure."

Angelo stopped short and turned. He brought his menacing face so close to Carl's that the smell of his peppery breath filled the air between them.

"First I'm gonna cut the phone line. When we get in, there's gonna be two guys. I'll take the first guy and you grab the second. I'm gonna talk to the first guy a little bit, and you just wrap the other guy up with that duct tape. When you're done, you come wrap my guy up. You don't have to pamper the little fairies, but I don't want you breaking nothing, not unless I say so. Got it?"

"OK," Carl said. "I won't break nothing on the guy until you give me the say-so. Uh, Angelo?"

"What?"

"You know, if you want to off one of these guys . . . uh, I'd really like to get to do it if you don't mind . . ."

Angelo grinned with understanding before he turned and said, "Come on."

The door was already open. All was quiet and one by one they slipped into the house. Carl shut the door quietly behind them. Angelo lit their way up two different stairways with a heavy-duty red-lensed flashlight. Before Carl could think, he was standing in the middle of a large bedroom. A king-size four-poster was set in the middle of the room and on it was a large blanket-covered lump that consisted of two intertwined bodies. Above the bed was an ornate chandelier that hung from a mirrored dome in the ceiling.

Angelo sat gently on the edge of the bed and he motioned Carl to the other side. Angelo fiddled with a Tiffany lamp next to the bed and it clicked on, illuminating the well-appointed bedroom. Angelo flipped back the crimson bedcover, exposing two men spooned together like man and wife. Morgan Lloyd was wearing a pair of striped pajamas; the other man was completely naked. Both of them began to shriek like women.

"Billy!" Lloyd screamed, reaching for his lover, whom Carl was dragging by his long golden locks toward the edge of the bed.

Angelo had his pistol out and quickly jammed it into Morgan Lloyd's mouth, silencing him of all except a pathetic whimper. Lloyd's eyes were as big as a snared rabbit's, and he rolled them toward Billy, who was frantically clawing at Carl's face with his hands as well as his feet.

"Fuck!" Carl bellowed and smacked his flailing victim in the face with a blow that spurted blood all over the bed linens.

"Fuck! Fuck! Fuck!" Carl said, punching Billy with each exclamation and speckling his own face with scarlet dots from the force of his blows.

"Billy . . ." Lloyd moaned past the barrel of the Glock pistol, and rolled his eyes away.

"Little fucking queer cut me!" Carl complained as he roughly began to wrap Billy's wrists with the tape.

"Shut up," Angelo said, and put his face up close to Lloyd's. Carl didn't know if he meant Lloyd or him.

"Now you listen to me . . . " Angelo's voice was low and guttural. Lloyd was quiet. Fear filled his eyes. Carl had Billy down on the floor now with his feet straight up in the air. Carl was winding the tape down from his ankles. Billy was moaning pathetically through a band of tape that cut across his face.

"You see this gun?" Angelo continued, jiggling the Glock in Lloyd's mouth.

Lloyd nodded and whined.

"Well," Angelo said, pulling back the hammer, "I'm going to fucking spray your brains all over this room with it.

"Open your fucking eyes!" Angelo screamed.

Lloyd opened his eyes.

Click!

"Aww, shit!" Carl said, tearing off the end of his tape job and sniffing the air like a mastiff. "What the fuck is that? Did he shit himself?"

Carl made his way over to the other side of the bed and began to tape Lloyd from the ankles up. "Aww, man," he said, wincing. "He did. That's fucked up."

"I told you to shut the fuck up!" Angelo said. This time Carl knew he meant him.

Angelo kept his face close to Lloyd's. He seemed not to notice the smell. He kept the gun in Lloyd's mouth.

"Now listen carefully, because I know you don't want me to have to pay you another visit to tell you again, right? Right!?"

Lloyd nodded his head and gave out a low cry that sounded like no.

"That's right," Angelo said. "Now, I'm going to let you live tonight and you know what? I'm going to let your little fag live, too. What do you think of that? Pretty fucking nice of me, isn't it? Isn't it?"

Lloyd nodded his head as violently as the big pistol would allow.

"Yeah, but you don't have to thank me. No, there's only one man in the world that's keeping you alive right now. Do you want to know who that man is? Yeah? OK, it's Grant Carter. Yeah, that's right. See, my boss says that you don't deserve to live. My boss says that I can have you for myself to kill in any way I want, and I got special ways to kill little fags like you. But then he tells me that a guy by the name of Grant Carter says that you're not such a bad guy, he says maybe I shouldn't get to kill you.

"But you know what I'm betting? I'm betting that you're gonna do something to piss off this Grant Carter. I'm betting a big-shot faggot like you's gotta throw his weight around . . . yeah. In fact, I'm betting that I'm gonna get to pay you a visit again real soon, and there ain't nothing that can keep you safe from me. You think you're safe? You got this big house, these gates, and lights, and alarms . . . You're never safe. You hear me? I'd love nothing better than to have to come back for you, 'cause next time it will be to fucking snuff you and whatever little fairy I happen to find you with. Now you just think about that. You just think about what a good friend you got . . . and if you forget, well, then I'll look forward to seeing you again real soon.

"Oh," Angelo said, pulling the pistol out of Lloyd's mouth so Carl could wrap a band of tape around his head, "another thing. If Mr. Carter finds out about my visit, if you so much as imply that maybe someone had to teach you some manners . . . well, then all bets are off. So you just be a good friend to Grant Carter and behave yourself, got it?"

Lloyd nodded emphatically.

"Come on," Angelo said to Carl, and the two of them left with Lloyd frozen on the bed amid his own stink and Billy thumping about on the floor in his own blood.

CHAPTER 18

Hunter walked alone down the empty beach. It was a weekday, early enough in the morning so that he had it all to himself. The sun was struggling to rise through a heavy bank of clouds and brilliant rays were beginning to creep over its highest peaks. A light breeze brought a fresh sea smell to his nose. It was a perfect summer morning in the Hamptons, but Hunter couldn't remember being so depressed in all his life. Even when his family was losing the farm they'd lived on for generations, he hadn't been as low as he was now. Hunter snorted. His brother would readily agree with that assessment.

He turned and peered back down the beach toward his house. He could make out Rachel moving steadily toward him. It was easy to tell it was her even at this distance. Her dark hair contrasted starkly with her all-white nylon sweatsuit, and the purposeful way she walked would have told him it was Rachel even if she had been wearing a disguise. He had left her asleep and was surprised to see her out and about this early. He began a steady pace back toward her, and in a few minutes he was kissing her lightly on the lips.

"Hi, honey," he said with as much cheer as he could muster.

Rachel returned his greeting with a look of concern, her pretty face turned up to his.

"Hello, honey," she said. "How are you feeling?"

"I'm fine," he replied. "You know, a little down about having to go to training camp is all. Besides that, nothing big. I'm fine, really."

"'He doth protest too much,'" Rachel said with a weak smile.

"What, I'm not protesting. I'm fine, Rach."

"Hunter, I know you. Remember? I'm the one who you say knows what you're thinking before you're thinking it. You said that," she reminded him, "not me, and for you to be out here at this time is unheard of. With camp in a few days you're usually like an old bear with your sleep, always grumbling about how you won't get any for a month. Since that party at the Carters' you've been mister early riser, acting like you've got the world on your shoulders."

"Oh, really, Rach," Hunter said, putting his arm around her shoulder and beginning to tug her down the beach toward their house, "you know how I get. You know I always get a little under the weather before camp. I hate to be away from you and Sara for a whole month. I swear, it's enough to make me think about quitting football."

"You'll get through it," she said. "But there's more than that, Hunter. I know your training camp mood. There's something else bothering you. Tell me . . ."

Hunter hesitated, thinking wildly. He slowed his shuffle and toed some wet sand into the advancing white foam of the surf. It wasn't like him to keep things from Rachel. She was his best friend and his best confidant, but he had never discussed his gambling with her at length. There had never been the need. It was never any big deal, until now. And now if she knew, she'd kill him. It was bad enough when she found out about the ten thousand dollars. If she knew the situation was compounded by threats from Tony Rizzo, she'd insist he call the police or something crazy like that. That's just how Rachel was. He didn't want that. He had no doubts that Rizzo would take him down. He was at the top of his career. He was finally going to make the kind of money that would set him free from everything. He couldn't let it get away.

"I guess it's the money," he said finally. "I'm worried about our money."

"This is something new," she said, though not sarcastically.

"I just can't stop thinking, with all my limited partnerships in the tank now, I was counting on those things to keep us going. Besides the houses and the farm—what's left of it—I've got everything I've made over my entire career invested in those damn hotels and apartment houses and all that other shit that's worth about nothing right now with real estate the way it is . . . "

Rachel laughed. "I'm sorry," she said. "I know it's not funny. But you've never given our finances the slightest bit of thought, and now, when you'll be making more than ever before, you're suddenly concerned about some bad investments made long ago. I can't figure you sometimes, Hunter, I really can't."

They were up on the softer sand now and the walking was harder. They made their way through the grassy dunes to the house.

"I'm just thinking worst-case scenario," he said. "I can't help worrying about the worst case. I don't want to let you down, Rach. I want to take good care of you and Sara."

Hunter reached inside the sliding glass door, glad to have sidestepped a major confrontation about his gambling. He hoisted a large duffel bag over his shoulder. Rachel picked up a deck chair and followed him silently as he went back down the steps. She sat in her chair as Hunter dug into the bag for a football. A local carpenter had rigged up a two-by-four frame and some netting with a tire suspended in the middle by four rusty chains. The awkward-looking contraption sat tucked between the slope of one of the grassy dunes and the back corner of their house. Hunter stood about thirty yards away from it. He began to zip the balls through the tire. Rachel loved to watch him. His motion was smooth and beautiful, and she loved to hear the sound of the footballs as they whistled through the air. She equated that sound with peace, probably because the two of them had had many of these moments together and Hunter, lost in the effort of something he did so well, would for a few brief moments shut down the internal engines that seemed to drive him through life.

After he'd thrown a half-dozen balls, Rachel spoke.

"There is no worst case," she said quietly. "So stop hanging your head and try to enjoy these last few days before you leave us for that god-awful camp. We have nothing at all to worry about."

The week after the Fourth crawled by painfully for Grant Carter. He was paralyzed by the impending meeting with Morgan Lloyd at First Bank. Guy Fitzpatrick, the Titans' general manager, had been after him to give his final approval to some rookie contracts, but he had no heart for it. The thought that the Titans might not even be his anymore invaded his every thought. He struggled diligently on the phones, seeking alternative financing from every source he could conceive of. No one was willing to help. The properties he owned had dropped so much in value that he had only his reputation to offer, that and the Titans. But when someone so much as mentioned his team as a possible bargaining chip, he would hang up abruptly. That was the only reason he was searching for a new source of money, to save the team.

After a week of no sleep and nothing but failures, Grant Carter once again found himself in the imposing offices of First Bank. Despite his precarious position, Carter maintained an air of dignity that in no way revealed his financial weakness. He had his pride, and if he had to go down, he would go down with his chin up. He would fight and scrape until nothing was left. He would take on First Bank in the courts and sue them for everything he could think of. He would destroy his records. He would pay off construction managers to abandon current projects. He would transfer the team to one of his shell corporations owned by Camille and file for bankruptcy. First Bank would ultimately get his team. But they wouldn't get it without a fight, and Morgan Lloyd wouldn't be the one to dole out options on the Titans. It would take years, and it would probably cost him everything he had. Grant Carter had built himself up from nothing and he could do it again. Surrender was not a word in his vocabulary.

There was no waiting this time, and Carter assumed Lloyd had eagerly awaited this moment. In a way, Carter was looking forward to this meeting as well. It had been clear to him a week before that he was backed into a corner, and he was eager to draw the battle lines. He would tell Lloyd that if he planned on taking him out, he'd better be ready to lose some sleep.

When Carter got his first look at Morgan Lloyd, he immediately thought the man was ill. Lloyd was pale and drawn. Dark bags sagged under lusterless eyes that twitched uncontrollably. The tick in the corner of Lloyd's mouth was going nonstop, like some broken child's toy. Carter smiled ever so slightly. It didn't bother him to see his enemy like this.

"Mr. Carter," Lloyd said fawningly, rising from behind his desk and showing Carter to a seat on the leather couch, "I'm glad you're here. I've been anxious for our meeting."

Lloyd sat down across from Carter on the edge of a wing chair.

Grant Carter eased himself comfortably back into the couch and began to assess the situation. He knew already that things had changed. He had been in enough negotiations to know when a man had lost his support. Carter could tell from his appearance alone, even without his beaten demeanor, that Lloyd had somehow lost a crucial component that was required to carry out Carter's destruction. Carter's mind raced with the possibilities. None made sense. Felix LaMonte was not a man to change his mind about something, and if he had, certainly he would be in this meeting himself, scrambling wildly to make up. Also, Carter knew he was vulnerable. He had been well aware of his situation even before his previous meeting with Lloyd. He had known that some pressure from someone high up within First Bank could ruin him. So what could it be?

The answer was not forthcoming, but that didn't bother Grant Carter. He knew that sometimes in business, things happened in unexpected and fortuitous ways. It was important when such aberrations occurred that the beneficiary go along with them as though it was expected from the start.

So when Morgan Lloyd said, "There's been a mistake," Carter simply nodded and smiled blandly and waited for him to continue.

"It's just that . . ." Lloyd seemed to be searching Carter's face for something. Carter gave him stone. "It's just that I realized over this past week that you have been an invaluable client to First Bank for years, and that the solvency of your financial position will most certainly resolve itself in time. Well, I'm sorry to have troubled you with all this, Grant. Please, let's just leave it at that and go on as though none of this has ever happened."

Grant Carter rose and waited for Lloyd to stand and offer his hand. "I'm glad you've come around, Morgan," Carter said with a vague note of condescension as he took the man's hand briefly. "It wouldn't have done either of us any good the other way."

Carter thought he saw raw fear in Lloyd's eyes. Why, he couldn't figure for the life of him. Whatever the reason, though, Grant Carter knew he liked it, and whenever he found out where it was coming from, he imagined he'd give Lloyd a few more doses of it before he was through.

Later that day, Carter's question was answered when his secretary told him there was a Tony Rizzo on the phone who insisted that he speak with him.

"He says he's a friend of Camille's, Mr. Carter, and that it was important. If he hadn't mentioned Camille, I wouldn't be bothering you, but I thought you might want to know," the secretary said apologetically.

"Ah, yes," Carter said, and because he was in a particularly good mood and it might humor his daughter to accept such a plea, he agreed to take the call.

"Hello," Carter said dully as he picked up the phone.

"Grant. This is Tony Rizzo." The voice was an arrogant one, and Carter had to replay breakfast in the Hamptons in his mind to match this voice to Camille's Tony. And he couldn't recall telling the young man to call him Grant.

"I met you in the Hamptons over the Fourth, with Camille," Tony said, immediately dispelling all doubt.

"Yes, Tony, what can I do for you?" Carter said with cool impatience.

"Well, I was just checking up on that First Bank situation to make sure everything was all smoothed over."

Carter almost fell out of his chair. How could Tony Rizzo know?

"Yes. Yes, everything's fine. Nothing to worry about after all," Carter said.

"Oh, that's real good, 'cause I made a few calls to some friends about that deal on Tuesday and I just wanted to check with you to make sure things were back on track."

Carter didn't know what to think. Could it really be possible that this young punk had something to do with Morgan Lloyd's turnaround?

"Well," Tony said abruptly, not giving Carter a chance to wonder any further, "I'm real glad things worked out for you, Grant. You just let me know if there's anything at all I can do for you. Anybody who's important to Camille is important to me, too. I want you to know that. Good-bye, Grant."

The phone went dead.

Grant Carter buzzed his secretary. "Where is Guy Walker?" he asked her.

"He's in Brockport with the team," she replied.

"Well, get him on the phone for me. Right now. I don't care what he's doing or what you have to do to get in touch with him. Call the damn Brockport police and have them drag him off the practice field if necessary, but find him and have him call me immediately."

Carter clunked the phone down to let her know just how serious he was. Walker was essentially useless, a washed-out ATF agent from Chicago who he'd hired on as a favor to a friend. Carter had wondered before why the league required every team to have someone in charge of team security. Well, maybe he could be useful now. For ten minutes Carter did nothing but think about Rizzo. What he came up with was not comforting, but then again, anything was better than what Lloyd had been planning to do to him. The phone rang.

"Walker?"

"Yes, Mr. Carter, they just got hold of me."

"Do you know someone by the name of Tony Rizzo?"

There was a pause, then Walker said, "How would I know him?"

"From around town. He's in the construction business, I think."

"I can't say I do offhand, Mr. Carter, but I can make some calls and have some people run a check on him."

"I want you back here now. I want you to handle this yourself. I want to know who this Tony Rizzo is. I want everything and I want to see it before the end of today. Now get back here."

Again he hung up the phone abruptly.

Grant Carter sat thinking for a few more minutes, then rose from his desk and looked out over the grass practice fields where the Titans carried on their in-season training. He stared at the sun-yellow goal posts and the bright orange blocking dummies. Without his players teeming about, sweating and knocking one another senseless, things just didn't seem right out there. But then again, things didn't seem right elsewhere either.

Ellis Cook spun and leveled his pistol at the advancing form. He fired and the figure dropped. From the gloom another figure sprang toward him, and again he fired. Now both lay in the muck that covered the concrete floor beneath his feet. He was in an old warehouse and it was dark with fog. Still, he could see enough to know that both the forms that now lay at his feet wore masks. There were three, though, where he thought there'd been only two and now their masks were off. Cook's scream came from deep within him. The horror was beyond anything he'd ever known. He drew a deep, quick breath and began screaming again, emptying his soul with the shriek. Beneath his feet were the lifeless faces of Tommy Keel, his girlfriend . . . and Naomi.

Cook's scream shook him from sleep. He sat up straight in bed. He hurt from the inside out. He ached for Naomi, and the unfairness of her death cut deep into him like a day-old wound. Even through the shock and dread and horror of his dream there was a certain joy in seeing her, even her corpse. Cook felt like mixing himself a drink, but decided not to. He poured himself a glass of orange juice and peered in on Natasha, his only comfort. Esther stirred and Cook shut the door quietly.

He got back into his own bed. The blankets were still in a heap on the floor. He pulled them back onto the bed and wiggled his feet in through the tangle in order to straighten them out. He pulled them up to his chin and shut his eyes. His mind began to turn. It was the same old thing for him. Possibilities and leads turned over and over in his mind as if by will they could help him to bring down Tony Rizzo. Tommy Keel came to mind, and Cook huffed to himself in the dark. He couldn't even dream in peace anymore.

Sleep would not return for Cook, so when the clock struck five he showered and dressed quietly. He phoned Conrad Duffy and suggested meeting him for breakfast. Duffy, Cook knew, was always up early, and Cook had in fact just caught him on his way out the door. They met at a Greek diner on Eighth Avenue. The place was packed with men wearing work boots and unkempt Cartwright overalls. Their faces were mostly rough and unshaven. Cook and Duffy, two black men in suits, drew stares as they sat down and ordered eggs and coffee.

"Thanks for meeting me," Cook said as the buzz of conversation that filled the place resumed.

"I'm glad you called," Duffy replied, sniffing the smell of bacon and toast from the greasy air around them.

"Listen, I want to know what you think about all this stuff with Grant Carter, Duffy. You've been in this city all your life. Sometimes I get the feeling I'm missing things, like things are different here."

"You don't seem to miss much, if you ask me," Duffy said as he dumped a package of sugar into his coffee and began to stir it with a battered spoon. "But since you ask, I think you should let the Carter thing go."

"I know, but I could squeeze Carter. If Fellows would only stop being such a prick."

"Let me tell you something about Fellows," Duffy said. "Prick that he is, he's right about Grant Carter. First of all, Carter wouldn't be such an easy nut to crack. If that motherfucker didn't want to help and you tried to pull some shit on him, he wouldn't scare so easy. He's a bad dude. You have to be to do big business in this city. I bet he could have your ass transferred to fucking Forsythe County if he had the itch to do it.

"You're trying too hard, brother," Duffy continued after downing another gulp of coffee. "If something is up with Rizzo and the Titans, we'll see it. All we have to do is keep watching and waiting."

"We're never going to see anything if Rizzo throws his tail every time he does business he doesn't want us to know about."

"He's only lost us a few times," Duffy offered.

"Yeah, but those few times must be the ones when he was doing dirty work. The rest of the time he's clean as a whistle. You know as well as I do he's on to us."

"I don't know," Duffy said, taking a careful sip from his mug. "It is possible that Rizzo is simply careful. We've had this conversation before."

"There's a leak somewhere," Cook said. "It could be Marrow."

They were both silent. Duffy knew that the thought had been floating around in Cook's mind. It had occurred to him as well.

"It could be anyone, or no one," Duffy said finally.

"You? Could it be you?" Cook said.

"It could be me. It could be you," Duffy replied flatly.

"What are you telling me?"

"I'm saying that you may have to fish around on your own. You may have to stop keeping everyone so informed. Just take in what everybody gives you and keep it to yourself."

"That's no way to handle a team," Cook said as he made room on the table for a platter of food. He didn't mention the fact that his fishing had already put him on notice with Fellows.

"You're the head coach," Duffy said. He had played college ball at Syracuse and he had the habit of using analogies from his bygone days. "You call the plays. The tight end doesn't need to know what the strong safety's doing. Why don't you try skipping the Monday morning meetings where everybody reports what they're doing to everyone else? Let it rest for a while. Tell everyone you want the time spent out on the street. That's where all the juice is, in those Monday meetings. That's how come everyone knows everything about what everyone else is doing."

"What about Marrow?" Cook said, digging into his food.

"Tell him some things but not all things. Keep some important details to yourself. You're the boss, don't forget."

"What about you?" Cook said, looking up.

Duffy flashed a brilliant smile of perfect teeth.

"Don't even tell me everything, OK? That's how I'd do it . . . Pass me that jelly."

Cook smiled back and passed a jar filled with purple goo. "I'm not keeping anything from you. Two heads are better than one. Besides, if I can't trust you, then I give up," Cook said, continuing to eat.

When both their plates were clean, Cook said, "I want to make some kind of contact with the Titans. I just have a feeling about it. I can't shake it. If I can get the drop on some kind of scam or something, I can make some people talk. That's what we need, people to talk. We need to get someone in the Mondolffi organization between a rock and a hard place, offer them witness protection, and watch them sell Tony Rizzo's ass down the East River. I know what you're saying about letting Rizzo run his course, but . . . well, damn it, I want to get the lay of the land."

Duffy seemed to consider something, and then he said, "I think I might have a way to make that happen. There's a guy by the name of Vince Peel. He's a good guy. He's in the Queens office, and he's the guy that goes out to the Titans training camp every year with someone from the DEA to read the players the riot act about drugs and guns and gambling. He's been doing it since I can remember. We could ask him if he needs a little help. Maybe we could even get him to let you stand in. I know he gets a chance to meet everyone when he goes out there, the coaches, the players. I don't know about Grant Carter, but I know he's met him some time before."

Cook was on his feet. He pulled a twenty from his wallet and flipped it on the table.

"What are you doing?"

"Let's go give him a call," Cook said.

Duffy shook his head. "It's only six-thirty. This guy's an old guy."

"That's perfect. Old men can't sleep past six-thirty anyway. Let's go."

Duffy shrugged and took one last gulp of coffee before he was on his feet. Cook was already out the door.

CHAPTER 19

Training camp was actually a relief to Hunter Logan. Normally it was the worst time of year, something he had dreaded since he was a kid when they used to have double sessions in the August heat when all the other high school kids were just starting to think about buying new school clothes. Now it was even worse. The NFL camps were at least a month long. It was a month of heat and pain and seclusion from your family. Hunter could not remember a training camp in his life when he did not think about quitting football.

This time, however, he welcomed the escape from New York. Since his encounter with Tony Rizzo, Hunter's days had been filled with worry. He worried about whether he should tell someone about Rizzo and what Rizzo wanted from him. Hunter was certain the guy would appear soon.

Now, though, stuck at Brockport State College in upstate New York, Hunter had no time to think of anything but football and his nightly phone call home to Rachel and Sara. When there was any free time, he spent it reacquainting himself with his teammates. Even the time he spent with Bert Meyer in the off-season was scarce compared to the intimacy of training camp and an NFL season. During camp your teammates became your family. And during the season, especially with a winning team, the guys were bound as tightly as college fraternity brothers. They lived a secret and privileged life that few others could imagine, and one that most people on the outside envied.

As Hunter walked slowly and stiffly from the athletic complex where they practiced to the mid-rise dorm where they ate and slept, he wondered how many people outside the league would really want to be a part of it if they knew what training camp entailed. He thought of the early morning wake-up call when Billy Knoll, the assistant equipment manager, wandered through the hallways of the dormitory sounding his air horn. That would be enough in itself for some people to turn back. But it was a fitting beginning for a day that went downhill from there.

After a quick breakfast there was the walk across campus to the athletic complex. There you got taped and dressed quickly for practice, which lasted from eight-thirty until eleven. After a shower and lunch there were meetings to review the morning practice and prepare for the afternoon. If you were lucky, you could get almost an hour to grab a much-needed nap. If not, you'd just walk right back to the complex and dress for the three o'clock practice. After that was weight lifting, then dinner, then meetings that lasted until about ten. Hunter would then rush to a pay phone, call home, and then spend another half hour bullshitting and playing poker or dice with his buddies until eleven o'clock curfew. Then it was lights out until the next morning, when the entire schedule would be repeated, usually without a variation.

"Hunter!"

Hunter turned when he heard Bert's voice behind him. He waited for his friend to catch up. Bert's painful hobble made him smile. He looked even worse than Hunter.

"Little sore?" Hunter said when his friend fell in beside him.

Bert groaned, "That was a bitch! What got into his ass? Pop would never have run us like that. It's bullshit. I'm telling you, we don't need that kind of running. And that live goal line scrimmage. This guy thinks he's still in college!"

Bert was referring to the new head coach, Martin Price, who'd come from Notre Dame. Unfortunately for the Titans players, Price had retained some of his hard-assed tactics from coaching college ball. These, Bert swore, included more hitting and running than any other NFL team in history. The riddle going around camp was: "What do you get when you cross a prick with a block of ice?" "That's easy: a Price." The riddle, and the regimen, left their coach with the clandestine nickname of "The Iceman."

"Oh, come on," Hunter said. "It's not really that bad, is it?"

"Huh! That's easy for you to say," Bert grumbled. "A fucking pretty-boy QB is all you are. You don't even get hit in practice! You guys go out there in your little blue jerseys so the rest of us stiffs in white won't bump into you by accident. I swear, man, when my boy grows up he's gonna be a quarterback or a fucking kicker, for that matter. What a life. You guys aren't even sore."

Hunter snorted. "Hey, I might not have my head bashed in, but I'm plenty sore. I have to do all that running, too. Plus my damn shoulder's killing me. It's no party throwing a hundred balls a day with a bum shoulder . . ."

Bert looked at the bag of ice that was bound to Hunter's shoulder by an Ace bandage. The bag must have leaked because there was a stain from the water on Hunter's blue T-shirt that left the arm a darker shade of blue. Icy drops fell from his elbow as they walked.

"Well, yeah, that's true. You got the bad shoulder," Bert conceded. "I forgot about that. Why the hell don't you lay off it a little?"

"Hah!" Hunter exclaimed. "That's a damn good question, but I've got a damn good answer—Broadway Blake."

"Oh, hell," Bert said, "he's not even in your league."

"Not right now," Hunter said, "and I like to keep it that way. Don't you see the way Price drools when the kid throws those long balls? I swear the man has to take cold showers after every touchdown pass the little bastard throws out there. Price loves him!"

Bert shrugged. "Yeah, but he ain't gonna put him in front of you."

"I know," Hunter said. "I just like to look good. That kid gets under my skin sometimes. I couldn't bear to stand around watching him run with the first team."

"Well, I'd rather have your bad shoulder than these fucked-up elbows anyway," Bert said, lifting his elbows to the sky like a big chicken, "and these fucking lumps on my forehead. You won't have the fucking brain damage I'll have in later life from all this head banging."

"What later life?" Hunter said, staring ahead and trying to keep a straight face. "Your brain is damaged pretty good right now if you ask me."

Bert began to nod in agreement, then realized what he was doing and scowled. "Fuck you," he said pleasantly.

As the two friends mounted the front steps of the large dormitory, Matt Brown, the Titans' best receiver, burst through the front doors. His eyes were wide and he looked wildly about.

"Did you guys hear?" he said, obviously aching to tell them the news.

"What?"

"Fucking night off tonight is what!" Matt said, nodding his head to reinforce his veracity. "Can you fucking believe it? The fucking Iceman called off the night meetings. We got to listen to a couple of stiffs from the FBI about drugs or some shit, but it's only until seven-thirty, then we're actually free from this shit until eleven! What you guys gonna do?"

Bert and Hunter looked at each other like convicts on a road crew left behind by some errant guard.

Hunter shrugged. "Play some poker, I guess."

"Aww, man! That's fucking pathetic," Matt moaned. "We get a few hours break from all this shit and you two hayseeds look at each other and talk about playing cards." Matt was clearly disappointed.

"Well," Hunter said, trying to recover, "what are you doing?"

"Me and some boys are getting the hell away from here, that's what," Matt said. "And you two better be with us if you want me to respect you in the morning."

"Where the hell are you gonna go?" Bert asked. "We're in fucking Brockport. If you blinked, you'd miss the place. It's got only one bar in the whole fucking town."

"And that, my man," said Matt, "is where we're at."

Bert shrugged and so did Hunter.

"OK," Hunter said as Bert nodded.

"We're with you," said Bert, and the two friends hobbled into the dorm to get themselves some dinner at the cafeteria before their seven o'clock encounter with the FBI.

Cook was disappointed. The drive from New York seemed to last forever. The DEA agent was a surly cuss by the name of Cutchins. He was a dumpy, overweight smoker with grayish, thinning hair and a face that looked like fifty miles of hard road. He wore gray trousers with an old blue blazer and a dull pink sports shirt. White flakes of dandruff were sprinkled about his shoulders.

The maroon cloth upholstery of Cutchins's Buick LeSabre stank from Marlboros, and Cook had to endure his smoking all the way from the George Washington Bridge until they unloaded at the Road Motel outside of Brockport. Cutchins let Cook know that he and Vince Peel had been making the trip to the Titans camp for the past seventeen years and that it was a kind of vacation that they both looked forward to. In fact, Cutchins lamented his sidekick's absence almost the entire length of Route 17. At one point Cook had tried to feign sleep, but the impervious Cutchins had simply poked him in the ribs until he opened his eyes.

"Hey," Cutchins had said, "Peel and me never slept on each other."

But Cutchins was no more than an annoyance. The disappointment came when he learned that Grant Carter wouldn't be within a hundred miles of the training camp.

"So," Cook finally said to make some conversation, "do you think we'll get a chance to sit down with Grant Carter?"

Cutchins looked at him as though he were mad. He guffawed and smoke spewed out of his mouth and nostrils.

"You think Grant Carter is gonna be there? In fucking Brockport?" Cutchins asked incredulously.

"Yeah," Cook replied. "When I talked with Peel, every other word was about what a hell of a guy Grant Carter was and how much I was going to admire the man. 'A man of wealth but great perspective.' Those were Peel's words, not mine."

"That's my fucking buddy Peel for you! What a fucking live wire. That's him, all right. He met Carter once when we got some locker room passes to a Raiders game for coming out here like this to talk with the team. The NFL takes good care of me and Peel. So this one game we run right into the old man himself, and I mean literally run into him. Peel steps right on the guy's Bally loafers and shits them all up with some gum that was stuck to the bottom of his shoe. Well, Peel says he's awful sorry and old Carter kinda grunts and says not to worry about it, but kinda pissed off like.

"That was it!" Cutchins howled. "And since that day you can't talk about the fucking Titans without Peel breaking out about what a hell of a guy Grant Carter is and how you'll really enjoy meeting him. That Peel, he's a pisser.

"I sure do wish he was here," Cutchins added just in case Cook had forgotten where he stood.

The only silver lining in that cloud was that it eased Cook's anxiety about not having told Fellows about his trip. He had played it over and over in his mind, and he'd come up with a thin but conceivable story to tell his boss. Had he met Carter, Cook would have simply explained that he had been doing a favor for an old friend of Duffy's who couldn't make the trip, and he had inadvertently run into Grant Carter. Cook wouldn't have leaned on the owner; he would have simply asked a few harmless questions and seen where they went. Certainly he wasn't going to bring Fellows with him like a baby-sitter. But the story was moot now that Cook wouldn't be meeting Carter.

So here Cook was, getting ready to give a talk about gambling to a bunch of pro ball players who he imagined would rather be anywhere else in the world. Cutchins, Cook could see, was unaware that the players didn't give a shit whether or not he was there. Cutchins had his speech down, and Cook bet himself that it was the same one he'd been giving for seventeen years. Cook didn't know how Peel addressed the players, but he was not one for public speaking, let alone speaking to eighty big, angry-looking ball players.

They were in a medium-size conference room in the dorm where the players were living. It was big enough to hold the whole team, but small enough to make it hot and cramped. Cook looked out at the mostly hostile crowd and recognized a few of the big-name players like Matt Brown and Rodney Smalls, and of course the quarterback, Hunter Logan. Logan looked up from his discussion with a thick-necked lineman and gave Cook a friendly smile, an oasis in a desert of disdain. Cook was surprised. Maybe he shouldn't have been. He'd heard that sometimes it was the biggest celebrities who were the most down-to-earth people.

Martin Price arrived and shook hands with both Cutchins and Cook. The coach was about forty-five with a slender athletic build, thick frameless glasses, and a gaunt face that was capped with a Titans baseball hat. Cook could see from the demeanor of the team as Price began to speak that his players were far from enamored with the man. He told his team to pay close attention to the speakers and that when they were done they were free from responsibilities until eleven o'clock curfew. This brought dramatic cheers, and then Price departed without so much as a nod.

Cutchins went first. Cook wondered to himself as the decrepit DEA officer droned on about the dangers of drugs and the legal restrictions on hand guns in the five boroughs of New York whether it was better that he was speaking last. On one hand, Cutchins wouldn't be a tough act to follow. On the other hand, it gave Cook time to be nervous, and it obviously increased the audience's already inauspicious mood.

"... I know you older guys will be disappointed that my usual partner, Vince Peel from the FBI, isn't with me this year," Cutchins finally said after asking for any questions and receiving none, "but I've brought a pretty decent guy with me to try to fill in. Gentlemen, this is Agent Cook, supervisor of a special task force on organized crime in the New York metropolitan area. Agent Cook will now talk to you about the hazards of gambling as it relates to professional athletes."

Cutchins stood to the side and Cook stepped up to the podium. There was no polite applause or welcome of any kind. The pervasive expression was one of having already heard it all before.

"Gentlemen," Cook began with a nervous edge in his voice, "I'm here to talk to you about something very serious . . ."

Someone in the back let out a resounding fart. Laughter erupted from all quarters, and Cook felt blood rush to his face. He stared coldly at the crowd until the last of the heckling subsided.

"Look out, dudes," someone said in a mocking tone, "this man is bad!" Cook found the source and stared directly at him. "I'll tell you something bad," Cook said with flat malevolence. "Bad is a kid about your age that I found a few months ago in Brooklyn with his head blown apart like a rotten melon, and his girlfriend, raped and laying right there alongside him and just as dead. That's bad, motherfucker, and that's the shit I got to deal with. So if you think I'm a joke, you just take your sorry ass on outta this room!"

There was dead silence and Cook knew he had their attention.

"Gentlemen," he continued, "I know you hear something about gambling every year at this time. I know the league mandates that you listen to this talk, and I know you're probably sick of it. But let me tell you something. If you think that gambling isn't a part of your world, then you're wrong. Billions of dollars are made in this country every year on the business of gambling. Billions. I know you men go to great lengths to make the kind of money you make in the NFL, and it's a lot, believe me. Gambling itself may not seem like any big deal to you people. But behind it all, the machinery that makes gambling happen in this country is organized crime. I'm not talking about a bunch of benevolent Italians with guns and fedoras. I'm talking about men who will rape your wives and murder your children. Believe me, gentlemen, they're all around you. The most dangerous of them are the ones that lead you to believe they're nothing more than businessmen. You'll know them by the questions they ask you: Who's hurt? Who's mad at the coaches? How's Hunter Logan look in practice? These kinds of things seem harmless, but if someone you meet starts asking you these kind of questions, you better clam up and give my office a call because chances are they're looking for some kind of edge on their line.

"For those of you who gamble yourselves, I'm telling you to stop. A few hundred here and there is maybe no big deal, but if you get caught up in it and you start trying to make a big comeback because you're down, well, let's just say that if you get behind on these people things can get ugly.

"Also, if you are caught gambling on NFL games, you will be suspended and in all likelihood, depending on the circumstances, you will banned from the NFL for life. That's the league's rule, not mine, but I understand it because if you're gambling on games within this league, you're compromising yourself. This league doesn't want that, and it shouldn't.

"Gentlemen, I know you're anxious to get out of here and I know none of you have any questions. But I'm leaving a stack of my cards here for you to take. If you have questions for me at any time in the future, or if you think you are being solicited for information that will be used in a gambling operation, please, give me a call. I am not the bad guy. I will help you gentlemen. The other guys won't. Believe me, they won't."

Cook put a stack of white cards on the podium and walked out of the room with a bewildered and slightly peeved Cutchins behind him.

The Titans hesitated only a moment before they realized that the strangely intense FBI agent was through. Then they broke for the doors to make the most of their few hours' reprieve from the doldrums of camp. Amid the animated conversation and the backlog of bodies waiting to get out the door, no one noticed Hunter Logan picking a card from the podium and stuffing it discreetly into his pocket.

By nine o'clock most of the Titans at the Ledge were half drunk. The Ledge was a rickety old building that had originally been a trading post built on the edge of the canal to take advantage of the commerce that once gave the town of Brockport a reason to exist. Now it was a dark, seedy establishment that was timelessly decrepit. It was dark inside, not so much by design but because of numerous burnt-out bulbs in the ceiling that went unreplaced. It was a place that could be described as an armpit, even in a place as dilapidated as Brockport.

The team had spilled out onto the sidewalk, and some of the more adventurous men had even scaled the steep bank and were skipping stones into the murky canal below. They began to grow rowdy. A few beer bottles were heard to smash. The occasional pick-up truck that ambled over the Main Street bridge would slow down to ponder the strange crowd before moving on into the country night.

Hunter was inside with six or seven others, sitting in a rough circle around a battered cocktail table. A haggard waitress milled among them, picking up empty beer bottles and replacing them with freshly beaded cold ones. Someone let out a belch. The waitress went on without a blink, as though that was par for the course. Hunter folded his hand and tossed in his cards. He had nothing and Bert's intoxicated grin told him his friend was holding at least three of a kind. Bert frowned when Hunter folded. The other guys began tossing in their hands one by one. They'd played enough with Hunter to know that you couldn't go wrong if you followed his play. Bert's fifty-dollar bill went unanswered.

"Fuck," Bert muttered, showing his three aces and scooping up the thirty-five-dollar kitty along with his fifty.

Hunter smiled weakly. Normally he would have taken special delight in foiling his friend's hand. But tonight he was preoccupied and still pulling on his original beer, the label of which was now tattered and the bottle warm. He couldn't stop thinking about the FBI agent's words. Hunter had never heard a talk like that before. It had shaken everyone up, and no one more than him. The team was used to the dynamic duo of Cutchins and Peel, who droned on amid cat-calls and paper airplanes. Cook had been all business, and what he said was sobering.

Hunter couldn't forget his words about the dead guy and his girl-friend. Maybe Cook could help him with Rizzo. Maybe that's what Rizzo was after, information from Hunter about the team. Rizzo was obviously involved with gambling; otherwise he could never have known about all of Hunter's and Metz's betting. Hunter couldn't get the notion out of his mind. It would be good to have a guy like Cook on your side, Hunter could tell that. The only question remaining was whether or not Hunter was in too deep already. If the league caught wind of his bets last season, it might be the end of his career.

There was some shouting and a movement of most of the players toward the door. The locals, entrenched on their stools at the bar, lifted their heads and peered dull-eyed over their flannel-covered shoulders.

"Come on," someone from the card game said, and together they got up and went outside to see what the commotion was about.

Matt Brown and House, the Titans' enormous left offensive tack-le, had coaxed a rookie wide receiver up onto the railing that sepa-rated the bridge's pedestrian traffic from the river twenty feet below. The entire team was outside now, forming a crowd around the pre-cariously balanced rookie. Hunter heard splashing below and looked over the edge to see a rookie tight end floundering in the murky water, making his way slowly toward the bank.

"Hell of a rookie initiation, huh?" Bert said to Hunter over his shoulder.

Hunter looked up at his friend and shivered. The night had grown cool and a foul breeze was blowing down the canal.

"That's crazy," Hunter said. He started toward the middle of the pack with Bert in tow. The rookie was pleading with House to let him down and not make him do it. House shook his head slowly and grinned from behind his dull, half-lidded eyes.

"Come on, rook!" Matt Brown said impatiently. "All you rooks is going over the edge at the Ledge, so you might as well get on with it. We're all waiting."

"Wait!" Hunter said amid the heckling from all sides. "Wait,

House." House turned with an angry glare that softened when he realized whose voice it was, but his face remained resolute. The rookie would go off the bridge.

"No, wait," Hunter implored. "House, let him down, man. I'm telling you, I saw a guy go off a bridge like this once when I was growing up. He got hurt bad. His head hit the water wrong and twisted his neck. It paralyzed him, man. He's in a chair now. Let that guy down, House."

At the mention of paralysis, the entire team seemed to retract. Those closest to Hunter actually stepped back, the others grew quiet. The thought of a life without motion was the ultimate nightmare for a ball player. The word itself was like Kryptonite, mysteriously weakening the resolve of those who were exposed to it.

"Come on, House," Bert said quietly, "Hunter's right. Let him down, man."

Suddenly Murphy, the team's center, Hunter's connection to the offensive line and the only other guy that was almost as big as House, staggered up and bellowed, "You heard Hunter, you big, fat slob! If Hunter says down, then it's fucking down. Who took us to the big game?"

House considered the faccs of those around him. Matt Brown shrugged in consent, and House actually gave the rookie a hand down from his perch.

"Gonna cut your hair off though, man," House said matter-of-factly to the grinning rookie. "You ain't getting away without that."

"That goes without saying," Murphy slurred, and then let out an enormous belch.

The rest of the team nodded in agreement.

Hunter looked at his watch. It was ten-fifteen.

"Come on," he said to Bert quietly.

"Hey, Hunt, we still got another half hour before we got to head back," Bert replied as he muscled a path through the throng.

"I know. I've had enough, though," Hunter said. "I'm too old for this shit."

The two of them walked silently through the quiet streets of Brockport toward the campus.

After a few blocks Bert said, "That was a good thing you did, Hunt."

"Huh? Oh, yeah, it was no big deal," Hunter said.

"Yeah, it was no big deal, but it could have been," Bert said. "That's the difference between you and most guys in this game. You think ahead to what might happen. No one else was thinking maybe that rookie could have gotten hurt. Hell, a couple of them already went over the side before you got there. Those other guys wouldn't have thought about the consequences until it was too late. That's why you'll make it even after football, 'cause you think ahead."

Hunter shrugged and said nothing. As they climbed the steps to the dorm where they were staying, Hunter thought about what Bert had said. For the most part he did think ahead and he had made the right decisions in his life. This gambling thing was something he had never expected, though. Who could have thought it? Everyone put a little money down. It was no big deal. Now, faced with the situation he was in, he had to make another choice. His instincts told him that the right thing to do was to call Agent Cook, tell him everything and beg for clemency. Hunter took the card out of his pocket and examined it as the elevator climbed to the eighth floor. There was a number on it that was followed by the words "twenty-four hours a day." He could go straight to the pay phone in the lounge on his floor and have it all out in the open.

But there were so many reasons not to make the call that when he stepped off the elevator, he was still undecided. When he was undecided about something, he always relied on some old advice that a rich Pittsburgh booster had once given him when he was in college. The slick-looking man with longish gray hair and a custom-tailored suit had been one of the most liberal contributors to the football program. He had come from the German ghetto in Pittsburgh, and without so much as a high-school degree, he developed a company that produced almost every ATM machine in the United States. He was renowned for his business savvy, and he had told Hunter that his key to success had been to do nothing at all whenever he was undecided about something. That was what Hunter would do now, nothing. It would turn out to be the worst advice he could have ever followed.

CHAPTER 20

Tony Rizzo got out of his limousine and stepped onto the sidewalk along Fifth Avenue. The sun was visible just above the trees in Central Park even though the pale August sky was littered with high cumulus clouds that would soon block its rays. That was OK. The clouds repelled the late summer heat, and a breeze from the west seemed to freshen the air. It was a beautiful day in the city, one Tony Rizzo would normally be enjoying.

Now, though, he ducked around the corner at Seventy-third and waited. A dark blue Crown Vic roared around the corner and slowed conspicuously as it passed him. It did keep going, even as Tony turned and went back to Fifth and headed south, but he knew all the same that he was being followed. He sighed to himself as he walked. He was tired of it. He wanted them to go away.

At first, being followed everywhere by the feds had been a novelty, and a badge of his own success. Weeks later, it was starting to take its toll on him. Deals were harder to make. And deals he had already struck were proving hard to keep. Tony thought about the row of town homes in Great Neck that had burned just last night. That wouldn't have been necessary if he could have responded immediately to the developer's irate phone call.

The guy was a red-headed pain in the ass by the name of Grossman, an Irish Jew of all things, and he had gotten out of line. The deal Tony struck with him had been that he would pay fifty thousand cash and hire all union labor for the job. There had also been a provision for one of Tony's new people to be hired on as a consultant for thirty dollars an hour. The guy was some new blood that Angelo was bringing along.

Carl Lutz was the new guy, and he began showing up almost on a daily basis. When Grossman asked him why he was always hanging around, Carl replied that he was keeping an eye on things. Grossman then told Carl that he could watch from across the street but to keep his pimply face off the site except for Fridays when he collected his paycheck. Carl took exception to the description of his face and had ended up flattening Grossman's nose. Grossman called Rizzo's office immediately and insisted Carl be terminated. Of course, no one insisted on anything to Tony Rizzo, but since his phone was wired he could only let the irate Grossman vent his wrath before saying, "I'm sorry you feel that way, Mr. Grossman."

Tony had raced out of his office and around the block to a clean pay phone to call Grossman back and rip him a new ass, letting him know that he'd fucked with the wrong guy. Grossman, however, had already left his office. Emboldened by Tony's apparent passivity, Grossman canned the union electricians on the site and brought in a nonunion group from upstate by the next morning. The damage was done. So much of the family's power was derived from its image, and Tony had been slighted by Grossman. He was left with no choice but to have the entire project burned to the ground on principle.

It had cost him the entire fifty grand to bring in an expert from New Orleans who did work of that caliber, so Tony was netting zero on a job that should have shown a nice profit. His uncle would not be happy about it, and Tony was sure that he would give someone else the new work on the Island because of it. Although it was good for the family's business overall to make a statement that told people they expected others to honor their deals, it would be bad for him personally because the other builders would tell his uncle that they'd prefer to work with someone a little more even-tempered. Tony knew just who that would be, too, his cousin Vincent, Jr., fresh out of business school and already making moves on the more legitimate end of the family's businesses. Tony was so angry that he would have had Carl's hands broken if Angelo didn't like him so much. Angelo was usually right about people, and besides, he had to be indulged in some things.

As if the legitimate part of his operations weren't going bad enough, the other end of things were not much better. People on the street knew he was marked by the feds and they weren't anxious to be brought down when the law finally caught up with him. This infuriated Tony. The Feds would never get him. His uncle, who always got information from people in high places, had told him to be patient and that if he could keep himself out of trouble for a while it would all blow over. Tony couldn't help wondering, though, if in fact his uncle wasn't feeling the heat of a young buck in the herd. He wondered if his uncle wasn't just telling him to slow down to keep him down. Of course, Tony wondered a lot of things. He was always wondering, always thinking.

Tony would stop every so often and turn quickly. There was no sign of the Crown Vic and no one he could tell was following him on foot. He knew they were there all the same, though. It seemed they were always there now, and he'd seen the Crown Vic before. Tony reached his building. A gloved doorman in green-and-gold livery opened the door. Neither of them spoke. That was how Tony liked it, and the help around the building knew better than to try to make small talk with him. Tony would meet even the simplest greeting with an icy glare.

Mikey, Angelo, and Angelo's new sidekick, Carl Lutz, were waiting for him in the lobby. Carl wore a double-breasted suit made by Angelo's tailor and a pair of alligator shoes. He looked like a new man. When they saw Tony, all three men snapped to attention and followed him into the elevator. No one said anything until they were inside Tony's apartment with the door shut.

"This place clean?" Tony asked Mikey, and then told Carl to get them some beers from the fridge as he kicked up his feet on the coffee table.

Mikey nodded furiously.

"I had the guy come through here this afternoon at four-thirty and he said that the place was fine except for the phones. The only place we couldn't check was the bedroom."

Tony was loosening his tie. He stopped abruptly.

"And why the fuck didn't you have him check the bedroom?" Tony demanded.

Mikey shrugged nervously and said, "Well, Tony, she wouldn't let me . . ."

"What the fuck does that mean, 'she wouldn't let me'?" Tony said in a mocking, wimpish tone.

Mikey shrugged. His face flushed. "You know how she can be, Tony, she told me . . . she said if I did not go away she'd rip my balls off and . . ."

"And what?" Tony said, grinning at Angelo, delighted now with Mikey's embarrassment.

". . . and . . . and, she said she'd crush them . . . in her teeth."

Tony howled. So did Angelo. Carl came in with the beers and he began to laugh, although he didn't know at what. Mikey snatched his beer from Carl.

"You shut the fuck up," he said to the behemoth.

Carl hung his head and obeyed, sitting in a chair that was outside the immediate circle. This made Tony and Angelo laugh harder. Anyone walking in on them at that moment would have thought them four successful uptown businessmen sipping imported beer in their custom suits, alligator shoes, and Rolex watches. But one would only have to stay a moment, hear their language, and see the insidious shadows lurking in their eyes to suspect that something about these outwardly dapper men was amiss.

Tony looked at his watch. "Well, I did just plan to have a beer with you guys and go over a few things, but it looks like my woman is going to be late as usual getting ready, and I ain't going in there to get her," he said, nodding toward the bedroom, "not if she's talking about crushing people's balls. Mikey, why don't you call for some Chinese food. Get me some of that fucking General Tso's chicken."

Mikey took orders and phoned out for the Chinese food. Tony finished his beer, and while Carl went to the kitchen for more, he pulled out a deck of cards and began dealing a game of five-card draw. The food arrived and the talk diminished into grunts, most of which were directed at the card play. When everyone was finished, Carl cleaned things up and brought more beer and sat down.

After a few moments of silent play, Angelo, who was sitting next to his understudy in a club chair, fished into his jacket, pulled out his pistol and cocked the hammer. Carl felt the cold barrel pressed gently against his ear. He felt sick.

"So," Angelo said calmly, looking at Tony, "you want me to kill my young friend for fucking things up with that builder?"

Tony looked long and hard at Carl. Carl's lower lip began to tremble involuntarily. Beads of sweat broke out along his hairline. Angelo took a sip of beer with his free hand. Mikey couldn't contain his grin.

Finally Tony said, "Nahhh."

The three of them burst into laughter again. This time Carl did not follow suit. Angelo slapped him gruffly on the back.

"Come on," Angelo grunted amid his laughter, "we was only kidding your ass."

Carl smiled tentatively and excused himself to the bathroom, where he began vomiting loudly to the delight of his companions. By the time they had settled back down to their game Tony was wiping tears from his eyes. It was times like this that he really loved what he did for a living. The times he spent with his friends were what it was all about. He was convinced that his ascension to power within the family would make these moments only more frequent and more enjoyable. He could envision the four of them reliving this very night while the rest of the family watched on with envy, wishing that they too were in the inner circle. Power, Tony believed, enabled one to truly enjoy the finer things in life.

"So, Tony," Angelo said, taking two cards and turning the conversation to business, "what's the deal with Hunter Logan?"

This was one Tony had been giving a lot of thought to, so he was glad when Angelo brought it up.

"I got this guy pegged," Tony replied, setting down his cards and leaning forward. "But I'm letting him stew right now while the team is away at training camp. I don't want to get him riled up right now. I want him to get nice and comfy. Then, when the regular season comes rolling around and the money on the Titans is heavy, then I'm gonna give that fucker a call."

Everyone nodded with satisfaction at the notion of their boss having one of the country's hottest sports figures by the balls. They felt that they too shared in this power, and to a small extent they did.

"How much you figure we can make off this deal?" Cometti asked.

"I figure this," Tony said. "With the team doing as well as they did last year, we were seeing about eight million in action every Sunday by the end of the season. A lot of it was lay-off that we had to take from other places because so many of the people in this town wanted money on the Titans no matter what we did with the line. With Logan shaving some points for us, we can fudge the line, back off on the lay-off action from the opposing city, and let the books go unbalanced at about two million to six . . ."

Tony paused dramatically for effect and then said, "That's four million a hit we can clear without anyone being the wiser. If I handle him right, I figure I can work Logan about once a month. That's sixteen million over the course of the season, and twenty if we get a shot during the play-offs."

The foursome sat quietly, each of them reflecting on the wealth they would be generating, and each wondering how much of it they would actually see go into their own pockets. For Tony, the feat itself would be as important as the money. It would show the rest of the organization that he had the creativity and the power to lead the family when his uncle was gone. The idea of his uncle being gone made him consider the large frame of Carl. Already, after the incident in Great Neck, he was building a reputation for himself as a loose cannon. Angelo would never kill Tony's uncle, but Carl . . . it could be the perfect coup. Carl could kill his uncle, and then Tony could have somebody kill Carl to cover his tracks. Tony put this into the back of his mind.

He took a long pull on his beer, then saw Camille through the corner of his eye emerging from the bedroom with a vodka tonic in her hand. She was dressed for dinner in a stunning, electric-blue sequined dress. She sauntered up behind Tony and rested one hand casually on the back of his neck while sipping her drink. Tony exposed his gold watch dramatically and cleared his throat.

"Well," he began, "it's eight-thirty. Good of you to rise from the fucking dead. I got news for you. If you want dinner, you can have what's left over from our Chinese. I got fucking hungry waiting for you to decide it was time to get your ass out of bed, so I ate with these guys."

His cronies smirked nervously. Camille's smile turned bitter.

"I wasn't in bed," she said coldly. "I've been getting ready."

"Yeah, well, you missed the fucking boat tonight, sister," Tony said with a yawn and a wink at his friends, "'cause my ass was up for work this morning, unlike you, who slept all fucking day."

Camille removed her hand from Tony's neck and picked up the phone.

"Yes," she said, "I'd like you to call car service for me and have them send a car. . . How long, do you know? Fine."

Tony chuckled at his friends, who looked on with embarrassed interest. Each of them sensed an impending storm as surely as an old man with a crooked leg. Mikey began to shuffle the deck of cards. Carl picked furiously at the label on his bottle. Even Angelo began to look around the room at interesting objects he hadn't noticed before.

Tony picked up the phone himself.

"Darren, this is Tony Rizzo. Cancel that car, thank you."

Tony gently replaced the phone and looked up, smiling at Camille. She'd made him wait, now he was going to do the same to her. He'd take her out when he was damned good and ready, and maybe not at all. He chuckled to himself at the thought of keeping her in after she'd gone to all the trouble to dress and primp herself.

"I'm going," Camille threatened, "with you, or without you."

Tony got angry. He was used to Camille's smart-ass remarks. He knew by now that she'd piss him off on purpose just to get him to play rough with her when they got to the bedroom. But he didn't go for that shit now, not in front of his friends. He'd told her that. He'd warned her. She was out of line.

"You ain't fucking going anywhere. I said I'm tired. I'm gonna play some cards with my friends, and you're gonna go back in that bedroom and wait for me."

"You can't keep me here. I'm outta here . . ."

Camille began to move for the door. Tony was up quickly and grabbed her wrist. Camille flung her drink at him, glass and all. The heavy crystal thudded off Tony's temple and smashed on the granite coffee table, spraying vodka and ice and glass everywhere. Tony swung his free open hand and cuffed Camille in the ear, knocking her off balance while he held her wrist tightly.

"You fucking son of a bitch!" she shrieked, swiping furiously at him with her claws and kicking violently at the same time with her high-heeled pumps.

Tony stepped back and dabbed the blood from the crimson tracks that marked his cheek. Camille scrambled to regain her balance, hair and make-up now disheveled, one breast almost hanging out of her dress. She was beautiful in her rage. She started for the door, turned back once, then grabbed the knob. That was when Tony lunged forward and put her in a headlock from behind with his knee in the middle of her back and his chest pressing against the back of her head. Tony closed his eyes and endured her slashing while he counted to six. At six, Camille went limp in his arms and he let her drop to the floor.

"Fucking A," Carl said, unable to contain himself. "He fucking snuffed her."

"Nah," Mikey said, trying to continue his shuffling of the deck as though nothing out of the ordinary had happened, "trooper's choke hold. Cuts the oxygen to the brain and ba-bing! out like a light. But not snuffed."

"Angelo," Tony said, "help me get this bitch into the bedroom."

The two of them dumped Camille's limp body facedown on the bed.

"Thanks, Ang," Tony said, loosening his tie. "Get those guys the fuck outta here. I'm gonna play with this bitch for a while, work on her fucking manners."

Angelo nodded and left.

Tony went to his drawer and took out some cut lengths of old panty hose. He'd used them before with Camille, but never like this. Tony smiled wickedly to himself. She was always getting off on excitement. He'd give her some real excitement and teach her a lesson in etiquette at the same time.

When Camille came to, Tony was sitting beside the bed dressed only in a silk robe. He had a drink next to him on the nightstand, and he was spooning cocaine into his nose. Camille began to shriek with rage and fight against the bonds. She had been tied up before, but at her own urging, never like this. She began to curse and cry.

"I'll fucking kill you, Tony! You let me up, you son of a bitch! My father will fucking kill you! I'll tell him if you don't let me up. He'll have you squashed like a fucking bug!"

Tony began to laugh maniacally. "I call the shots with your fucking old man, you bitch!" he bellowed. "And I call the shots with you! I can end his world with a phone call. I can take his precious fucking team from him in a week!"

Tony stood and spooned another mound of powder into his nose.

Then he opened his robe so she could see him and see what was coming to her. Camille fought ferociously as Tony climbed on top of her.

CHAPTER 21

H unter lurched from his bed. The buzzing alarm had ripped him from a sound sleep. It was seven o'clock. Bert was still a lump under his covers. He had wax earplugs that cut out all the noise, even the alarm. Hunter crossed the tiny dorm room and shook his friend. Bert moaned.

"Come on," Hunter said, "get those damn things out of your ears, and let's get some chow."

"Whadya say?" Bert said, removing the yellow-stained globs of wax.

"Let's eat," Hunter said. "What would you do if I wasn't here to get you up?"

Bert smiled from behind his sleep-swollen face and said, "You're always there, Hunt, you know that. You're the guy everyone counts on."

"Yeah, that's what I'm afraid of sometimes."

"What's that mean?" Bert asked, standing and pulling on a pair of shorts and a T-shirt.

"Nothing. Can we go now?"

The two friends lurched and limped out of their room and made their way downstairs to the dining hall. They were both plagued with the aching muscles and joints of a long, hard training camp. Bert loaded his plate with eggs, bacon, and grits. Hunter had some cold cereal and fruit.

"Better eat something man," Bert said through a mouthful of eggs when he saw Hunter's tray.

"Nah, I'm trying to keep my weight down. Besides, I've got to start getting used to eating better so when I'm done with this game I won't balloon up like Metz or something."

"Metz was a fat slob to begin with, though, wasn't he?" Bert said casually.

Hunter shrugged. "Guess so."

Someone had left a newspaper at the end of the table, and Hunter fished through the stack for the sports section.

"Besides," Bert continued, "you're not leaving this game so fast anyway. You got a lot of years left in you, at least until the end of this big contract you've got. You're the life of this team, man. You're the world champion quarterback."

"Well," Hunter said, looking up from the paper and rubbing his aching shoulder, "right now I wonder if I can get through this season, let alone the end of my contract. The way I've been playing in pre-season's got me wondering if they'll even keep me around for the money they've got to pay me."

"You're crazy, Hunt," Bert said. "So you've had a few bad throws. You haven't even had a chance to get into a groove. They only play you in the first quarter of these pre-season deals. Everyone knows you're saving the good stuff for the regular season."

"I hope that's what it is," Hunter said, "me saving it. I'd like to think so anyway, even though if you'd have asked me, I would have told you I was giving it my damnedest. The truth is that all I want to do is get this camp over with and get home. In a way, I don't even give a shit about football right now."

"Yeah, well, everyone feels like that now," Bert said, "but camp is as good as over. After this week we go home. When the season gets going, you'll start to rock and roll."

"I can't wait," Hunter said almost wistfully. "I miss Rachel and Sara badly. It hurts, I miss them so much. It's enough for me to think about making this my last year."

"Ah, bullshit," Bert said through a mouthful of bacon.

Hunter shrugged and went back to his paper. Bert chewed and watched his friend. He saw Hunter's face drop. He read on for a while. Bert watched with interest.

"Holy shit," Hunter said quietly, tapping the paper with his fingertips. "Did you see this?"

"How could I see it? You're the one reading it."

Hunter said nothing, but Bert could see the distress on his face as he continued to read.

"What?" Bert said. "What's in it?"

Hunter had a blank look on his face.

"This guy in San Diego. A lineman named Chadwick . . ."

"The All-Pro end?" Bert said.

"Yeah, he's gonna get banned from the league for life."

"Life?" Bert screwed up his face as though this was something too horrible to be true.

"That's what it says. It says he was doing those off-season junkets to Vegas and I guess getting put up and taken care of all the time. Says he got in with the wrong crowd, made a lot of money, but then lost it all. Then he started giving these guys from Vegas information on his team, you know, injury reports, player morale, stuff like that, to help them with one of those nationwide gambling services that people call for good bets. It says he did it to help pay off his debts, which were—" Hunter looked back down at the paper—"four hundred and seventy thousand . . ."

Bert whistled. "Can you imagine gambling away that kind of cash?"

"No," Hunter said.

"Well," Bert said, "I'd have hated to be in Chadwick's shoes."

"It says he did it for them all last season. They caught him when the FBI busted some big shot in Denver for tax evasion. It says the guy blew in this whole gambling thing. One thing led to another and they pulled Chadwick right off the practice field. The league says if it's substantiated, he'll be barred for life."

"Let me see that," Bert said, grabbing the paper from across the table.

Bert scanned the page, murmuring, then he read, "the commissioner said, 'The league will not tolerate any member that calls into question the integrity of even a single game.' He went on to say that 'even the appearance of impropriety on behalf of a player will result in expulsion, and each player is warned of the seriousness of such conduct every year as part of a mandatory meeting during preseason camp . . .' Holy shit! Can you imagine that! It's just like that guy was saying the other day. Remember that guy, Hunt? Hunt?"

"Huh? Oh, yeah, I remember," Hunter said, his mind a million miles away. It was as though he had almost been in a deadly car wreck but avoided it in a last-minute swerve that was caused by some stroke of luck totally unrelated to him. It was just luck. Hunter had been so close to making that call to the FBI and certainly ending his career. If he kept his mouth shut and something like what happened to Chadwick happened to him a year after the fact, he'd already be at least three or four million dollars richer. Things wouldn't look so bad with that kind of cash in the bank. The thought of ending his career—something he had referred to casually just moments before—now gave him a chill. He could actually see that Pittsburgh alumnus and hear his words. "When in doubt, do nothing." When this was all over, Hunter would have to look the guy up and tell him how valuable his advice had been.

Cook listened intently. He was sitting at a conference table in his office with Duffy and Marrow. Marrow was giving him the latest progress on the team's pursuit of Rizzo.

"So," Cook said when Marrow was finished, "besides a possible tax fraud, which you seem to think is nothing more than an accounting oversight, we've got nothing on Rizzo? I can't believe it, John."

Marrow shrugged and looked to Duffy for help.

"Sir . . ." Duffy began, addressing his friend formally since they were in the office and Marrow was there, "I know you don't want to hear this, but I think maybe we should drop Tony Rizzo and shift our focus to Mondolffi himself, maybe even Angelo Quatrini. He's the dirtiest guy in that whole family."

Marrow nodded in agreement and said, "We could put our surveillance on Quatrini and probably come up with any number of felonies within a week. Then we could put the squeeze on him and maybe get to Rizzo or the old man."

Cook met these suggestions with a neutral expression. He seemed to consider his men's words. Finally he spoke.

"Angelo Quatrini is from the old school, he'd never talk. We'll continue to keep Rizzo under surveillance. He's got fresh blood on his hands from Tommy Keel, and he's up to something with this Carter girl. He'll slip up. We just have to make sure we're there when he does."

Cook stood up, signaling an end to the meeting. Marrow shrugged and began to stuff papers back into a folder that lay in front of him.

"Duffy," Cook said, catching him just as he walked out, "come back. Shut the door."

Duffy did and sat back down at the table.

"Why?" Cook asked.

"Because I want to see you succeed," Duffy said.

"Why did you say that in front of John?"

"Because every time I bring it up when we're alone, you just brush it aside. I want it on record. I want you to drop Rizzo.

"I know about the calls you've been getting from D.C.," Duffy said. "I know the pressure's on."

"How's that?" Cook asked, looking intently at Duffy. "How do you know?"

"I don't know what's been said, but I've seen the calls coming in. I see all that kind of stuff."

"I didn't know part of your electronic surveillance included this office," Cook said sternly.

Duffy raised his eyebrows and said, "It was you yourself who said someone in this office was dirty. I'm just keeping an eye out."

"I'm sorry," Cook said. "I didn't mean to sound as harsh as I did."

"I know how this stuff works," Duffy said. "This operation is unprecedented. They want results yesterday. The Bureau doesn't like to do things differently as it is. Ellis, I think you're being emotional about Rizzo. There are other ways to assail this organization. Rizzo is like a cause with you. It's obvious that the reason you're on to him is more than him being our best shot at the Mondolffis. He's not our best shot. We know that now. We're coming up dry with him. You need to come up with a new strategy. That's why I said it."

Cook thought about what Duffy said. It was true he wanted Rizzo. It was true he was emotional about it, yes. But he did genuinely feel that it was because Rizzo would slip up. He was too arrogant, too violent and volatile. Cook knew if he just hung with Rizzo, it would pay off. On the other hand, he had sat here in this office that had been specially constructed for him and his team, expending Bureau resources at an enormous rate for more than three months now, and had nothing to show for it other than a possible fine for an incorrect tax return. It was a joke to call it fraud; it was simply a mistake. Cook wondered if he, too, wasn't making a mistake. Duffy was right about the pressure, it was there. People high up wanted progress.

"All right," Cook said, "we'll pull back on Rizzo. But I still want the taps going. I want you to stay on top of him as much as you can, Duffy. I'm going to go ahead myself and see what I can come up with. I'm going to have Fellows set up that meeting with Grant Carter and follow up what I can on that end of things. I'll take the rest of the men and let John do what he thinks best. Let me see the new surveillance plan before you do it, though.

"You're right," Cook said, shaking his head and casting his eyes down to the floor, "my judgment has been clouded."

Then he looked up. "I have to make this work, Duffy," he said almost desperately. "I have to."

Duffy stood and put his hand on his friend's shoulder, giving it a squeeze. "You will, Ellis," he said. "Something will happen."

After the Titans' final pre-season game, the seemingly relentless "Iceman" finally gave his team a reprieve. The game had been on Friday night against Denver in New York, and afterward the Iceman told his players they were free until the following Tuesday. Elation was an understatement. Hunter went straight home after the game, and only Rachel's insistence on not waking Sara could dissuade him from jumping in the car and heading straight for the Hamptons. Hunter tossed and turned until about three and then woke at seven with his wife and daughter, anxious to get on the road.

"We'll stop at the deli and eat in the car," he told his wife as he pulled on a pair of jeans.

After a restful day on the beach, they decided to go out for dinner. Hunter insisted on going out alone with Rachel on a date, as he called it, but he was equally adamant that he be the one to put Sara to bed. That wasn't until eight-thirty, so after he'd read to her and tucked her in, they turned the house over to Rachel's mom and dad, who were more than happy to keep an eye on things and give the young couple some time to themselves.

The Rococo was built on piers that overlooked one of the inland waterways of Quogue. It was an exclusive place, so much so that Hunter could look like himself without concern for interference from some sunburned fat guy in flowery shorts who wanted to congratulate Hunter on a fine season last year, would pull up a chair as he did so, and then mull over this year's possibilities. Dinner would cost them at least four hundred dollars. The tables were set apart in different bay windows overlooking the water. The service was impeccable, if a little snobby. A string quartet played Vivaldi and Pachelbel. The people who went there were Hampton old money who would never stare at a professional athlete, let alone ask for an autograph. Anyone having dinner at the Rococo usually considered themselves too important to get excited about anyone but themselves. It was the perfect place for Hunter and Rachel to have a romantic evening alone.

After a full meal and two bottles of wine, Rachel drove them back to their beach house. Her parents were asleep on the couch and awoke as Rachel and Hunter walked in. They shuffled out the door, rubbing sleep from their eyes. Rachel checked Sara while Hunter stripped himself and flopped naked and drunk onto the bed.

"I'm gonna be sorry tomorrow," he said when Rachel appeared and then stepped into the bathroom.

"Sometimes I like you like this," she said, her voice echoing off the walls of the tiled room and into the bedroom. "I can take advantage of you."

Hunter laughed in a lewd way. "I like the sound of that," he said. "Hey, Rach, while you're in there, get me one of my pills from my shaving kit, will you?"

Hunter was feeling too good about the night and the freedom from the team to even realize that he'd just blown it.

"What?" Rachel said in an angry voice. She appeared in the doorway holding up a bottle of pills she had pulled from his kit. "You said you weren't going to let them give you this!"

"All right, Rach," he mumbled, "take it easy, will ya? We're having a good time. This is our night. Take your damn clothes off and come here. We'll talk about that in the morning."

"No," she said. "We'll talk about this now."

Rachel stamped her foot on the floor and Hunter rolled over with a moan and pulled a pillow over his head. Butazolidin was a powerful anti-inflammatory drug that was known for its possible dangerous side effects. It was also the best thing Hunter had ever taken to help alleviate the pain and swelling in a damaged joint.

"We talked about this, Hunter. We agreed that you wouldn't use Butazolidin."

"OK," he said, throwing his legs over the edge of the bed and sitting there in a slumped position. "OK. You saw how bad things were going in those first couple of pre-season games," he said, looking up into her eyes and then back down. "This thing was killing me . . ."

Hunter reached up instinctively and began rubbing his shoulder.

"It hasn't looked like it's been bothering you," Rachel said.

"It isn't," he said, "not much anyway, so long as I take the pills."

"Hunter, I can't believe it," she said, shaking her head and sitting down next to him.

"They've been testing my blood every week," he said. "Everything looks pretty good so far."

She looked at him with disbelief. "Every week? How long have you been taking it?"

"After the second game in Chicago," he said. "I had to, Rach."

"You didn't have to, Hunter," she said. "You don't. We talked about this. We're going to be around together a long time after you're through with this game. At least I hope we are, but not if you take stuff like this. You know that it kills off blood cells. How do you think that could be good for you? They don't even give it to average people anymore. Don't you think there's a reason? Hunter? Talk to me."

He shrugged. "I got to be ready to play, Rach. You know that."

"Why is it that you have to be ready? If your body won't let you, then you don't play, Hunter. Other guys don't."

He looked up at her. "Not many," he said quietly.

"It's the incentive money, isn't it?" she said flatly.

"No."

"It is, Hunter, I can see it in your face. No wonder you've been acting so strange all through camp. Every time I've talked to you, you've sounded . . . I don't know, but I knew something was wrong. I can't believe you'd let them put this crap inside your body. I can't believe it."

"It's not just the money," he said, looking up at her. "The money's part of it, but it's not just that. You don't understand, honey, it's what players do. When you get hurt, you do what you have to to play. Especially when you get paid the way I do."

"The way you do? They haven't paid you well for the past twelve years in this league. Now you take them to a Super Bowl and they pay you. You deserve every cent of it and more. I see what this has done to your body. I see you wince when you get up in the middle of the night. You can't even tie your shoes without groaning. You've earned this money, Hunter. You don't have to prove anything."

They sat quietly for a long while. The window was open and Hunter gazed out at the night sky, feeling the ocean air on his face.

Quietly he said, "Give me the pills, Rach."

She still held the bottle, clutched tightly in her hand as if keeping them away from him would save his life.

"I'm not in the fucking mood," he said in a low guttural tone.

She heard the angry influence of his drinking and threw the bottle down next to him on the bed. She went to the other side and got under the covers, turning her back to him and closing her eyes. Hunter reached down and extracted a little blue pill, so small but so effective. He popped it into his mouth and swallowed, then fell back onto the bed with his head on the pillows. Within minutes he was breathing heavily. Rachel, however, stayed awake. She brushed away the moisture that was brimming in her eyes and turned over to cover him with the comforter. She kissed his lips and held him tight. He never knew.

"If you've dropped the tail on Tony Rizzo," Fellows said blandly, "why is it that you've insisted I set up this meeting?"

Cook knew Fellows was more than a little annoyed with his insistence on the meeting, mostly because Cook had forced the issue by bringing it up in the Saturday supervisors' meeting, which really gave Fellows no choice but to agree.

"I just think that it might pay off to have Grant Carter aware of exactly who Tony Rizzo is and to keep his eyes open to any contact he might try to make with any of his players—or anyone in the entire organization, for that matter," Cook said.

Fellows answered this with a knowing frown.

Cook was driving them in one of his task force sedans out to the Island to meet Grant Carter at the Titans' complex. It was Monday and the team was off until Wednesday, when they would begin their regular in-season routine and preparation for the opening game against the Detroit Lions. Fellows had arranged the meeting, and he wasn't telling Cook much about how the owner had received the idea.

All Cook knew was that they were going and Fellows was still holding firm on his being present to make sure that Cook stayed in line. The distaste the two men had for each other grew between them like a fungus, thick and insidious. Cook knew Fellows was delighted at his lack of progress, and in a way Cook almost wished for Washington to pull the plug on him and his task force and end the little game that was being played out between him and Fellows. As a superior the man had become so distasteful to Cook that he had begun to think he preferred failure to continuing under this malignant supervision.

The Titans' complex was singularly unimpressive. It was a single-story concrete structure that reminded Cook more of an elementary school than the home of a world champion football team. Carter's office, however, was no disappointment. It reeked of excessive opulence. Green marble covered the floor and walls. Brass-trimmed mirrors backed shelves that were laden with plaques, trophies, and photographs that chronicled Grant Carter's life in the world of sports. The furniture was all dark brown leather, overstuffed and comfortable-looking. The man's desk was a solid block of black granite, the rough-cut sides juxtaposed dramatically with the smooth, glossy surface where Grant Carter had laid his hands with their fingers intertwined to suggest one powerful appendage.

"Sit down," Carter said, making no move to rise or shake hands with the FBI agents.

There were two chairs facing Carter's desk, and Cook and Fellows did as they were told.

"How can I help you?" Carter said with the same lack of hospitality as his first words.

Fellows, normally the first person in a room to assume a tone of condescension, surprised Cook by the humility of his response. "I hope we aren't disturbing you, Mr. Carter. I am the assistant special agent in charge from the Manhattan office of the FBI. Agent Cook here is a supervisor for a specially designated task force on organized crime. We are here only to give you information. We have no interest in inconveniencing you in any way."

Cook figured Carter must own politicians on the highest levels to be able to affect Fellows in this way.

"In the case at hand, as I said, we are here merely as a service,"

Fellows said, nodding to Cook as a cue for him to begin his pitch.

"Mr. Carter, we have been following a man by the name of Tony Rizzo." Cook paused to look for a reaction on Carter's face. There was none, so he continued. "Tony is a member of the Mondolffi crime family, a very prominent member."

Still Carter remained as blank and as still as the desk at which he sat.

"Well, we know that he has been seeing your daughter, and we also know that he's been to your house."

"Just a minute," Carter said, holding up one hand and picking up his phone with the other. "Susan, get me Marty Higgs . . . Now!"

Carter knew full well who Rizzo was. He'd learned that days ago. He also knew that his empire was hanging from a very precarious thread. To save himself and all he'd worked for he needed only time. Tony Rizzo was giving him that time. Carter was not about to let the FBI come into the middle of it all and start making wild conjectures. To him, the FBI was simply another government entity to be dealt with accordingly. As in every other appendage of the government, the men could be bought and sold. He knew how to handle men such as these. He would attack.

"Hello, Marty, I want you in my office . . . yes, now, I have two agents from the FBI who have violated my privacy, and I want you here so that you can know just how we can best end their careers within a month."

Carter hung up the phone and looked impassively at Cook, who was beginning to sweat. Cook hadn't dreamed of something like this. When Fellows had warned him of flustering the owner, he never dreamed that such careful phrasing of the situation could prove to be upsetting. Cook had the sinking feeling he'd made a mistake. He felt like a man dumped over the side of an ocean liner. His help had already begun steaming away at full speed, leaving him alone in unknown waters.

"Mr. Carter," he began, holding up his open hands in a gesture of peace and submission, "you don't understand, sir. We're not here to give you a problem of any kind. We're here simply to inform you of who Tony Rizzo is and to ask you to call us if in any way you feel he is disruptive or potentially disruptive to your organization."

Cook looked to Fellows for help, but only received an I-told-you-so expression. Just then a middle-aged, portly man with ruddy skin and freckles about his wide-eyed face came steaming into the room. Cook assumed it was Marty Higgs. Carter motioned for Higgs to sit down in a chair behind the agents, where they could only hear his huffing and puffing. "As I was saying, Mr. Carter," Cook continued, "I merely hoped that I might be of service to you in fending off any difficult situations that might arise from Tony's presence around your team."

"Is Tony Rizzo a convicted criminal?" Carter asked coldly.

Cook looked at Fellows again for help. His boss was busy trying extricate a hangnail with his teeth and didn't appear to be paying the slightest bit of attention. Cook thought about the question. He looked over his shoulder at Higgs, who now had out a yellow legal pad and pen and was waiting patiently for his response.

"No," Cook finally said, "but . . ."

"Has my daughter committed any crime?" Carter said.

"No," Cook immediately replied.

"Well, then," Carter said, "I see no reason to continue this discussion any further. I won't have the FBI making accusations against me or anyone I may have associated with when there is no basis for them."

Fellows stood and opened his hands, palms up, to signal the FBI's capitulation. "Mr. Carter," he said, "we in no way meant to disturb you or make any accusations of any kind. We have no desire to trouble you. That's not why we're here. But as you know, organized crime is constantly trying to make inroads into the world of professional sports. We know that you and your daughter are completely innocent of any wrongdoing, but we do think it is our duty to let you know just exactly who Tony Rizzo is. Now, that said, Agent Cook will simply leave a card with Mr. Higgs here, and we will be on our way."

"Please call me if there is anything I can do at all," Cook added before trailing his boss through the door.

"Well, Cook," Fellows said when they were in the car and on their way back to the city, "I hope you can see what I meant when I told you that men like Grant Carter aren't to be trifled with."

Cook wanted to say that if Fellows had gotten a little heavy with Carter in the first place, he might not have walked all over them, but instead he merely nodded.

"That man gave the president ten thousand dollars in his last campaign," Fellows said. "That is a man that neither you nor I should trifle with in any way."

Cook bristled at this notion. He believed what they had taught him at the academy: No man was above the law. That's how Cook saw things, but he wondered how it could be true if a man in Fellows's position was so willing to concede otherwise.

Vincent Mondolffi received another phone call soon after the word spread among Cook's task force that the surveillance on Tony Rizzo would be dropped. Mondolffi was also told that in all likelihood, resources formerly expended on his nephew would be redirected on himself and other members of his organization. This was nothing but good news to Mondolffi. Tony was the weakest link in his family. As soon as he got off the phone, Mondolffi told Ears to find Tony and bring him to the restaurant that Mondolffi used as his headquarters.

When Ears found him, Tony was supervising the beating of a nightclub owner named Burke who had falsified his receipts for the past three months and thereby cheated the Mondolffi family out of its share of the profits. Tony leaned back in a comfortable leather chair that he swiveled about on its rollers. He was animated and cheerful when Ears came through the door into the back room of the establishment.

"Watch this," he told Ears with a grin.

Carl and Angelo were having a contest. Their jackets were laid neatly over a chair and their sleeves were rolled up to their elbows. The object was to see who could knock Burke farther across the room with a single punch. Blood streamed down Burke's face, which without connection to the body would certainly have failed to be identified as human. Except for the blood, snot, and torn flesh, Burke's head looked more like a Halloween pumpkin than anything else. He was tied to a chair, and numerous chalk marks told the tale of just how far he and the chair had been propelled by the previous blows from Tony's friends. Carl glanced up, then slugged Burke, connecting solidly with his chin and actually lifting the chair off the floor, beating the previous best mark by ten inches.

"Fuck!" Angelo exclaimed. "That's gotta be it. I can't believe you got him that far."

"Tony," Ears said, obviously unimpressed, "your uncle wants to see you. Now."

Ears's words cast a pall on the festive group. To be summoned unexpectedly by Vincent Mondolffi was somber news. Unless something extremely good had transpired that would justify special recognition from his uncle, Tony knew such a summons was usually a bad sign.

When Tony saw the smile on his uncle's face, he knew his star was rising. When his uncle rose from his plate of cheese and melon to kiss his cheek, he knew he was unstoppable. And finally, when his uncle loudly praised him in front of Ears, Dominic, and several other underlings for defeating the careful efforts of the much lauded Federal Bureau of Investigation and its special task force, Tony knew that his uncle's death and his own ascension to power would not be a long time in coming. He had weathered the storm. The powers against him had waged a campaign of stealth and deception. He could finally relax a little. They had dogged his every move, uncovered every legal and financial document that bore his name. They had come up with nothing. Tony would be perceived throughout the organization as a careful, cunning, and indestructible power. When he made his play for power, this image would be every bit as valuable as the millions of dollars he would make on the New York Titans.

CHAPTER 23

The pressure on the Titans was high. After being the world champions the year before, there was only one thing they could do to have their season considered a success. They had to win it all again. Anything less would be a disappointment. Hunter Logan was feeling this pressure as much as anyone. In the team's two pre-season losses Hunter had performed poorly, leaving the game after the first quarter without so much as a single touchdown. Even in the two games that the Titans had won, Hunter's performance had been less than exciting. In one, he led the offense to a single touchdown, and in the other, by only ten points in the entire three quarters. Without great defense, everyone knew, that game, too, would have been lost. To make matters worse, Broadway Blake, Hunter's backup, was looking like a superstar. Even Hunter had to admit that his younger understudy was playing great ball.

Now it was for keeps. The Titans faced Detroit on opening Sunday afternoon on national TV. The word around town and around the country was that Hunter Logan was a one-trick pony. He'd had a single season where he'd played above himself. What had happened in the previous year, wrote the sports writers, was dumb luck, something that was unlikely to happen again in a million years. It was obvious to everyone that the Hunter Logan who had led the Titans through training camp was not the same Hunter Logan who had taken them to Miami only five months before.

Some said Hunter was simply too old. There was talk of his bad shoulder needing surgery if he was to be revived. Others said the money had gone to his head. Still others said he'd never been that good to begin with and that he'd only cashed in on the incredible talent that had surrounded him. There were a few, however, and Hunter was among them, that knew he had merely been in a funk, one that he would pull out of now that the games were for real.

The interviews had been relentless. Across the country, football fans of all ages had their eyes on New York to see what fate held for the man who held the mantle of success. It sickened Hunter to know that there were many who wanted him to fail. He knew they were out there. He could hear it in their voices. They were the reporters who were frustrated athletes themselves and who deep down resented the hero status that was afforded to any athlete. They asked him questions like "Do you feel like you've let down your team with your performance so far this season?"

Those were ugly words and they made Hunter seethe with anger. But he held himself in check, knowing full well that if he led his team to victory against Detroit, the tide would turn in his favor and the same ones who had injured him with their insults would be lauding his greatness on Monday morning.

It was six-thirty Wednesday evening when Hunter was finally ready to leave the Titans' complex. After practice he'd done three TV interviews, talked to five writers, and given soundbites to four radio reporters. After all that, he'd spent another hour watching Detroit film until he could stand it no longer.

His stomach growled. He flicked off the projector and left the dark meeting room. The locker room smelled of stale sweat and wet towels. It didn't bother Hunter. He put on his jeans jacket and stopped at the phones on his way out to call Rachel.

"Where have you been?" she asked. "Bert was home two hours ago."

"Bert," Hunter huffed, knowing Rachel had gotten the information from Bert's wife, "is a defensive lineman. No one wants to interview defensive linemen, and they don't have to study game film. All they have to do to get ready for a game is eat raw meat and grunt. Yours truly, on the other hand, is the prima ballerina of the gridiron . . . a quarterback. I have to—"

"—I know," Rachel interrupted, "use my mind, my body, and my soul."

"Did you play QB in high school?"

"When are you coming home?" Rachel said in a flat tone.

"On my way," he replied. "Just checking in."

"Well, I don't like you so late, but I'm glad to hear you getting back to normal," she said.

"Have I been abnormal?" Hunter said in mock surprise. "Me? I can't figure out why. I have no pressure on me or anything. Hmmm . . ."

"I hear you. Come home."

"See you in a few."

"Oh, Hunter."

"Yeah?"

"Stop at the Food King and get decaffeinated coffee, will you?"

"Got it. Love you."

"Love you, too."

Hunter hung up and pulled his jacket up over his head. He ran through the lot to his car. A steady, heavy rain fell from the dark gray sky. The air was cool for September. It felt more like November. Hunter made his way through the late rush-hour labyrinth of headlights, taillights, and dented bumpers. Even the air was wet and Hunter had to turn on the defrost. People hurried in and out of the Food King to and from their cars. There were no spaces close to the entrance and Hunter toyed with the idea of bagging the whole thing and getting home. Maybe he'd make a fire tonight. Sara would like that. He'd make popcorn, too. Coffee was a must.

He parked on the outskirts of the lot and stepped close to his car to avoid being hit by a van that had pulled in next to him. The passenger door of the van opened before it stopped, and a large man in a long black raincoat jumped out in front of him. The side door swung open and another large man, dressed the same, only younger and more stupid-looking, got out to block his retreat. Hunter's mind raced with the possible mistakes that were being made. It wasn't an instant before he knew that this had to do with Tony Rizzo.

"Get in," Angelo Quatrini growled with a malevolent smile.

"Why?" Hunter heard himself saying.

"Get in. Tony wants to talk to you," Angelo said.

Carl took Hunter's arm in a firm grip and helped him into the back of the van. Hunter would later think of all the things he could have done but didn't. Instead, he was like a barely animated puppet. Carl got in next to him and sat with his hands in his pockets. Angelo got in, too. At first Hunter thought it was Rizzo driving the van, but Angelo called him Mikey, so Hunter knew it wasn't. They rode in silence. Hunter thought of trying to escape, hitting the man next to him in the head and jumping out of the side door, like in the movies. But his limbs felt heavy, fear oppressed him.

In five minutes they pulled down a broken road amid the wetlands that separated the Five Towns from Rockaway. A limousine sat like an angry monster in the rain; its red-eyed taillights shone through the puffing smoke from its exhaust. The van pulled up behind the long black car. Angelo got out and opened the side door. Carl got out and they stood waiting for him.

"Come on," Angelo said.

Hunter got out into the downpour. It was almost completely dark now. Across a field of cattails, Hunter could hear wet tires hissing on the pavement of Atlantic Avenue. The two men walked on either side of him as they approached the limousine. Hunter's whole torso was constricted with fear. His mind drifted as if he were breathing nitrous oxide. The three of them stopped outside the rear window of the car. It opened about six inches.

"Come here" came the muffled voice from within the car.

Hunter tried to peer into the gloom. He could see nothing. The window opened a little more, and he moved his head closer and closer until his wet head was out of the rain. Tony Rizzo sat in the dark staring straight ahead. His hands were placed carefully on his knees. Under his dark raincoat he wore a dapper suit and tie with a white shirt. He looked like a Wall Street executive.

The two men beside Hunter each grabbed one of his arms and held him where he was. Tony calmly pushed his finger forward, raising the window until it jammed itself up under Hunter's chin. Hunter's instincts took over and he struggled in vain to extricate himself, kicking viciously at the men that held him and cursing Rizzo.

"You fucking son of a bitch!" he bellowed.

The two men outside tightened their vice grips on his shoulders and jammed their fingers painfully into his armpits. The pain was so great that Hunter could struggle for only a few more moments before his body went limp.

"That," Rizzo said, "is what you don't do. You don't fight me. You do as I say, when I say." He turned on the light and stared wickedly at Hunter. "You got that?" Tony asked in his thickest Brooklyn accent.

"I said, 'You got that!'" Tony screamed.

"Yes," Hunter managed to squeak out. The feeling of confusion was back, confusion swimming in fear and shame. His armpits and his throat hurt. The rain had completely soaked through his clothes. This wasn't supposed to happen to someone like him.

"Good. Now I ain't gonna say this twice to you"— Tony reached up and placed his palm against Hunter's cheek—"so you listen carefully. You play Detroit this weekend and you're favored by eight. Here's what you do. You can win the game. I wouldn't ask you to lose, that would be criminal." Tony chuckled through the nose at his own humor.

"I can't," Hunter heard himself say.

Tony's eyes flashed with an insane light. He pulled a pistol from his jacket and pushed the barrel against Hunter's upper lip. He could feel the metal against his teeth. Hunter's eyes spun with fear.

"You're past can and can't, big shot!" Rizzo bellowed. "I'm not fucking around. This is the real shit. You got nothing to worry about. You ain't even gonna let anybody down. You just make fucking sure as your life that you don't win by more than a touchdown. You fuck this up and you won't see us coming next time. You got that?"

"Yes," Hunter said.

The window opened and Rizzo pushed his face back out with the barrel of the gun. The window hummed shut again, and the limousine rolled away slowly in the darkness. The two men beside him were already halfway to the van. Hunter just stood in the road until the van lurched toward him as though it might run him down. He jumped to the shoulder of the road and slipped in the ditch. In a moment of thoughtless anger he grabbed a rock and rifled it at the van as hard as he could.

The rock clumped loudly off the back door. For an instant Hunter was afraid at what he'd done, but the van never even slowed. He was sure he'd seen the faces in the van howling with delight as he sprang from their path. Hunter pulled himself up and sat cross-legged on the shoulder of the road. Rain and night were all around him. He put his face in his hands.

"My God, Jesus." he growled in anger and frustration. The helplessness in his voice made him choke and almost vomit, and he clenched his fists, uttering guttural noises like a cornered animal.

He let a cold resolve fill the void of fear and agony. However much he didn't deserve this, it was his. It wasn't going away. He'd deal with it and be done. His mind made up, he rose and walked briskly back into Cedarhurst. He found a cab and got in.

"Damn," the driver said, "got a little wet?"

"Take me to the Food King," Hunter said.

Hunter kept a sweatsuit in his trunk. He put it on in the car and even went into the store for the coffee. His story was simple. He went over it in his mind again as he drove through the harbor. He'd gotten to his car when he realized he'd forgotten his bag. The doors were locked and everyone had gone. He'd walked back to the car and realized he'd locked the keys in it. He had only one quarter and used it to call a locksmith from a pay phone down the street. Hunter waited at the car so he wouldn't miss the guy. By the time the guy got there, Hunter was soaking wet. It was a good story and it would work. It was no longer a matter of Rachel being mad at him for gambling with Metz on football games. He didn't want Rachel to know the shame he'd endured. More than that, he never wanted her involved. He would just take care of it and make it go away. It was a nightmare, and he wanted to keep it his nightmare.

By the next morning the gray sky had spent its moisture. Dirty puddles at every street corner rippled in the warm breeze. Tony Rizzo steered his Benz around the corner of a burned-out Brooklyn factory and drove until the street ended at the edge of the East River. Even though it was a side street, it was lined with cars, so Tony parked in front of a hydrant and let himself in through a gate in the dirty chain-link fence that surrounded what looked like an old warehouse for an adjoining factory. The warm breeze off the water was fetid with the rotten smell of river fish. Wet garbage of various colors stuck to the ground like mold on month-old Wonderbread.

Tony pranced through the garbage and hopped over puddles

until he reached the concrete steps that led to the loading dock, where years of loading and unloading toxic chemicals from out-of-state tractor trailers had left cracks and stains in the concrete. With his knuckles, Tony rapped a code on a steel door whose blue coat of paint bled rust from multiple wounds. There was no sign of a handle. It looked like the kind of door that was never meant to be opened. Tony repeated the code, and the door did open, just a crack. The pockmarked face of a greasy-haired man in his forties stuck out and murmured, "What?"

Tony's expression was malignant until the man realized who the knocker was.

"Tony," the man said deferentially, pushing the door wide open and stepping aside so the man could enter with ease.

"Where's your gun, Pete?" Tony said coldly to the man.

Pete shrugged apologetically and said, "In my car. Aaron doesn't like guns. He made me leave it. He says it makes everyone nervous. He told me to push that button there if there's ever any trouble, and he'll take care of things better than any gun could. You told me to do what he says, Tony, otherwise I'da told him to kiss my ass."

Tony tightened his lips. He left Pete standing in the doorway and made his way through an inner door into the open warehouse. Two rows of desks facing one another went almost from one end of the warehouse to the other. At every desk sat a man or woman who wore a headset like an AT&T operator and punched away at a computer keyboard in front of them. At the opposite end of the warehouse was a glass cubicle that contained a single desk and chair. On the desk sat two phones and a laptop computer. In the chair sat a skinny young man in a wild shirt. His curly black hair was receding quickly up his skull. The shirt, the wild, half-bald head of hair, and a thick pair of round spectacles gave Aaron Weiss the look of a mad clown. His eyes were narrowed at a Rubik's cube, which he spun wildly in his hands. By the time Tony reached the glass cage, the puzzle was solved. Aaron looked up with a goofy smile and pushed his glasses back up to the bridge of his nose and hopped to his feet.

"Tony," the clown said with an uncertain giggle, "what brings you here?"

"I wanted to see how things are going," Tony said, sitting on a corner of Aaron's desk.

Aaron pulled down the corners of his mouth and said, "Fine, fine. How's it going with you?"

"Good. I just want to go over these numbers again," Tony said. "I don't want any fuck-ups. Sit down."

Aaron sat down.

"Tell me again how this shit works."

"Well," Aaron began, "by integrating our variables by computer, we can actually predict the resultant ratio given the existing odds at any—"

"Not that shit," Tony said, waving his hand impatiently. "Tell me how you make sure we take more money on the Titans than the Lions. I don't want any fuck-ups on this."

Aaron seemed to consider the tip of his nose. He took a deep breath, considered how best to communicate the complex system that he'd devised to a guy who hadn't finished high school, and started again.

"All we want to do is achieve a ratio of approximately three to two. We take three dollars on the Titans for every two on Detroit. Since we know the Titans will lose, we put the imbalance in our own pockets. I adjust the line hourly to achieve that ratio at all times. I can give you any ratio you want, Tony. All the computers out there feed information into this one here on my desk. It's simple, really. There's a mathematical formula that adjusts the line to keep a one-to-one ratio of the bets that we've been using for the past three years. All I had to do was change the ratio in the formula for just the Titans games. I do it by adjusting the line. I don't know how you're doing it, Tony, but if you deliver on this game, we're going to have a serious cash problem. I mean as in what to do with it all."

"So we could end up with four or five million after the game, right?" Tony asked.

"Like I told you before, the lower the line goes on the Titans, the more aggregate action we get on the game. It becomes a favorite bet when people know that the line is, say, nine in Vegas and we're giving eight. Based on the past numbers and my projection for what the false line will do, and figuring in the juice on top of it all, we should have no problem bringing that kind of money in. Just lowering the line by a single point brings 'em out of the woodwork. It's like a fire sale."

"Speaking of fires," Tony said, glaring at Aaron, "what's the deal with you telling Pete to leave his gun in the car?"

"Really, Tony," Aaron said. "I've got people out there who lead normal lives. They don't want some guy waving a gun around at the door. They're nervous enough as it is. And you know as well as I do that Pete can't have a gun and not wave it around."

"Yeah, well, I want this place secure. We got a lot into this operation."

"Tony, I told you before . . . Any irregularity at the door, Pete pushes the warning button, and I dump every bit of information into a security file. By the time anyone could get from the door to this desk, every record we have would be beyond anyone's retrieval but mine."

Tony grumbled but got up off the desk and ambled out of the office. Aaron got away with things other people wouldn't dream of. But Aaron was a genius. Three years ago Tony had hired him to overhaul the family's gambling system. Since then, all they had done was grow. Bookies everywhere wanted to lay off with the Mondolffis. Since Aaron had arrived, it was a no-fuss, no-muss operation. Everything always balanced—until now. But now the imbalance would make Tony richer and more powerful than ever before.

He watched his employees carefully as he sauntered past them through the warehouse. Most of them, he saw, despite being busy fielding calls and punching information into their terminals, warily observed him from the corners of their eyes. He was the big boss to these people, someone to be feared. He liked that feeling and took his time getting out.

He chucked Pete on the shoulder as he passed through the outer office, but said nothing to him about getting his weapon back. The older man looked at him sadly and shrugged, a toothless dog without his gun.

Later that same day, across the river and all the way downtown, Ellis Cook sat looking out through the blinds of his office window as the workday drew to a close. Past some old buildings and a decrepit water tower, Cook could actually see a slice of the Hudson River. It wasn't much, but it was the closest Cook had ever come to an office with a view in his entire life. Of course, he hadn't chosen the building for that reason, but when he had been on site one day last winter with the designer who was helping him with the renovation, he'd seen the view out of the then cracked and dirty window and asked that she put his office there. As time went by, Cook noticed that a multitude of pigeons lived in the air space between him and the river. Often, especially in the evening when the sun was going down, the birds animated the squalid scene of broken-down buildings and a dirty river with magnificent aerial feats.

On his way out, Cook stopped by Duffy's office.

"You got the stuff?" Cook asked.

"Yeah, I got it," Duffy said. "You gonna tell me what you want with it?"

"No."

Duffy nodded with a thoughtful look and said, "Good."

Duffy picked up a briefcase from beside his work area and laid it out on a table in the middle of the room. High-tech electronic equipment of all kinds winked like Christmas lights behind him as he bent over the open case. Then he held up a metallic wafer about the size of a quarter. One side was covered with smooth white paper.

"It's magnetic," Duffy said, "but you can peel this paper off and there's some sticky shit that will bond to a fish's belly. There's another one in the case. I'll show you."

Duffy handed Cook the disc and popped up what looked like a notebook computer inside the leather case.

"Here's the other disc. I've got it set up so you just put this little switch here on the side to COMPORT 2, and you'll home in on this other one instead of the one in your hand. I don't know if you'll need it, but in case Rizzo, or whoever it is you're following, buys a new car or something, you can switch over and you'll be OK. You can even go back and forth between the two if you need to.

"Power is here," Duffy said, flicking a little switch on the side that lit up the screen. "I've got it programmed for a fifty-mile radius from this office. It's as simple as turning it on and looking for the red dot of light. Used to be you'd have two antennae on your car and they'd triangulate with the disc. With this new setup though, the case triangulates with a cellular phone cell and the disc. A computer program gives you a map location. It's the latest . . . I ordered it from Washington when we were having problems keeping tabs on Rizzo. See here, it's on our office. If you have to go outside the radius, you'll have to tell me where you want to go. I'd have to set up the reception center in that other place. I can do it, it's no problem. The phone dishes we use to pick up the signal are just about everywhere these days. That's all you need."

"Wow," Cook said, "I feel like James Bond."

"Yeah," Duffy said, "this stuff just came out. The only weakness is obviously if the subject leaves his car and takes off. That's why you'll never see the traditional tail replaced. That is, until they can come up with something you could plant on the person himself. Who knows, they'll probably do that too one day."

"Don't worry, Duffy," Cook said. "As long as there's bad guys they'll need good guys to chase them."

Duffy smiled. "I get my pension in three years anyway," he said. "I got nothing to worry about."

Cook looked at his man thoughtfully, then closed up the briefcase. "You got those other things I asked for?"

"One 35mm camera with telephoto lense, one telescopic mike for listening in from up to two hundred feet, and one pair of Zeiss miniscopes that make a mosquito look like an elephant, yup, I got it all," Duffy said, and hoisted a duffle bag from under his counter giving it to Cook.

"Thanks," Cook said and headed for the door.

"Hey, Ellis," Duffy said before Cook was gone, "everybody in the office is starting a football pool. Half the money goes to the homeless shelter around the corner. Everybody's too scared of you to ask, but I figured I could. You want in? It's only ten bucks a week."

Cook stopped just outside the door and furled his brow. "Why didn't anyone want to ask me?"

"'Cause you're such a hard-ass, I guess," Duffy said casually.

This surprised Cook.

"You are kinda tense, man," Duffy explained. "Tense or intense. And I think they thought with this whole Rizzo thing that gambling of any kind might kinda set you off."

"What do I have to do?" Cook said.

"Just fill this out and give it back to me with ten bucks," Duffy said, reaching into his desk and pulling out a parlay sheet. "Whoever has the most correct picks wins the pool."

Cook took the sheet from Duffy.

"I'll get it to you tomorrow," he said, waving the sheet over his head as he walked out the door. It shouldn't have bothered him, but Cook thought about being a hard-ass all the way home.

Before Cook even got out of his office, Grant Carter, who also had a tendency to work late, got a phone call from Camille.

"Hi, Daddy," she said, sweet as sugar.

"Hello, Camille . . ." He paused. "I know you want something, dear, so just tell me. I've got a million things to do and a dinner meeting at seven all the way in the city."

"Well, traffic won't be bad going in," she said, refusing to be as gruff and businesslike as he.

"No, I guess not . . . Now, what is it, Camille? I know you don't call me 'Daddy' unless it's something. Otherwise it's 'hey, Dad.'"

"I can't even talk nice to you without you giving me a hard time, Daddy," she complained with a little laugh.

This time Carter remained silent, reviewing some notes for his dinner meeting while waiting for Camille to get to the point.

"Are you there?" she asked.

"Yes dear, I'm waiting."

"Well, it's not a big thing for you, I don't think," she said emphasizing the I.

"Then tell me what it is and we'll hang up. Honestly, Camille, I don't mean to put you off, but I do have a lot to do."

"OK, Tony has a good friend who's crazy about the team."

"Everyone's crazy about the team right now," Carter interjected sarcastically, "we're the world champions."

"Well, Tony asked me to see if I could get him a pass to go into the locker room before the game. Not to bother anybody," she added quickly. "He just wants to see it. I don't know, to see the players. How they get ready or something."

Grant Carter fixed his attention on the silver championship trophy encased in oak and glass on the wall opposite his desk. Everyone wanted a piece of that trophy, something to do with it, anything at all. People came out of the woodwork just to get near it, or near the players who'd won it. Grant Carter understood that. There was something that trophy represented that money could not buy. It was something that had to do with the desire for greatness, that feeble human attempt at immortality.

But there was something about his daughter's request that was more immediate and important than all that. Rizzo was asking a favor of him, but not in a way that suggested he was owed anything. That was good. Carter knew who Rizzo was, and he'd spent more than a few moments worrying that Rizzo might make a demand for reciprocation. Carter had wondered to himself how far he would go to ensure Rizzo maintained his hold over Morgan Lloyd until he could get his empire back into the black. Now it was apparent that he needn't answer that question. Rizzo, whether it was because he hadn't really done that much to put Lloyd at bay or because he'd simply done it to impress Camille, was obviously not going to call in his favor.

"Daddy?"

Camille's voice roused Carter from his reverie.

"Oh, of course, Camille," he said. "That's no problem. I'll give you to Annette and she'll line it up for you. Tell her she can leave the pass for Tony's friend."

"Thanks, Dad," Camille said. "I'll let you go."

Grant Carter's gaze returned to the trophy his team had won for him. He grinned. Rizzo was the one complication in his life lately that had bothered him the most. Maybe Rizzo wasn't such a tough guy after all. Carter knew he was bad. That much he'd been able to find out. But like much of even the worst human element, Rizzo knew better than to cross the lines of wealth and social level and tamper with someone as important as Grant Carter.

CHAPTER 24

That evening Cook rented a car without telling anyone. He had a ready supply of cash that he had to account for, but he could keep his expenditures under wraps until a final accounting at the end of the year. Everything he planned on doing now outside the office would be kept to himself. He would, of course, keep a careful record of his activities and be able to explain his secrecy later because of his, and others', strong suspicions that someone, somewhere was giving up information that was finding its way back to the Mondolffi crime family.

After reading some stories to Natasha and putting her to bed, Cook gave his sullen aunt a nod.

"Work," he said as an explanation for his departure and his shabby dress. Cook wore an old pair of gray slacks and a black T-shirt covered by a ratty gray hooded sweatshirt. On his feet were black hightop sneakers that had also seen better days. The only thing that could give away the fact that he was an agent was the bulge from the Glock that was strapped under his arm. Esther uttered one humph and turned her attention back to the TV. Cook chuckled the whole way down the street to his car. Just wait until she learned of his new schedule. Esther would have more than a humph for him then, but they'd get by. One thing Cook knew about Esther, as tough as her exterior was, deep down she loved him almost as much as Natasha. She'd simply had a difficult life, and she felt she best served him by keeping him on his toes.

Cook drove uptown with the flow of traffic, letting the yellow cabs scream by and around him without getting perturbed. When he reached Rizzo's building, he took the next right and drove across town until he found a spot to park. He walked back through the New York night, which was alive with lights and noise and people, to the garage of Rizzo's building. The garage was a yawning cave in the solid rock slabs of high-rise buildings and regal town houses that lined the street. Cook knew that at night only one attendant would be on duty, so he found a dark corner between some buildings across the street and waited about fifteen minutes before a car finally pulled off Fifth Avenue and turned into the garage.

Cook darted out of the shadows and walked halfway down the ramp. He finally heard the door slam shut and the car go back into gear. Cook carefully edged down the rest of the ramp. While the attendant backed the car into its spot, Cook eased himself down behind the first row of vehicles. After a minute the attendant whistled back to his booth, kicked up his feet, and began flipping through the pages of a *Penthouse* magazine. Cook fished his way through the garage for an hour. Rizzo's car was not there. Cook had expected as much, and he hunkered down in a corner behind a Rolls Silver Spirit to wait.

Every time Cook heard a car pull in, he peeked up through the window of the Rolls to see if it was Rizzo's Mercedes. As the night went on, Cook had less and less cause to look up. At midnight he fished a box of No-Doz from the pocket of his sweatshirt and popped two tablets. They kept him alert until two, when he hit another. The whole while Cook sat thinking. It was the idle time of a stakeout that reminded him of why he really needed to be out of the field. Much of an agent's time on the job, especially when surveillance of any kind was involved, was spent simply waiting.

When you wait, there's nothing to do but think. And for Cook, whenever he had more than ten minutes to think, no matter what tricks he employed, his mind turned to Naomi. A shrink that he had gone to see immediately after her death had told him that one day he would think of her and be filled with warmth from the fond memories of the times they'd spent together. The shrink had said there would one day be no pain. Cook had come to doubt that shrink, and every shrink, in fact. For him, time to think meant inevitable pain. So Cook suffered.

At three-thirteen, Rizzo pulled into the garage. He and Camille Carter got out and walked straight to the elevator without a word to the attendant or each other. Cook watched where the car was parked and humped over to it when the attendant was again ensconced in his booth. He took the homing disc Duffy had given him and stuck it up under the car's wheel well. This would make following Rizzo on his own possible. The only problem he'd have would be when Rizzo took a limousine somewhere, which he did three or four times a week. Rizzo didn't have his own limo, but he had an arrangement with a service that provided him with one on demand. Because the car was usually not the same, another disc would be pointless. Of course, a limo was a lot easier to tail than a Mercedes 500SL.

When he'd finished, Cook simply stood up and walked out of the garage. The attendant didn't even notice him until he was almost halfway up the ramp.

"Hey, man!" the attendant barked, not even bothering to get up from his seat within the safety of his booth. "You get your ass outta here!"

Cook had the same thing in mind.

Since his Wednesday encounter with Tony Rizzo and his thugs, Hunter had done nothing every night but toss and turn in bed. Rachel figured it was the pressure he was under from football. She could read the papers and their speculation that Hunter was a burned-out comet by virtue of his bad shoulder, or age, or lack of talent, or all three. A win on Sunday would go a long way toward silencing the critics. That was how Hunter explained his gloom.

With the game looming like some Shakespearean specter, Hunter tried harder than ever to prepare. He watched so much Detroit game film he saw it whenever he closed his eyes. He balanced the fine line between practicing enough to be ready for the game and resting his shoulder so it would allow him to throw well. He kept pumping in the Butazolidin and got a cortisone shot in the bad joint on Friday.

Saturday night the team stayed at the Meadowlands Marriott near the stadium. Hunter was determined to get some sleep. Instead of counting sheep, he drank four cold Rolling Rocks with Bert, then slugged down two Halcyons. Twenty minutes later, Bert and Hunter were lying in their respective beds under the flimsy hotel covers talking of nothing other than the game. Hunter, nervous that even drugs couldn't suppress his anxieties, began to finally feel himself float. As he drifted off, images of the Lions defense turned slowly in his mind, and then nothing.

Hunter woke from his deeply drugged sleep at eight o'clock on Sunday morning. The good feeling of finally having gotten some rest was almost instantly supplanted by the worry of what the day would hold for him. Every player was nervous on game day. Each wanted to do his best and perform in a way that would help the team win.

Hunter had more to think about than most players even on a normal Sunday. He had to know not only the responsibility of every player on his own offense, from the offensive linemen's calls to the wide receivers' pass routes, but he had to know what everyone on the opposing team was doing, or likely to do. The opposition's formation determined the weakness in their defense. Hunter needed to recognize the subtle signs that told him what their play was in the few seconds he had before the ball was snapped. If he saw that the play called in the huddle was running or throwing directly into the other team's strength, he would call at the line, changing the play to something entirely different.

All that now was coupled with a strategy within his strategy to win the game. The inner strategy was to make sure the Titans didn't beat the Lions by more than a touchdown, thereby placating Rizzo and hopefully making him go away. Hunter didn't like it, but morally he could rationalize what he was going to do because his intent was still to lead his team to victory. That was his main responsibility on Sunday, and if he had to shave a few points in the process, no one would really be the worse for wear.

Without getting out of bed, Hunter reached over to the night stand and grabbed the phone. He dialed home, and Rachel answered on the first ring.

"How did you sleep?" she asked, not even trying to hide her concern.

"Awesome," he replied.

"Oh, good," she said. "Did you have to take those pills?"

"Yeah," Hunter said, "and I'm damn glad I did. I was a wreck."

"Well," she said, "you needed the rest, that's for sure."

"So you're not going to give me any grief about the Halcyon, huh?"

"Oh, come on," she said, "I understand what you're going through, Hunter. I know how the media affects you no matter what you say. I just don't like to see them pumping that Butazolidin into you and those cortisone shots. If you need some Halcyon to get some rest, well . . . hey, even Bush used to take it."

"Now you're comparing me to a Republican," Hunter said. "You must be really pissed."

They had a small laugh, then went through their weekly game-day routine of questions that they both knew the answers to: "How's Sara?" "Fine." and "You going to eat now?" "Yes, as soon as Bert gets his ass out of the shower."

Bert finally did get out of the shower, and Hunter said good-bye to Rachel. The two of them headed down to the ground floor, where one of the banquet rooms retained an elaborate pre-game meal for the Titans. They didn't talk. They didn't have to. Both were thinking about the game, their assignments, and what they would have to do if they were going to go to bed that night and consider it a success. Hunter took a pile of eggs, then shoveled on two baked potatoes with his fork, added a couple of spoonfuls of cottage cheese, and smashed it all together to come up with what he claimed to anyone who'd listen was the perfect pre-game concoction.

Bert was more of a traditional eater. He claimed he needed breakfast and lunch since he wouldn't get to eat again until that evening. He started out with pancakes and bacon drowned in syrup and then got a clean plate for his filet and baked potato with sour cream. Hunter had once tried to warn his friend that the protein and fats he was ingesting could never convert into energy in time for the game and would only serve to slow him down. Hunter should have known better. The food an athlete eats before a contest is as personal as religion, and like religion, it should not be talked about among friends who want to stay that way.

Across the Hudson River, Cook sat in his maroon Dodge Dynasty with a thermos of coffee, a bag of bagels, and a tub of vegetable cream cheese. He was waiting outside on a corner of Fifth Avenue where he could see both the front entrance to Rizzo's building and the yawning darkness of the parking garage. Today he looked like the quintessential FBI agent with a dark suit, dark tie, and Ray-Bans. It was a beautiful day. Cook couldn't help thinking of the things he could be doing with Natasha. It had been a real temptation to take the day off. Only his dedication to a greater purpose had kept him from a drive to Jones Beach, out on Long Island. Natasha loved the beach. Cook could have used a day of rest, too. He'd followed Rizzo around the Manhattan nightclub scene until the wee hours of the morning and gotten home smelling of smoke and sticking to his clothes with sweat.

But Cook knew that to do it right, he needed to dog Tony Rizzo's every move. It was like fishing. You can't see underneath the surface of the water. You don't know when you're going to get a bite. It can happen any time, or not at all. But one thing was for sure. No one ever caught one when their line wasn't in the water. That's how Cook felt right now, like his line was in the water, but there were no bites.

When Rizzo did come out of the garage in the red Mercedes, Camille was right beside him. It wasn't hard for Cook to follow the two of them downtown, through the Lincoln Tunnel, and finally to the Meadowlands, where a crowd was building for the season opener between the Titans and the Lions.

Cook was stopped as he tried to follow Rizzo past a line of cones that blocked most cars from the lots right next to the stadium.

"I'm following them," Cook said to the attendant, a big, burly woman in a Titans cap who was missing a front tooth.

"You ain't following anybody, mister, unless you got a gold pass," she said in a disgusted tone.

Cook sighed and pulled out his badge.

"This good enough for you?" Cook said as he watched Rizzo's car actually disappear into the bus tunnel that went under the stadium.

"Uh-uh, buddy," she said in the voice of the obtuse drone that she was.

Cook was tired of this New York routine of even the lowest people on the totem pole asserting their authority with a joyful vengeance. Down South, an FBI badge meant get the hell out of the way. He put the car in gear and drove over the cones. The woman began shouting insanely into her walkie-talkie, and she chugged after his car as fast as her beefy frame would allow. Cook glanced back through the rearview mirror and smiled at the big lady's face, which was comically distorted with anger. The fatty handles that hung over the side of her pants shook wildly as she ran.

Cook buzzed past another set of guards, laughing out loud now, and drove straight into the tunnel where Rizzo and Camille had disappeared. A squad car pulled up with its lights flashing before he could get through. When he reached for his wallet, the two New Jersey state troopers pulled their guns on him.

By the time Cook got everything worked out, Rizzo and Camille had parked their car and were lost in a stadium of eighty thousand people.

When their meal was over, Hunter and Bert collected their overnight bags and hailed a cab for the stadium. The team provided buses, but those didn't leave until a little later in the morning. Like many veterans, Hunter and Bert both liked to get to the stadium early to go through their rituals of taping, dressing, stretching out, and reviewing their game plans one final time. For three hours before the whole team was ready to go out, Hunter usually fussed like an old lady getting ready for church.

The cab they'd caught at the hotel let them out at the mouth of the tunnel. Hunter breathed deeply. The smell of popcorn and hot dogs cooking mixed with the stale smell of spilled beer gave him a sense of belonging. For most of his life those smells meant football, and football was his life.

On their way down the ramp a maroon Dodge Dynasty went screaming by them and screeched to a halt. A cop car was close behind, and the two friends pulled up short to watch the action. They saw the cops draw their weapons on the handsome black man in a suit and dark glasses who'd gotten out of the Dynasty.

"Must be a fucking drug dealer or something," Bert said out loud.

"In a Dynasty?" Hunter said.

Bert shrugged. "This New York is a fucked-up place. Where I come from, you don't see crazy shit like this happening," he said.

The cops and the man exchanged a few words, and all three of them disappeared into the security offices at the bottom of the tunnel. Hunter and Bert rubbernecked as they passed the office on their way to the locker room, but they could see nothing through the battered blinds that hung in the office windows.

Once in the locker room, Hunter almost began to forget his problems. The routine was everything, and for years he had used it to reduce even the most intense stress. He took comfort in dressing in his uniform the exact same way he'd been doing it for fourteen years. The obsession with the routine was more a distraction from the anxiety of the game than deep-seated superstition, as many people thought it to be. Hunter didn't think they'd lose if he made a mistake like looking into the mirror on the way out of the bathroom. But it was part of his routine not to look, so he didn't.

Hunter was taped and dressed by the time most of his teammates were arriving from their bus ride. Now he was into the part of his routine that included a complete review of the game plan, followed by a personal prayer. The team always prayed together, of course, but he habitually said his own beforehand. Hunter was seated on the stool in front of his locker, looking at the carpet in front of him and saying his prayer when two large black wing-tipped shoes came to rest directly in his line of vision. This annoyed Hunter. He tried to ignore the distraction, but the shoes didn't move.

Hunter looked up and found himself face to face with the cold, rodent-like eyes of Carl Lutz. He felt a nervous urge to revisit the bathroom. Carl smiled.

"How did you get in here? How did you get that?" Hunter said, shifting his eyes to the blue-and-yellow locker-room pass that hung fastened to the button of Carl's suit coat.

Carl only continued to smile and stare at Hunter.

"I'm here to make sure you don't forget you got a job to do today," Carl said in a low, threatening tone. "You got a nice little family. I'd hate to see you fuck up and have something bad happen to them."

Hunter just stared at Carl's pass.

"I remember," Hunter said quietly in a voice that was tinged with nausea.

"Good."

Hunter looked up to watch the burly thug walk calmly out of the locker room. Hunter gazed around him, nervous that someone might have seen their exchange, but the rest of the team was more than a little busy getting ready for the season opener.

Hunter was in a daze. The nightmare was fresh again in his mind. How could the thug have gotten such a pass? Then Hunter remembered that nothing was beyond those kind of people. That thought scared the hell out of him. It was all he could think about.

Before he knew it, Hunter was out on the field, standing with his helmet under his arm in an assemblage of warriors. Out of habit, he sang "The Star Spangled Banner" under his breath. Moisture welled in his eyes at the final words of the song, and the crowd roared. The usual feeling of noble battle, where the rules are clearly set out and the contestants cross the field after the game to shake hands, of being one great country, under one flag, normally touched Hunter before each game with the same kind of sentimentality that inspired Norman Rockwell. That and the thrill of the impending contest were typically a high.

Today he had no such thoughts. Bewilderment and fear clouded his mind. That he was going to shave points in this contest was unquestionable. Just to hear his family mentioned from the mouth of Carl Lutz almost made Hunter want to find Rachel, get their daughter, close out what cash they had, and run. The outcome of the game seemed suddenly meaningless to him. The only thing that was important was to lose on points. Hunter decided he wasn't going to take any chances.

The referee tossed a coin and Detroit called tails. Under normal circumstances, Hunter would have smiled when he saw the heads. He loved to take the field first, to get right into the thick of things instead of standing around while the defense drew first blood. Now Hunter jogged listlessly to the sideline with the other Titans captains. He headed for the Gatorade table to get the same last gulp of water he always got between the coin toss and the kickoff. The mouthful of water went sour and heavy about halfway down. The sickness stayed with him as he recalled his rain-soaked encounter with Tony Rizzo on Wednesday night. Here he had been all morning, acting as though this was just another game. Like everything was just fine and all he had to do was go out there and win. But that was not all he had to do. Carl Lutz's appearance had reminded him of that. He had to cheat. Yes, it was cheating, what he was going to do. With a sudden cold certainty, Hunter knew that doing anything for someone like Tony Rizzo was wrong. But as he heard the thud of the kickoff amid the cheering throng and watched the ball turn slowly end over end through the air, Hunter also knew that he had no choice.

A fter Cook was able to verify to the troopers who he was, they became extremely helpful. The older of the two had a brother who was a Treasury agent, and he showed a respect for Cook that Cook hadn't seen from any of the locals since he'd arrived in the New York area. The troopers instructed the stadium security people to give him whatever he needed. They gave him a pass that allowed him to go wherever he wanted and a map on which they marked the location of the owner's sky box. Cook thanked the troopers, who said they'd see to his car, and he insisted on taking down the name of their superior. He intended on sending a letter of thanks. He knew that kind of thing went a long way in law enforcement, and he intended to repay the troopers for their assistance.

Instead of going to the side of the stadium where Grant Carter's sky box was located, Cook did just the opposite. When he was directly across from the owner's box, he went up an escalator and found himself on the lower level of the stadium. People were everywhere by now, pushing, shoving and cursing their way to their seats before the game began. Most were dressed in the green and gold colors of the Titans, and many were already weaving from too much drink. Cook wormed his way up one level and out the nearest entrance to the seats and the sunshine that was quickly warming the day. A surly usher stopped him and asked for his ticket.

"Oh," the usher said in surprise when he saw Cook's pass. "How can I help you?"

"I just need a place to sit and observe," Cook said.

"Well, all the seats will be filled today," the usher said, "but you can just stand here with me if you want. This is the best view in the house.

"There, you can stand right there if you want to," the usher said, pointing to a small space between the entranceway and the seats that rose above it.

Cook thanked the usher and wedged himself into the little nook while the mob filed past, looking for their proper seats. Cook pulled a small pair of Zeiss field scopes—nothing out of the ordinary at a football game—from the side pocket of his jacket and began to scan Grant Carter's box. There were plenty of people in there, and it took Cook almost until kickoff to determine that Rizzo and Camille were not present. Cook thought it strange. Both Camille and Rizzo struck him as the types to be in a box where they wouldn't have to rub elbows with the common man.

He knew they had to be in the stadium somewhere, though. He began to pan the crowd opposite him. If the daughter of the team's owner was in the crowd, her seats would be the best in the house. He started at the fifty-yard line in the first row and began working his way up. He found them about thirty rows up, almost directly opposite him, right on the fifty. Rizzo and Camille sat side by side, dressed as though they were going shopping on Madison Avenue, and both of them pensively stared at the field below. Cook examined the people who sat around them, all of whom were dressed in the typical garb of football fans: T-shirts, shorts or jeans, Titans baseball caps, and sneakers. The people talked and joked among themselves, leaving Rizzo and Camille to their apparently sullen silence. Cook wondered if the two of them had simply had a quarrel and were cooling off. As the game began, their expressions remained impassive. Camille seemed bored with the whole thing, and Rizzo had the intense, expectant expression of a man waiting for bad news.

The Titans took the ball on the initial drive and began to move down the field. Hunter completed on a few underneath passes that gave them no more than five- or six-yard gains, but the running game was on the money and before he could think twice about it, the Titans were on the Lions' twenty-three-yard line. This made

Hunter nervous. He knew he was in scoring position. If the Titans scored right away, he would have to compensate for it later. The next play that came in from Price was a pass. Hunter was glad for the chance to slow things down. By simply throwing a bad pass, he could greatly reduce the chances of his team scoring.

As much as it bothered him to do it, Hunter dropped back on the next pass play and fired the ball just out of Weaver's reach. Weaver lunged and dove through the air, just tipping the ball. Up it went, lazily spinning end over end. A Detroit linebacker held out his arms to make the easy catch and raced down the field into Titans territory before he was tackled by Murphy.

The crowd, who until then had been in a fevered frenzy, grew quiet. There was a little booing but not much. It was, after all, the opening game, and the crowd had as much tolerance now as it ever would, especially coming off a world championship season. Everyone around the game of football knew that an unlucky start didn't mean anything. In the game of football a team could be beaten soundly for three solid quarters and then come out and win it in the fourth. The sprinkled boos came only from the harshest Hunter Logan critics.

After that Detroit made Hunter's job easy. The Lions went right down and scored to make it 7–0. After two more stalled Titan offensive series, Greg Peterson, the Titans fullback, fumbled the ball on a third and one. Detroit recovered and drove down the field to make it 14–0 with less than two minutes to go in the half.

Hunter knew that if things got much worse, he might have trouble giving his team any chance to win at all, and his plan was to do what he had to to keep the Titans close until right at the end. Then he would try to pull the game out for them with some last-minute scoring that would give them the win, but only by one touchdown or less.

Coach Price was signaling the plays to Hunter from the sideline. For the entire game until then, Hunter had simply run the plays that had been called, letting the chips fall where they may. He had done this at times, despite seeing a defense at the line of scrimmage that would undoubtedly stifle the play. Hunter really couldn't be criticized for running the play. Martin Price had the type of ego that could not admit he'd called the wrong play, so it was the safest approach for Hunter to take that would allow him to keep the game in check. If Price did call a big play, like the pass to the tight end down near their own goal line, Hunter could simply throw a bad pass or an interception. Things like that happened.

Now, though, Hunter was determined to get his team a field goal before the half. Even three points would give his teammates the lift they needed in order not to self-destruct completely. Price signaled in an 80-Y-Go—the tight end would be the primary receiver in the post. Hunter called the play, told his line to give him time, and broke the huddle. At the line of scrimmage, Hunter could see that the Lions were in a three-deep zone with man-to-man coverage underneath. An 80-Y-Go was the wrong call.

"Idaho fifty-five! Idaho fifty-five!" Hunter bellowed to his team. Idaho was the hot word that let every Titan player know that the play was being changed from the huddle call. A fifty-five put three of his receivers to one side and crossed them underneath in a way that would pick off the man-to-man defenders. The slot, who was the primary receiver, would cross the field to the weak side where the X receiver had hopefully run off his defender and the deep safety with a go pattern where he raced for the end zone. His team adjusted and shouting filled the air from both teams. The Lions scrambled to adjust to the new formation, and the Titans line began barking out new line calls for a different pass protection.

"Set, hut! Hut!"

Hunter took the ball from the center and dropped five steps. The slot came streaking across the field, wide open. Hunter hit him with the ball right in the hands, and the receiver ran for twelve more before being knocked out of bounds. In this way Hunter worked his team down the field to the Lions' ten-yard line with eleven seconds left on the clock, time enough for only one more play.

Price signaled in an H-Out with the receivers running flag routes that would clear the end zone for the running back. Hunter called the play and ran it from scrimmage. The H-back was wide open, but Hunter held the ball an instant too long, then gunned it wildly over his receiver's head as he was hit from the side by two Detroit defenders. The field goal unit came out onto the field, and the Titans went into the locker room at halftime, well behind, but energized by getting on the scoreboard.

After the game began, the stadium usher planted himself next to the agent to avoid the constant flow of fans to and from the concession stands.

"Get too much beer spilled on me if I stand there," the usher said as an explanation, pointing at the concrete platform at the top of the steps. "You don't mind, do you?"

"No," Cook said, but that was all. He continued to observe Rizzo through his scopes, only setting them aside every so often to rest his eyes. As the game went on, Cook became aware of the usher's expletive comments regarding the action of the game. Hunter Logan's overthrown pass into the end zone seemed particularly upsetting to him.

"You're a big fan, huh?" Cook said in the way of polite conversation.

"Yeah," the usher said. "I got a C-note riding on this."

"Wow," Cook said.

"Yeah, you ain't shitting," replied the usher. "Hunter Logan better get his head out of his ass or I'll be eating soup for dinner all next month."

Cook thought about that, then ended their conversation by bringing the scopes back up to his eyes. At halftime, Camille got up from her seat. Rizzo remained where he was, sitting almost like a statue, impervious to everything around him, as if nothing mattered but the resumption of the game. Cook wondered at Rizzo's obvious engrossment with the game and if there was any meaning to it.

In the locker room, Hunter sat and listened to Price exhort his team to pick up their intensity. Normally unemotional, the coach was now a frenzy of hand waving and yelling. The prospect of losing the opener to a team they were favored to beat by nine points was infuriating. It all went by Hunter as though he were watching a movie. His mind was on the task at hand. Right before the team went back out for the second half, Bert walked up to Hunter's locker and offered him a can of Gatorade. Hunter took the can and drained it.

"You OK?" Bert asked.

Hunter stood up and took his helmet off its hook. "Yeah," he said blandly.

"Sure? You seem a little out of it. Is your shoulder OK?"

"Yeah," Hunter said, then as if he were reciting a script, "let's go win this one."

Bert nodded and followed his friend out onto the field. The Titans defense responded to their coach's call and stuffed Detroit on the opening kickoff. Hunter and the Titans took over at midfield. Hunter decided to let things happen for a while and just play. The first series took his team right down the field and connected to Matt Brown in the end zone. After that he moved his team at will, but would come up short of the end zone to ensure only field goals. His play was brilliant until his team got inside the Detroit twenty-yard line. The Titans kicker made three out of four short field goals, and before Hunter knew it his team was winning 16–14. There were only about ten minutes to go in the game, and Hunter felt that he was right where he wanted to be. If the defense kept Detroit shut down as they had the entire second half, he could simply slog along without a score, win the game, and keep the score under a touchdown.

Hunter was actually starting to relax a little about things when a Titans defensive lineman hit the Lions quarterback from behind, knocking the ball loose. Bert, who was close by, scooped it up and ran the fumble all the way down to the Lions' one-yard line before he was tripped up by a Lions running back. Bert came off the field with the ball held high for the roaring crowd to see. A touchdown now would put them up by nine and all but ensure a Titans victory.

Hunter jogged onto the field, his stomach knotted with anxiety. The play was a dive up the middle. Hunter bobbled the snap. The ball came out of his hands. A Detroit defender grabbed for it but only batted it back into the Titans' backfield, and a melee ensued. There was a pile of bodies over the ball, and Hunter stood back to let the referees sort it out while he stared at his hands incredulously and rubbed them on his pants like some little league baseball player blaming his glove for a mishandled grounder. Hunter cursed quietly to himself. When the last player was pulled off the pile by the officials, all that was left was Murphy, the Titans' center, hunched protectively over the ball.

Hunter began to chastise himself for even worrying about winning this game. For what was at stake didn't matter. The team could easily lose this and go on to win the championship again anyway.

Too much was at stake for him to have taken a chance. Unexpected things were commonplace in the game of football. He shouldn't have taken the chance of letting it get this close. His mind whirled with the possibilities of what he could do now. If he fumbled again, it would make obvious what he was actually doing. If a running play was called, he'd simply have to change the play by calling an audible at the line of scrimmage and throw a pass.

Since Murphy had recovered the ball on the five-yard line, Price called a pass play. Hunter called it, broke the huddle, and set his team on the line. Briefly he assessed the defense. He knew how they'd cover the pattern. He took the snap and dropped back. The strong safety was playing underneath on his X receiver, and Hunter gunned the ball just behind the X, right into the safety's hands. The unexpected ball bounced off the defender's hands and into the air. The X, who'd stopped in his tracks, now leaped for the wayward ball. It was actually between his hands when the Lions' big inside backer hit him from behind, upending him and sending the ball harmlessly to the ground. The play had been so close that Hunter almost vomited.

It was third down and five from the goal now, and everyone in the stadium knew it would be a pass. Price called a roll right throwback to the tight end. Hunter dropped back, but this time he wasn't going to take any chances. He held the ball for a painfully long time, waiting for the Lions' rush to take him down. But his own line had risen to the occasion, and Hunter was jogging to his right, unmolested by defenders, with his tight end waving his hands wildly on the other side of the field in the end zone. In this brief instant of time Hunter thought he could even hear people in the nearby stands shouting, "Throw it! Throw it!"

Finally Hunter gunned the ball with such velocity that it rocketed over his wide-open man and almost went into the crowd. Hunter jogged off the field, passing the kicker who would make the field goal and extend their lead to just five. It was better than nothing. Detroit would have to score a touchdown now to win where before a field goal would have been enough. But had Hunter connected on what was an easy touchdown, the game, with only four minutes left, would be all but over. Price met Hunter at the sideline and took hold of his arm.

"What the hell was that?" Price said coldly.

"Hey," Hunter replied, shaking himself free from the coach and starting for the bench as if he were a million miles away from what was happening, "we're winning, aren't we?"

Price followed his quarterback with a malignant stare, then turned his attention to his defense.

Even from across Meadowlands Stadium, Cook could see without his scopes that Tony Rizzo was upset when Bert Meyer recovered the fumble. While the rest of the crowd, even Camille, were on their feet, gesticulating, cheering and celebrating, Tony Rizzo remained frozen in the same position he'd been in all game. A closer look confirmed Cook's suspicion. Rizzo wore a stone-cold frown and had begun to gnaw on a knuckle. Only when Hunter Logan blew the pass did Rizzo seem to relax. At least he stopped chewing his knuckle.

"Fucking shit! Son of a bitch! Damn it all to hell!" bellowed the usher as the field goal team went out onto the field. Cook put his scopes aside and looked at the middle-aged man, who was in much need of a shave. His face was almost purple, and Cook quickly reviewed his CPR technique in his mind, thinking that this guy was surely going to blow a valve.

When he finally stopped fuming and the blood left his face, Cook said, "Take it easy, buddy, the defense hasn't let them do a thing all second half. Detroit might get a field goal, but they aren't going to score six."

The usher looked at Cook as though he were mad. His bright green eyes shone from amid his bloodshot whites and his gray, saggy face.

"It don't matter if they win or lose now," the usher said, his voice cracking with phlegm.

"I thought you got a hundred on the Titans," Cook said without thinking.

"Man," the usher said in his deep, rough voice, "the Titans got to win by eight. There's a line, man. Titans by eight was a sure thing. Detroit wasn't shit last year and besides, their quarterback got hurt in pre-season. All fucking Logan had to do was hit that fucking wide-open tight end in the end zone and I was laughing."

The usher shook his hung head and jammed his thick hands into the bright yellow windbreaker that was part of his uniform.

"Man," he said, "this game was a sure thing."

Cook thought about that, then put up his scopes to watch Rizzo for the rest of the game. The Titans defense held and the final was 19–14, Titans. Cook saw Rizzo smile for the first time, then rise with Camille on his arm and disappear into the crowd.

CHAPTER 26

Rachel was waiting for Hunter in the tunnel just outside the locker room. The air was filled with the electricity that always resulted from a victory. Everyone was happy. The upbeat attitude of the players would spill over into their lives at home. It would be a good week. All the Titans' wives and girlfriends were there, gossiping among themselves and waiting for their mates to shower and finish with the media. Since Hunter was always one of the last players to appear, Rachel was used to the wait. Bert and Amy Meyer would usually keep her company. Sometimes, especially after a win, the four of them would go out to eat before heading home. When Hunter appeared, dressed typically in a pair of jeans, cowboy boots, and a white T-shirt, they had already decided where they'd go for dinner.

"Nah, I don't feel like it tonight, you guys," Hunter said sullenly when they informed him.

Bert and Amy looked surprised. Rachel looked concerned.

"Hey, man," Bert said, gripping Hunter's shoulder in his familiar way, "we won! Don't start getting down on us, you had a good game."

"Yeah," Hunter said sarcastically, meeting his friend's eye, "two interceptions, a fumble, and only one time did I get us in the end zone. That's real good. Anyway, I just don't feel so hot."

Rachel took her husband's arm and began to walk with him out of the tunnel. The four of them didn't say much. Bert had tried, but they all knew it was no use when Hunter felt he'd played poorly. The strange thing was that he'd really had a pretty good game. He'd made few big mistakes, but in the end they hadn't cost the team its victory. Usually Hunter got down only after a loss. Now they had finally gotten off to the start they had been waiting for, and Hunter was morose.

Rachel knew not to argue about it or try to change Hunter's mind. After a game he was either in a good mood or a bad one, and nothing could be done about it except for him to get a good night's sleep.

They finally got to the team's parking lot, which was a fenced-in area just outside the tunnel. Hunter looked around anxiously.

"You looking for someone?" Bert said innocently.

"Huh? No," Hunter said. "I'll see you tomorrow Bert. Bye, Amy. Come on, Rach."

Over her shoulder, Rachel said to Amy, "I'll call you this week and we'll get together with the kids."

"Hunter, what's with you?" she asked, trying to keep pace with him as he made his way through the rest of his teammates, who were milling around the parking lot.

"Nothing," he said, still looking around. "I just want to get out of here."

They sat in their car in traffic for almost forty minutes before the road opened up a little and they began to move. Hunter deflected Rachel's every attempt at conversation before finally switching the radio on. When they crossed the Verrazano Bridge, Hunter suggested they stop at a deli in Hewlett and eat before picking up Sara at Rachel's parents' house.

The deli was crowded with people of all ages eating everything from stuffed cabbage to roasted chicken. It was a brightly lit place, and the animated buzz of conversation gave it a communal air. The bad news was that Hunter was recognized instantly. Parents and kids of all ages lined up at their table to get him to autograph napkins and scraps of paper that Hunter suspected would be lost or thrown away by the following week. Still, he signed and smiled, and generally played the part of the All-American football hero. Once in a while Hunter actually enjoyed a limited amount of attention. But it was never something he sought.

Soon every autograph was signed, and Hunter signaled for the waitress and gave her their order. When she left, Hunter and Rachel lapsed into silence once again. With apparently nothing to say to each other, their attention was drawn to an elderly couple seated at the next table. The man was complaining loudly about the coleslaw while his wife tried to quiet him.

"There's too much mayonnaise," he bellowed in a thick European accent.

Hunter looked up and met Rachel's eyes. Something about the despair in the man's voice over something as innocuous as the coleslaw set them both to laughing. Then the man started up about how the pickles were so hard they were going to break his teeth and that he'd sue if they did. It was one of those rare moments when laughter compounded by silliness brought them to tears. When their laughter finally subsided, Rachel reached across the table and took Hunter's hand.

"What's wrong, honey?" she said in a conspiratorial tone meant to suggest that there was nothing he couldn't say to her.

Hunter paused, frowned, and seemed to consider the water in his battered glass. He drank up the water and then swirled the ice.

"It's just football," he said blandly. "The pressure's getting to me, I guess. My shoulder, all the bullshit in the papers about whether or not I'm the man everyone thought I was last season . . . it gets to me."

"It's more than that," Rachel said with a certainty that made him wince. "I know how football affects you. I know that this is more than that. The way you were looking around today after the game . . . what is it, Hunter? Something's bothering you."

Hunter smiled nervously and squeezed Rachel's hand. "Nothing. Really, Rach, I'm fine. It really is football," he said, thinking to himself that it wasn't a complete lie. Football was the center of the problem if not the problem itself.

Rachel just stared. Tears started to well up in her eyes. "I can't believe you're keeping something from me, Hunter," she said finally, almost choking on the words.

Looking up with incandescent eyes, she said, "You've been so—so distracted. You're somewhere else half the time, Hunter. You're not with me . . . since before camp started. I know how you get about camp, but when you got back, instead of getting better, you got worse. Then I told myself you just needed to get the first game behind you, to win it and silence the critics. But now you did that, and today all you could do was look around after the game like you were guilty of something."

"I'm not doing anything wrong," Hunter said almost angrily. "You know better than that!"

"I don't know what I know, Hunter," she said with tears running down her cheeks now, "unless you tell me what's going on."

Hunter reached out and wiped the tears away. "Don't cry, honey," he said quietly, looking around. "Don't."

Hunter took a deep breath and told her everything in a guarded whisper, from the betting with Metz to his first and second encounters with Rizzo, and finally what had happened today, what he'd been thinking, how he'd felt.

"That's who that guy was," Rachel said, suddenly.

"What?" Hunter said.

"That guy I saw outside the house that day," Rachel said quietly, staring at her husband's face. "I knew something was wrong about that guy."

Hunter looked confused.

"Forget it," she said, "go on."

Hunter continued to tell her about what had been going through his mind. When he was done, the food came. It sat untouched while the two of them sat silently holding each other's hands.

Then Hunter said quietly, "I didn't tell you because I didn't want you to worry, Rach."

Rachel met this with more silence. "We have to tell someone," she said.

A forkful of kasha, halfway to his mouth, fell back onto Hunter's plate. "No!" he hissed. "That's one thing we definitely can't do."

"We have to, Hunter," Rachel said. "It's the only way."

She responded vehemently to his hesitation.

"I'm talking about our lives, Hunter."

"So am I," he responded, still whispering. "If we go to someone, I'm done."

"Football might be done," she whispered back, "And if it is, well . . . it's football. I'm talking about you and me and Sara. These people don't go away, Hunter. They come to stay. You can't get rid of them. We need to get help."

"But they will go away," Hunter insisted. "They'll go away as soon as I'm no longer any value to them. If I can just get through this season, Rachel, we'll be set. We won't have to worry."

"Ha! Worry?" she said with a crazed expression of disbelief. "What do you call what you've been doing since the Fourth? What do you think I'm going to do knowing those people are out there? That they've already been to our house?"

"You don't know that for sure."

"I know, Hunter."

"I did what they asked me to do," he explained quietly. "That should be it with them anyway. Rizzo said 'a' favor. I've done it."

"Hunter," she said, "you don't make the rules with these people. They make the rules. The only way to get away is to get help."

"I'm not throwing this season away!" Hunter hissed with a scowl. "I've worked my whole life . . . I've spent fourteen years in this league busting my ass, hoping, praying to make the big money and set myself, set us, up for the rest of our lives. If I have to take a few points off the outcome of a game, what's the big deal? Like you said, we won. Everybody's happy. It's not like I really did anything wrong."

"Can you hear yourself?" Rachel said. "Did you hear what you just said? You're not doing anything wrong? Hunter, you're working with the Mafia—"

"—I'm not working with anyone!" Hunter said, slamming his fist down on the table and drawing stares from all around.

He leaned across the table and said in a lower but equally fierce tone, "I'm doing what I have to to protect what I've worked for, Rachel. You don't know what it's like! You've always had it. You've always been taken care of. You haven't had to scrape and save and eat food from cans. You haven't had to watch everything your family owns stripped away from them while you stood by!

"I've seen all that, Rachel," Hunter continued in a desperate voice. "I've seen it, and I won't see it again! I won't see it happen to you and to me! Not when we're so close!"

He sat back now but held her eyes. He knew they were going to do battle over this.

Rachel met his stare and held it. "No," she said, shaking her head. "No way, Hunter. Don't give me that crap about your family and my family. That's not what counts here. We've got to get help . . . no matter what happens."

"Huh!" Hunter snorted in disbelief. "You're taking yourself a little too seriously, Rach. You don't make that call. That's my call. This is my career, and you aren't fucking telling me that it's over. Uh-uh."

Rachel said nothing more but simply got up and walked out. Hunter scrambled to his feet and threw a couple of twenties on the table amid their plates of half-eaten food. He caught up to her halfway to the car and grabbed her wrist.

"Don't pull that shit," he said. "Don't walk away from me!"

Rachel pulled free with a violent twist of her arm.

"I'll walk away if I want! I'm not going to listen if you're going to talk macho bullshit to me! Those people will eat you up! You think they care who you are, Hunter? You're nothing to them! You're so used to everyone groveling at your feet because you're Hunter Logan that you can't understand that these people will use you up and then kill you! I'm not going to sit around while they do it, either."

"What's that supposed to mean, Rach?" he said, almost yelling as he followed her along. "Huh? What's that? Don't you talk about not being around, Rach, that's not part of what we talk about . . ."

Rachel got into the car and sat silently. Hunter got in, too. He started the car and screeched out of the lot and down Central Avenue. Then he pulled over suddenly and stopped. Hunter shut off the car and threw the keys against the windshield, then pressed his palms tightly against the sides of his head.

"My God," he whispered quietly. "What's going to happen, Rachel? What the hell is going to happen to me? I feel like I'm going insane."

Rachel reached over and pulled his head to her breast. She could feel the energy draining from him. The stress, she knew, must be unbearable. She knew, too, that he was doing it for them as much as for himself. He really believed that they needed to live the way they did. She had told him time and time again that it wasn't necessary. She realized that it was he who could never live the other way. She held him for a few moments before picking the keys up off the dashboard and quietly handing them back to him.

Then gently she said, "Let's go home."

The paperwork on Cook's desk was beginning to pile up. He buzzed his secretary and asked her to bring him another coffee. It was his eighth cup of the morning, but he'd been out very late the night before watching Tony Rizzo celebrating the Titans win. Cook had never known Rizzo was such a fan, Maybe it was Camille. Maybe it was something more . . .

"Hey, man," Duffy said, peering in through his door with Cook's coffee in hand. "Clara says this is your eighth cup. I'm getting ready to call a buddy of mine who works narcotics in the NYPD."

Cook waved Duffy inside. His friend shut the door behind him and sat down, setting the coffee on the edge of Cook's desk.

"I do like this view," Duffy said, gazing out the window. "That's what you get when you're the boss man."

Cook chuckled at his friend's southern po' folks intonations.

"Good to see you can still laugh a little," Duffy said, "'cause you sure can't keep your eyes open."

Cook stifled a yawn. "I'll be OK."

"From the looks of this desk, you need another you," Duffy said, hefting one of the many heavy stacks of paperwork. "You need to lighten up on whatever it is you do when you skip outta here at eleven o'clock every day. By the way, what is it you do?"

"Now, you know I'm not telling you," Cook said, "so why don't you just stop asking me, man?"

"I'm just making sure," Duffy said. "I like testing you."

"Hmmm," Cook said.

"But seriously, man," Duffy said, "you better get at this stuff, whatever you're doing. This is the kind of backed-up paperwork that can get you retired from your supervisor status early in this bureaucratic Bureau."

"If we don't come up with something on the Mondolffis soon," Cook said, raising a sheet of paper from his stack as evidence, "I'm not going to have to worry about supervising anything but Natasha's homework."

"What's that?" Duffy said, innately distrusting any official-looking document.

"This is a letter from Miles Zulaff himself," Cook said in a serious tone. "It appears the director has asked Zulaff to make a personal assessment of the viability of the Special Task Force, or STS as they're calling it. I've got to meet with him and Duncan Fellows."

"When?" was all Duffy could think of to say.

"Next week," Cook said. "So I'm assuming that if we don't have something concrete real soon, I can simply put a match to all this paperwork, get a job as a Brinks armored truck guard, or a BATG as I'm sure the Bureau will fondly call me, and kiss my pension good-bye."

"You wouldn't really leave the agency, would you?"

"No," Cook said, tossing the letter back into its pile. "No, but I might as well leave. If this doesn't work, I'll be pulling some kind of guard duty in Podunk, South Dakota, somewhere with the KKK knocking on my door late at night and Natasha coming home with a white boyfriend when she's twelve."

"My momma was white," Duffy offered.

"I didn't mean it like that," Cook said. "I just meant I got plans, plans that end in D.C., man. If we could just get a hook into these bastards, just a start, I could get Zulaff to give me more time."

"Well," Duffy said after a moment, "let me buy you a slice of pizza."

Cook looked up with a surprised expression on his face. "That ain't like you, Duffy," he said, "to talk about buying lunch before we even get the tab."

"Yeah, well . . . remember that football pool?"

"Yeah, don't tell me you won it."

"Uh-huh," Duffy said, nodding his head. "I got nine of those games right. Can you imagine it? I oughta start taking action on these things for real. Victor got eight right, I got him on the Titans game. Every sap in this city went for the home team. Damn fools, though, it ain't often one NFL team beats another by nine points, you know. If you're gonna bet, you gotta bet your mind, not your heart. I can't say as I blame Victor, though, he grew up in the—"

"Duffy," Cook interrupted, "what did you say just now? About the Titans?"

"I said you got to bet your mind, not—"

"No, not that, about nine points, what about nine points?"

"Just that it doesn't often happen that one team beats another by nine points in this league since free agency," Duffy said.

"I thought the spread was eight on that game," Cook said, rummaging through his desk drawer until he came up with his half of his losing parlay. "How come this is nine?" Cook asked Duffy, pointing to the +9 that appeared next to the Titans on the card.

"Because that's what it was," Duffy said. "I get that parlay from a guy I know out in Vegas."

"Could the line be different here in New York?" Cook asked.

"Sure," Duffy said. "If you were betting with a different syndicate. It probably would be different here, too."

This knowledge seemed to deflate Cook. He rested his elbows on the arms of his chair and put his fingertips to his lips. "Why's that?" he asked anyway.

"Well, if you had some kind of local syndicate—" Duffy began.

"Like the Mondolffis?" said Cook.

"Yeah, like the Mondolffis, then you'd have a hell of a lot more action on the home team, the Titans, so you'd probably have to raise your line to balance your books."

Cook dropped his hands and lifted his head. "They'd have to raise it, right?" he said excitedly.

"Yeah, they'd probably raise the line anywhere from a half to a whole point higher. This way they'd get the same amount of money down on the Lions as they did on the Titans. They never lose money. Each bet on the Titans is covered by a bet for Detroit. The syndicate makes its money on the juice, the ten percent service fee from both sides, just for taking the bets. Why? What are you thinking?"

"Nothing," Cook said, and was silent.

"So, what about lunch?" Duffy reminded him.

"I can't," Cook said. "I got something I have to do."

"If I didn't think I knew you, sir," Duffy said, "I'd think you didn't like me anymore."

"That's not it, my man," Cook said as he got up, drained his coffee cup, and put on his jacket. "I just don't want to end up in Podunk."

As Tony Rizzo entered Crab City, a trendy seafood restaurant on Park Avenue South, he never even noticed Ellis Cook watching him from the opposite sidewalk. Rizzo sat down at a table where Mike Cometti, Carl Lutz, and Angelo Quatrini were already waiting. Rizzo didn't acknowledge the other men but spoke directly to Angelo.

"Anyone follow you here?" he asked.

"Nah," Angelo replied. "I remembered what you said, Tony. Whenever I meet with you I toss those feds like a salad. I lose 'em in the subways. They hate those fucking subways."

"Good," Tony said. "They'll be gone before you know it, Ang. Just hang tight. It's probably no big deal, but you never know with those motherfuckers. They see us sitting here talking like this, they're liable to pop a bug in the salt shaker."

"Isn't that illegal?" Carl said, knitting his brow as though he were trying to recall one of the finer points of the legal system. "Isn't that like entrapment or something?"

"Holy shit," Tony said to Angelo, "where the fuck did you get this guy, Ang? Is he for real?"

"Nah, he's just fucking around," Angelo said, signaling his protégé to shut up.

Tony looked at Carl suspiciously and signaled the waiter to come take their order. As the waiter left, Tony leaned forward and said, "OK, here's the deal. We made over four million on the game yesterday." Here Tony paused for the proper effect. "Everybody big in our organization knows about it. In fact, my uncle wants to see me tonight at his house, and I know that's what it's about. I'm going to recommend that he cut each of you guys in for a hundred grand.

"That's above the share of the business you already get, Ang," Tony said, making sure that Angelo knew he wasn't being treated the same as Cometti and Carl, both of whom looked as though they might swallow their tongues.

"What I want to work on is this," Tony continued. "Ang, I want you to arrange a meeting with me and Scott Meeker."

Meeker was the owner of The Star casino in Atlantic City. He always comped the big Mafia bosses when they came into town. He was on excellent terms with everyone and was one of the few men who could arrange meetings between men of different families without raising eyebrows.

Angelo looked at Tony with a questioning expression.

"You just tell him I need to see him about something important," Tony said. "I'm going to have him set up a meeting between me and Mark Ianuzzo and Sal Gamone. There's no way I can talk to both of them at the same time without getting Scott to set it up. What I'm thinking is this: I want to throw a bone to these guys, let them in on the action for our next game."

Tony saw three puzzled faces. It was what he expected, but he wanted to run this by his men to see if he'd considered all the angles. Mark

Ianuzzo and Sal Gamone were the heads of New York's other two prominent Italian crime families. The Bronx belonged to Ianuzzo, and Gamone ran Staten Island. They were the capos, the bosses. They were like corporate CEOs whereas Tony was only a capo regime, which was akin to a corporate VP. Normally the lines of communication weren't open between the two different ranks. But Tony, whose father had dealt with these men and whose uncle was currently dealing with them, and whose reputation in the city was growing every day, was close enough to the top to request such a meeting. But without the intervention of Scott Meeker to keep the whole thing under wraps, Tony's uncle would be sure to find out. If he did find out, he would see what was coming and probably have Tony knocked off.

But if Tony was going to whack his uncle, he would need to have already established a good relationship with Mark Ianuzzo and Sal Gamone. Once Tony made the bold move, it would be up to the commission, the governing body made up of the heads of all the crime families, as to whether he would be allowed to take over the family, or be a marked man for upsetting the order of things without their prior consent. Since his uncle was not a controversial member of the commission, it would be foolish to approach the capos with the idea of eliminating him. But if he did it on his own, he would then have the right to ask the commission for their approval to take over the family and thus become a member of the commission himself. If Tony could ingratiate himself to Mark Ianuzzo and Sal Gamone beforehand, his chances of success would be excellent.

The cooperation of Scott Meeker would be the key to keeping these men's mouths shut. Once the meeting took place, Tony would rely on the lure of money to keep things quiet. For the privilege of giving these men an NFL football game, and thus millions of dollars, Tony would be asking only for their silence in return. In the process, however, he would undoubtedly be softening these men for when they had to make their future decision regarding his fate. It would be his peace offering. Beyond that, the manipulation of something as big as an NFL game would be a signal to these men that they were dealing with a man of power and vision.

"First of all, Tony," Angelo finally said, breaking the stunned silence, "your uncle won't like you meeting with these guys without him knowing, and second, what makes you think they'll meet with you anyway? They don't deal with anyone but your uncle, and when we go to them, they'll probably just laugh in our faces."

"First of all," Tony said, "Uncle Vinny isn't going to know that I'm meeting with them. You guys are going to keep this real quiet. Second, the key is Meeker. He can set it up and keep it confidential. I'll let him in on the action to make sure he does. Third, as far as Ianuzzo and Gamone are concerned, after they get in on the action, they'll be damn glad they met with me, and they'll look forward to doing business with me in the future."

"Why not tell your uncle?" Angelo persisted.

"Because, Ang," Tony said, knowing that although Angelo was his most valuable weapon, at the same time he was possibly his most dangerous obstacle, "I want to surprise Uncle Vinny like I did with this four million dollars. I don't want my uncle getting in the way of what I'm doing when it's ultimately the best thing for him. I want to help him position the family in a role of leadership among all the families. Once we do that, if we all work together, we can take back the drug trade from the Colombians and the Jamaicans."

"But your uncle don't want anything to do with drugs," Angelo pointed out.

Tony sighed, "Yeah, Ang, but that's just for now. My uncle will change his mind about that. I know he will. Believe me, he'll see the value of it.

"I've already talked to my cousin Vinny, Jr., about it," Tony lied, "and me and him know that between the two of us we can bring Uncle Vinny around. Once we do, we'll have everything with the other families in place. You gotta think ahead in this world if you want to make it big."

"It's fucking brilliant," Mike said, and Carl nodded.

"OK," Angelo shrugged. "I just know how your uncle is, Tony. He won't like not knowing about something like this . . . but he's your uncle . . ."

"That's right," Tony said, "blood's thicker than water."

All the men nodded their heads at the wisdom of this remark.

"So when we gonna do it again?" Mike asked.

"Always thinking ahead," Tony said to Mike as their food was laid down before them. Then to Carl he said, "You can learn something from Mikey. See how he's thinking ahead? That's just what I was talking about.

"We'll wait until the Tampa Bay game," Tony said, slurping down raw oysters with red sauce between each sentence. "That'll give me time to set things up with the big guys, and I want to give Logan a couple of weeks to settle down. I want to let things get back to normal for him. This guy right now is like a . . . like a racehorse to us. We want to rest him up good before running him again. Otherwise, he might crack and do something stupid. The head game I'm playing with this guy is the key to everything.

"By the way," Tony said, "so I don't forget. Mikey, remind me tomorrow to have you take a hundred thousand dollars in cash and dump it in Hunter Logan's savings account. I want you to go in there and make a lot of fuss too, demand to see the manager and all that, so people remember you were there."

"You gonna cut Logan in on this?" Mikey said, mystified.

Tony slurped down his last oyster and chuckled. "Yeah, you could say that. That's exactly what I'm gonna do. This way, if Logan gets any ideas about not coming our way in the Tampa game . . . Well, it looks kinda bad for him that someone's dumped a big load of cash in his account. It looks real bad in fact."

The others nodded and fell into their food. Tony Rizzo was handling Hunter Logan masterfully. It thrilled them all to be a part of something so big and so daring. They knew that one day everyone in their world would know the story about how they rigged the NFL games with a big-time quarterback. They each fancied that the part they played in it would give them a place in mob history.

H unter Logan spent his week preparing for the Titans' second game. It was hard work, concentrating on the upcoming game with Cleveland. It seemed that each time he got himself mentally into the Browns' defense, Tony Rizzo would pop into his mind. When he finally boarded the team plane at Kennedy Airport, Hunter breathed a sigh of relief. If Rizzo had planned on talking with Hunter, he'd have done it already. During the flight, Hunter delved into the intricacies of his game plan that he'd overlooked during the week. When they arrived at the hotel in downtown Cleveland, Bert wanted Hunter to go out for dinner with him and some other Titans players.

"No," Hunter said, looking up only briefly from his notes. Upon entering the hotel room, he'd thrown his bag on the bed nearest the window and planted himself at the small desk that sat opposite. "I'm gonna stay here and go over this stuff."

"Come with us," Bert said. "You gotta eat anyway."

"I'll get some room service," Hunter mumbled.

"Man, you're acting weird as hell," Bert said. "You can't let that bullshit in the media get you down."

"I'm not," Hunter said honestly. "I just want to make sure we win this game tomorrow. I want to make sure I'm ready."

"Hunt, we been doing this stuff all week. You're as ready as you'll ever be."

"Nope," Hunter said.

Bert knew his friend well enough to give up.

Hunter studied for a full hour before his phone rang. It was his mother.

"Where are you, Ma?" Hunter asked.

"In the lobby downstairs," she said. "We wanted to surprise you! We drove out this morning."

Cleveland was only about four hours from where Hunter had grown up. With everything that had been going on the past few weeks, he had forgotten to call and see if his family was coming and whether or not they needed tickets. He should have. The Titans weren't playing in Pittsburgh this season, and this was the closest he'd get to his hometown. Now he was in a vise. He wanted to study. He needed to study. But his mother had made the long drive to surprise him.

"Is Henry with you?" Hunter heard himself ask without thinking.

"No," his mother answered quietly, "he had some things to do. I came with Julia and Freddy. I hope it's all right."

"Of course, Mom," Hunter said. Freddy was his sister's husband, a quiet, husky farmer whom Hunter had known since he was a kid and whom he had always liked. "I'm sorry, I didn't mean it to come out that way. I'm glad you came. It was really nice. I should have called you this week to see if you needed tickets."

"We got them from cousin Frank. He's a season ticket holder."

"Sure, I know," Hunter said. "Well, let's see . . . it's six. I've got a meeting at eight, so how about if I come down and take the three of you to dinner?"

"That's fine, Hunter, but we didn't want to disturb you—"

"Come on, Ma, I'll be right down."

Hunter hung up and pulled on his jeans and his boots. He'd been studying in his undershorts and socks. In the lobby, he was swarmed by kids. Each one had a page or two filled with at least a dozen different types of football trading cards bearing his image. Hunter could see his mom, his sister, and her husband over the throng. He smiled apologetically to everyone and said, "OK, guys, one card each. I'll sign one for everybody, but just one."

The kids looked at this as a boon and cheered their hero. Hunter could see his mom smile with pride and settle down to wait until he'd finished. "That was a nice thing you did," she said when she was on his arm and walking out the door with him. "That's why things have gone so well for you, Hunter, you've never changed."

This prompted Hunter to think of the precariousness of his current situation. Had it not been his mother who'd made the remark, he would have laughed openly and bitterly at the irony of what she'd said.

There was a good restaurant close by that Hunter knew from his many trips to Cleveland with the NFL. It was also casual enough so that his family wouldn't feel uncomfortable. Freddy was wearing his work boots and a flannel shirt, and Hunter knew that any place that was fancy enough to have a maitre d' would have made them uneasy. Hunter's presence created a stir the instant they walked into the place. He did his best to act like people weren't ogling him, despite the fact that their young hostess couldn't keep her mouth from hanging open as she led them to a corner booth that Hunter had pointed out to her. They talked about things from home; how the crops were looking, Freddy's bull that won a blue ribbon at the fair in August, and how much money its sperm would bring in. Hunter was painfully aware of how distant his own world was from these people who had once been at the center of his universe.

When their food came, the conversation lagged. They ate like people who worked outdoors for a living. By the end of the meal, Hunter felt the silence draw him, like a rabbit to a snake's eyes, to the familiar subject that any thought of home inevitably brought him to.

"So, Ma," he said, composing his features and wiping his mouth carefully so as not to show any anxiety, "how's Henry?"

The question jarred Hunter's mother in a way that let him know she had expected it but hoped that it would never come.

"Oh, he's fine," she said lightly.

Hunter nodded. "Good," he said quietly, as if he were ready to move on to the subject of cows.

"How's his job?" he asked suddenly, apparently unable to help himself.

Hunter saw his mother's face cloud over and then brighten as if with a new idea. "Well, he's not at the gas station right now, but he's got some good opportunities," she added quickly.

Hunter leaned over to his mother and said in a low voice, "Ma, do you guys need some money?"

Hunter's mother looked across the empty plates at his sister and started to cry quietly. Then, before anyone could say or do anything, she jumped up from the table and rushed off to the ladies' room. Julia followed. Hunter looked at Freddy, whose down-turned face was red.

"Freddy," Hunter said, "what the hell is going on? Come on Freddy, talk to me."

Freddy reluctantly looked up and met Hunter's eyes. "Things is kinda tough on everyone, Hunter," he said as sheepishly as a two-hundred-fifty-pound farmer could.

"Meaning what?"

"Well . . . Julia and I, we do what we can for your ma and Henry, but, well, even with my prize bull . . . well, we ain't on no food stamps anyhow," Freddy said with a note of defiance.

In that one proud statement Hunter saw how bad things were for his family. They were not the kind of people to take hand-outs. They wouldn't stand in a welfare line. They wouldn't buy their food with stamps, even if everyone around them was calling it OK. That's the way they were. Maybe for the first time, Hunter felt the great distance that really separated him from his family. In his world the dilemma was how to hang on to the beach house; in theirs, it was whether or not they would eat and be warm through the winter, or whether the bank was going to come in and take their land away. It was happening all over America. It was the rule now rather than the exception. It was the working people who were suffering, the farmers, the factory workers, the laborers.

Hunter looked at his Rolex. He had only twenty minutes before his meeting. He looked at the hallway where the bathrooms were and supposed his mother would be in there a long time. She wouldn't want to face him now anyway, and it would be easier for her to take what he was leaving if she didn't have to thank him. Hunter pulled his wallet from his back pocket, flagged down their waitress, asked her for a pen, and handed her his gold card to take care of dinner. Then, from an inner fold in the alligator hide, he extracted a folded check. He made it out for the sum of fifty thousand dollars and handed it across the table to Freddy.

"Freddy," Hunter said in a serious tone. "Freddy!"

Freddy finally looked up from the check, his mouth still agape.

"This is between me and you, Freddy," Hunter said, then waited until Freddy nodded. "You know Lance Anderson, the man who runs that River Savings Bank in town?"

Freddy nodded again. The waitress returned with Hunter's credit card, and he signed the bill before speaking again.

"You give this check to Mom and tell her to take it down to Lance Anderson and have him put it into something safe that'll kick out some good interest. You tell her to take that money and use it for all of you whenever she needs it. You tell her . . . you tell her to keep it, Freddy. You tell her it's the right thing to do. It's what she should do, that I'd be hurt bad if she didn't use it. Will you tell her?"

Freddy nodded for a third time, and Hunter rose, tossing his napkin on the table and taking one last look toward the rest rooms.

"Bye, Freddy," Hunter said, shaking his brother-in-law's callused hand. "If I don't see you all tomorrow, I'll know you had to get back in a hurry. Thank Julia and Ma for coming to see me. Tell them I'll win this one tomorrow just for them."

Then without another word, Hunter hustled himself out to the street and made his way back to the hotel for the team meeting.

Rachel had a large bowl of popcorn and a large ice bucket filled with four Diet Cokes in front of her on the coffee table. The security system was turned on. The phone was pulled across the room from the end table and was set on the table next to the supplies. Sara sat next to her on the couch, and together they settled down to watch the game. Rachel liked to have everything right there so she didn't miss a moment of the game. She had never been a football fan. In fact, it was Hunter who'd taught her the game. When she finally knew what was going on, she realized what she'd been missing all these years. It was the most visceral and exciting sport she'd ever seen, all the more because her husband was the focus of everyone's attention and usually the star of the game. To her every game was an emotionally wrenching experience, and although it was Hunter who had the rights to exhaustion the night after a game, she was also glad to finally rest her head following an afternoon of cheering, hollering, and anxiety over whether or not the Titans would prevail.

On this day, in the city of Cleveland six hundred miles away, her husband shone as brightly as in any game he had ever played. The field seemed to belong to Hunter. He spent the afternoon directing receivers down field, avoiding swarms of defending Browns, and when all else failed, he would simply run the ball like a deer, dodging, leaping, and accelerating with a grace that was almost poetic. Rachel had seen enough football to know that on this day, everything was right for Hunter. He could do no wrong. At one point, down near the Titans' end zone, he threw a pass that was tipped up by a defender. Instead of watching it fall to the ground, Hunter, to the amazement of everyone including the Cleveland Browns players, dashed across the line of scrimmage and caught what was technically his own pass. Then he sidestepped a linebacker, lowered his shoulder, and ran over the Browns free safety to score a touchdown. The announcers roared with praise. The thrill of it all made Rachel forget the bigger problems in their life.

"I can't remember the last time I've seen a football player play such an inspired game," Bob Costas gushed from the announcers' booth. "Hunter Logan can do no wrong! It's like his whole life is charmed, and he's just daring someone out there to try to stop him!"

There was more, but Rachel stopped hearing it. Suddenly she was cold.

"What's wrong, Mommy?" Sara asked, sensing her mother stiffen beside her.

Rachel gave her daughter a startled look, as though she had forgotten Sara was there at all.

"Nothing, dear," Rachel said, "nothing at all."

Ellis Cook sat nervously pulling at his tie. He was waiting outside Duncan Fellows's office. He supposed he could live without the Bureau, the stuffy hierarchy of rank, the plush decor that was so much wasted taxpayers' money. Cook smiled to himself. He didn't begrudge those above him the finer things in life. All he wanted was his fair crack at getting a taste of the same. Well, no one in their right mind could say Cook wasn't getting the chance. He thought of all the things he could say to Zulaff to buy more time. Something was rotten in his group, that was for sure. But just how rotten was uncertain. If he played that card, he might look like a whiner. No, Cook would just play it straight and hope Zulaff would give him just a little more. Damn, it bothered him just being there now. He should be out tailing Rizzo.

But on the other side of that door were Fellows and Miles Zulaff, probably discussing just what Cook's future held. Cook wondered how Fellows was playing it in there. He knew Fellows wanted to be rid of him, if for no other reason than the man flat-out didn't like him. But just how far Fellows was willing to go remained to be seen. The way things were going, Cook suspected that Fellows would have to do little more than stand back and watch. The Bureau liked results, and it liked them fast. The director was a sworn enemy of organized crime. It was his pet project. Cook, it appeared, had killed the pet.

Finally Fellows's secretary was buzzed. She picked up the phone, listened, and then said to Cook, "You can go in now, Agent Cook."

Cook stood up and straightened his tie one last time, then marched through the heavy oak door to meet his destiny. The two senior men were sitting at one end of the conference table, where Fellows held his Saturday meetings. Zulaff stood to shake Cook's hand. Fellows followed cue, but only as a perfunctory gesture.

"Sit down, sit down," Zulaff said warmly.

Cook hadn't had much contact with Miles Zulaff before, even though it was he who had been directly responsible for selecting Cook to head up his task force. Cook wondered whether Zulaff might not want to try to distance himself from the whole task force idea if it appeared that Cook was going to fail. Zulaff, however, seemed quite at ease with Cook.

"I understand things have been a little slow," Zulaff said in an even and easy way.

Cook nodded and said, "We've had some setbacks, sir, and the climate is tough right now."

"I thought things were ripe with Tony Rizzo. Isn't that why you were so in favor of assailing the Mondolffi organization? But now I see from this file," Zulaff said, tapping the file that lay open in front of him, "that you've recently suspended observation of Rizzo altogether."

"That's right, sir," Cook said, trying to wet the inside of his mouth. "We just weren't getting anywhere at all with Rizzo. We're pretty sure he was on to us. A couple of times he shook our tail, and the conversations he did have on his private phones were either personal or spoken in code."

Zulaff raised an eyebrow and said, "Any ideas on why that might be?"

"I can't say for certain, sir, so I'd rather not make any rash speculations. But in my opinion it was clear that Tony Rizzo was simply waiting us out. When he did have to make a move, he was able to lose us using intricate and well-planned deceptions. It wasn't just chance when we lost him."

Zulaff nodded and seemed to consider what Cook was saying.

"I can get to these people if you can give me more time, sir," Cook said, breaking the silence. "I'm sure if you can give me until the end of the year, I can give you something concrete."

Zulaff looked at Fellows. Cook couldn't read his immediate supervisor's expression, but he seemed to be communicating something silently to Zulaff.

"Well," Zulaff said, "I'll be candid with you, Cook. There are a lot of people who think this has been one big bomb."

Cook glanced at Fellows, who was grinning like a cheshire cat.

"The Bureau hasn't operated like this before, as you know," Zulaff continued. "This is an experiment, and it seems that it's coming up short. I'll give you until the first of November, but no more. With the resources we've put into this, it just doesn't make sense to keep going without making even the slightest inroad. If we don't have something by then, I'm closing you down."

"I think that even by then I'll have something for you, sir," Cook said optimistically.

"I hope so, Cook," said Zulaff. "Believe me, I hope so."

CHAPTER

IIII IIIIIIIIIIIIIIIIIIIIIIIIIIIIIIIIIIIIIIIIIIIIIIII

I t was ten days before Scott Meeker could arrange the meeting with Mark Ianuzzo and Sal Gamone. Meeker was eager to help Tony when he learned that the young capo regime was going to deliver an NFL game to him. Besides being owner of The Star casino, Meeker was a notorious gambler, and the thought of getting in on a fixed game and an easy quarter million, his typical Sunday bet, was too much to pass up. Also, he was a man who knew the underworld as well as anyone. He knew that Tony Rizzo's star was on the rise, and a favor right now could be something of great value in the future.

The meeting was arranged in a suite at the Waldorf-Astoria hotel. Tony arrived with Angelo and Carl at five minutes to twelve. Meeker was waiting for them. He was a large man and easy to spot. He wore a red jacket over a beige shirt and pants. His hairpiece was jet black to match the thin mustache that was a lonely line in the middle of a reddened face. Heavy gold bracelets and chains hung from the man like a pro athlete. His appearance was almost comical, and Tony would have laughed if not for Meeker's influence and usefulness.

"Tony!" Meeker said with a beaming smile and an outstretched, bejeweled hand.

Tony shook the fat man's soft, tiny hand and smiled thinly.

"Angelo! Good to see you," Meeker said to Quatrini.

"This is Carl," Angelo said. "Carl Lutz."

Meeker nodded and said to Tony, "I'm sorry, these guys will have to wait for you down here."

Tony shrugged and pointed his men toward the bar. "I'll be down," he said to them.

This was what he had expected. He was not Ianuzzo's or Gamone's equal. He wasn't the head of his family. They would each have a man with them at the meeting, but not him. He would go into their presence unprotected and unarmed. At the door he was frisked by two men. A big lug with thick, shaded glasses took his Beretta from him while a tall, lean man with an ugly scar across his angry face ran his hands over Tony's body. Meeker smiled apologetically while the frisking went on, but Tony was unmoved. It was the way things were. One day soon he would be above this sort of treatment. The big lug motioned him into the dining room where an elaborate lunch had been laid out for the four men. Both Ianuzzo and Gamone remained seated as Tony entered. He could see from the gnarled black shells stacked on their plates that they had already begun working on the large bowl filled with crushed ice and oysters on the half shell. They did, however, shake hands and greet him warmly.

"Tony," said Gamone, a plain-looking man in his mid-sixties, sporting a dab of bloodred cocktail sauce in the corner of his mouth, "it's good to see you. When was the last time? Your cousin's graduation party?"

Tony nodded. His uncle had thrown a spectacular affair for Vincent, Jr., upon his graduation from Wharton. All the most important men in the city had been invited. This reference to his family made Tony uneasy.

"Sit down, Tony," Ianuzzo said, waving to a chair at the end of the table. He, too, was an unremarkable character, small in stature, handsome and dark-skinned, dressed in a simple gray three-piece suit that one would expect to see on an older man like Gamone. Ianuzzo was only just past forty. "Sit down and eat with us. We can talk after we eat."

Tony sat at one end of the table and Meeker placed himself on the other end, nearest the two capos. The effect was to isolate Tony in a subtle way. What was said during that lunch Tony would never remember. He could think of nothing but the proposal he was about to make to these men, and whether or not it would suffice in convincing them to ignore the protocol that normally dictated they inform his uncle of his activities. Finally there was espresso and a plate of fruit. The uniformed waiters from the hotel staff were cleared out, and the two bodyguards closed the doors to the dining room as they themselves left.

"So, Tony," Sal Gamone said after stirring and sipping his hot drink, "what can we do for you?"

"It's what I want to do for you, Mr. Gamone," Tony said, reaching for his water glass and hoping the slight shake in his hand was not noticeable. Both men met this statement with silent stares.

"I simply have something to offer that I believe can benefit all of us," Tony continued, "without harming each other in any way. I—I just think it is good practice to share our fortunes with good friends around us."

Both men nodded as though this certainly was a noble idea.

"What is it you have for us?" the younger capo said.

Encouraged, Tony said, "I have the ability to determine the outcome of some professional football games. I know both of you have gambling interests just as we do. It's as simple as adjusting the line to unbalance the books. I've made over four million dollars so far."

Tony let that sink in. He watched as the two older men digested what he'd said. They were quiet for several minutes, each one calculating in his mind the risks and benefits of proceeding. Meeker sat between them, flushed and perspiring lightly from his vigorous assault on the food only moments before. He smiled at Tony confidently. But then, he had nothing to lose and much to gain.

"I'm concerned," Gamone said finally with a frown, "as to why it is you are offering us this gift and not your uncle."

Tony cleared his throat. He felt naked and vulnerable without his gun and wished he had it.

"I, uh, my uncle and I have been having a series of disagreements lately as to just how the family business should operate. He has not been agreeable to mutually beneficial ventures with other families that I have suggested to him in the past. But I think that is the direction we must go in. I think cooperation will benefit us all, and . . ."

Tony stopped talking. These men didn't like talking. The less said the better, and he had probably already said more than was necessary.

"What do you want in return from us?" Ianuzzo asked pointedly.

"Beyond keeping this venture between the three of us," Tony paused, "I only seek your friendship."

"Friendship is a big thing," Gamone said, sipping his espresso.

Tony hesitated. Respect was good, but he'd shown enough of that to get his point across. Now he had to show some balls.

"So is four million dollars," he said flatly.

Both men scowled at this.

"Tony, I think we need a few moments to consider what you've said," Gamone told him.

Tony got up and let himself and Scott Meeker out before closing the large mahogany dining-room doors behind them. Together they went into the adjoining living room and sat down. Tony remained calm on the outside in a way that would have impressed the two men in the other room, but his mind was reeling. He had just put himself at the mercy of these two men. If they disclosed to his uncle what he was up to, it would be the end. He didn't have the strength to fight his uncle. Even most of his own soldiers would side against him in a battle like that. Even, he suspected, Angelo. Although he spent most of his time with Tony and was extremely loyal, Angelo had some old-fashioned notions about the family. He would never go against Tony's uncle.

If his uncle died, Tony knew he could count on Angelo in the struggle for control of the family. But to take on the existing capo was tantamount to suicide and everyone knew it. The only way Tony could take over the family was to hit his uncle before he knew what was happening. His recent success, which had left his uncle greatly pleased, would give Tony the advantage of surprise. But once his uncle was killed, the other families would traditionally go to war with the usurper. Ianuzzo and Gamone could change that.

The scar-faced man came in and told Tony that they would see him. He entered the dining room but didn't bother to sit down.

"We would like to accept your gift, Tony," Mark Ianuzzo said with a warm smile, "but on a condition . . ."

"Certainly," said Tony, unable to hide his relief.

"We would like to watch a game be controlled first," Ianuzzo said, "to see how it's done. We will put up some personal money, both Sal and I, as I assume Scott is going to do. We will see how that turns out . . . and if it succeeds and it looks good to us, then we'll move some big numbers around. It's not that we don't trust you, Tony, it's just that these things are easier said than done. We want to see it first. If you can do it once, then you can do it twice.

"If this all works out," the older man continued without a smile, "then we see no reason to interfere with your family business. We look at it simply as a gesture of good faith and friendship."

It was a bad week for Hunter. The Titans lost their road game to Miami, and Hunter felt the loss was due to the three interceptions he'd thrown. There were two types of athletes in pro ball. One lost and looked around him for the reason; the other lost and looked within himself for the reason. Hunter was one of the latter. This made him a natural leader on the field, but it meant a lot of sleepless nights the week after a loss. At first, Rachel couldn't understand this. "It's one game," she would tell him. "You didn't lose it by yourself. There are fifty other guys out there with you."

Now, however, she knew better. She knew it was because he cared so much when his team lost that he could help them so much to win. When things were on the line, everyone knew that Hunter Logan could be counted on to leave everything he had on the field. No one seemed to suffer more when the Titans lost.

If a loss wasn't enough to haunt him, Hunter's shoulder was acting up. And if those two things weren't enough, there was always Tony Rizzo to think about. Hunter had imagined that the longer Rizzo remained silent, the better he would feel. This was not so. Hunter had not forgotten Rachel's words about people like Rizzo not going away so easily, and the more time that went by, the more anxious Hunter became. He couldn't go anywhere without looking over his shoulder. Every time he pulled into a parking lot, he expected to see a van racing up next to him and the goon squad popping out to surround him. At every intersection Hunter would nervously scan the traffic around him. Every noise in the night woke him. It got so bad that he found himself wishing Rizzo would just appear so it could be over with.

Because Hunter was so acutely aware, he saw Carl before Carl saw him. He was stuck at a traffic light, making a left off the Sunrise Highway. It was not uncommon for him to have to wait at this spot for three changes of the light on Wednesdays. Because of his long post-practice film sessions in the middle of the week, he usually did not leave for home until six o'clock, and the traffic was always bad.

Carl was walking slowly toward him down the middle of the median that divided the traffic. His size and gait made him stand out from the shabby old guy selling papers, the Asian woman holding a white bucket of roses, and the other occupants of this small territory set between the opposing lanes of the rush-hour traffic.

Hunter instinctively ducked when he saw Carl scanning the traffic. He felt like a fool when he heard the thug's beefy knuckles rapping on the window. Hunter looked up. What else could he do?

"Let me in, man," Hunter heard Carl say through the glass. "You fucking better."

Hunter hit the power locks and watched helplessly as Carl crossed in front of the Town Car and climbed in through the passenger-side door.

"Go to Atlantic Beach," Carl said. "Tony wants to see you. I'll tell you how to get there when we get over the bridge."

Then Carl reached over and changed the radio station to KROC. AC/DC was playing "Hells Bells."

"Cool," Carl said, pumping up the volume and settling back into the leather seat as if Hunter wasn't even there. Carl was comfortable with who he was. By sheer luck he had been taken under the wing of a powerful Mafia assassin. Carl had been transformed. From the clothes he wore to the way he talked, almost nothing remained of his former self, the goofy, steroid-using gym rat that ran errands and numbers for Jimmy the Squid. Carl was a member of an elite club, not just a street thug.

Right now Carl was on a kind of probation. If his work and his loyalty impressed the others, he would be in. Angelo assured him that he was talking with Tony about it personally and that he had taken Carl on as his protégé. He knew that one day, maybe in a month, maybe in a year, or two years, Tony Rizzo would come to him and give him a very difficult task. The completion of that task would mark his entry into the family. Carl could not wait for that day. He knew he would be worthy.

"Stay on the rotary and head east," Carl said when they'd finally crossed the bridge.

"Now turn at this light and go all the way to the beach."

Hunter did as he was told.

"Park it over there," Carl said, pointing with a thick finger. "Tony's on the beach. Get out and follow that path."

Hunter looked over his shoulder as he made his way down the path that led through the dunes. Carl followed. Just past the dunes, Tony Rizzo sat on a worn bench, his eyes shaded by a pair of dark sunglasses. He was slumped in his seat with his hands in his pockets and his feet crossed in front of him. He looked out at the ocean. The surf crashed loudly against the shore and gulls wheeled in the air, landing momentarily to tear a rotting piece of flesh from a large fish carcass. For years to come, Hunter would associate the pungent ocean smells of Atlantic Beach with Tony Rizzo.

"Sit down," Rizzo said without looking up.

Hunter sat and glanced over his shoulder to see Carl take his position behind them a few yards away.

"Now," Rizzo said, "isn't this nice? Isn't this a nice way for you and I to be doing business?"

Hunter didn't say anything as his anger and frustration started to boil inside him.

"This is how you and I will meet from now on," Rizzo said, still intent on the seascape in front of him. "What I did before the Detroit game was to make sure you and I were on the same wavelength. Now I know we are.

"By the way," he continued, chuckling, "I got a fucking laugh when you tried to throw an interception right into that Detroit guy's hands and he dropped it! But you did good, though. I was pleased with the way you handled yourself.

"Oh, that reminds me," Rizzo said, reaching down beside him and lifting a brown paper bag from the sand. "This is for you." Hunter looked at the bag that Rizzo held out for him.

"It's ten thousand dollars," Rizzo said. "A little post-game token of my appreciation. Go ahead, take it. You earned it."

"I don't want your money," Hunter said with disgust. "I'm not taking a cent from you. You and I aren't in business together."

Rizzo laughed, "Oh, yes, we are. We are in business. In fact, this money here is just a little something extra. We already dumped a hundred grand into your bank account a few days after you threw the Detroit game.

"Yeah, that's right," Rizzo continued. "It looks kind of bad for you, I know, throwing a game like that and then having one of my men walk right into your bank and make a big fuss about dumping that kind of money into your account. But I didn't want you to think you could walk away from me. No one does that. I say when things are over and when they're not, and right now, they're not. So go ahead and take the money."

Hunter sat staring straight ahead with his arms crossed in front of his chest.

"Take the fucking money!" Rizzo said threateningly.

Hunter took the bag and set it down on his lap.

"Look at it," Rizzo said. "Look at the fucking money."

Hunter pulled a tightly wrapped stack of twenties from the bag.

In a calm voice Rizzo said, "You work for me, Logan, and if I decide to give you something extra for the effort, you take it and be fucking thankful.

"I said fucking thankful!" Rizzo said, turning his face toward Hunter.

Hunter slowly stuffed the stack of bills back into the bag.

"Thanks," he muttered, spitting on the ground in front of them.

"Good," Rizzo said. "Now, you're favored to win this weekend by six, but I don't want you to make it by more than three points. You got that?"

Hunter said nothing as he watched Rizzo's eyes move behind the dark lenses.

"You see, because even though I'm acting all nice with you, and even though I'm cutting you in on some of the action, the same shit goes . . .

"In other words, if you fuck up, I'll not only end your career, I got some sick fucker that works for me who loves little girls—just like the one you got."

Blind rage flooded Hunter's brain and he lunged for Rizzo's throat. Hunter could feel the soft flesh between his fingers and the ridged tube of the windpipe as he tried to crush it beneath his thumbs.

Carl jerked Hunter's head back by the hair at the base of his neck. He felt the air rush out of his body. Carl had him in a choke hold and Rizzo was standing in front of him, rubbing his throat. Rizzo hauled back and punched Hunter in the stomach, forcing the air from his body a second time. Carl increased the pressure on his neck and Hunter collapsed.

Rizzo had pulled his Beretta from its holster and jammed the gun into Hunter's gasping mouth.

"Now," Rizzo bellowed with hatred, "you got that now, don't you? Because I mean what I say. You do it, or you're fucked, and so is your family. You got that?"

Hunter closed his eyes and nodded.

"And never," Rizzo screamed, "Never do you touch me again!"

Rizzo jammed the gun deeper into Hunter's mouth and cruelly twisted it around. Hunter felt the pistol's sight tearing up the soft tissue on the roof of his mouth. He tasted blood. Then Rizzo yanked the gun out, chipping the backs of Hunter's front teeth.

"Come on," Rizzo said to Carl.

Carl let Hunter fall to the ground. The men walked slowly away, leaving Hunter to choke in the sand.

When Cook saw Hunter Logan sitting alone on the bench with his head in his hands, it was all he could do to keep from running over and cuffing him on the spot. This was the break he had been waiting for! Cook could see the headlines now. What he was about to uncover would be talked about for years to come. It was bigger than Art Schlester, bigger than the Boston University basketball scandal. He would not only bring down one of the country's biggest crime organizations, he'd throw in a superstar as well. Cook knew who Hunter Logan was. It didn't surprise Cook that Logan was involved. He'd seen it time and time again with these professional athletes. He'd seen it firsthand, the drugs, the guns, the gang rapes, the hookers—they were into it all, athletes were. And it pissed Cook off, too. These were the same guys whose pictures hung on the bedroom walls of kids across the country. They were respected, admired, idolized.

And Hunter Logan was supposed to be one of the best role models. Cook had read about him, a hardworking guy who had grown up on a farm and still did charity work for farmers in need; and that was only one of the many charities that he was involved in. Every time Cook turned around, he saw Hunter Logan's face or heard Hunter

Logan's voice. The guy was on billboards and TV. He was in the newspapers and on the radio. When Cook saw something like this it made him want to spit.

"Charities my ass," Cook mumbled under his breath.

A gust from the ocean blew some sand up into his face and he wiped it off with the back of his sleeve. When he looked up, Hunter Logan was on the move. Cook packed his camera with the zoom lens into his duffel bag and scrambled down the side of the dune, through the sea grass, and onto the concrete walk that led back to the street. He kept himself distant from Hunter Logan so he could watch without being noticed; it was now only curiosity. He really should be back in his car and following Rizzo to wherever he was off to next. But something about Hunter Logan attracted him. It was like the big one that swam lazily under your boat just past your line. You had to watch it swim until it disappeared into the murky depths of the water. Hunter Logan was a big fish.

But Cook would not take him today. He could do that any time. He had the pictures of the two together. He had a shot of Logan with the money in his hand. He could implicate Logan with the mob and their gambling and end his career. Of course, Cook didn't really want Logan. He was of no value without Rizzo. Ending an athlete's career wouldn't put him any closer to D.C. But bringing down Rizzo with implications of a scandal within the closely guarded world of the NFL, now that would give Cook some clout.

As Cook watched Hunter Logan's Town Car pull away from the curb, he thought about all this. Logan was the key. He could simply threaten to destroy Hunter Logan, thereby securing the quarterback's cooperation in taking down Rizzo.

If he got Logan to help him, he could create an airtight case against Rizzo. Once he had Rizzo, Cook was certain that the whole Mondolffi organization would soon follow. Rizzo was too egotistical to sacrifice himself for the good of others. What Cook needed to insure Logan's help was leverage. If he was wrong about Logan's involvement with Rizzo, then Logan might set off all sorts of bells and whistles within the league, and the media, the mob, and the Bureau would be certain to hear them. Fellows would end his operation instantly, and Rizzo would run for cover again. If, however, Logan was really on the take, he would fold under Cook's pressure.

Cook needed to make sure . . . and he had a strong feeling he'd know if he was right after watching Logan's performance this coming Sunday.

H unter didn't have to tell Rachel that he'd been contacted by Rizzo again. She knew the moment she saw his face when he walked through the door. All week he'd been low. His performance in Miami and his aching shoulder had revitalized the media criticism of the pre-season. Now he didn't even say hello to her. Sara jumped on him, screaming, "Daddy! Daddy!" and led him by the hand into the playroom. Hunter went as if under a spell. Rachel followed and watched as Sara sat him down on a tiny chair next to her table and began to lay out a pretend tea party.

Sara chattered away, completely unaware that anything was wrong with her father. She pretended to pour tea from a pink plastic pot and then paused to dig a rubber croissant out from underneath her plastic sink, placed it on a plate, and set it before him, asking if he wanted jam. The expression on Hunter's face was dull. His eyes were glassy and he responded to Sara in a monotone. He was trying his best to be normal. It made Rachel want to cry.

"Honey," Rachel said to Sara as she entered the room, "why don't you let Daddy sit down at the big table in the kitchen and have a drink before dinner? You can watch a tape while we're eating."

Sara had already eaten a grilled-cheese sandwich, one of the few meals she would even consider these days. She frowned at the notion of ending her tea party.

"Come on, honey," Rachel said, coaxing, "Daddy's had a very hard day and he needs to relax. He'll play with you after dinner.

Why don't you go in the other room now, and you can put on your new *Beauty and the Beast* tape."

"Yeah! *Beauty and the Beast*! And can I have some ice cream, too?" Sara asked, sensing that she held some kind of advantage.

"Yes," Rachel said, leading her into the TV room.

"Julie," Rachel yelled into the kitchen, "will you please bring Sara a dish of ice cream?"

When Rachel returned, Hunter was sitting just as she'd left him, with his knees tucked up close to his chest and absently turning his plastic teacup over and over on the little table.

"Hunt?" she said.

He looked at her as though he hadn't noticed her until then. "Yeah?" he said quietly.

"You OK?"

"No."

Rachel walked over to him and he wrapped his arms around the backs of her knees, burying his face in her thighs. She reached down and held his head tightly. He moved it slowly back and forth in a silent no. For a time they said nothing.

"We should tell someone," she said finally.

He seemed to be thinking about it, then said, "We've been through this."

"I know we have," she said, "but look what it's doing to you."

"I'll be OK. I just have to get through it. I just have to get through Sunday. How many more times can they try to do it?" he said. "It has to end."

"We're making close to a quarter of a million dollars a week," he said, reminding himself just as much as her. "Just this season. I just have to get through this season."

"But what if something bad happens?" Rachel said.

"What? Like what? All I have to do is shave the games. What could happen bad?"

"What if you couldn't shave the game?" she said. "What if something happened? Like last time . . ."

She was referring to the way his team had almost scored at the end of the game and taken away the point spread.

"I can control the game," he said, not sounding all that confident. "I can throw interceptions. I can fumble the ball. I can cause a delay of game. I control the game more than anyone in that stadium. Nothing's going to happen. I'll be all right."

"I just say forget the money, Hunter," Rachel said. "We can live without the money."

Hunter let a long time pass. He was thinking about what she'd said and about all the things he'd said to her after the Detroit game, when she'd first found out. They were all still true.

"I can't," he said finally.

"Do you want a drink?" she said, pulling away and raising him up.

He looked up at her from his small seat. "Don't be mad," he said. "Look at me, Rachel. Don't be mad."

"I'm not," she said, "but if you're not going to tell someone about it, then let's not talk about it anymore. Not right now. Let's just have a drink and dinner. We can put Sara to bed and watch a movie. Like you said, we'll get through this game and a few more and it will be over. This can be your last year. You can retire. Your shoulder . . ."

Hunter nodded and stood up. He put his hand on the back of her shoulder and followed her out into the kitchen.

That night Hunter lay awake until finally he got up, shuffled through the dark to their green marble bathroom, and found a Halcyon in one of the many prescription bottles that filled his black leather shaving kit. Within a half hour Hunter was sleeping.

It was nearly four in the morning when Rachel's screams woke him from his drug-induced sleep.

"What? What?" he yelled almost angrily at her.

He looked. She was sitting up but still sleeping. She was pulling her cheeks down with the palms of her hands, and it gave her eyes a sunken, ghoulish look. Tears streamed down her face. "No, no, no-o-ooo," she moaned. Hunter shook her until she awoke.

"Hunter, they're here," she said wildly. "I saw them! Where's Sara? I saw them!"

This scared the hell out of Hunter. He looked at the control panel for the security system on the wall next to the bed, trying to think straight. There were no flashing lights, no alarms, nothing, only the soft, harmless light that fell into the room from the full moon that had risen late in the sky and now hung just over the tall trees that protected their home. He looked through the mullioned window and out into the front yard. There were no strange cars, no

shadows lurking about, only the luxurious rolling lawn and the finely trimmed shrubs amid the heavy old trees whose leaves the wind
rustled peacefully. Reason told him no one could be there, but
Rachel's cries couldn't keep his heart and stomach from constrict-
ing with fright.

"No," Hunter said to her calmly but firmly. "No one's here,
honey. No one's here."

"Where's Sara?" Rachel said. She was starting to come around,
but she was still nearly hysterical.

"She's sleeping," Hunter said.

"Go check her, Hunter," Rachel implored. "Go make sure."

Hunter got up out of bed and crossed the hall to Sara's room. She
was sleeping soundly, undisturbed. Hunter brushed the hair back
from her beautiful face and kissed her cheek. When he returned to
his bedroom, fresh tears were flowing from his wife's face.

"Honey," he said in a pleading tone, "honey, don't. Everything is
OK. Everything's going to be fine."

"I dreamed they came for us," she moaned. "I dreamed they were
here. I dreamed they wanted Sara . . ."

"No, no," he said, holding her and rubbing her back in big, slow
circles. "No, they don't want Sara, or us. It's just money. They want the
games, for the money. They don't care about us. It will be all right. It
will be over soon. I promise, honey. It will all be over soon . . ."

Cook followed Rizzo and Carl by way of the homing device. Rizzo
dropped off Carl at his car, which he'd left on a side street near where
he'd waited for Hunter Logan. Rizzo then went straight to his own
apartment and, Cook assumed, began preparations for whatever
evening activities he had planned. Cook decided to give himself a
reprieve from his relentless schedule of work tailing Rizzo, and
grabbed a few hours' sleep. Today was a breakthrough. He was sure. In
fact, the entire week had been unusually productive. Cook was beginning to think that his perseverance with Rizzo was going to pay off.

He'd seen Rizzo go into the Waldorf on Monday and waited
around after he'd left to see just who was important enough for him
to leave Carl and Angelo waiting in the lobby. It was only fifteen minutes after Tony had departed before Mark Ianuzzo and Sal Gamone
quietly left the hotel with their respective bodyguards and climbed

into waiting limousines that sped off through the Manhattan streets. There was also a loudly dressed man who Cook didn't recognize, but who he later learned was the owner of The Star casino in Atlantic City.

Cook took photos of all these characters in their different poses at the Waldorf. He would add them to the file that he was putting together in his room at home. He'd set up a mini-headquarters for himself there. His notes and photographs were starting to add up to something that he knew would eventually lead to the downfall of the Mondolffi crime family. Right now he was also the only one who knew about it, and he imagined that the hints of success he was getting were a direct result of his secrecy. It bothered him that there was a leak somewhere in his organization. It was something that he knew would not just go away, and he knew he had to fix it. But the truth was, if he didn't get something on Rizzo fast, there would be no need to worry about it. His task force would be dissolved, and whoever the rat was would be moved into some other area of the Bureau.

It burned Cook to think that one of his own could be bought like that, but it wouldn't be the first time. Crooked cops were as common as crooked citizens, Cook knew that. He'd seen it plenty. Being a cop, in fact, had allowed him to see more of it than most people. The Bureau, like any other kind of police force, kept its dirty laundry to itself whenever possible. Crooked cops were usually just asked to leave without their pension. Only in the most extreme cases, when there was an airtight case, would an agent be punished for his ill deeds. It was something that was just too hard to prove. So much of what the Bureau did required its agents to go undercover or trade information with existing crime elements that it was often difficult to know where and when to draw the line. Thus it was always easier, when it became obvious that an agent was compromising himself, just to let him or her go and be done with them. For anyone who'd worked his whole life in the agency, being booted without a pension was just as bad as going to some federal prison anyway.

Cook parked his rented car in a garage around the corner from his apartment and walked back home, enjoying the balmy late September evening. When he walked through his door, Esther and Natasha were at the kitchen table working on a report for Natasha's history class. Actually, Esther was fulfilling the role of companion more than anything. Cook knew that although the woman was mentally as sharp as a tack, she had never gone past the eighth grade in school. But he was certain that her silent interest in Natasha's prattle about the Revolution was an invaluable study aid for a girl whose mother was dead and whose father was working almost twenty hours a day.

"Daddy!" Natasha shrieked when she saw him.

Cook opened his arms and his daughter filled them. Esther looked up at him over the rims of an old pair of ill-fitting reading glasses. Cook smiled at her as warmly as he could. He knew Esther was mad at him for his absence these past few weeks. There was no way he could explain it to her and nothing he could do, so he simply made the best of it and smiled at her as much as she would allow. Cook took over for Esther, who grumbled her way out of the kitchen and into the bedroom that she shared with Natasha. Natasha was too excited about the time she was getting to spend with her father to notice her grumbling aunt. Another way, Cook thought, that the little girl was so much like her mother. Naomi had always seen only the bright side of things, even when she had had to look through the gloom of poverty and oppression to do it.

Cook explained to Natasha that the work he was doing at the moment was extremely important, but that soon, very soon, he figured he would be able to spend more time with her again. He assured her that was what he desperately wanted. They worked on her report some more, then played eight games of checkers while eating an entire pint of vanilla ice cream together before Cook finally told Natasha to get ready for bed. She frowned but did as she was told, and Cook read to her from *Charlotte's Web* before tucking her into bed.

Esther, who had waited in their small living room while Cook put Natasha to bed, looked like she had something to say. Cook sat in the big chair opposite the couch and bowed his head to take his medicine from the tough old lady.

"Ellis," she said in a calm way that surprised Cook, "I want to ask you something."

"Yes, Esther," Cook said looking up, "of course."

"There was an old woman down the street who got killed just two days ago." Esther paused to see what kind of impression that made on Cook. "She was an old woman, like me, and she lived alone. Almost like me. They broke into her apartment late at night, and they killed that old lady for her TV."

Now Esther looked at him with her dark, piercing eyes in a way that made him feel he should know what the meaning of all this was, but he didn't.

"Yes, Esther?"

"So, if you're gonna be out until all hours of the night every damn night, doing God only knows what . . . Well, then I want some protection."

"Esther," Cook said in a pleading tone, "that's why I carry my phone with me wherever I am, so if you need me, all you got to do is call. I carry it for that reason alone. I'm never very far."

"This is a damned mean and ugly city you got us living in, Ellis," she said with a firm nod of her head, "and I want some protection."

Cook thought about this for a moment, then said, "Aunt Esther, do you want a gun? Is that what you're saying?"

"That or a damn big dog," she said spiritedly, "and they don't allow dogs in this building."

Cook couldn't help chuckling. The notion of his aunt with a gun was, well, . . . actually, when Cook thought about what it took to shoot another human being, he supposed that Esther would benefit as much as anyone from having a gun. He could see that she had taken his chuckle as a sign that he was not taking her seriously, so he quickly added, "Of course, of course, Aunt Esther, you can have a gun if you feel like you need it."

"I do," she said with finality.

Cook nodded and went to the top shelf of the closet in his room. He returned with a nickel-plated .38.

"Where do you plan on keeping it?" Cook asked. "I don't want Natasha knowing where this is. I don't want her touching it."

"I plan to keep it under the mattress," Esther said with a tight little smile. "I'm surprised, you being so good about it," she added.

Cook smiled. He was giving in rather easily to his longtime household nemesis, but he felt it was the least he could do. He knew Esther well enough to know that if he didn't give her a gun, she'd go out and get one somehow. She was that way. Once she got the notion in her head that she and Natasha were in danger staying here alone so much, and that a gun would make them safe, well . . . Cook doubted there were many forces on the good earth that could stop her.

"These bullets are called glazier points," Cook explained, loading the shells carefully into each of their five chambers. "They explode on impact, so they will pretty much kill whatever they hit. And if you miss, they won't go through the wall and hurt someone you don't intend to shoot.

"Not that I think you'll need it," he added. "Those kind of things happen, but they're rare, even in a city like this."

Cook looked up to see if Esther was getting all this. She was, so he handed her the loaded weapon. "Thank you, Ellis," she said, and patted him on the shoulder as she passed by on her way to bed.

When Cook put his tired head down on his pillow that night, it was the first time in a long while that he felt like he'd had a good day on the job front as well as on the home front. He was very much looking forward to the day when that was the rule, rather than the exception.

Tony's infatuation with Camille Carter was beginning to wane. Her spirited insolence, which had at first intrigued him, was now beginning to annoy him. And his notion that she was the most beautiful woman he'd ever seen was also growing old. More and more he noticed that other women would catch his eye in the way they always had before he'd fallen in with Camille. He was growing restless. But the fact that Camille had essentially moved in with him, although they had never discussed it, combined with the fact that he still wanted to keep her for business purposes because of her easy access to the team, meant that getting rid of her would be no easy task. The time would come, however, when he would simply tell her to leave and then change his locks.

Because of this Tony couldn't help himself in treating Camille a little more harshly than she had already become accustomed to. It meant that his roughness began to go beyond the bedroom, where she had shown a great fondness for such treatment since their first encounter. One thing that particularly annoyed Tony was Camille's refusal to keep her nose out of his business. It seemed the more he told her to butt out, the more interested she became.

Often he had to slam the bedroom door in her face to keep her there when he was discussing business with his cronies in the living room. She would respond by throwing shoes, and even a lamp once, at the closed door. Also, Camille refused to obey his direct command that she not answer his telephone. She complained that she now got calls at this number as well, and would regularly disregard his demands. Tony had taken to cuffing her harmlessly when this happened, and a fight always ensued. He was tired of all this. The thrill was no longer there, and the resultant sex, for him, was becoming more of an exercise in anger than anything else. He knew it wouldn't be long before he bedded someone else, and the thought that he'd have to hide his activities rankled him.

Their relationship had deteriorated so much that Tony actually winced when he asked Camille to get them two fifty-yard-line tickets and Carl a locker-room pass for the upcoming Titans game against the Colts. He knew she was going to give him grief about asking her. She'd said more than once that the only time he treated her with any respect at all anymore was when he wanted something. It was a mystery to Tony why Camille would continue to live on at his apartment if she really felt that way.

"So that's why you're taking me out tonight?" she crooned. "I knew it was something. It's never just to be together anymore, Tony. There's always a catch with you."

"That's not why we're going out tonight," he said angrily. "The day I need to trade favors with you is the day they put a fucking bullet in the back of my head."

"Oh," she replied snottily, "you don't need my favors? That's bullshit, because if you don't need something from someone, Tony, you don't say shit to them, in case you haven't noticed."

"I'll get the tickets from your old man if you don't want to do it for me," he said. "But if I do, I ain't taking your ass with me. That's as simple as it is. So, you want a nice day at the ball game? Get me those tickets and Carl the pass. You want to stay home by yourself, or go up to the box to hold daddy's hand? Then don't get them. I can do it myself."

"Since when can you call my father?" Camille said with as much condescension as she could muster. "Do you think my father deals with criminals like you? The only reason he'd even talk to you is because of me!"

Tony chuckled softly, enjoying the humor of what she'd said. He got up from his chair, walked over to the couch where she was sitting, and put his hand gently on her cheek, stroking it softly.

"Just get the tickets, Camille," he said quietly, still stroking her face.

Then Tony grabbed a handful of hair at the back of her neck and twisted his hand up in it good. He lowered his face down to within inches of hers. "And don't ever, ever call me a criminal," he said maliciously through his clenched teeth. "I know I let you get away with a lot of shit, Camille, but don't push me on that. You don't talk like that, in front of me or anyone! You got that?"

Tears welled in Camille's eyes despite her anger. She thought of a million things that she could say to goad him, to insult him, and put him in his place. But there was something dark in his eyes, something she'd seen before but only in an unfocused sort of way. She saw murderous hatred, and this time it wasn't just a vague emotion. This time it was all for her.

Camille nodded and whispered, "Yes . . ."

"Good," Tony said, returning to normal and gently letting go of her hair. "Now get dressed because I want to leave here in an hour."

Camille did as she was told without a word of protest. She had always prided herself on her spirit. Why had she not fought against him just now? Did she love this man? She didn't think she knew what love was. She had never been sure. She lusted for him. She thought about him all the time, and when she wasn't with him she felt drawn to him, like she needed to be with him. She knew he was no good, she wasn't a fool. She'd been with him now for months, and she couldn't help seeing little things here and there that told her he was a feared man and that he had what were called "soldiers," men who would do absolutely anything he commanded. She saw fear in the faces of these men from time to time. That told her a lot.

She knew what it all meant. But then, why didn't it matter to her that he was obviously a devious and ruthless criminal? She couldn't say. Certainly she hadn't been raised that way. But she hadn't really been raised in any way at all, just grew up surrounded by people who were paid well to watch after her. That was the way it had always been, and she had always sought to make her own way, her own rules. This, however, was the first time in her life that she felt that somehow she didn't have a choice. Now here she was, Camille Carter, daughter of Grant Carter, one of the richest and most powerful men in the city, and helpless in the grasp of a criminal. She had just been cowed. No one had done that to her, ever. And because of that strange force inside her, the one that prevented her from slapping Tony Rizzo in the face and walking out the door, she had the feeling that the worst was yet to come.

T he air was cool that Sunday, even for early October. Some of the players for both the New York Titans and the Indianapolis Colts wore long-sleeved thermal tops to ward off the chill. The linemen like Bert, of course, wore nothing on their arms, preferring to brave the cold for an opportunity to show off the massive muscles that they'd worked so hard to develop all their lives. Besides, it was considered a weakness for a lineman to succumb to the elements. For Hunter's part, he always did what was most comfortable. There were some quarterbacks around the league who liked to fancy themselves tough, as tough as the linemen that protected them, but Hunter was not one of these. He was too pragmatic.

He began his charade early in the day during warm-ups, before the stands filled and while kickoff was still an hour away. Instead of throwing his typical spirals on a string, he put some air under the ball and wobbled it a bit. He would dramatically stop to rub his shoulder every so often too, just for good measure. He wanted an excuse for what he was about to do. After being tormented by Rizzo's words over the past few days, Hunter had decided that winning the game meant nothing. He wasn't taking any chances. If there was any danger to his little girl, or his wife, he wasn't going to risk it just to win a football game.

His team could lose this one and still get to the play-offs and even win it all. It was only one game, and it sure as hell didn't matter to Hunter in the grand scheme of things. It was strange how suddenly the whole notion of winning and losing had been put into perspective for him by Tony Rizzo. Really, what did it matter? To anyone? Yes, coaches and players could lose their jobs by losing games, but only lots of them over an entire season. Each single game in itself meant nothing. The world would wake up Monday morning and life would go on. No one would live or die because of the outcome of a football game. No one would be a better or worse person. When you broke it down to the essentials, it was a meaningless exercise.

These thoughts allowed Hunter to plot his team's defeat without remorse. He'd make it up to them next week anyway. Still, he'd have to play his role and make it look good. He wanted everyone around him to believe that it was his shoulder that would be responsible for his erratic and at times downright despicable performance. When the game began, Hunter lived up to his own worst expectations.

The Colts didn't help matters much. They could do almost nothing against the Titans defense. Every time during the first quarter the Colts got into the red zone and in a position to score, they would turn the ball over to the Titans. It was a bizarre feeling for Hunter to be secretly rooting for the opposition's offense to score. But without a score from Indianapolis, Hunter had absolutely no intention of putting his own team on the board. He had only three completions in fifteen attempts, and twice he had to throw interceptions to stop potential scoring drives. Two times he let the play clock run out to get a five-yard delay-of-game penalty, and once he had fumbled a snap.

Still, for all his blundering, the Titans defense was rising to the occasion and apt to score themselves on an intercepted pass or a blocked punt, and if they did . . . Hunter couldn't even consider it. Crazed by this thought, that the Colts might in fact give up points to the Titans defense, Hunter decided to take matters into his own hands. Right before halftime, with the offense driving down the field, Hunter called an audible at the line of scrimmage, changing the play from a run to a pass. It was third and one, a down when most teams would run the ball. The percentages for gaining one yard were clearly in favor of a run. Hunter had no business changing the call Price had signaled in from the sideline. He dropped back and threw an interception on the screen pass he had called. A

Colts linebacker picked the ball off with ease and practically waltzed into the end zone, giving the visiting team a 7–0 lead.

To have the Titans defense play so well, only to see their efforts foiled by Hunter Logan, who had done nothing all day except fuck up, was maddening to the crowd. They booed wildly as Hunter shuffled off the field, avoiding the irate Price on his way to the bench. From the stands Hunter could hear the murderous cries for his head.

"Logan! You stink!" someone shrieked.

"Logan! You're killing us!"

"Take that contract and stick it up your ass!"

"My mother could do better than you! Go home!"

The obscenities and insults poured out from the stands like a flood. Hunter tried to ignore them. He pretended not to hear. Then Price was in his face.

As much as Hunter wanted to be absolved from having to shave points in the game, he had no intention of letting things reach the point where he was taken out of the game altogether. But that's exactly what happened.

"I'm putting Stevens in," Price said, then turned to walk away.

Hunter grabbed him by the arm and spun the coach around. Price stared incredulously at the player's restraining hand.

"Take your arm off me, Logan," Price said. "You're done for the day."

"You can't," Hunter heard himself say. In the split second after he'd heard the coach's words, Hunter realized that although he could not be blamed for getting benched, it was not something Rizzo would forgive.

"I can and I will," Price said. "That audible was the last straw. There is absolutely no excuse in the world for that shit! You made me look like an ass!"

"They're not going to let you pull me," Hunter said desperately, referring to the owner's obvious bias for a player he was paying so much money to.

"I'm the coach here, remember?" Price said maliciously. "And if Mr. Carter calls down, well, your shoulder obviously can't take it. Now let the hell go of me."

"It's not my shoulder," Hunter heard himself saying.

"I don't care what it is really," said the coach. "I won't have you out there playing like this, especially after Miami last week. I've got a game to win and I sure as hell can't do it with you playing the way you are. Now get a cup of Gatorade and come keep the stats for Stevens.

"Besides," Price added with a vengeful grin, "the crowd won't mind . . . they've been asking for Broadway."

Hunter let his hand fall to his side. He didn't even feel the sting of the insult of having the young rookie supplant him. He felt paralyzed, as if in a dream, as he watched Price make his way back to the sideline to pat Blake Stevens on the rump and send him in with the rest of the Titans offense. Hunter looked vaguely around him at the crowd as if to plead with Tony Rizzo, wherever he was, that what was happening was beyond his control. He couldn't help it. Surely Rizzo would understand that?

But the only thing that came into his mind was the leering face of Carl Lutz in the locker room before the game. Hunter knew from that face that he was the sick son of a bitch that Rizzo was referring to when he talked about someone who liked little girls. Hunter felt sick, sicker than he already was. He tried desperately to think of ways that he could protect his family. If Rizzo was in front of him at this moment, he thought he would try to kill him with his bare hands. That wasn't happening.

He'd take them away, he'd have to. He could go to the bank and cash out everything he had. He could contact Madigan, his financial adviser, and have him convert his investments to cash within a week, then wire it somewhere. He'd take Rachel and Sara and run. They could go somewhere, maybe even out of the country. It wasn't his fault. If he hid somewhere good, they wouldn't look too hard. They'd realize it wasn't his fault. It was mad! But what else was there? He wouldn't have another moment's peace if he stayed.

Tony Rizzo was nervous. Even though his man was doing everything he could to keep the game within the spread, things looked bad. He could see it the same way Hunter could: The Titans defense would score a touchdown and it would destroy him. When Hunter threw the interception, Tony couldn't help himself from standing on his feet and cheering madly. The crowd around him glared vengefully.

He glared back. He'd kill every fucking one of them! He had four million dollars on this game, and he didn't give a good fuck what these people's sentiments were. He sat back down.

Camille glanced at him nervously and said nothing. He looked at her and shook his head. She was really beyond worthless. He preferred her nagging to the mousy deference she now gave him. It was like something had snapped in her the night before. She bored him now to no end. He turned back to the game. The Colts kicked off. Tony's face dropped. The crowd roared with approval as Broadway Blake trotted out onto the field amid the rest of the Titans offense. Tony searched frantically for Hunter Logan. He'd kill that piece of shit! What was Logan trying to pull? He spotted Logan on the sideline, gazing absentmindedly into space.

"What the hell is going on?" Tony said out loud.

"It's about time they pulled that bum out of there," Tony heard a fat woman in front of him say to her long-haired, chain-smoking husband. "The son of a bitch killed us last week in Miami."

It hit Tony hard. The coaches had pulled Hunter Logan from the game. He had never considered it! Who ever heard of taking out your starting quarterback? But Price, the coach, he was supposed to be some tough guy. Iceman, they called him. The tough-guy coach was showing who was boss. Tony's face flushed. He'd kill the fucking coach, too! His mind spun. How could he get to the coach? He turned to Camille.

"Take me to your father's box," he ordered, pulling her to her feet.

Camille knew better than to ask why. The demonic determination shone on her boyfriend's face.

Grant Carter's luxury sky box was actually directly above them on the fifty-yard line. They climbed up two levels of stairs without a word between them. People were already milling about the concourse in thick numbers, trying to beat the halftime rush to the bathrooms and hot-dog stands. Tony became impatient at the top of the second stairway and pushed an older man out of the way, almost knocking him over the railing. A few people made some indignant noise about this, but they, too, could see the resolute and angry look on the face of the young, well-dressed man. And, after all, it was a New York and New Jersey crowd, and people didn't think much of getting themselves into a scuffle or shot over an affront to some unknown man.

Until she'd met Tony, the sky box was the only place Camille had ever pretended to watch a Titans game, so she didn't waver in the crush of people but went right for the unmarked door that was guarded by a uniformed police officer. The cop must have been a regular, because he recognized Camille instantly and stood aside. The inside of the box was like a transplanted uptown cocktail party. People stood toe-to-toe, talking and drinking and paying little attention to the game itself. It was the affair that they were there for. Since the Titans were the reigning world champions, it was exceptionally fashionable to be seen in the team owner's sky box. There were a few die-hard football fans among the fray of tweed jackets and turtleneck sweaters. These people, men mostly, included Camille's father, and they were given the reverence of space and comfortable chairs pushed to the outer limits of the lavish room overlooking the playing field.

Grant Carter was sitting pensively in his favorite chair, flanked by a senator, a movie star, and a middle-aged woman whose bloodline was as blue as the crisp autumn sky. It was obvious from the stress that lined his face that Grant Carter was completely engrossed in the workings of his team and whether or not they were going to prevail. When Carter was brought from his reverie by the voice of his daughter, he broke into an immediate smile. But when he saw the impudent Tony Rizzo standing next to her, bending down to whisper in his ear, his smile faded quickly.

"I need to speak with you," Rizzo said. "Now."

Grant Carter looked quickly from side to side, although his expression didn't show anything but detached calm. He stood up to speak to his new guest and leaned close to his ear.

"You're a damned fool coming here like this!" he hissed between his teeth. "I've got three people from the NFL office here in this box!"

"I don't give a flying fuck if you've got the pope and the chief of police!" Rizzo said, his voice rising above its original whisper, causing a few heads to turn.

Grant Carter excused himself momentarily from his immediate guests and led Rizzo over to a corner that was somewhat private.

"You owe me, Carter," Rizzo blurted out rudely. "Don't give me that indignant look like you're some kind of high-society asshole! I saved your ass, and I can fuck you over just as easily, so you just listen to what I'm going to tell you and you do it."

Carter's face turned red, almost purple. His upper lip trembled slightly with rage. Still, he listened. It wouldn't be long before he could put this trash in his place, he told himself. It would not be long . . .

"I want Hunter Logan back in that game," Rizzo said, pointing down at the field where the teams were both milling towards their locker rooms for halftime.

The words hit Carter like a cattle prod. Hunter Logan? Carter had a million thoughts go through his mind.

"I'll wait here until I see it," Rizzo added, planting himself firmly with his arms folded across his chest.

Carter calculated for only a moment, then said, "I'll do it, but don't stand around here. It's damn foolish for both of us if you do. I'll do as you ask because I had the same thought myself. Why you want him in I don't want to know. Don't say anything more to me."

"How are you going to make it happen? I'm not fucking around here."

"Listen," Carter said, bringing his icy stare close to Rizzo's face, "I'm not a fucking street thug! I'm a businessman. I don't fuck around. If I say I'll do it, then it's done. Now don't be a damned fool!"

Carter stalked away, not even noticing his daughter, who was standing by ashen-faced, shocked at having seen the power that Tony Rizzo could exert over her father. Tony stood long enough to see Carter sit back down and pick up one of three phones on a small cocktail table next to his chair. Then he turned and left with Camille trailing behind him like a tattered kite.

When Cook saw Rizzo jump up and drag Camille with him up the stairs and out of sight, he immediately shouldered the duffel bag that lay at his feet and made tracks for the locker room. Cook was in such a tear that he didn't even think to say anything to the usher, who by now considered himself a friend to Cook. As he skipped down the concrete steps inside the stadium two at a time, Cook hoped he was guessing right. But what else could Rizzo be doing if not going to have some words with Hunter Logan? Why else would he jump up and disappear right before halftime? If Cook could catch Rizzo and Logan together—in the locker room, of all places—he would certainly have all the leverage he would need to get Hunter Logan's cooperation. Certainly the way Logan had been performing on the field until this point in the game told Cook that his suspicions were entirely correct.

Cook had another stadium pass from the security office, and it allowed him to penetrate the depths of the stadium, down into the protected reaches where the teams dressed and prepared for the game. The same pass allowed him to walk right by the security guards at the door to the home locker room. Cook was surprised at how easy it was. He imagined it was even easier for Tony Rizzo when he was being accompanied by the owner's daughter.

Inside the locker room the team was separated into two distinct groups, one being the offense players and the other the defense. They were on opposite ends of the large room, and each were clustered around a chalkboard listening to coaching instructions and sometimes rising to illustrate a point of their own in chalk. A few of the players and the equipment people were roaming in and out between the bathroom, the equipment room, and the locker area, so Cook was not noticed by anyone. A quick scan told him that Rizzo was nowhere around. Cook didn't think it was possible that he'd already been there and left, so he simply found the most innocuous place to stand and settled down to wait. Hunter Logan was easy to spot. He was sitting just outside the circle of offensive players in front of his own locker. Instead of paying attention to the coaches at the board, Hunter was staring blankly into space as though none of what they had to say mattered. Cook assumed the superstar's conscience was weighing him down. That was good. If the guy had any kind of conscience at all, Cook would have no problem securing his assistance.

But then Cook overheard something that explained Rizzo's sudden irate disappearance from his seat as well as the look on Hunter Logan's face. Two players had stopped on their way into the bathroom right in front of Cook as though he wasn't there at all.

"Bert," said a linebacker named Johnson, pulling a blood-soaked glove off of his hand and tossing it into the bottom of his locker, "what the fuck? What happened to Hunter? Is it his shoulder?"

"Nah, man," Bert said bitterly. "Fucking Price just pulled him, man. Just fucking pulled him!"

"No shit?" said the linebacker incredulously.

Those were Cook's sentiments exactly.

"Did you hear the fucking crowd?" Johnson went on. "What a bunch of assholes. They forget that he's the guy who won it all for us last year."

"Fucking assholes is right. The only thing I can't figure is who's a bigger asshole, the fans or the Iceman," Bert said and walked away in obvious disgust.

The only question that remained for Cook now was where Rizzo had gone. He understood Rizzo's predicament exactly, if in fact Hunter Logan was working with Rizzo. Rizzo probably had a tremendous amount of money on this game, maybe millions. Suddenly his ringer, the only man who could control the entire outcome of a game single-handedly, had been pulled off the field. Rizzo would have to do something to try to get him back on—that or pray, and Cook knew Tony Rizzo wasn't the praying sort. Cook decided to keep close to the team and see if Rizzo showed his face. "Excuse me," Cook said to the player named Johnson, who was now alone at his locker pulling on a pair of fresh gloves, "could you tell me where Coach Price would be?"

Johnson looked up at the source of the voice. "Down there," he said, eyeing Cook with suspicion, "through that doorway and halfway down the hall is the coaches' locker room."

"Thanks," Cook said and slipped through the door and down the hall until he came to a door that was marked Coaches Locker Room. Cook looked around, then pushed the door and stuck just his head inside the room. Price was sitting alone smoking a cigarette. It looked funny to Cook, seeing someone so closely tied to the world of sports sitting there with a butt hanging out of his mouth. There was a shattered red phone hanging off the hook on the wall just off to the side of the bench. The broken phone was dangling, as though it had just been thrown. Price suddenly looked up at Cook.

"Who're you?" Price demanded without getting to his feet.

"Oh, I'm sorry," Cook said, not wanting to blow his cover, "I'm looking for the bathroom. I'm with the media. Is everything OK, Coach?"

"Yeah. What the hell do you mean by that?" Price said like a man whose problems could never be solved. "Get the hell outta here!"

Cook had no way of knowing whether or not Rizzo had somehow contacted the coach, either in person before he'd gotten there, or over the now-broken phone. He knew one thing for sure, though. By the time he got back to his post with the usher, Rizzo was sitting calmly in his seat, and Hunter Logan was jogging out onto the field with the Titans offense.

CHAPTER 31

Hunter knew from Price that the call had come from upstairs. Nothing else on earth could have gotten Hunter back in the game. Price had stormed into the locker room just before the end of halftime and angrily told Hunter that he would be starting the second half.

"You better get it together, Logan," Price had said, "because even Mr. Carter won't put up with that kind of shit for long. I don't care how much he's paying you. You'd almost have to try to look any worse."

The coach's last words had shocked Hunter, but there really was nothing to think about. Hunter was in too deep. Everything in his world—his finances, his career, and now apparently the well-being of his family—depended on his keeping Tony Rizzo happy. As much as he'd like to, Hunter didn't give a damn about what Price, or Carter, or anyone thought. He would do what he had to.

As if in answer to his prayers, the Colts came out after the half like a team possessed. Whatever their coach had said, it did the trick. Hunter had seen things like that before. During one half, a team looked like they didn't belong on an NFL field; in the next they were kicking the hell out of the defending Super Bowl champions. In this case, that was exactly what was happening.

Responding to his anger with Hunter, Price began the half by calling three running plays in a row. On third and two, the Colts stuffed the runner at the line and the Titans had to punt. The Colts offense then quickly and methodically marched down the field and kicked a field goal to expand their lead to ten. Hunter began to breathe easier. Still, Price insisted on running. Hunter got the message: His throwing had been so unpredictable that the coach would rather take his chances on the ground. Under normal circumstances it would have been an infuriating insult. Now, though, Hunter was glad to oblige. This possession the Titans actually got a first down, but only one before they had to punt again.

On the next Titans offensive series the first two plays, again runs, failed utterly and left the team with third down and nine to go. Price signaled in an underneath pass play. Hunter dropped back to pass and threw to his deep receiver, who was wide open. To everyone but Hunter, Cook, and Rizzo, the ball looked like it was just barely overthrown. To those three men, however, it was an athletic feat of extraordinary skill. This is because each of them knew that Hunter threw the deep ball with such accuracy that everyone thought he was trying to complete it when he was actually making the ball truly uncatchable. Hunter couldn't help smirking to himself as he passed Price on the way to the bench. Even the incensed head coach could not blame Hunter for going deep to the wide-open receiver.

For twenty more minutes the game slogged on without another score. There were only three minutes and twelve seconds on the clock. Hunter felt almost safe. He actually toyed with the idea of trying to bring his team back and win the game. But two touchdowns would put him over the three-point limit that Rizzo had allowed him. He could score once, then get a field goal and then try to win it in OT by another field goal, but decided against it. He wasn't taking any chances. Football was a funny game, and strange things happened. This decision turned out to be one of the best he'd ever made. Desperate to score points, even the spiteful Price had to call passing plays if he hoped to win. Hunter obliged by completing a short underneath pass for five yards, then throwing two incomplete so that the Titans had to punt.

The game was essentially over. After heartily booing Hunter for this and every preceding pitiful series of play, people started to file out of the stadium. From his spot on the sideline Hunter could see them filling the aisles, people who knew that the game was now hopeless and who themselves had hopes of beating the worst of the traffic. Hunter had done so poorly that even Bert had averted his gaze when the two friends passed on the sideline before the defense went out onto the field. Hunter was so relieved that the morbidity of his friends and teammates made him want to burst out laughing. If they only knew what was really important.

But this in turn depressed Hunter. He felt like he was cheating them, cheating everyone. He knew that somehow he must have cheated himself just to end up in the position he was in. But he couldn't think exactly how that had happened He had been going along, playing football for as long as he could remember. He'd never had to think about such things before. His whole life had been defined by football, and until now it had simply been a matter of winning games on Sunday.

A cheer from the remaining crowd jolted Hunter out of his reverie. The defense had stuffed the Colts' attempts to run the ball, and using all three of the Titans time-outs they had only allowed twenty-seven seconds to expire. The Titans still technically had a chance to win. The Colts got into punt formation and it happened. The Titans blocked the kick. Someone scooped it up and took it all the way into the end zone for six. Hunter felt a twist in his gut. If he had scored a touchdown before the blocked punt, the Titans would have won by four. The idea made him queasy.

Now the Titans lined up for an onside kick. Hunter clenched his fists. The odds were one in a hundred of recovering an onside kick, but it happened. Hunter was buckling his chin strap and jogging out onto the field before he could think. It was like he was in a dream. That was probably the only reason he let the first play happen as it did. The Titans had the ball on the fifty-yard line. Even though they had no time-outs, the two-minute warning would stop the clock. Because of this, Price signaled in a draw play. Everyone would be expecting a pass with the Titans having depleted their supply of time-outs. Price had chosen to roll the dice. He was thinking that even if his team didn't score, they only had to go about twenty yards to get into field goal range. They could tie it up and try to win it in overtime. They certainly had the momentum after the last two plays.

Hunter called the play in the huddle as it was called. He went up to the line. He wasn't thinking, he was in a daze. It was incredible. The only thought that filled his mind was that he would gun the ball into the ground every time he dropped back to pass. He wasn't going to let his team score any points at all. He wasn't taking any chances on overtime. The draw to him was an exercise in futility, a ten-yard play at best to preclude the passing game that would be essential after the two-minute warning. So when Garrison Morgan took the ball up the middle, Hunter simply turned to watch him go down instead of carrying out his fake as he had been coached to do for over twenty-five years.

What he saw was incredible. It was one of those runs that made the highlight film for the entire league. Morgan bounced off tacklers, reversed his field, and literally jumped over bodies on a run that lasted forever in Hunter's mind. He found that he was moving down field, watching, willing some Colt defender to somehow drag his teammate down. It just didn't happen like this. It was too much. No one could have luck this bad. No team could have luck this good. Then it happened.

The Colts free safety finally caught up to Morgan, and even as Hunter's teammate was raising the ball in the air in celebration of an amazing, game-winning athletic feat, the free safety dove, reached out, and just clicked the back of Morgan's heels with his hand. The running back tumbled, and Hunter searched madly for the closest official to tell him whether or not Morgan had scored. It seemed like eternity. A second passed, then two. Not one of the officials raised his hands to signal a touchdown. A signal finally came for a Titans first down.

The clock stopped for the two-minute warning. Price was furiously gesturing Hunter over to the sideline. Hunter practically staggered. He would never remember what Price's words were. He had the vague impression that all was forgiven in the flushed thrill of imminent victory. He forgot the play that Price called, but did know that it was a run. It didn't matter. Hunter called a thirty-two trap in the huddle. His voice, like the rest of him, shook uncontrollably. He didn't look at a single teammate's face in the huddle. He kept his head down and mumbled the call so that Morgan had to demand he give it to them all again.

Hunter went to the line and took the snap. He dropped back into the backfield, passing Morgan, who reached out expectantly for the ball. Hunter turned and stumbled. His line, who had been blocking for an inside run, allowed the Colts defenders to come streaming through into the Titans backfield. Hunter waited until he was completely engulfed and then simply opened his arms, allowing his opponent's big, burly defensive end to pluck the ball from his grasp. The lineman lumbered for a couple of yards before tripping on his own teammates and being swamped by Titans players who had turned to see the disaster and come running in vain pursuit. The game now was over. The Colts offense trotted out and fell on the ball three times to run out the clock, handing the world champions a 10–7 defeat. Hunter, relieved almost to the point of tears, didn't even notice or care that his entire team avoided him like a leper as they made their way off the field and back into the locker room.

At The Star casino in Atlantic City, Scott Meeker, Sal Gamone, and Mark Ianuzzo sat clustered around a big-screen TV in a large penthouse suite. The view through the sweeping, tinted windows was of the Atlantic Ocean. The expanse of blue water was broken by white triangular sails of recreational boaters heading for the harbor, and every so often a helicopter lifted straight into the sky before heading out over the water on its way back to New York City, carrying the high-rollers who'd spent their weekend at the tables. Of the three men in the penthouse's expansive living room, only Scott Meeker had shown any emotion during the game. The final minutes, of course, had meant nothing to these men. They had placed their money on the point spread, which was six. They were in no danger that late in the game, but they watched with interest because they knew that Tony Rizzo was. They knew that if Morgan had run the ball in that final yard and scored, Rizzo would have had to come up with several million dollars.

"Did you see that?" Mark Ianuzzo said to Gamone after the final gun. "If that guy goes in, it's kaput!"

Sal Gamone remained silent.

"What?" said Ianuzzo.

"Just this," Gamone said quietly, "you saw what Hunter Logan did. How likely are the chances of the Titans blocking that kick . . . then getting the onside kick . . . then, to top it off, have Morgan run through the Colts like shit through a goose? That wouldn't happen like that in another hundred years. And even if it did, Logan learned something. He wouldn't let it happen like that again. Next time Morgan never gets that hand-off on the draw. I think what our friend Rizzo has is a good opportunity.

"The only thing that concerns me," Gamone continued after taking a drink from his glass of straight scotch, "is how long Logan can go on doing things like this and not get run out of New York, or benched by the team. People are going to start asking questions if this happens too much."

"It's a funny game, though," Ianuzzo pointed out. "Lots of times guys have bad games. As long as we don't try to go to the well too often . . . but I agree with what you said about that game not coming out like that again."

As the two men talked, Meeker began to flit about the room like a three-hundred-pound songbird, refilling his guests' glasses and clapping his hands gleefully with every other step he took. For him the game was a grand win. He was playfully considering just how he would spend the easy money he had just made, and greedily anticipating an even bigger take on the next game. Beyond that, he was delighted to have acted as the broker for what was looking like a very successful venture for everyone.

"I've got to hand it to Rizzo," Ianuzzo said. "He's got either the coach or the owner in his pocket. Did you see how they yanked Logan in the second quarter and then came out and put him back in the second half? No wonder Rizzo is so damned confident."

Sal Gamone simply nodded thoughtfully.

"The Titans play the Giants in two weeks," he finally said.

Ianuzzo knew what his counterpart meant without his having to explain. There would be more action on that game than anything short of the Super Bowl. It would be a tremendous opportunity.

"So," Ianuzzo said, "we're going ahead with Rizzo?"

Gamone tilted his head and lazily raised an eyebrow before he said, "If he delivers like he did today in two weeks? Then I think the young man will have shown us that his intelligence and efficiency make him an excellent candidate for the council. If, of course, the day should arrive when his uncle is no longer able to run the business."

Ianuzzo snorted, "Yeah, if, of course."

"Scott," Sal said, "you set up a meeting with Tony for tomorrow. I want to give him plenty of time to get the things he needs in place."

Meeker nodded eagerly.

"I always knew you never liked Vincent Mondolffi," Ianuzzo then said pensively.

"I like him," Gamone answered, sipping his drink, "but he's got strange notions, like there's something wrong with the kind of business that we've all built our fortunes upon. It's not good to forget where you came from."

The Titans' schedule during the working week required players to report to the facility on the day after the game to get treatment for their injuries, lift weights, run, and, as a team, watch the game film of the previous day. It was a light-hearted fun experience when the team won, and it was absolute torture when they lost. When they won, everything was good. Mistakes were overlooked. Good plays were lauded by coaches and teammates alike. When they lost, every mistake was accentuated to the point that each man was made to feel as though something he specifically did had caused the entire team to lose. Hunter dreaded the film after the Colts game more than any other he'd ever had to watch. He knew how bad it was going to look, and he couldn't help worrying that someone might find him out. Because he knew that the mistakes he'd made were intentional, and he couldn't help thinking that others would see that as well. He couldn't imagine what would happen. No one could prove it certainly, but he'd be ostracized by his entire team if they ever suspected him of such a thing.

The reality of the situation was that everyone thought Hunter had simply played an awful game. His teammates knew that his shoulder was hurt, and they hadn't forgotten that he was the same guy who had taken them all to the championship last year. Still, the entire film session was painful for Hunter. Price was openly brutal with his criticism.

"That's so bad," Price had said, replaying Hunter's final game-losing fumble over and over again, "that it's embarrassing."

Under normal circumstances, Hunter would not have allowed Price to berate him like a schoolboy. He would have had words and even fists with the coach right there in front of the team. Instead Hunter sat there and humbly took what was coming to him. He felt that he deserved everything that Price gave him. With the danger now behind him, Hunter found himself wishing he had somehow managed to help his team win and keep Rizzo happy.

His teammates thought they knew how Hunter felt, and they gave him his space during the few hours he was at the complex working out and treating his shoulder. Only Bert had any words for him at all.

"Don't worry about it, buddy," his friend said as Hunter was drying off after a shower. "We're all behind you. You just get that shoulder well, and you'll get us right back on top."

Hunter only smiled weakly and said, "Thanks, buddy. I feel bad I let everyone down."

"Shit happens," Bert said.

"Yeah, shit happens."

"Get together this week?"

"Sure, I'll have Rachel call your boss," Hunter said, cracking his first smile.

"Kiss mine."

Hunter spent the rest of the day with his daughter out back on her swing set while Rachel worked with Julie in the kitchen, where she could watch them through a window over the sink. Hunter had had an elaborate playground built for his daughter well before she was old enough to use it. It sat between some of the old trees in the backyard and was an intricate maze of swings, ladders, towers and slides that spanned a large area filled with wood chips. Hunter and Sara could spend hours at a time out there and never get bored. Around six o'clock Rachel called them in. She gave Hunter a cold beer at the kitchen table before Julie served dinner.

As they began to eat, Sara said abruptly, "Mom, what's wrong with Dad?"

Hunter looked up at his wife.

"Why, honey? I thought you and Daddy were having fun all afternoon," said Rachel. "Daddy's fine."

"Are you fine, Daddy?" Sara said, looking at him innocently.

Hunter put on his best smile, "Of course, honey. Why?"

Sara shrugged as if to say she'd been wrong before, then said, "I don't know, you just seem sad."

Hunter leaned over to his daughter and hugged her. "I'm fine, honey," he said.

Hunter and Rachel did their best to make light-hearted conversation throughout the rest of the meal, and if they didn't pull it off, Sara was too polite to say so.

When Sara was finally off to bed and Julie had retired to her apartment over the garage, Hunter and Rachel settled themselves down for a quiet evening in the living room. This was the heart of the old house. It was paneled in mahogany, and thick beams crossed the high ceiling. Dark, heavy wood and leather furniture, along with a large cobblestone fireplace, gave the room a cozy feeling despite its size. Hunter carefully laid a fire and lit it before sitting down on the couch next to Rachel.

"Is the alarm on?" she asked as he cracked open a bottle of Rolling Rock that she'd left for him on the coffee table.

"My God, Rachel," Hunter exclaimed in a more exasperated tone than he meant to, "do you think I can relax for even one damn minute? I mean, I go through hell at work, I get home and play with Sara until bedtime, I make us a fire, then I finally get to relax and you want me to get up and put the alarm on at nine o'clock at night?"

"Forget it," she said quietly, but he was already up.

Hunter came back, apparently cooler than when he'd left, but no sooner did he bring the green bottle of beer to his lips than a nasal electronic voice blurted out: "Someone has entered the rear outer perimeter."

Hunter gave Rachel an exasperated look.

"Maybe just some kids playing around," she weakly suggested.

"Someone has entered the rear inner perimeter" came the voice once again.

Hunter stood up and went toward the back of the house, digging for a moment in one of the kitchen drawers and coming up with a can of Mace. Rachel followed him nervously to the back door, crouching behind his back and peeking over his shoulder as though they were in the middle of some horror movie. Security lights flooded the entire backyard. A well-dressed black man carrying a briefcase and shielding the spotlights from his eyes with his free arm slowly climbed the worn slate steps of the patio off the kitchen and knocked softly on the thick wooden door.

"Who the hell is that?" Rachel hissed. The two of them could see out through the small window in the door.

"I don't know," Hunter said.

"Is it someone from the team?" Rachel asked.

"Who is it!" Hunter demanded through the glass. Before Cook answered he lowered his arm and showed his face. Hunter's stomach dropped as he realized it was the FBI agent who'd spoken at the team meeting they'd had back in training camp.

"My name is Ellis Cook," the man said in a strong, educated voice that was also slightly impatient. He held his badge up to the glass. "I'm with the FBI. I need to speak with Hunter Logan."

Cook apologized for coming to the back of the house in such an unorthodox manner, but said he would explain. He asked if he could sit down, and together they sat at the kitchen table. Hunter's feeling of sickness was almost overwhelming, and he felt as though he were in some crazy dream, caught in the act of committing some heinous crime. Cook had read up extensively on Hunter during the past few days by doing a NEXUS search. There were hundreds of articles written about the quarterback over the past few years, and through them Cook had gained a feeling for the kind of man he was dealing with. He had decided to approach Hunter as a friend, someone he could confide in and rely on. This is why he had chosen to first meet with the quarterback at his own home, with his wife present. He wanted Hunter as calm as possible.

"I'm going to give it to you straight," Cook said, addressing both Hunter and Rachel at the same time. "You're in a lot of trouble, Hunter."

Hunter looked Cook in the eye. The blank look on his face was replaced with an acuity that encouraged Cook. The look told Cook that he wasn't going to have to go through this step by step and start taking photographs out of his briefcase.

Hunter nodded and said, "I know."

"I'm not here to scare you," Cook continued. "If I'm not mistaken, you're probably pretty scared already. But I have to inform you that if convicted for what you've done, you could do ten to twenty.

When things like this shake down, the wise guys all start to talk. They give up other people to save their own ass, and the athletes are the ones who end up doing the time.

"They've got nothing else to give," Cook explained. "Like that deal with the B.C. basketball players back in the early eighties . . . The wise guys gave up their pals who pulled off the Lufthansa heist and got into the government witness-protection program. They also dropped the dime on the players. They did ten years."

Cook saw the blood drain from both Hunter's and Rachel's faces, just what he'd wanted. "I don't want to see that happen here," Cook said.

"I didn't have a choice," Hunter said quietly, looking up again and meeting Cook's stare.

Cook nodded. "I suspect not, but you must have done something. These guys don't go after someone unless they've got something on them."

Hunter quietly explained how Rizzo had proof of his gambling through an old friend on NFL games and how it would end his career if it came out. "I thought if I gave up a couple of points on a game and didn't lose it that they'd leave me alone and no one would really be hurt by it," Hunter explained. "I was actually going to call you. I've still got your card in my wallet. Here," he said, pulling the card out and tossing it onto the table as proof of his veracity.

Cook only nodded sympathetically. He wanted to let Hunter continue, to get it all out. Rachel was saying nothing, but she had taken Hunter's hand and held it now as it rested on the table. There was a moment of silence. Only a large cuckoo clock ticked noisily on the wall. Then Hunter went on to explain how the very day after Cook's visit he had read about a player who'd been suspended from the league for a suspected connection with gambling.

"It would have been the end for me," Hunter finally said. "I guess it is now anyway . . ."

Then he fell silent.

"I don't know about your football career," Cook admitted, "but I can tell you that with me, you can have a life after all this. You can help me put this Tony Rizzo away, maybe for good."

"Huh, what, in a witness program?" Hunter scoffed. "You think I could go somewhere where someone didn't notice me? You think I want to?"

"I didn't say anything about a witness program," Cook said.

Hunter glanced nervously at Rachel, then decided to speak anyway. "You think these people are going to let me help you put them away and not do something to me? Isn't that how all this works?"

Cook shook his head, "No, that's not how it works. You're somebody. They won't just harass you or hurt you. They do that to people in their own world, or somebody who could disappear without too much commotion. Someone like you? They're not going to do anything. Look at Art Schlester. He blew in a bunch of wise guys to get out from under his debts. Nothing happened to him. It just doesn't work that way. They only want you to believe things like that so you'll do what they want."

Hunter looked skeptical.

"Look, Hunter," Cook said, "it's up to you. If you wanted us to move you someplace and help you change your life, to get away . . . we could. But if you help me, I can help you keep your career. Believe me, if we go to the commissioner and say, 'Here's a guy who did very little wrong, then got himself into hot water because he was scared and being threatened,' and then we convince him that you were integral in helping us take these guys out . . . Maybe you get a fine or a couple of games suspension, but believe me, we can help you put your life back to normal. I can guarantee you the commissioner will be getting calls straight from Washington to tell him how you were integral in helping us out—and how you came to me personally, of your own volition."

Hunter wondered if that was possible. He wished it was, but did not know.

"We don't really have a choice, do we?" said Rachel suddenly. She realized that Cook was giving them the opportunity to make it look as though they had initiated everything and not him. It was a magnanimous gesture that could save not only Hunter's career but his reputation.

Cook paused, thinking, then said, "No, you don't."

She nodded and looked at Hunter. She would never say that she had told him to call Cook in the first place. She didn't have to. He knew it better than anyone.

Hunter shrugged and said, "What do I have to do?"

Cook forced himself not to smile. "How does Rizzo meet with you? How does he contact you?"

"I never know," Hunter said, frowning. "They just appear and take me to him, once in the parking lot of the Food King and another time the guy just climbed in my car at a traffic light."

"Hmm," Cook thought about that, "and Rizzo's never told you how to contact him if you needed to?"

"Our conversations are never that long. He tells me what he wants me to do, makes some threats, and that's it. Then he sends some goon into the locker room right before the game. He must get the pass from Rizzo through Grant Carter's daughter, Camille."

"Yeah, I know all about her," said Cook.

"She's not in on this, is she?" Hunter asked.

"No, not as far as I can see." Cook said. "I think she's just in the wrong place at the wrong time with the wrong guy. Now, what about the guy you used to place the bets through? The bookie. He could get you in contact with Rizzo. I want you to call him so I can wire you. If we get Rizzo talking about the whole thing, if we can get him to threaten you, we'll have him in the bag."

"I never placed the bets myself," Hunter said. "I did it with Metz, like I said. I never even asked who he placed them with."

"So where's Metz?" Cook asked.

Hunter shrugged. "I haven't seen him or spoken to him since I found out that he bet on that Titans game last season. That was in July."

"OK, you get in touch with this Metz and find out who his contact is. That way you can get a message to Rizzo that you want to meet."

"What about Rachel and our daughter Sara?" Hunter said suddenly. "I want them to get away from town. I don't want them around while all this is going on."

Cook frowned and shook his head. "No, we can't move them around. We can't do anything out of the ordinary. That was precisely why I came to the back door tonight. Rizzo's got someone watching you all the time, following your every move to make sure nothing funny is going on. He's sitting out on the street in the front of the house right now in a black Town Car with tinted windows."

This news made Rachel visibly shudder.

"Tony Rizzo knows he's exposed himself with all this," Cook said, "and with everything that's at stake, they're keeping an eye on you to see if you do anything out of the ordinary."

"That's all the more reason to get them out of here," Hunter said.

"No, that's all the more reason to keep them right where they are," Cook said. "Everything's fine just as it is. You just go on about your life as you always do. Nothing's going to happen. Then, the minute we get the tape on Rizzo, I'll have him and his men in the bag before they know what hit them."

"How many men do you have with you?" Hunter asked.

"I've got twenty agents directly underneath me, but I can have a small army if I need it," Cook said. "Right now, though, I'm working alone. I didn't tell anyone I was going to meet with you. Right now everything we do is best kept between us. The time will come when we'll call in all the troops, but what we need more than anything is stealth. Don't say anything to anyone. Like I said, just live as you always do. Talk on the phone like you always do. Go to the store, work, whatever, just look normal. We can end this whole thing in a couple of weeks if we're careful."

"Are the phones tapped?" Rachel asked.

"I don't know for sure," Cook admitted. "I haven't checked the main box on the pole, but if they wanted to hook in, I'm sure they can do it. But like I said, you shouldn't be saying anything to anyone anyway."

"So what do I do?" Hunter asked.

"Tomorrow," Cook said, like a general laying out his plan of attack, "make a call to your friend Metz. Get his contact and then call whoever he is and tell him you want to get a message to Tony Rizzo. Have him tell Tony that you need to see him because you've got a problem that you need to talk to him about. Use those words so Rizzo doesn't think you're walking around with loose lips. Tell whoever it is that Tony will want to know right away so he calls Rizzo right away. I'll be back tomorrow night and show you how to wear the wire. You'll have to keep it on you all the time since Rizzo probably won't let you know when he's going to see you. I imagine he'll do what he's been doing, just have someone pick you up somewhere and drive you to him. I'll tell you tomorrow night all the things I want you to say to him and we can go over them until you're comfortable.

"If you need me," Cook said, picking up his card from the table and writing on it, "call me at this number. It's my home. I'll be back tomorrow night. I'll come in through the back again. Don't call me at the office. In fact, I'll scratch the number out. Like I said, until we're ready to call in the troops, this operation will stay between the three of us. It's safer for us all."

On that ominous note Cook stood to leave. He glanced around quickly at the beautiful interior of the regal old home, then looked at the couple sitting in front of him holding hands at their kitchen table. They seemed frozen in their seats. Cook waited patiently for them to come around and let him out through the same door he'd come in. They weren't much younger than he was, but they looked like children to Cook. Of course, they hadn't seen the same things in life that he had. They didn't know the horrors that were out there. This was their first taste of the way things really were. Cook marveled that people could go through life so thoroughly out of touch. But then, he guessed that a lot of people did.

After Cook left their house and the alarm system was back on, Rachel and Hunter went upstairs to talk in their bed. After about ten minutes of going over how Cook really was the best and only way out of their dilemma, Rachel started to nod off. She had always had the unique ability to sleep in times of extreme stress. Hunter didn't chide her for it. He wanted her to sleep. He felt bad enough that he had gotten them into the mess they were now in, and he considered it his lot to remain wide awake, tormented by the events of the past few months. As he wandered aimlessly about the house, he clung to the one notion that gave him any peace at all: It would be over soon.

Cook had said that in a few weeks Rizzo and his crew could be behind bars and that Hunter's celebrity status would give them immunity from repercussions with the mob. Hunter wondered about that. It scared him to think about. The only thing he knew about organized crime was what he'd seen in the movies. He thought that if you crossed them, you were finished. But Cook seemed unconcerned about that.

Hunter had a good feeling about Cook. He always thought he could get a good feeling for the type of person someone was in the first five minutes of meeting them, and he had a feeling that Cook was straight up. In fact, he couldn't get away from the notion that Cook was some kind of guardian angel. He gave off the sense that he'd seen so much and been through so much and come out knowing how things like this really worked.

Hunter took another bottle of Rolling Rock from the fridge, cracked it open, and wandered upstairs. He went into the front bedroom that they used for guests and pulled back the lace curtains, trying to peer through the thick old trees to the street. Cook had said someone was out there in a dark car. It gave Hunter the creeps. He couldn't see anything, but he didn't doubt Cook.

He wandered into Sara's room. She was sleeping peacefully amid all her dolls and stuffed animals in the pretty, pastel-colored room that Rachel had worked so hard to decorate. Sara, peaceful in her sleep, lay there without any idea in the world that their lives were balancing delicately on the brink of disaster, and hopefully she would never know. The thought that this beautiful young thing and his wife were in danger brought tears of frustration and grief to Hunter's eyes. He wanted it all to go away, to wake up tomorrow and have everything back to the way it was.

He would appreciate things then, things he had taken for granted. The simplest things came to mind: dinner with his family, driving home from practice with the windows down and the radio on, walking on the beach, throwing passes at his tire machine, and a dozen others that he would ordinarily not think of as special in any way. Now, though, everything in his previously "normal" life was special because of nothing more than the fact that the ominous threat of Tony Rizzo was hanging over them.

Hunter left his daughter's room and dug a Halcyon out of his shaving kit. He stole a furtive glance at his sleeping wife as he washed it down with a glass of water from the sink. The clock read 1:48 when Hunter lay back in the bed. Tomorrow was a big day. He closed his eyes and waited for the drug to lift him away.

Hunter sat in his shorts at the desk in their bedroom with the telephone in hand. Rachel, he assumed, was downstairs, having already taken Sara to kindergarten classes that were only a minute from the house. She always let him sleep in on Tuesdays since it was the only day of the week he had off during football season. Not that he had slept that long—the Halcyon had gotten him only six hours of sleep—but it was six more than he could have gotten without it. Hunter's fingers trembled as he dialed the phone. His feet were cold. He hadn't bothered to put on socks or even a T-shirt. The instant he woke up he had only one thought in mind, to call Metz and get things started. Hunter counted twenty rings before placing the receiver back in the cradle.

He pulled on a sweatsuit and went downstairs. Rachel was sitting at the kitchen table with a cup of coffee, reading the paper. She looked the same as she always did, and Hunter wondered briefly if Cook's visit hadn't been just a dream. But when Rachel looked up, Hunter saw fear in her eyes.

"Hi," she said. "Sleep OK?"

"Yeah," he said, "I called Metz's house but there was no answer."

"Why don't you call him were he works?"

"I will but not until nine. They don't open until nine."

Hunter sat down and Julie brought him a cup of coffee and asked him what he wanted for breakfast. Hunter said nothing and he and Rachel just sat for a while looking at each other.

"It's all going to work out," Rachel said finally, trying hard to smile.

Hunter nodded and said, "You know, I'm sorry, Rach—"

"Don't," she said. "I know. It's OK."

At nine o'clock exactly, Hunter dialed Metz's office.

"Dan Metzler no longer works here," said a perky female voice on the other end of the line.

"Could you tell me where he is?" Hunter asked, twisting the phone cord with his fingers.

"Hang on," the girl said, putting him on hold.

"Personnel" came the lispy voice of a bitchy young man, "can I help you?"

"I'm trying to find out where Met—Dan Metzler is. Can you tell me?"

"What department?" the man huffed.

"Uh . . ." Hunter tried to think. Even though he'd known Metz for years, he never was sure exactly what he did for a living. Metz rarely talked about his work, as if it was a nasty habit that he just couldn't shake. "I think he visited stores and checked on accounts, or something like that . . ."

"Oh, something like that?" the man said sarcastically. Then in a flat tone he said, "That would be Quality Assurance Department, probably an assistant manager. A real V.I.P. Hang on."

Hunter was put on hold again. After almost ten minutes he was told that Metz had taken a job up in Syracuse with U.S. Tobacco.

"Do you have a number or anything?" Hunter asked.

"I'm sorry, that's all I can tell you," he said, and Hunter was disconnected before he could ask another question.

It was the kind of phone conversation that always burned Hunter. It didn't matter who you were when you called some businesses. People were rude, apparently without fear of losing their jobs. He knew from reading the papers that it almost required a court order these days to can someone from any job, especially in a large corporation. That was one of the good things about football, there was no pandering about. When someone screwed up they were gone before they knew what hit them.

But his concern was with finding Metz, so he forgot about it and called information to get the number for U.S. Tobacco in Syracuse. There was no such listing. He called the corporate offices in New York, and in anticipation of the sarcasm and rudeness that were sure to come, Hunter started throwing his name around. He had to talk a little football, but he got results. Seven phone calls later, he was dialing Metz's office upstate.

"Heeell-o, U.S. Tobacco," Metz answered cheerfully.

"Metz, it's me, Hunter."

Metz was quiet, figuring just how to proceed.

"Hi, how ya doing, Hunt?" Metz said cautiously. "Everything OK?"

Hunter snorted and said, "Yeah, fine. Listen, I need the name and number of the guy you used to place our bets with."

"Wow! You starting back up?" Metz said enthusiastically.

"No," Hunter said flatly. "I just need to get a message to someone."

"Oh. Well, I got it here in my book. Just give a minute to find it."

Hunter waited silently. He could hear Metz digging through drawers and then flipping through his book.

"So how's it going up there," Hunter said to fill the silence.

"Oh, great!" Metz said excitedly, glad for his old friend's concern. "You'd love it up here. No crime, no smog, pretty scenery. Here it is! Jimmy the Squid. It was under B for betting. That's why I couldn't find it, but here it is."

Metz gave Hunter the number.

"Thanks, Metz," Hunter said. "Well, I gotta go. I hope everything goes well for you up there."

"Hey, Hunt," Metz said quickly, "I'm sorry, man. I'm really sorry. I never meant anything bad to happen. I didn't even think about betting on your game, about what it could do. I—I know it was wrong, I just didn't think. I'm sorry."

"Yeah, Metz," Hunter said, his voice sounding suddenly tired. "Well, shit happens."

Later that same morning, on the upper east side of Manhattan, Tony Rizzo was shaving in his bathroom. He whistled as he worked. In fact, he had been whistling since the alarm went off at ten. Camille had been unable to get back to sleep, and since Tony seemed to be in such a good mood, she decided to break their recently established pattern of silence.

"Got something important today?" Camille asked tentatively.

Tony popped his head into the doorway, the surprise in his face showing between patches of shaving cream.

"Yeah," he said almost pleasantly, "I do. How'd you know?"

"Oh, the whistling, I guess."

"Was I whistling?" Tony said, furrowing his brow. "Yeah, I guess so."

Cook had been in his office since six A.M. He hadn't slept well the night before and decided to go in to work early rather than fight it. Besides, he was behind in his paperwork and wanted to keep his i's dotted and his t's crossed until he broke the Tony Rizzo case. The way things looked from his viewpoint, he was going to be keeping his office running in New York for a while. It would probably be at least six months before he'd have all the loose ends tied up on the Mondolffi family, maybe more. But he had the feeling that once he had Tony Rizzo, things would start to move. He knew Rizzo was the only one who mattered in Rizzo's life and that he would turn on others in a heartbeat. Once the organization started to crumble, Cook was certain that someone would drop the dime on Tony's murder of the Fat Man. Then he could put Tony away for good.

At eight-thirty, Cook had a meeting with Duffy and Marrow. They were updating him on the progress of the investigation. The news was all bad, but Cook maintained an even expression as he listened.

He could hear the undertones of both of these men. Their hearts were no longer in it. No real progress had been made and the writing was on the wall. Cook knew they were backpedaling, preparing for the inevitable disbanding of the task force, probably spending more hours on making calls around inside the Bureau to land a new assignment than concentrating on the Mondolffis. Cook really couldn't blame them, and he was tempted to tell them that he was going to save the day in the eleventh hour. Cook hated the thought that these men considered the project a failure.

But discipline and secrecy had taken him this far and he wasn't about to take any chances by letting the cat out of the bag. He said little during the meeting. When it was over, he told them he would not be around for a few days. "I've got some things I'm working on that are going to keep me away."

By ten, Cook had plowed through a mound of paperwork and had the essential things in order. He worked through lunch and by late afternoon had composed a seven-page report outlining the situation he had with Hunter Logan and where it fit into the plan to bring down Tony Rizzo. He would send a copy of the report to Zulaff in Washington. He knew it would give him as much time as he needed to get the job done. Cook congratulated himself on a good morning's work. He proofread the report and went to see Duffy about the electronic equipment needed to wire Hunter Logan. On his way down the hall he bumped into Duncan Fellows and another man whom Cook didn't recognize.

"Hello, sir," Cook said, caught completely off guard.

Fellows smirked and said, "Cook, this is Marty Lazinski. Marty is doing an inventory of all the equipment we've got here to see what we can salvage and what we've got to sell. Isn't that what you do when we close down an office, Marty? Liquidate?"

Cook gave his boss a blank look. Fellows was obviously getting a jump on things by taking the preliminary preparations needed to close down his operation, and he was clearly enjoying it. Cook gritted his teeth. Fellows wasn't making the slightest effort to conceal his delight.

"By the way, Cook, while you're out of your office, maybe it would be a good time for Marty to look at your desk. I told him he could have it, if he liked it."

This was too much for Cook.

"I'm glad you're here, sir," Cook said, offering a genuine smile of his own. "I need to talk with you about something very important."

Fellows assumed a haughty air of indifference and chuckled lightly as he followed Cook back down the hall and into his office.

"I'm sorry, Marty," Cook said, gently closing the door on the accountant. "This will only take a minute."

Fellows winked knowingly at his sidekick and said, "I'll be right out, Marty."

Cook closed the door and went around behind his desk.

"So, wondering what the Bureau holds for you next, Cook? Too bad you can't take this view with you," Fellows said, gazing out through the canyon of buildings toward the Hudson River in the background.

"Sit down, sir," Cook said, still smiling.

"I really don't have time, Cook," Fellows huffed. "Marty and I want to finish up here. We've got a tee time at four."

"I think after you take a look at this you'll be able to get out to the driving range in plenty of time. That is what you do, isn't it? Go to the driving range when you've got extra time on your hands?"

Cook flipped his report to Zulaff across the desk. Fellows picked it up and began to read. Cooked watched as his superior's face turned red, then white. Cook was delighted. The sick look on Fellows's face only confirmed how much the man had been gloating over what he'd assumed was Cook's failure.

"I told you none of this cowboy stuff on your own, Cook!" Fellows tried to sound stern, but the report had taken the wind out of his sails and his words came out sounding more like a protest. Both men knew that Cook's ends justified the means. The bottom line was simple: Cook was going to bring down Tony Rizzo, and possibly the entire Mondolffi organization.

"I want to see the rest of this file," Fellows said, looking as though he had been punched in the stomach.

Cook's bright smile lit the room. "I'll be happy to accommodate you, sir," he said, "when I get it all together. It's not here right now. I've been doing some work at home . . . on my own time."

Fellows said nothing. He turned and started for the door.

"Excuse me, sir," Cook said, rising to cut him off and lifting the report gently from his hands, "but I'm sending this by courier to Mr. Zulaff, eyes only, of course. But," Cook added, opening the door for his boss and bowing sarcastically, "I thought you might like a peek at it first . . . to save you and Marty the trouble."

Tony Rizzo knew things were going as good as he'd hoped when he walked into the suite at the Waldorf and there were four places set at the dining room table for lunch instead of just two. Mark Ianuzzo and Sal Gamone were already sitting when Meeker ushered him into the suite.

"Tony!" Mark Ianuzzo greeted him warmly. "Sit down. We were waiting for you."

Tony knew better than to begin the discussion with business. Ianuzzo and Gamone would let him know when the time was right, probably after the espresso was served. The four of them casually discussed politics, taxes, and the fate of the country's economy under the new administration. When the table was cleared and the room emptied of all except themselves, talk turned to Hunter Logan.

"We're very impressed," Sal Gamone said. "You should know that up front, Tony. Especially the way you got Logan back on the field after they'd pulled him. That showed us that not only have you come upon a great opportunity, but you've thought over every angle carefully. We appreciate the fact that you're willing to share this opportunity with us."

"We know that times are uncertain," said Ianuzzo. "We understand that sometimes things happen to people at the top of any organization and . . . they have to be replaced. Naturally, when the time is right, we'd like to work closer with you."

"Before we can assure you of our complete cooperation," Gamone broke in, "we would like to see you take care of the upcoming Giants–Titans game, as a guarantee. All of us will be able to make the kind of money on that game that will help us to soften the rough times ahead.

"After that," Gamone continued, "whatever happens, you can count on our friendship."

"We would like to mention to you now that we'd also like to be involved in another one or two of these games before the end of the season," said Ianuzzo. "And we were thinking that if the Titans could make it to the Super Bowl again, it would be the first time anyone could control the outcome. You can imagine the possibilities."

"Of course, we'll have to make sure we don't let Logan lose too many to keep them out of it in the first place," said Gamone. "So?"

Both men looked at Tony. He couldn't hide his smile.

He nodded and said, "I can give you the Giants game, and one or two more after that. It's no problem at all. The idea about the Super Bowl is something I hadn't thought of. I like it. And if they get in, we can make history."

Tony saw that these men were pleased, though not in the same way he was. He liked the idea because it would put him into the forefront of organizations like theirs around the world. It could mean more power. They liked it because it would mean an incredible amount of money. Every school teacher, businessman, factory worker, and secretary in the country bet on the Super Bowl. Everyone. No one was exempt from putting action on the show.

Tony took a final sip of his coffee and, in order not to overstay his welcome, rose to leave. He appreciated the fact that these men had sat down with him to eat. It meant he was almost an equal. Two things remained for him to do. First, he had to fix the Titans–Giants game. Second, his uncle had to meet with what Ianuzzo had called "uncertain" times. Both were well within his grasp. He could see the peak of the mountain, and all that remained was one last sprint to the top. Of course, if he failed in either one of these, he would be cast down, probably to his death. That, however, was not even a consideration. Tony Rizzo believed in his own destiny.

CHAPTER

Cook decided to take Natasha and Esther out for dinner to celebrate. Esther could not remember the last time she'd seen him so jubilant. Natasha sensed the difference in him, too, and during their cab ride down to the Village, took advantage of his good mood to show off some Spanish words she had learned. She explained that Alejandro had taught the words to her and Lucy during recess so they could greet their teacher, who was also Hispanic, in her own language tomorrow morning.

"Ready?" she asked, concentrating to remember the exact phrase.

Cook smiled affectionately at her and nodded.

"Vese mi cula!" she barked proudly, smiling from ear to ear.

Cook's face sunk. The cab driver was looking back in the rearview mirror, smirking and searching for a glimpse of the little girl. Cook scowled at the driver and glanced at Esther. She remained, as always, passively staring straight ahead.

"What, Daddy?" Natasha asked, sensing her father's disapproval.

"Don't say that, Natasha," he said in a sterner tone of voice than he'd intended.

"Why not? Good morning is a nice thing," she argued back.

"I said no!" Cook bellowed in a voice that got even Esther's attention.

Tears welled in Natasha's eyes, and her lower lip began to tremble. Cook watched her fight back the tears. It reminded him so much of her mother that he was lost for a moment in his own world.

Esther broke his reverie by staring at him with as much malice as she could muster.

"No, honey, I didn't mean to yell," Cook said softly, reaching out to stroke his daughter's cheek, "but those words aren't nice. They— they don't mean good morning, they mean something not nice."

Cook realized how silly he sounded, talking about "not nice" in the kind of world they lived in. He reflected that his daughter probably heard a lot worse every day, at school, on TV . . .

"It means 'kiss my butt,'" he told her suddenly. "You don't want to say that to your teacher."

Natasha giggled at his words. He never spoke like that. Cook scowled at her. "OK?" he said.

Natasha nodded, trying her best not to keep giggling. Cook could see that even Esther was amused. He turned his attention to the people going by on the sidewalk. The practical joke Alejandro had attempted to play on his daughter was no big deal. He was sure he'd done worse in his day. But it reminded him that things were not always as they seemed. Suddenly, he was no longer in a celebrating mood. The case was not wrapped up yet. He remembered Tommy Keel. The thought of the boy and his girlfriend lying there in the kid's apartment with their heads blown open like summer melons took Cook's appetite away. As he knew it might be the last time for a while that he would see his family like this, he did his best to be pleasant and cheerful during dinner. But Esther and Natasha were acutely aware that although Cook was there, his mind was already working far away.

The dinner put Cook behind schedule. He had wanted to be at Logan's house by nine, but it was nine-fifteen before he even got off the Nassau Expressway in the midst of the Five Towns. The weather had turned cooler, so Cook had the windows up until he drove past the entrance of Hewlett Harbor. He wanted to be alert to everything around him as he drove through Logan's neighborhood. He went past the front of the house. The black Town Car was parked just past the driveway, on the other side of the road. It sat right on the boundary line between two homes so that each neighbor would think the Town Car had something to do with the guy next door. It was a good choice of car, too, common and unassuming.

Cook never slowed as he passed. He knew he'd learn nothing and only give himself away if he did. His only purpose was to make sure that whoever was watching the house was actually in the car. The last thing he needed was to bump into some guy of Rizzo's out in the shrubbery.

He wound his way through the back roads of the Harbor to the street that would allow him to access Logan's house from the back. He parked in the same manner that Rizzo's man had, on the boundary between two homes. He got out of his car and slung the bag with the wire in it over his shoulder, then worked his way through some lawns and shrubbery until he came into a grove of towering old trees that marked the end of the Logan property. He peered up the slight rise, past the playground, past the pool, and into the warm yellow light of the house. He could see Hunter peering out of the bay window in front of the kitchen table where they'd sat last night.

Cook cast a glance around quickly, taking in the dark outlines of the enormous neighboring homes that sat like dark shrines, silhouetted against the moonlit night sky. He exhaled slowly and started to walk toward the house. He collected his thoughts for the plan he was about to unfold and wondered if Hunter had had any success with getting the number of the bookie.

Hunter shook Cook's hand at the door, actually stepping out into the night to greet the agent.

"Agent Cook," Hunter said.

"Just Cook, call me Cook."

Cook stepped into the house and saw that Rachel was waiting for them at the kitchen table. She had a full pot of coffee in a silver urn and a crystal cake plate covered with delicious-looking baked goods laid out on the table. The sweet smells filled Cook's nostrils. He gave Rachel a smile and they exchanged pleasantries. The food seemed superfluous. Here Cook was, about to unfold a plan that could put Hunter's life on the line, and the table was laid out as if a tea party were about to begin.

"Can I get you something to drink?" Rachel asked. "I made coffee."

"Coffee would be great," Cook said, sitting in the same chair he sat in the night before.

"Did you get the number?" Cook asked Hunter.

"Yes, I tracked Metz down in Syracuse. He still had it. The guy's name is Jimmy. Metz said it was Jimmy the Squid."

Cook nodded and took a sip from the mug Rachel handed him.

"He's one of Tony's soldiers," Cook said. "He runs the numbers in the Five Towns for the Mondolffis, got shot up a few years back and he's been in a wheelchair ever since. Can you call him any time tomorrow?"

"Yes," Hunter said, "we break for a half hour at lunch."

"Good," Cook said. "Give Jimmy a call and tell him who you are. Tell him that you need to get a message to Tony Rizzo and that it's important you speak to Tony right away. Tell him that you won't talk to anyone but Tony. Tell him that Tony will be mad if he doesn't get the message right away. That'll insure he calls Tony immediately. Nobody wants to get Tony mad, especially one of his henchmen."

Cook picked his bag off the floor and took out the wire. There was a small microphone with a peel-off back that Cook told Hunter to stick to the inside of his shirt near the collar. A thin wire connected the mike to a small transmitting pack that Hunter could strap around his waist inside his pants. The pack was only two by three inches and a half inch thick.

"Wear the pack in front like this," Cook said, strapping the pack around his own waist. "It can go underneath your pants and no one will ever know it's there. The transmitter will send the signal to a receiver I'll have nearby in my car. There's a homing disc I've put on the back of the transmitter. I can follow you wherever you go. I'll tape everything once I hear that Rizzo has made contact with you. You'll have to wear this all the time. I'm sorry, but we can't be sure when or where Rizzo will have you picked up."

Both Hunter and Rachel looked more worried with each passing moment.

"I don't want either of you to worry," Cook said with confidence. "I've done this hundreds of times. It's no big deal and it will be over before you know it. You'll be able to go back to living your lives the way you always have."

As Cook expected, this seemed to be exactly what the couple wanted to hear. He kept things simple, as though what was going on was no more than an ordinary task like washing a car, and his easy yet upright manner, his good looks, and his smart wardrobe helped him to put even the most endangered civilians at ease. To prove the point to himself, he reached out and plucked a sweet bun from the plate.

He chewed a mouthful casually, then swallowed and licked some sticky icing from his fingers before saying calmly, "Do either of you have any questions?"

Hunter reached across the table and picked up the wire. He turned it over slowly, testing the sticky surface on the back of the mike. "Just wear this all the time?" he said.

"Yeah, except the shower and in bed."

Cook had meant it as a kind of joke, but he could see that Hunter was taking the whole thing very seriously. "So you'll be there, I mean, around wherever it is that Rizzo meets me?"

"Yeah, I'll be right there, close by," Cook said.

"And you think everything's OK with Rachel and Sara?" Hunter said. "You're sure you don't think we should send them somewhere?"

"Would they ever go away anywhere during the football season?" Cook asked.

"No," Hunter said. Rachel shook her head in agreement.

"Then, like I said, the best thing to do is what you'd normally do. The most dangerous thing would be to start changing the way you behave. Believe me. I'm not coming in the back door for nothing. If Rizzo knew you were up to something, I might not get my chance to nail him."

Hunter looked directly into Cook's eyes and said, "Maybe that would be the best thing of all, for him to just go away."

This caught Cook off guard. He thought his message the previous night was clear. He held Hunter's gaze. "The problem with that is, if I don't get Rizzo, well, I've already got you."

"Why is it you don't already have Rizzo?" Hunter said.

"If you go down, which you could easily do," Cook said firmly, "and you try to bring Rizzo in, he'll sell you out and say you approached him to pay off some gambling debts. I can get Rizzo on bookmaking, but that's chump change. He'd barely get a warning for something like that. Bookies need a revolving door at every court-house across this country. They're in and out, in and out. It's no big crime. But threatening a player who tells him he's going to back out of his fix—that's extortion, that's bookmaking, that's fraud, that's racketeering . . . and that's more time than Tony Rizzo will be willing to serve. He'll start serving up his buddies and hopefully, his buddies will serve up him."

Cook could see that the message was now loud and clear.

"Hey," Cook said, almost apologetically "you're not the only guy with a family. I've got things in my life that need doing, too. Believe me, the best thing is for you and me to work together."

Cook stood to go.

"Mrs. Logan," he said, "thanks for the coffee and the roll."

"Hunter," Cook said, holding out his hand to shake with the quarterback, "I'll be right there if you need me. After tomorrow at noon, you just talk into the mike if you want me to appear for any reason. I'll figure out the best way to make contact without our friends finding out."

Hunter stood now and shook the agent's hand. "So you think this is safe?" he said again.

"Listen," Cook said, putting on his most serious face, "everything will be fine. I'm the only one that knows you've got this wire. You just tell Rizzo that the deal's off, let him rant and rave at you, threaten you a bit, and you say OK. He'll leave you alone and that's it. You're done! The hard part will be over, and you and your family will be fine. I promise."

With that final assurance, Cook said thank you once more to Rachel and faded out the back door into the darkness.

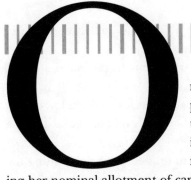

On Saturday morning, Hunter packed his bag for the team's trip to Kansas City. Rachel stood leaning in the doorway with her arms folded. Sara was downstairs watching her nominal allotment of cartoons.

"Rachel, everything will be fine," Hunter said, then stuffed in an extra pair of socks and zipped his bag.

"I know," Rachel said. "I just want them to call already. It worries me that nothing's happened. Maybe they know about Cook. Maybe they're waiting until you make this trip and Cook's not there."

"Rachel," Hunter sighed, "we've been through this. Cook can't get on the charter plane. Neither can Rizzo. Cook's going to keep close to Rizzo while I'm gone, just in case he does try to zip out to Kansas City to make contact with me, but like Cook said, it just doesn't happen that way. These guys aren't that sophisticated. Rizzo doesn't know about Cook, and he's just waiting until he's damn good and ready before he contacts me. He's making me sweat, that's all."

Hunter looked at his watch and said, "Bert's late. Shit! It'll cost us two thousand if we miss this plane."

"I don't know, Hunter," Rachel said, following him down the hallway to the stairs, "this whole thing . . . I mean, who ever heard of an FBI agent who worked alone? I mean, he seems like a great guy, and the real thing. But what if this Cook guy isn't on the level?"

"Rachel," Hunter huffed as he chugged down the stairs, "will you stop all this? He's OK. I told you. He was the guy who came to the team during camp. He was there with the DEA guy. He's the real thing, believe me."

"I'm just worried about you," Rachel said, right behind her husband as he bent down to kiss Sara on the couch. "You can't blame me for that."

Hunter stood up and put his arms around his wife.

"A car has entered the outer drive" came the monotonous electronic voice of the security system.

"That's Bert," Hunter said.

"Why are you worried about Daddy?" Sara asked her mother after coming to life at a commercial break.

"I'm . . . I just don't want him to get hurt in the game, honey," Rachel said.

"He won't get hurt," Sara chirped. "Audrey said Daddy's got a glass shoulder, but I told her that her dad probably never put the pads on."

Hunter smiled at his daughter and tousled her hair. "Putting the pads on" was a common football term she must have picked up from him. Players were always questioning the manhood of the general public by pondering whether or not they had ever "put the pads on."

"A car has entered the upper drive" came the voice, and then a horn beeped.

Hunter bent down and kissed his daughter one last time. "I love you, sweetheart."

"I love you too, Daddy."

Rachel followed him to the front door.

"Love you," Hunter said, opening the door.

"So Cook's following you two all the way to the airport, right?" Rachel said, then tugged on Hunter's collar and said loudly, "Make sure you follow them, Cook!"

"Rachel!" Hunter said, tugging back his collar. "Will you give me a kiss? I've got to go. Stop worrying about me."

"OK, go. Good-bye, you'll be late. I love you."

Hunter gave her a final kiss and hurried out to Bert's car. "I'll see you soon," he said as he shut the door with a wave.

Bert punched the car and they took off down the driveway in a great hurry.

"Not soon enough," Rachel said, but Hunter didn't hear her.

Later the same day, Vincent Mondolffi emerged from his favorite Brooklyn haunt. His eyes were adjusting to the dark evening sky when he spotted a white van parked at the curb just down the street. He silently pursed his lips in annoyance. He was beginning to feel like a man in the deep woods without a hat. The FBI was buzzing around his head like a swarm of deer flies. They wouldn't kill him, they wouldn't even slow him down that much. But there they were, a constant irritant. He had spent the week in Philadelphia on business, and they had even followed him there. He knew they were listening to many of his conversations, and he had to go to great lengths to keep many of his conversations private. He had to have Ears rent him a car every few days, then have Dominic sit in it all day so that the feds couldn't put some tracer on it. Back doors, pay phones, and speeding cars had become a way of life for him in the few weeks since the call announcing that he would be the focus of the special task force rather than Tony. He couldn't imagine what it would be like if he wasn't one step ahead of them all the time.

He did admit to himself, though, that whatever the inconvenience, it was much better now than when they were scrutinizing Tony. He knew that this task force was desperate, and he also knew that he wouldn't make any mistake that would allow them to write him even a parking ticket. Vincent Mondolffi had always been careful. It was one of his strong suits.

He was on the sidewalk getting into his car with Ears when Martino, the owner of Romans, came bustling out of the restaurant in his shirtsleeves calling his name.

"Vincent! Vincent!" he cried. "There is a man on the pay phone who says it's urgent that he speak to you."

Mondolffi nodded to Martino and followed him back into Romans with Ears in tow. There were only a few people who knew to call him at the pay phone. Over the past few weeks he had gotten only two calls on it. The last thing Mondolffi wanted was the feds to find out about the pay phone and start bugging it. The phone's security was so critical to him that he had a man run a check on it every day at six o'clock just to make absolutely sure. He picked up the phone, confident that the call was a private one.

"I've been calling you" came a voice that was becoming too familiar and too expensive as of late. "We've got a problem."

"Tell me," Mondolffi said impatiently.

"I mean a real problem."

Mondolffi could tell that the caller was nervous, almost desperate. This made him very uneasy.

"What?" he said.

"Tony's been fixing Titans games, you know that." Mondolffi said nothing. "So now, the black agent—"

"The same one with that Keel kid?" Mondolffi cut in.

"Yeah, he's gotten to Hunter Logan. Logan's going to wear a wire. If Tony meets with Logan and he talks . . . it's over, you can kiss Tony good-bye, and I know you don't want Tony turning into a federal witness."

"Did Tony already talk to Logan with this wire?" Mondolffi asked gruffly.

"No."

"So, what's the problem? I tell Tony to shut his mouth and lay off the Titans and everything's fine."

There was silence. It was obvious to Vincent Mondolffi that his informant had not thought things through. This was not a good sign.

"There's already a file on Tony and Logan," the voice said.

"Get it," Mondolffi said flatly.

"Get it for you?" the voice said, breaking as if that was a joke.

"I said, get the file. For me. I want it. I don't want anybody putting heat on Tony for anything. I don't want that. I'll pay for it."

"Something like that," came the slow, careful response, "would be hard to get."

"You listen to me," Mondolffi said in an angry tone, "I've had it up to here with all this shit! I don't want to hear about it! You get me that file. If something goes down on my nephew, something's going to go down on you, too! You got that?"

"Yes," said the voice in a distant way that made Mondolffi wonder if the man was thinking of something else.

"All right? Are we all right?" Mondolffi said.

"Yes, of course," the voice said with regained composure. "I'll arrange to have it delivered."

"Good," Mondolffi said and hung up the phone with a sigh.

He turned to Ears and said, "Come on. We've got to lose that FBI van and find Tony."

Outside, as he was getting into his car, Vincent Mondolffi again eyed the white NYNEX van halfway down the block. Ears, he noticed, was smiling as he pulled on a pair of driving gloves he used whenever he had to do some fancy driving. "I'm too damn old to be doing this kind of shit," he mumbled as he slid into the backseat beside Dominic.

Ears Vantressa knew that the hardest part about losing a tail was knowing exactly who was following you. Most times when someone wanted to tail you, they had at least two vehicles in constant communication with each other. You could always flush the first, but the second could be right there beside you and you'd never know. In this case Ears knew exactly what he was looking for. Besides the NYNEX van there was a dark blue Crown Vic. To get them both in line, Ears got onto the BQE and started to speed. He knew somewhere in the sea of headlights behind him, the two FBI vehicles would come into line together. After a few miles Ears swerved off the BQE and onto the LIE for the Midtown Tunnel. He raced toward the tunnel and jumped off the express at the Green Point Exit. This left him in the heart of the Brooklyn river docks, and after a couple of quick turns and a final dodge around a corner into a dark garage they sat and waited with the lights off, facing out into the side street. Within a minute the van raced right by. A minute later the Crown Vic followed.

The three men got out of the rental car and got into an old Chevy Caprice. Dominic and Vincent Mondolffi slouched down in the backseat until they were crossing the Fifty-ninth Street Bridge into Manhattan. A few minutes later they pulled up in front of the Palladium. Dominic hopped out of the car quickly and jogged up to the oldest bouncer at the door. They exchanged a few words, then Dominic turned around and gave his boss a thumbs-up before disappearing into the nightclub. Five minutes later, he emerged with Tony behind him. Tony got into the backseat of the car while Dominic remained standing outside like a sentry.

"Tony," Vincent Mondolffi said warmly, kissing his nephew on the cheek.

"Hello, Uncle Vinny," said Tony, forcing a smile. He was dressed as always in an expensive, dark-colored suit. His tie was electric blue and he had a matching handkerchief in his breast pocket. His hair was pulled back in a tight ponytail.

"I've got some bad news," Mondolffi said, "but . . . it could be worse." Tony's face clouded over with concern, and he glanced at Ears nervously while he waited to hear what it was. "You've got to lay off of the Titans game, Tony," he said. "The FBI's gotten hold of Hunter Logan and he's working with them."

Vincent Mondolffi thought he saw a flicker of relief on his nephew's face, and then, as if he hadn't understood what his uncle had said, complete shock.

"You're kidding," Tony said quietly.

Mondolffi shook his head and said, "No, they're going to have Logan set up a meeting with you and wear a wire. They've already got some things linking the two of you, but I should have that file in my hands before the weekend is over."

"I'll kill that fuck Logan," Tony said to quietly to himself, seething with rage.

"No," Mondolffi said. "No, what's done is done. You played the game and made us a lot of money, but it's over. You did a good job, and now I don't want you doing anything foolish, Tony. The feds are all over us right now, and something like that would only complicate things. Stay clear of Hunter Logan. You've gotten enough out of him. The game is over. Don't take it hard. Be glad we found out when we did."

Tony looked searchingly at his uncle, as if maybe he expected something more.

"That's it?" he asked.

"Yes, why? Should there be more?" said the uncle.

"No."

"So we're straight on this," Mondolffi said. "I don't want another incident like the one with the drugs. I don't want to tell you twice on this, Tony. It's for your own good more than anything else."

"We're straight," Tony said. "Who's the guy feeding you all this information?"

"That's not important," Mondolffi said, dismissing the question. "I'll let you get back to what you were doing."

Tony got out of the car and said good-bye. As he walked away, Vincent Mondolffi wondered to himself what would cause his nephew to be relieved, bewildered, and enraged all in the course of their simple conversation. He shrugged to himself. He had one more thing to think about tonight that turned his mind away from his nephew. His man inside the Bureau had given him an uneasy feeling. It was just a feeling, but he always followed his instincts, and they told him that someone should be keeping a close eye on the dirty agent. Someone should be there when he got his hands on that file. Vincent Mondolffi didn't want to leave something as sensitive as the file to someone who he felt was losing control. That's what was happening, too. He realized it for certain, thinking back to the sound of the agent's voice.

He pursed his lips together tightly, thinking. A bad agent in trouble . . . that was dangerous. That was something that needed fixing. He waved Dominic inside the car.

"Dominic," he said when his man was sitting beside him and listening attentively, "I've got a job for you . . ."

Mondolffi leaned close to Dominic and spoke softly into his ear. Ears glanced in the mirror and saw this. He averted his eyes immediately. He wasn't insulted. That was the way Vincent was. Ears knew that his boss trusted him and Dominic more than anyone in the world, and still there were things he kept from them. It was probably one of the reasons why Vincent Mondolffi was the boss.

Ears heard Dominic get out of the car and slam the door shut. Then he watched as Dominic weaved through the crowded sidewalk outside the Palladium and hailed a cab. Despite all the years of conditioning not to wonder about anything, Ears couldn't help but wonder where his partner was going.

"All right, Ears," Mondolffi said abruptly. "Take me home."

A unt Esther liked to watch "Gunsmoke" reruns on Saturday nights. It was one of the few luxuries she allowed herself. She'd seen each episode three or four times, but that didn't matter. She hustled Natasha to bed and settled down on the couch with a can of Coke and a white sugar-powdered doughnut. Everything was right in Esther's world. The only thing that could have been better was if she knew where her nephew was and when he'd be back.

"Cuss that Ellis," the old woman muttered to herself and then briefly touched the small, simple wooden cross that hung around her neck.

Festus was dragging his wounded and bleeding leg through the marshal's office door when a knock came at Esther's own door. She looked up from her show like an angry owl. The knock came again and she returned her half-eaten doughnut to its plate, then licked the white powder from her fingers. She was halfway to the door and muttering ceaselessly under her breath before she was struck with the notion that whoever was at the door might be there to harm her.

Esther stopped dead in her tracks. It was late Saturday night. No one should be here knocking. Her heart began to gallop, and she shuffled into her bedroom to get her pistol from under the mattress. She returned to the door and quietly put her eye to the peephole, pointing the gun at the door all the while.

There was a man in a suit out there, and Esther almost jumped out of her skin when he rapped loudly once more.

"Who is it?" she cried, stepping back from the door and leveling the gun. She closed her eyes, scared of the noise the gun would make if she pulled the trigger.

"Are you Aunt Esther?" came the man's voice. "I'm Duncan Fellows. I'm with the FBI. Your nephew works under me. I need to come in. Are you in there?"

She opened the door a crack and stared at the man called Fellows.

"He dead?" she asked in a shocked voice.

"No," Fellows said. "No, he's not. But he's in some trouble, and I need to help him. Can I come in?"

"Let me see your badge," Esther said stubbornly.

Fellows whipped out his badge and his ID and held them up to the wedge of light that shone through from Esther's side of the door. Esther pretended to examine it carefully despite being unable to read anything at all without her glasses. She felt ludicrous, standing there with the gun. She quickly stuffed the firearm in the pocket of her tattered old housecoat, then unbolted the door and opened it the rest of the way.

Fellows came in. Esther could see that his hands were trembling slightly, and she thought she smelled peppermint schnapps on his breath. He looked around nervously.

"Are you alone?" he said.

"What kinda question is that?" she said, sliding her hand discreetly into the pocket of her housecoat.

"I . . . nothing, I just wondered if you were all right, staying here, alone . . ."

"What you want?" Esther said, stepping backward into the living room.

"Cook, your nephew, has some papers here. I need to see them. It's important. He may be in great danger," he added.

"Ellis sent you?" Esther asked.

"Yes," Fellows nodded, "I'm his boss."

"I know that," Esther said, looking as though she might have bitten into a lemon.

She thought for a moment. She thought of her nephew's words about her overreacting. She pointed toward Ellis's bedroom.

"He keeps all his things in there," she said.

Fellows's face seemed to relax. He almost smiled.

"Good," he said and went into Cook's bedroom.

Esther followed him. She reached across the hall and shut the door to her bedroom, then watched Fellows silently from the doorway.

"You're making a mess," she commented sharply.

Fellows looked back at her and smiled in a wicked way. "I'm sorry," he said. "It's important."

Esther began to think that she'd done the wrong thing to let Fellows in. She had a bad feeling about the way he was ripping through her nephew's things. He was digging through the bottom drawer of Ellis's battered old desk when he suddenly stood erect with a thick manila folder in his hand. He began thumbing through the pages and photographs inside. He smiled and snapped the folder shut, setting it down on the desktop. Then he proceeded to go through the rest of Ellis's things.

"You find what you needed?" Esther said.

"Yes," Fellows murmured without looking at her. "But I need to make sure I've got everything."

In another minute, the room was in a complete shambles. Fellows had extracted two packets of photos and their negatives from the top shelf of the closet, and he now held them with the file.

"Now," he said, looking at Esther, "are you sure this is the only place he keeps his papers? It's important, very important . . . for him."

Esther shook her head and said, "If it ain't in there, then it ain't Ellis's."

"Good," Fellows said.

Esther suddenly came to her senses and remembered Ellis's cellular phone. She backed into the living room and quietly picked up the phone while Fellows was doing a final take of the bedroom. She heard the phone ring twice, but before Ellis could answer, Fellows was on top of her, snapping down the receiver of the phone. "What are you doing?" he growled.

"Calling Ellis," she said, glaring at him. "He said call if I needed him. I don't know if I like what you're doing."

A twisted smile appeared on Fellows's face. He reached into his coat and pulled out an automatic handgun. It had a cylindrical tube on the end of it, a silencer. Fellows pointed the gun at Esther's forehead and put the index finger of the hand that held the file up to his lips.

"Shhh," he whispered. "If you're quiet, and if you do what I say . . . no one will get hurt."

Cook was sitting at the upstairs bar of the Palladium. Besides his brief encounter with Vincent Mondolffi, Tony Rizzo's night had been uneventful. Tony seemed to be engaged in a game with Camille Carter. Cook called it the "See How Much She Can Take" game. Rizzo, with one arm around Camille, was engaged in a lively discussion with a beautiful brunette whom he had flagged down about an hour earlier. Cook couldn't help wondering how long Camille would put up with Rizzo's obvious flirtations. He had bet himself she would slap Rizzo's face and walk away before his fourth drink. He was working on his fifth soda water with lime, and Camille was still there when he felt more than heard the small cellular phone in his coat pocket ring. Popping it open, he heard only a dial tone.

The call made him nervous. Only Esther had the number and she was to call him only in the event of an emergency. Cook's heart pumped adrenaline through his body. He started up from his chair, then sat back down. He had made a promise to Logan that he would stay on top of Tony Rizzo. It was certainly possible that Rizzo could take a plane to Kansas City and make his rendezvous with the quarterback there. It was unlikely but possible, and Cook didn't want to jeopardize Logan.

Besides, Cook reasoned, it could have been a caller who had dialed the wrong number and hung up when he realized his mistake. Just as likely, it was Esther. Nervous about the recent killing down the block, she could have heard a noise and called him in a panic, then realized she was being foolish before he had time to answer. Cook was getting jumpy from sitting, that was all. If Esther needed him, she would have stayed on the line. Cook was determined to see Rizzo to bed. After that he would make a quick trip back downtown to check on Esther and Natasha. There would be plenty of time for that.

Esther involuntarily staggered backwards into the hallway and bumped against the bedroom door. She looked up at Fellows. His eyes were crazed, and his tongue darted nervously over his lips as he kept the gun at her forehead. Her legs felt wobbly and she dropped to the floor. Before she heard the gun go off, Esther's last feelings were of disgust with herself. She was disgusted that she couldn't do a thing. She wanted to take the gun out of her housecoat pocket. It was there for her protection, and now, with a chance to use it, her limbs felt too heavy and she was sluggish with fear, as though she was living out a horrifying dream.

The silencer's spit sounded like the burst of an underwater scream. Esther's face was sprayed with blood, and she heard the pistol clatter to the floor. She looked up and watched Fellows's faceless body drop lifelessly. She felt the warm pool of her own urine beneath her. Too terrified to scream, she looked up with a gaping mouth at the large man who stood only a few feet away in the living room. He was dressed in dark pants and shirt and wore a dark blue windbreaker. His face was distorted under the tight covering of a woman's stocking.

The big man stepped forward into the hallway and leaned down over Fellows's body. He suddenly jammed the cylindrical barrel of his gun tightly behind Fellows's ear and pulled the trigger in three quick short bursts. Esther heard the bullets hitting the floor like three raps of a hammer. The underside of the dead man's head was a pudding of blood and brains. The big man quickly and quietly stuffed the bloodied papers and photos Fellows had taken from Ellis's room back into the file. He picked up the packets of photos too and stuffed everything into the front of his pants before he zipped up his jacket.

When he finished, he checked his appearance, then seemed to notice Esther for the first time. He aimed his gun at her head, then paused and tilted his own head ever so slightly, like a dog that hears a silent whistle. He stood that way for almost a minute. Tears filled Esther's eyes and ran pellmell down the crags in her old face. Her mouth was twisted, but she made no noise. She prayed to God, not for her own life, but that the man would kill her and go away, leaving Natasha to grow as old as the aunt who would willingly die in her place.

The man backed into the living room and reached down. With a gloved finger from his free hand he popped off a pair of cheap rubbers that Esther hadn't noticed until now. Then he straightened and held his finger to his lips much in the same way Fellows had, signaling her to be silent. He tossed the pistol down on the floor beside Fellows's body. Esther's eyes followed the clatter of the gun in disbelief. When she looked up, the man was gone.

Before *Aladdin* was over, Sara had fallen asleep on the couch with her head on Rachel's lap. Rachel let the movie run even though she'd already seen it a dozen times. She was waiting for Hunter to call. When he did, they talked for almost an hour, Rachel carefully avoiding the subject of Cook and Rizzo. She knew Hunter would want to keep his mind as clear as possible for the game tomorrow. That would be hard enough without her fretting to him over the phone. All she wanted was to hear his voice.

"OK, Rach," Hunter finally said, "I'm turning in. I'll call you in the morning."

"All right," she yawned. "I'm going to bed now, too. If you don't get me here, I'm probably on my way to the Hamptons to surprise Mom and Dad for breakfast, then watch the game out there. I won't call you before I go in case you're still sleeping."

"No problem," Hunter said. "I love you, honey."

"I love you, too."

"Rachel?"

"Yes?"

"Don't worry. I'll be fine."

"All right . . . good luck."

At midnight Duffy got a call from an agent named Brotz, the desk agent at the Manhattan office. Duffy and Brotz had worked together on several occasions through the years.

"Duffy?"

"Yeah? Who's this?" Duffy said, his voice hoarse with sleep.

"It's me, Brotz. I'm working the desk tonight. I know it's late, but I thought you'd want to hear this . . ."

"Go ahead," Duffy said.

"It's unbelievable, really," Brotz said. "We just got a call from NYPD. They found Duncan Fellows dead as hell . . . shot through the head."

"What?" Duffy said increduously.

"But get this—they found him in your boss's apartment." Brotz's words seemed to hang in the air.

"Cook's?" Duffy asked finally.

"Yeah, I thought you'd want to know," Brotz said in a nearly apologetic tone. "I mean . . ."

Duffy waited to hear what Brotz meant, but the whole thing seemed too bizarre to have any meaning.

"I . . . yes. Brotz, thanks," Duffy said, then hung up.

Duffy sat there in the dark for several minutes shaking his head and thinking. He swung his feet out of the bed and began to dress. He hoped Cook wasn't in any trouble, but after what he'd just heard he doubted that was possible.

Rachel heard a strange yet familiar voice in her dreams. She sat upright in the bed. Her bedroom was dark except for the pale moonlight coming in through the windows. A storm was blowing in from the ocean. The wind howled violently outside, and the moon-lit shadows of the trees fell in from the window and swayed wildly across the bedroom floor.

"Someone has entered the front inner perimeter."

The electronic voice cut through the sound of the swaying trees and hung eerily in the darkness. Rachel was terrified. She must have heard the first warning in her sleep. Someone was out in the front, on foot. Sensors in the driveway would have specified if it was a car. In the darkness she fished through the night table drawer for her Mace. Before she could get her hands on it, the security system began to wail. She looked up at the monitor above the bed. ZONE 3 flashed on the digital readout in bright red letters—it was the service door near the garage. The phone rang, and Rachel picked it up. She shook her head, still trying to come completely to her senses.

"This is Regal Security" came the bored voice on the other end of the phone.

"My God! Someone's here!" Rachel screamed into the phone. "Send the police!"

The voice quickly came to life, "All right, Mrs. Logan. Are you OK?"

"Just send them!" she shrieked. "Someone is in my house!"

Rachel heard the man talking calmly over the phone.

"This is Regal Security," he was saying, "I have a break-in at two-fifty-seven Meadow View with residents in the home. Please dispatch immediately. Yes, I have them on the line. I will."

". . . Mrs. Logan, I'm staying with you. Are you still all right?"

"Oh, my God, I've got to check my daughter," Rachel said and scrambled from her bed with the phone still in hand.

"Mommy! Mommy!" Sara burst into her room, sobbing. "Stop the noise! Make it stop!"

Rachel grabbed her daughter and held her tight. She punched the code into the monitor and the house became eerily silent. The ZONE 3 light still flashed, illuminating the bedroom with a bloodred glow.

"Mrs. Logan? Are you there?"

"Yes. Yes, I'm here."

"Just stay calm, Mrs. Logan," the man said. "The Nassau police are on their way. They'll be there in just a few minutes. Is your daughter with you now?"

"Yes."

"Is it just the two of you in the house?"

"Yes."

"And you're still in your bedroom?"

"Yes."

"All right. Do you have a lock on the door?"

"Yes."

"All right. You stay there in the bedroom and lock the door. You'll be fine. I'm right here, and the police are on their way."

Rachel locked the bedroom door and moved back toward the bed, gripping her can of Mace tightly and squeezing Sara with her arms.

"Mrs. Logan," the man said, "my name is David. Now, don't worry. The police will be there any minute. If there is an intruder, he's probably already gone. That's the beauty of a security system. It's like a big dog, and when a burglar hears it, he runs. It might not even be anyone, Mrs. Logan. Most of the time it's a door that just wasn't shut, but if it is someone, the police will be right there, so don't worry. Are you OK?"

"Yes," Rachel said, drawing strength from the fact that her

daughter was scared and the security man was obviously very nervous. Someone had to keep cool, and it would now be her.

She breathed a sigh of relief when she saw the flashing lights through the curtains of her window. David had chattered at her nonstop, but now he was repeating her name.

"Mrs. Logan?"

"Yes," she said, "I'm right here."

"Now, I've got the police on the other line, and they want you to stay where you are while they go through your house. OK?"

"OK."

"Yes," she heard David saying into another phone, "it's the side door near the garage, and the residents are remaining in the master bedroom on the second floor with the door locked." Rachel heard the police-car door slam. She waited patiently as the policemen worked their way through the downstairs of her house. Twenty minutes later, they were outside her bedroom door. There came a gentle tap, as if they were afraid of waking someone.

"Mrs. Logan?" came the soft voice of a young man through the door. "I'm Officer Wolkoff from the Nassau County police. Are you OK?"

"Yes," Rachel said, tears suddenly streaming down her face. "I'm fine."

"You can open the door, Mrs. Logan. We've checked the house and everything's fine. I think I can show you the problem. It looks as though your alarm system is on the fritz, ma'am. The side door was unlocked but shut tightly, and so were all the other doors . . ."

CHAPTER 36

lthough Officer Wolkoff was only twenty-two, he was the epitome of his profession. He was clean-cut, had a fresh red face, and refused to call her anything but "ma'am." By the third alarm malfunction that night he had thoroughly checked the entire Hewlett Bay area for any suspicious vehicles and repeatedly offered to take Rachel and Sara to her parents' place in Quogue even though it was an hour and a half away. But Rachel refused to upset her parents—or her husband, for that matter—by calling in the middle of the night. It was obvious to her that Wolkoff and his older partner, who was no less than a sergeant, had everything under control. It was three A.M. when she finally told David with Regal Security that she would just disengage the alarm. David fretted that he wouldn't be able to get someone there until Monday to fix the problem, but Rachel said not to worry, her husband would be home tomorrow night anyway.

She apologized to the officers for one final time from the front steps and wished them good night. They assured her that they would keep a close watch on the neighborhood for the rest of the night.

"Don't worry," the young officer added before he disappeared into his patrol car for the last time, "we get this kind of thing all the time. It's always just a bad system."

Rachel was proud of her rational acceptance of the situation as she settled down beneath the sheets with Sara snuggled up close beside her, already breathing heavily with sleep. She had locked the bedroom door again and left the Mace out on the nightstand. She was safe. Sleep, however, would not come. She tossed and turned for thirty minutes, then sat bolt upright in bed. Without the police right there, assuring her that everything was fine, the prospect of waking her parents didn't seem so ludicrous. She went back and forth in her mind a minute before she picked up the phone. The line was dead.

It all fell together instantly for Rachel. The phone line could be cut only if the alarm was off. Otherwise a cut line would signal the alarm, just like any zone violation.

"Sara!" she whispered, shaking the little girl. Sara moaned, irritated at another disturbance in her normally peaceful child's sleep.

"Sara! Wake up!" Rachel hissed, refusing to stop shaking her daughter's shoulder.

"Mommy, stop," Sara complained.

Rachel thought she heard a noise at the bottom of the stairs. "Sara, quiet! Do as I say!" she said as forcefully as she could without raising her voice. "Now!"

Sara came to life at the tone of her mother's voice. Rachel thanked God she saved that tone for times when she really needed it. "Come with me," she said, leading her daughter quietly to the bedroom closet.

She heard the knob on the bedroom door rattle loudly. Someone was there!

Rachel pushed aside her husband's clothes and clawed desperately for the hidden handle to the old trapdoor. She'd never used it herself, but she'd seen Hunter go through it when they first bought the house. He'd wandered through it every day for almost a week before he got bored and forgot about it. Her teeth chattered and her heart thumped wildly with fear.

"Mrs. Logan." She heard a gruff voice coming from the hallway outside the bedroom. "It's the police again, Mrs. Logan. Everything's fine. We just need to talk with you, so come out."

The voice didn't belong to Officer Wolkoff. She knew that much.

"There!" Rachel muttered to herself triumphantly as the door sprung open.

Rachel dragged Sara into the pitch-black passageway and pulled the door shut behind her.

"Mrs. Logan!" she heard the man shout. "Unlock the door, Mrs. Logan! We need to speak with you."

Rachel felt her way cautiously along the passageway. She jumped at the sickening crash as the intruder violently kicked in her bedroom door. She jerked Sara forward, and they both tumbled down several steps in the darkness to a small landing. Sara let out a shriek.

"I hear them!" she heard someone yell. "They're here somewhere!"

Rachel found her daughter's mouth and held it tightly. Sara began to sob and pawed gently at her mother's hand, but Rachel would not let go. The men's footsteps pounded loudly about the upstairs. Rachel looked up at the thin line of light as one of them flipped on the light in Hunter's closet.

"You must be quiet!" she whispered frantically in her daughter's ear.

Sara nodded. Rachel's hand was wet with the little girl's tears, but still she held her mouth shut.

Someone was rummaging around in the closet. Rachel's eyes were riveted on the thin outline of the trapdoor. She expected it to burst open any minute.

Then she heard a man's angry curse and his footsteps leaving the closet. Slowly she removed her hand from Sara's mouth. Carefully she untangled herself from Sara.

"You must be absolutely quiet," she whispered. She felt Sara's head nod in acknowledgment and began to inch her way forward.

"We'll find you, Mrs. Logan!" one of the voices bellowed. "You come out now and we'll leave the little girl alone!"

The mention of her daughter made Rachel panic. She choked back a sob and hurried down the rest of the stairs, bumping loudly into a wall.

"She's downstairs!" someone cried.

"I heard her up here!"

"They're downstairs now! I heard them!"

Rachel navigated down a long corridor, feeling ahead with her right foot until she came to another set of stairs. She heard the closet doors in the entryway being flung open, the crash of the pantry doors being ripped off their hinges.

"You bitch! Come out! We'll kill your little fucking girl if you don't!"

Rachel was crying now, too, and was almost glad for the darkness so Sara wouldn't see the panic and tears that covered her face. She felt the hard concrete of the basement under her bare feet. They were down! A maelstrom of footsteps pounded above them. Rachel scurried across the basement floor between the walls of the wine cellar and the foundation until she came to the end. She felt the seams of a doorway and gently pushed it open. A section of the wine racks swung open, and Rachel stepped into the musty cellar. She stopped in her tracks. These men would not stop hunting, and Sara couldn't run very fast or very far in her tiny bare feet. If the men saw them running from the house, or if there were more of them out there, they would catch Sara quickly and both would be caught.

"Sara," Rachel said in her most imploring tone, taking her daughter's face in her hands, "listen to me carefully! I know you're just a little girl, and I know you don't want me to leave you, but you have to do as I say! I'm going to run for help. I want you to stay in the secret passageway. You'll be safe there, and you have to do it."

"Mommy, I want to go with you," Sara whispered fiercely.

"No!" Rachel said without wavering a bit. "You stay here, Sara! I'm telling you to stay. Daddy would be very upset if you don't do what I'm asking you now."

"Daddy?" Sara said, and Rachel could see that she'd hit a nerve.

"But I'm scared," Sara whimpered.

"Honey, I know," Rachel whispered as she stroked the little girl's cheeks. "I know you're scared, but I want you to be brave. I want to tell Daddy how brave you were when I needed you to be."

Sara thought about this and said, "Daddy will think I'm brave if I stay?"

"Yes, honey."

Sara was thinking, and Rachel tried to be patient.

"OK."

"Good, honey! Now listen to me, this is very important. I want you to stay in a secret hiding place until you hear me or Daddy or Nana and Poppa, no one else. You're going to hear me yell in a few minutes, but don't worry about that. You just stay here until everything is quiet again. Then when you hear one of us, you come out. Even if they say they're the police, Sara, don't come out. Don't let anyone know you're there. One of us will come. I promise. Are you OK?"

Sara nodded.

"OK, good. Be brave, honey."

"For Daddy, right?"

"Yes, honey, for Daddy."

Rachel gently pushed her daughter back behind the wall and closed it. Tears were streaming down her face, but she brushed them aside and started up the cellar stairs, letting herself out into the backyard. Choking back a sob, she tried to think rationally. This was the only thing that could protect her little girl. She had to think clearly.

She carefully closed the cellar door and circled around to the front of the house. Their van was parked neatly in the driveway like an overnight guest's. The service door to the house was ajar, and she could hear the men rushing around inside her home.

"I'll find you, you bitch!" a voice bellowed suddenly from within.

Rachel jumped at the sound and trembled. She had to do what she was about to do. It was the only way, she told herself. The thought of her little girl made it easy. She stepped into the entryway and turned herself about, so she could get out as fast as humanly possible. She was afraid with the wind and the loud hissing of the trees that the men inside might not hear her, so she backed in to the house a little more and yelled over her shoulder.

"Run, Sara! Run!" Rachel screamed at the top of her lungs. She waited only an instant, until she was certain that the thunder of footsteps was headed her way.

"She's getting out!" someone yelled.

Rachel ran. She got out of the house and halfway across the front lawn before she looked over her shoulder to make sure the men were following her. They were just emerging at a full sprint from her house. She thought she could outrun them. She veered toward the driveway to save herself from having to go over the stone wall that marked the perimeter of their property. The wall might slow her down.

That was her last thought before she went down in a heap on the lawn. She was numb from the shock and suddenness of her fall. A wiry man with a grip of steel had tackled her by the ankles and was holding her tightly around the waist. Rachel was aware of the other two men closing in on her fast. She kicked and screamed, fighting wildly. Her cries wafted up uselessly amid the howling wind. No one would hear her.

Carl got a hold of her legs, and Lonny finally pinned her arms to her sides. Rachel recognized Carl as a changed version of the brute she'd seen at her mailbox in the summer. Her eyes widened with fright as Angelo Quatrini's hand closed over her mouth. She tried to bite him instinctively. He only smiled, taking a rag from the front of his windbreaker and replacing his hand with it. The moment before Rachel lost consciousness seemed to hang in time. She used it to try to read whether or not these men had bought her ruse and would abandon their search for Sara in order to escape as quickly as possible. The faces of the three men and the swaying branches of the trees above them began to spin slowly. They were carrying her toward the van.

"Let's go," a voice said. "Forget the girl."

Rachel smiled. Then everything went black.

Cook parked his rental car in a garage on Sixth Avenue. It was his habit to keep the car away from where he lived and walk a few blocks. He saw the flashing lights when he turned the corner at Twelfth. He sprinted the rest of the way down the street and broke through the yellow police tape without bothering to duck. He went unnoticed amid the blinking NYPD squad cars and an ambulance, but there was a crowd of law enforcement personnel on the steps and he held his badge high. The throng of officers and detectives parted silently for him without asking for an explanation. They already knew that this had something to do with the Bureau.

Cook pushed himself by two forensic men who were plodding up the narrow stairway, yawning sleepily and toting black bags like doctors making midnight house calls.

He barged through his own front door and was halfway into the living room before anyone recognized him. Duffy was on his haunches, gently poking the figure of Duncan Fellows whose blood was splashed all over the little hallway. Duffy rose when he saw Cook. Cook's stomach sank.

"Natasha?" he croaked, his eyes pleading with his friend for news that she was alright.

Duffy looked around nervously, but the police were busy at work and didn't seem to notice Cook. He took his boss by the arm and led him into the bedroom.

"Natasha?" Cook repeated. "Do you know what happened?"

"They're not here, Ellis," Duffy said in a low voice, "and I don't know if you should be. I have no idea what the hell is going on, but when the boys from the office get here they're going to want some answers."

Cook glanced into the hall. Cops were everywhere. A camera flashed repeatedly like an erratic strobe light. Technicians from the forensic lab were carefully scraping up minute samples of everything from the blood to the carpet and putting them into little plastic vials. The whole thing was like some bizarre dream.

"What do you mean, answers?" Cook heard himself say. "Where's Natasha?"

"I mean, Cook, the boss is dead and his brains are splattered all over your hallway like a spilt dish of pudding. What the hell was Fellows doing here?" Duffy said.

"I don't know," Cook said. He looked around the mess and crossed the room to examine his desk. The Rizzo file was gone. He went to the shelf in his closet.

"Gone," Cook murmured.

"What?" Duffy said.

"No one knows where Esther and Natasha are?" Cook asked without bothering to answer.

"No," Duffy said. "No one saw them. One of your neighbors came home and saw your door wide open. They called for Esther and when no one answered they looked in and found Fellows."

Cook nodded. "OK," he said, and moved toward the door, then quickly slipped through the throng of police and out of the apartment.

"Ellis," Duffy called after him.

Cook didn't seem to hear him. Duffy hurried down the stairs and grabbed Cook's arm tightly as they reached the stone front steps of the building.

"Ellis!" Duffy hissed. "Where the hell are you going?"

Cook turned and looked Duffy in the eye. "I've got work to do. Either Esther's taken Natasha and run, or somehow Rizzo has got them. Either way, the best way for me to settle this is to do my job."

"Well, you can't just walk out of here, Ellis," Duffy said frantically. "You can't just disappear again! They're going to want to talk to you."

"Who?"

"Who? Everyone, that's who," Duffy said. "NYPD's gonna want you. The guys from Fellows's office are gonna want you. Washington's gonna want to talk to you. Hell, this is a mess!"

"I gotta go," Cook said, turning abruptly and starting down the stairs. "I can't wait around until they figure out what's going on."

Duffy ran to catch up and had to jog to match his friend's pace. They ducked under the police lines.

"Ellis," Duffy said, huffing now. "If you walk away from this, you'll be on your own, man. Don't do it! It looks bad, you understand me? You can't just leave!" Cook pulled away.

"You give me as much time as you can, Duffy." he said over his shoulder. "Keep them away from me. You're right, this whole thing looks bad, and I don't have the time to sit around for three days answering questions. Got it?"

Duffy stopped and watched Cook as he continued to put distance between himself and the mess at his apartment. He bit his lower lip, angry with himself for all the questions he wanted to ask Cook but didn't.

Duffy cupped his hands around his mouth just before Cook rounded the corner.

"I'll try!" he called.

Without looking back, Cook gave him a wave, then disappeared.

Cook forced himself to think objectively. Someone had killed Fellows. That same person had taken the files on Rizzo. Cook had no explanation for why Fellows was at his apartment. It was inexplicable.

He guessed that someone in the agency was a lot further gone than he had imagined, and that person had figured what Cook was doing and then took the files. Either way the killer was linked to the Mondolffis. Esther and Natasha might have escaped the apartment during the fray with Fellows and were running somewhere. Cook hoped that was the case. He knew Esther would get them someplace safe and stay there. Another possibility was that whoever had killed Fellows had taken the two of them for some reason.

Everything led him right back to Rizzo. If Esther and Natasha had been taken, Rizzo could get them back. If his family was safe, he still needed Rizzo's head on a platter to help clear up the mess that would be waiting for him when he surfaced. Things didn't look good. There would very likely be no prints on the gun used to kill Fellows, and Cook would be a prime suspect. His relationship with Fellows was strained, and the body was found in his apartment.

Cook was so close to having the goods on Tony Rizzo that he could feel it. He wouldn't stop now. He wouldn't let the FBI and the NYPD slow him down with their questions. He scouted the garage for another Dynasty. When he found what he was looking for, he switched its plates with his own car's. In all likelihood, this would buy him some more time. Most people never noticed their car plates as long as they had them. But it wouldn't be too long before the police traced the credit card numbers he'd be using. Cook didn't have much time. Hunter Logan would be back later in the day and Cook knew something would happen soon. He would follow Logan from the airport as planned and proceed with the quarterback as though nothing else had happened. For all Hunter Logan knew, things were just the same as they had been.

In Kansas City, Hunter Logan played like the Super Bowl MVP he was. The Titans' defense played below themselves, allowing Joe Montana to gun the ball up and down the field almost at will. The result was a high-scoring shoot-out. The Titans had the ball on the last possession, however, and Hunter was able to orchestrate a two-minute comeback to win the game 42–38, throwing a touchdown with only eleven seconds left on the clock.

The Titans players were ecstatic with their last-second win, and Hunter was their man. Everyone forgot about his disastrous performance only a week earlier. Cans of beer and bottles of vodka were broken out on the plane trip home, and the festive mood was heightened. Hunter sat in his usual place next to Bert, slowly working on a frosty can of Bud Light and staring out the window as the plane lifted off the ground. Hunter worked his jaw to pop the pressure from his ears.

"You gotta tell me what's up, Hunt," Bert said suddenly, leaning across the empty middle seat so they could talk in confidence.

Hunter looked down at Bert. "What do you mean?" he said lamely.

"I mean, come on, man!" Bert said, obviously irritated. "You mope around these days like a damn street bum. Something like last week I can see. I know how much pressure you put on yourself to win. I can understand last week. But now? You just pulled off a fucking miracle, and you outgunned one of the legends of the NFL."

Hunter just listened and nodded. He took another sip from his beer.

"So?" Bert urged.

"So, what?" Hunter replied. "I've got things on my mind. That's it. It happens sometimes, you know?"

"Hey, are you and Rachel having some problems?" Bert said, his voice suddenly softening.

"No. Everything's fine with Rachel. Everything's fine everywhere.

I've just got things on my mind, and I don't want to talk, OK? Come on, Bert."

Bert nodded. "Yeah, but this is different. This is because I am your friend. I want to help you."

"You really want to help?"

"Yes," Bert said, nodding vehemently, "I do."

"OK," Hunter said. "Just be my friend and stop asking me questions. Everyone asks me questions."

"OK," Bert said, trying to hide his disappointment. "Let's play some poker."

Hunter turned his gaze back out to the window. It was beginning to get dark out, and he could just see his reflection in the window. He realized he hadn't shaved in several days.

Bert pulled out a deck of cards and popped the middle seat's food tray down between them. He shuffled and dealt out a hand of cards.

"OK," Bert said when the cards were all out. "Five-card draw, kings are wild, ante's twenty bucks. How many you want?"

Hunter didn't say a word.

"Hunt, come on . . . let's play."

Hunter turned to his friend and pushed his cards away. "No cards," he said. "I'm not playing."

"See what I mean?" Bert huffed. "You're not yourself, man! You're just not yourself."

Hunter turned back to the window. He frowned, remembering that he'd forgotten to put on the wire when he dressed after the game. He had actually felt a little free from it all this past day and a half. When he had boarded the plane he had known he was leaving Tony Rizzo and Agent Cook and the whole mess behind him, even if for just a day. That was why, Hunter thought, he'd been able to play so well. The game, the trip with the team, it was his reprieve, and it had been wonderful.

Now Bert wanted to play cards. The idea of any gambling turned his stomach. Without it, he and his whole family would be safe right now. Things would be easy, wonderful. It frustrated Hunter. Whenever he finally achieved his dreams on the football field, something in his life got fucked up. In college it had been his family's ruin. Now it was Tony Rizzo.

Hunter sighed and got up from his seat to go back into the rest room and strap the wire to his body. Time to get back to reality.

The team unloaded from the plane slowly. Most were half drunk. Others wanted to finish up card or dice games before they disembarked. Bert and Hunter were two of the first to go after the front of the plane was emptied of the coaching staff and management people. They walked through a raging crowd of fans, cordoned off by police tape, who had come to greet the team at the airport. There were only a few hundred, nothing like the mobs that the Titans had experienced when they'd made their way through the play-offs in January. After a few waves and a few autographs that Hunter signed as he walked, he and Bert were free from the crowd and made their way through the terminal quickly so as not to give the gawkers and finger-pointers a chance to stop them for autographs.

They both leaned to one side as they walked, off balance because of the bags slung over their shoulders, but Bert was weaving a little more than usual, and Hunter asked him if he could drive.

"You can," Bert said, wisely tossing his friend the keys.

Hunter navigated through the garage and then across the Island back to the Five Towns. He had downed a few cold ones himself, so he was driving extra carefully. He eased the car off the Beltway and onto Rockaway Boulevard. Because of his care, it surprised him to see the flashing lights of an unmarked police car in the mirror.

"Oh, shit," Bert moaned. "Are you OK, man?"

"Yeah, I think I'm fine," Hunter said, pulling over to the side of the road. "I only had a couple. I didn't do anything. Maybe you've got a bad taillight or something."

The uniformed cop walked up to the car, and Hunter rolled down the window with his driver's license in hand.

"Are you Hunter Logan?" the cop asked.

He was an older guy and he wore dark sunglasses despite the fact that the sun had already gone down.

The question surprised Hunter because it wasn't asked in the normal way, of someone who was confirming the identity of someone who they suspected was a star. It was more like the guy had been looking for Hunter.

"Yes," Hunter said, dropping the hand that held his license to his lap, "I am."

The cop looked around, then nodded. "OK," he said. "Can you get out of the car and come with me?"

"Why?" Hunter asked. He saw this irritated the cop.

"I don't know, Mr. Logan," the cop snapped, "I was just asked to bring you in . . . something to do with the FBI."

The cop looked into the car at Bert and said, "I think that if you want to help your friend out, you won't ask him any questions about this. That means keep quiet."

Hunter quickly looked at Bert. His friend's mouth was agape. Hunter wanted to tell him that he'd done nothing wrong, but he knew that would sound silly.

"Bert," he said, sliding out of the car, "I'll see you tomorrow. Don't say anything, OK? And don't worry. Everything's OK."

"You want me to call Rachel?" Bert whispered so the cop couldn't hear.

"No, just . . . I'll see you tomorrow . . . Don't do anything."

Hunter followed the cop to his car and started to get in.

"Get in the back," the cop said rudely. Then, without apology he said, "Those are the rules."

The cop shut his light off and put it down on the seat. He swung out across traffic and back toward the Belt.

"Isn't the headquarters back that way?" Hunter asked, unable to help himself.

The cop glared back at him in the rearview mirror and said nothing.

"Hey, come on," Hunter said after a while, "what's the deal?"

"Look," the cop said, "we'll be there in a minute and you can ask all the questions you want. My job was to pick you up, OK?"

Hunter shrugged. The whole thing made him nervous, but Cook must know what he was doing. Maybe they'd even gotten something else on Rizzo, and Cook was just bringing him in to tell him the whole thing was off.

The cop headed back toward the airport at about a hundred miles an hour. Suddenly he jammed on his brakes. After screaming to a near stop, he wrenched the wheel and gunned through a fishtail, making a U-turn at an emergency break in the highway and then gunning the engine again. The cop's gaze alternated maniacally between the road ahead and the rearview mirror. They stayed on the Beltway toward the Verrazano Bridge and got off an exit in Brooklyn that Hunter didn't recognize. His nervousness increased, but he figured that was the way things would be for now until the FBI and Rizzo were out of his life. They pulled into the parking lot of a motel, and the cop stopped in an empty spot in front of a row of light-blue doors whose paint was cracked and worn.

"In 107," the cop said. "They're waiting for you." Hunter got out of the car, and the cop lurched out and squealed away. Hunter wondered how the hell he was going to get back home, but told himself that Cook would take him.

The door to Room 107 opened before he could knock. Carl reached out and yanked him inside with his free hand. In the other hand he held an automatic handgun with a silencer attached. Tony Rizzo sat propped against the headboard of the bed farthest from the door. He was watching Sunday night football on TNT and seemed not to notice Hunter's arrival.

Carl kicked the back of Hunter's knees and he stumbled forward, catching himself from a fall on the edge of the bed. Before he could turn around, he felt the cold barrel of the gun pressed up behind his ear. He froze.

"Get down on your knees," Carl said.

Hunter eased himself down on his knees, already sick with anxiety. This was it! He prayed that Cook had stayed with Rizzo and was out there, somewhere, getting it all. Then he remembered what the cop had said about the FBI wanting him. Something wasn't right. Hunter felt a nervous sweat break out under his arms.

"Now unbutton your shirt," Carl said with joyful menace in his voice. Hunter hesitated. Carl bumped the gun against his head and said, "Your fucking brains are gonna look real good on that wall."

Hunter fumbled with his shirt buttons, numb with fear. He closed his eyes and cringed, anticipating the shock of the gun going off when they saw the wire. When his shirt was only half unbuttoned, Carl reached around him and tore the wire off his chest, ripped it free from the transmitter, and tossed it onto the empty bed with a grunt.

Tony Rizzo waited for a break in the action before he flicked off the TV and got up from the bed. Calmly he picked up a baseball bat that he'd kept leaning against the wall and stood over Hunter.

"I'm not fucking around with you anymore, Logan," Rizzo said.

"This is the way things are. You fucked around with the FBI, we know that. You tried to fuck me. I don't like to be fucked, so this is what I did. I got your little fucking wife . . ."

Hunter looked up at Rizzo in shock.

Rizzo's face twisted into a smile. "Yeah, that's right," he said gleefully, "I fucking got her. You know what that means?"

Hunter looked down at the floor. The carpet was a worn-out red and orange shag. Hunter's mind froze on noticing the carpet. He wondered how many bad things had happened on this ugly carpet.

"Do you know?" Rizzo screamed, losing his patience with Hunter's lethargy.

"No," Hunter said, shaking his head and looking dully back up at Rizzo.

"Aw, does that make you sad? Be fucking sad, Mr. Hero," Rizzo said.

Hunter heard Carl behind him, guffawing, "Haw, haw, haw."

"You should be pretty fucking sad, because if you fuck up in any way at all from here on in, your little cunt wife will fucking disappear. You got that? I mean, fucking gone! I mean, no one will ever know what the fuck happened to her. That's my treat for you, you fucking asshole! That's what you get if you try me again.

"Now," Rizzo continued, "the Titans are gonna be favored this weekend against the Giants. You lose that fucking game, you hear me? You lose it."

Hunter nodded.

"And I'm going to be watching you, too," Rizzo said. "I'm going to be watching everything you do. Now, your little girl is somewhere and I don't know where. That bitch wife of yours did something with her, but she's not around because we looked for her. You find that little brat and you put her someplace quiet because here's the thing. If something goes down again with the FBI, or the police, or the fire department, or the fucking Boy Scouts of America, if any noise starts getting made, that's it. Your wife is gone. Now you just go about your business and lose that game Sunday, and bing! everything in your life is gonna be back to normal just like nothing ever happened. But if you fuck up . . . then good-bye, little Rachel . . . oh, and I will give her a nice little fucking before I snuff her, too."

Hunter raised up from his knees instinctively, driven mad with fury. A roar came from deep in his body. His vision was blurred with the primal urge to kill. Rizzo wound up and hit him square in the stomach with the bat. Hunter collapsed in a heap on the musty carpet.

"That's good," Rizzo said, standing above him. "That shows you've got enough balls left in you to pull this off. But you see what you got? You tried to get me, and I fucked you up before you got off the floor. Don't you forget that."

Hunter heard the men leave and the door shut behind them. He rolled on the floor in pain for several minutes before he could catch his breath. A low, guttural animal noise escaped from Hunter's throat. It grew louder and louder until it was almost a scream. He pulled the hair on his head and shook his entire body back and forth like some crazed cobra. It was all like a nightmare. It was too much to believe.

Hunter finally calmed himself and got a cab that took him to Hewlett. He mumbled to himself in the backseat, and the driver glanced back at him nervously, a disheveled, unshaven loony whose hair was standing almost on end from being tugged so violently. If it wasn't New York and if Hunter hadn't flicked a fifty at the cabby from the start, it was likely he wouldn't have been driven all the way home. Hunter clung to the idea that maybe Rizzo was just having fun with him after all. Maybe Rachel was fine, but Rizzo just wanted him to consider the possibilities.

But how had Rizzo known? That was what haunted Hunter. What had Cook said? That they would be safe? That no one but him would even know? Hunter hoped he'd get the chance to pay Cook back. In fact, his anger was completely focused on Cook and not Rizzo. The mobster was an evil force in the universe that simply had to be reckoned with, something that Hunter just wanted to go away and then avoid for the rest of his life. But Cook? He was supposed to be one of the good guys. Hunter had trusted him, counted on him.

The cab stopped suddenly.

"This ain't your place," the cabby said incredulously. Hunter did not argue. He jumped out of the car and raced into the service door of the house, which was still ajar. He yelled for Rachel. He began running through the house, wishing, more than he'd ever wished for anything, that she'd just be there, somewhere, reading, or playing with Sara, or taking a bath, doing anything, just so she was there as she should be.

When he got to Sara's bedroom, he yelled instinctively, "Sara? Sara!"

By the time he got to his own bedroom at the end of the hall, Sara was pulling herself free from some clothes in his closet, screaming, "Daddy! Daddy!"

Hunter almost didn't recognize her. Her face was dirty with dust and tracked with tear lines. Her nightgown was smudged and grimy. She looked like a child's doll cast aside long ago, pathetically awaiting someone's attention in some forgotten corner of the attic. Hunter surrounded her with his arms and held her tightly to his chest. She began to sob hysterically, reliving for him the awful moment when their house had been invaded by the bad men. Hunter stroked her hair and whispered calmly to her that everything would be all right.

"Daddy," she cried, "I want Mommy. Where's Mommy, Daddy? Did the bad men get her?"

Sara continued to cry for her mother, and Hunter was able to deduce much of what had happened by her rantings. She was sobbing something about being brave and having to pee in the cellar when she suddenly let up and said, "Daddy, I'm hungry."

Hunter carried her downstairs to the kitchen and made her a peanut butter sandwich. The simple act was a relief from the constant thought of Rachel being taken from him. But when Hunter sat down to watch Sara gulp down the sandwich, the horror flooded in again. How could it have really happened?

"Daddy, can I have another?"

He made another sandwich and thought about where he would go from here. He knew only one thing: He wanted his wife back. He'd do whatever it took. If it meant throwing another game and keeping his mouth shut in the meantime, that was something he was prepared to do. He had to get Sara away. That was a problem.

"Sara, honey," he said, "I'm going to have you stay with Nana and Poppa for a few days, is that OK with you? It's not that I don't want to be with you, but I need to be able to work so I can get Mommy back."

Sara's eyes brightened at the mention of Rachel's return.

"You're going to get her?"

"Yes, honey," Hunter said, sick with uncertainty but trying not to be. "I am."

Hunter called Rachel's father, Morty, and told him as much as he could without being too specific. He told him he was having problems with the Mafia because they wanted to force him to throw some football games and that they were keeping Rachel from him until he delivered. Her father was frantic, but Hunter rammed home the idea that the only way to get her back was to keep things quiet for a week and do what they asked.

"What about the police, the FBI?" her father said desperately.

"The FBI is the reason why they took Rachel in the first place," Hunter said. "Look, you've got to trust me on this. She'll be fine, really. These people are businessmen. I give them what they want, and there won't be any trouble. The worst thing you or I could do would be to make any noise about this."

After a long conversation, Morty agreed. He told Hunter he would be there as soon as he could.

Sara was asleep on Hunter's lap long before his in-laws arrived. They loaded her into the car, and Hunter tried to assuage their worried looks with assurances that everything would be fine. Like Rachel, he was at his best when those around him needed his strength. Rachel's parents, usually rosy and robust, were now bent and pale.

"Hunter," Morty said to him before getting into his car, "I want you to know something."

Hunter nodded. The older man had allowed his small wire glasses to slip down his long nose. He looked as though he'd aged ten years.

"Many people look to their sons as the ones who will carry on for them after they have gone. But in the Jewish religion, it is the woman who passes on the lineage. This is the way it has always been. What I'm saying is that Rachel is my only girl. I love my sons, but she has always been the light of my life. I think you know that.

"What I mean to say is this. I know that if there is danger for my girl, I couldn't think of anyone other than you that I would rather have responsible for getting her back. You ask me not to go to the police, not to say anything about this to anyone, and I won't. I won't because I know that you will bring her back. This is why my Rachel married you and why it was so easy to accept you into our family, because you're a mensch. It means you're strong . . . and you are good."

Morty turned slowly and shuffled around to the other side of the car. He got in without another word. Rachel's mother sat quietly in the front and gave Hunter a pained and burdened smile. He saw his daughter go by as the car pulled past him around the circle and out the drive. His father-in-law's words spun inside his head like brightly colored tops in an empty room. Strong and good. He wondered how long they would spin before they lost momentum, wobbled, and dropped lifeless in their own tracks. He wondered if in fact they had done this long ago.

C ook followed Logan from the airport and watched and listened over the transmitter as he and Bert Meyer were pulled over. Cook suspected that Rizzo was making his move the minute he saw the "cop" get out of the car and start looking furtively around him. Cops worried about only one thing when they pulled someone over, and that was who and what was inside the car. This guy was more concerned with who was watching him. When Cook heard the cop talk to Hunter, he broke out in a sweat.

Cook followed at a safe distance as Hunter was driven onto the Belt Parkway. He was right behind them when suddenly the cop doubled back on the expressway. Cook didn't jam on his breaks and try to follow. That would have given him away. He kept his cool and doubled back as safely as he could at the next exit. Losing audio contact because of the distance between him and Logan would have made a less experienced agent panic. But Cook could afford to be patient. The homing disc that Hunter Logan wore on the underside of the transmitter would tell him where the quarterback was being taken, and they would have to stop somewhere before Rizzo could talk to Hunter. When they did stop, Cook could catch up and get in audio range again.

Cook popped open the computer case and followed the homing track toward Brooklyn. He was led into the parking lot of a seedy motel off the highway. He was in range now, and the audio came back. Cook stopped quickly and flipped on his recorder. He heard a rough voice saying, ". . . gonna look real good on the wall . . ."

Suddenly there was a sharp cracking sound and then nothing.

Cook frantically punched buttons and twisted knobs on the recording device, then the receiver. Something was wrong!

"Shit!" Cook cursed, going over the equipment again and again. "Son of a bitch!" he screamed, slamming his hands on the steering wheel.

This was it, he was sure. Whatever was faulty was on Logan's end. Cook couldn't help wondering if the quarterback had backed down at the last moment. Or maybe he'd done something dumb to give away the wire. Cook had seen that before. Once in a rural Georgia town Cook had wired an accountant who did the books for a country bar that a white supremacist leader was using to launder drug and gun money. The guy couldn't keep himself from nervously touching the transmitter. The bigot asked the accountant three times what was wrong with his chest before he figured it out, and when he did, Cook had to start his whole investigation from the ground floor again.

Cook fumed the whole time Logan was inside the motel room. Finally Rizzo and Carl came out, got into a black Blazer, and drove off. Cook almost went right in, but the habit of cautious patience paid off. In the corner of the lot was the dark Town Car with a wiry, cigarette-smoking guy who looked like a ferret leaning against the hood. He seemed to be paying a little too close attention to Room 107. Cook held tight and continued to fume.

When a cab pulled up to the room and Hunter appeared, Cook could see that the player had been roughed up a little. He followed the cab and the Town Car, at a very safe distance, back to Hewlett.

Hunter went into his house by himself and sat down on the couch in the living room without bothering to put on a light. His sense of being completely alone was almost tangible. Morty's words haunted him. Good was getting Rachel back, but strong—was he being strong? It was more like weakness. He had done nothing but go along with Rizzo since his appearance three months ago. Strength would have been if he followed Rachel's advice back in the very beginning and gone to the FBI. The money, his career, his reputation, the things he had tried to protect back then now seemed so meaningless. Hunter had made decisions he wished he could make over again. He tried to push it out of his mind, but he was certain of one thing. If he didn't get Rachel back, he might as well die himself. His life would be nothing but a living hell. He would never know another moment's peace if anything happened to her.

Hunter sat up straight. He thought he had heard a noise. Maybe it was . . . no, there it was again, a soft rapping at the back door by the kitchen. Hunter's first thought was Cook, but then he wondered if it wasn't just one of Rizzo's cronies taunting him. It had been painfully obvious that Rizzo had something very big riding on Hunter's performance in next week's game. Hunter snuck up on the door and opened it suddenly. He thought he heard the FBI agent gasp.

"What the fuck do you want!" Hunter said maliciously.

Cook was taken aback, but only for an instant. He had a few choice words himself that he wanted to share. He started to push his way past Hunter into the quarterback's home, but Hunter jarred him with a stiff arm.

"You just hang on a fucking minute, man," Hunter growled, giving the agent another shove. "You and I don't have anything to talk about. You can fucking kiss my ass, Cook."

Cook grabbed Hunter by the shirt and pushed his way in the house. "This is stupid, man!" Cook blurted out. "Those people are still out there watching you!"

Hunter took the invasion as his cue. He threw a roundhouse punch that landed squarely on Cook's jaw, knocking him down to the floor. Cook's reaction was instinctive and he lashed out instantly with his foot, hooking Hunter's leg behind the knee and bringing him down with a crash. Hunter was on Cook fast, but Cook boxed Hunter's ears and squirmed out from under his stunned adversary to stand above him like the victor in a wrestling match.

Hunter got to his knees slowly, wobbling. Suddenly he lurched at Cook with his head down and barreled into his solar plexus, knocking out Cook's wind with a violent huff. Hunter windmilled his fists at the same time and landed punches to Cook's face and body, but the older man was still in control. He tucked himself up into a ball and used Hunter's momentum to roll backward and pull the quarterback's entire body over the top of him. Then Cook spun quickly and sprang to his feet, ready and waiting for Hunter's next move. Hunter got his bearings and rose to face Cook. Then he stopped.

"Just get the fuck out," Hunter said flatly.

"Hey," Cook said, "I know they pinned you with the wire, but it wasn't anything I did. You must have given it away, Hunter, but we can do something. We can still get Rizzo—"

"Ha! Given it away!" Hunter said, rubbing some blood from his lip with the back of his sleeve. "You're the one that gave everything away, Cook! You're the only one, unless you told someone, which you said you wouldn't do.

"They knew everything," Hunter said, his face going blank with the exhaustion of all the day's emotions as well as a full sixty-minute game in Kansas City. "They knew it all, and now they've got Rachel."

"That's not . . . they couldn't know. I didn't tell anyone. They didn't know from me, but there was no one—"

Cook stopped abruptly. Instinctively he felt for a chair at Hunter's kitchen table, pulled it out, and sat down. Cook furrowed his brow and asked himself if what he was thinking was at all possible. There had been no leaks. Only one man had known how Cook and Hunter were going to take down Tony Rizzo. The idea that Duncan Fellows was the dirty player was as unthinkable as it was appealing to Cook. He never had liked Fellows, but he had always attributed his bad feelings to the way Fellows had handled the Keel situation. Now Cook knew why Fellows had put him on the defensive. He had been trying to cover up his own deceit by putting the blame on Cook for failing to stick to procedure with a possible witness.

"There was someone," Cook said. "One man, my superior, who knew about you . . ."

"Cook," Hunter said, "I want you to leave."

Cook turned his gaze back to Hunter. "I can help you," he said. "I'm probably the only one who can."

"I've seen your help," Hunter said. "Just leave me alone. I know how to get my wife back, and if you want to help, you'll just stay away. Forget it. You lost. Rizzo's too big."

"If you think you can get Rachel back by just giving Rizzo a game, you're wrong. You'll need more than that. If he knows he's got you, he'll keep her until things get too hot for him. Then he won't be giving her back. That would be too dangerous for him. The only way your wife won't be a problem for Rizzo is if she disappears."

"Nnnnnoooo!" Hunter screamed, grabbing Cook by the shirt and pulling him up from his seat.

Cook remained impassive. Hunter Logan looked like a shell of the man he'd seen only two days ago. He was exhausted, frantic, and beaten. The whole thing was driving him mad. "I can help you," Cook said quietly. "I can get her back."

Cook saw a flicker of hope in Hunter's eyes.

"You want to believe that you can go out and toss a game to Rizzo and he'll give you your life back, but think about it. Think about how this whole thing has played itself out. What did Rizzo want from you at first? A favor? A little information? Then once he had that, he wanted some points, am I right? Then a game, each time probably promising you that the way to get rid of him was to do as he said."

Cook paused, then said, "Look where you are now. Look at the pattern. Rizzo doesn't think like you and me. He's an animal. He doesn't care that Rachel is your wife and that you love her. He does not care about people. He'll kill her, Hunter."

Hunter flinched at Cook's last words. He was torn apart with guilt and an overwhelming feeling of inadequacy. He felt helpless against Rizzo. He had worked all his life to be someone, someone that mattered. Now, here he was, one of the most well-known celebrities of his time, but helpless against a criminal like Tony Rizzo.

"How can I get her back?" Hunter demanded.

"I can get her back. When are you supposed to throw the game? This weekend?"

Hunter nodded.

"Sure," Cook said, "more money will be going down on this game than any but the play-offs. That gives me a week."

Hunter relaxed his grip on Cook and said, "What are you going to do?"

"I'm going to find her . . . and get her," Cook said.

Hunter thought about that. It didn't make sense. FBI agents did not "get" people, they arrested the bad guys.

"No," Hunter said, "Rizzo will find out. He'll see it coming. Your boss, or someone, talks too much."

"My boss is dead," Cook said.

This neither surprised nor worried Hunter. Everything was crazy.

"I'll go after her alone," Cook said.

His determination was like a breath of fresh air. This was how Hunter had always lived, by seeing a problem and attacking it. Since Rizzo had come into his life, Hunter had been dangling helplessly on a string. He didn't know how to act against someone like Rizzo. But guns and bodies and threats—those were Cook's world.

"Are you sure about Rachel?" Hunter asked. "Are you sure Rizzo wouldn't just let her go?"

"It's possible," Cook said. "But I don't see it. Tony Rizzo is on the verge of something big, and he's acting instinctively. If he thinks he's better off losing your wife, she'll be gone. Then it will be too late to do anything. I always favor action if there is any hope at all."

"And do we have any hope?" Hunter said.

Cook shrugged. "If I can find her, I can get her. Hunter," Cook said, "I'm sorry . . ."

Hunter's shoulders slumped. "It's not you, Cook," he said. "I'm the fool, from the beginning. It was such a stupid thing to do, but everyone does it. I didn't think anything of it. I know what the league says, but it . . . but the real fuck-up was not going to you as soon as Rizzo approached me. That's what Rachel said to do. I just never thought all this could happen, to me especially."

"It happens to people like you a lot easier than anybody else," Cook said. "And don't blame yourself. We all make small decisions that lead to big and painful consequences . . . it just happens."

Hunter sat down next to Cook on the end of the table and said, "How do we start? I'm going with you."

"That's not possible," Cook said. "Rizzo's still got someone watching you. I need to move fast and freely. Even if they weren't watching, you'd stick out like a sore thumb."

"If you're going to find Rachel, I'm going with you, Cook," Hunter said. "I'm staying with you. She's my wife, and if something did happen and I wasn't there . . . That's the way I've been my whole life. If things are on the line, I want to be the one making it happen. I want to be the one making the decisions. The winning and losing comes down to me. That's the way it has to be, especially with my wife. I won't let you go without me. I'll let Rizzo know you're out there before I let you go poking around and risking her life without me. Besides, I can disguise myself so that no one will notice me. I do that all the time. I've had to over these past few years just to have some peace when I walk down the street. I'm the master."

"But listen to yourself," Cook said. "You're not rational. Even if you could mask who you are, you can't go anywhere. That guy out there is gonna expect to follow you to practice tomorrow and then home. He's gonna watch everything you do. You can't be at two places at the same time."

"Yes, I can," Hunter said.

Camille pulled her car off the Roscoe exit and headed north on 206. The sky was just starting to turn pink in the east. There was a slight autumn chill in the air, but the forecast was for fifty-five, so she'd dressed in a light jeans jacket and a T-shirt. She shivered a little and turned up the heat. The mountains were colder than the city by almost fifteen degrees. She could see Bear Spring Mountain looming in front of her. She recognized the surrounding landscape and began to slow down. She saw the dirt road that led uphill toward the cabin that belonged to Tony Rizzo. She debated whether or not she should just drive right up the two-mile road to the front of the house and lean on her horn until he came out with whoever it was he had in there beside him, maybe wrapped in a sheet or wearing one of her silk nighties.

Camille saw red. The image made her murderous. She had stayed up the entire night before. Tony said it was business that he had, but she'd seen the Timberland boots in his bag. She knew what that meant. He was going to the mountains. He always brought the boots. It was the only time he used them. And since she'd known him, the only times he had gone to the mountains was with her, so the two of them could relax and be alone together. Tony always said sex was best in the mountains. Those were the words that had stuck in her mind when she had seen the boots on Sunday afternoon. She tried to escape it. She even went out to the clubs that were hot on Sunday nights. But that did her no good. She was marked as Tony Rizzo's woman, and only the most daring men would even steal a furtive glance at her long, hard figure and streaming blonde hair. She was off limits until Tony was done with her. She had been around long enough now to know the rules.

She'd gone home and tried to sleep. She even took a downer, but it only made her depressed and anxious. Finally she simply decided to find out for herself. She took a hit of speed to counteract the downer and set out. She was determined that if she found Tony up there with another woman, it would be the end. Part of her wanted that almost desperately. But much of her was still obsessed with the power and strength that oozed from Tony. Her obsession went beyond his Adonis looks. She could have that with many men. The link that held her was psychological. She knew it. She knew what it was and why, but that did nothing to help her break it. She wanted a dominant male as her mate and that was Tony. Even among wealthy and famous and successful men, Tony stood out. He exuded something that innately generated fear and respect in them. She had even seen her father succumb to him. Her father, one of the most powerful men she knew, had treated Tony with respect from the first, even though Tony had annoyed him. Then, in her father's sky box during halftime of a game, she had seen the fear. It was a power Tony had over people. She knew it was a bad thing, but she was drawn to it nonetheless.

His cruel games with her only heightened the notion of his dominance. No man had ever dared to cross the line with her, knowing that she would simply toss them aside and move on. But she could not do that with Tony, even if she wanted to. She would be free only when he set her free, and all the other males in the pack knew this and kept their distance accordingly. Still, his teasing games with other women in public were one thing, but taking them to his retreat, that would end it. She would leave New York if she had to, but she would end it.

Camille turned up into the drive before fear overcame her. She was almost relieved when she saw that the pipe gate that blocked the drive was chained and locked. She backed out and drove a half mile down the road to a sandy path into the woods where an old country dump had been. She parked her car and bent down to tighten the laces on her sneakers. She puffed her breath like smoke into her hands before jamming them back into the pockets of her jacket and starting off. She would go, but she wouldn't make it so obvious. As she stumbled through the woods in the gloom, she planned her escape. If there was another woman there, she wouldn't confront Tony. She would just leave. She'd go to her bank and wire a lot of cash to Switzerland. She could kick around Europe for a while until

Tony settled down. Then she'd come back and start over. It was not an unfamiliar plan—she'd pondered it before—but nothing had as yet brought her to enact it. If she caught him now, though, she knew she would go.

It was a long hike uphill to the cabin. Camille was breathing like an old dog, huffing and wheezing by the time she reached the perimeter of trees that surrounded Tony's hideaway. She stopped to rest. In the gravel drive was a Blazer and a sleek new Cadillac Seville, both of them black. Camille knew the truck was Mikey's, and she thought the car belonged to Angelo. Maybe it belonged to the other woman, but maybe Tony really was here having some kind of business meeting with his right-hand men. She felt the speed beginning to wear off, and weariness overcame her like a fever. She cursed to herself for not having brought another hit. Suddenly the whole thing seemed scary and a little ridiculous, but she had come too far to turn back. She would find out for herself and end it. Carefully Camille approached the cabin.

There was a covered porch that wrapped around the entire dwelling and Camille went quietly up a set of side stairs. Her and Tony's bedroom was around in the back of the house, and as she edged her way along the porch, she looked nervously into the windows. Her worst fear was to see Angelo leering out at her unexpectedly from within. She peered around the edge of a window into what she knew was an extra bedroom. She froze. There on the bed was a woman lying on her side. She was dressed in only a long T-shirt. Her legs were bare, and there were no covers on her. Camille raged with jealousy and brought herself into full view of the window. The idea that at least Tony hadn't fucked her in their bed crossed Camille's mind.

Then she saw something that didn't make sense. The dark-haired woman slept with one hand stretched over the top of her head, and it was handcuffed to the brass headboard. Camille tiptoed around to the back. She peered into Tony's bedroom and there he lay, alone and sound asleep. She went back to the side room where the girl slept. Camille looked carefully. She recognized this woman, but she had to think from where. Suddenly the door to the bedroom burst open. Camille dropped down quickly, but saw that the intruder was not Tony but Carl Lutz. After only a moment Camille heard the door shut, and cautiously she peeked back up over the windowsill. On the night table beside the girl was an orange, two pieces of bread, and a bottle of water. The girl had shifted in her sleep and Camille got a better view of her face. Camille studied the face carefully and it hit her suddenly. There was a thick band of tape across her mouth. The woman was the wife of Hunter Logan. Camille backed away from the window quickly, her head swiveling from side to side. When she got to the stairs, she turned and ran.

CHAPTER 39

Hunter sat waiting. He hadn't slept since Saturday night before the game, but he didn't feel tired. Exhausted, yes, but not tired. There was no way on earth he could sleep. He wondered if he'd be able to at all before he got Rachel back. He would get her back, he believed that now. He got up and went to the back window by the kitchen. It was only eight-thirty. He didn't expect Cook much before nine. He went back to the front of the house and peered out into the darkness. There was nothing there. He went back to the couch and sat down. He needed to do something, but there was nothing to be done right now except wait.

He thought about the call he'd made to Henry last night and shook his head. Why was it that it took a tragedy to bring a family together? When they were growing up, he and Henry had been best friends. There was a time when their parents had worried about them each having their own identity. That was before football. It started in high school and then went from bad to worse to even worse as Hunter went through college and into the NFL. Maybe that was why he and Henry had such a hard time for so many years, because they had been so close. After Cook left last night, Hunter had taken his car out and driven to a little Italian place called La Viola. He sat down to eat just to make a show of things for whoever was in the dark Town Car that he watched pull up right outside the front window of the restaurant. He knew that the restaurant had a pay phone in the bathroom, so after he ordered, he went back there to call his brother. Henry had answered the phone.

"Henry," Hunter had said, "I need you to help me with something."

"Time for me to pay back your last cash infusion?" Henry had said sarcastically, referring to Hunter's recent financial assistance. "I knew there would be something you'd be wanting me to do when I saw that check. Well, I didn't ask for it, Mr. Hot Shot, so don't think I've got this need to do something for you—"

"Hank . . ." Hunter choked the word out past a lump that had lodged in his throat. He hadn't called his brother that since they were thirteen, and he didn't do it intentionally now, it just came out. Hunter realized that there was nothing he wouldn't do to get Henry's help. Rachel's life depended on it. "Hank, I need you. It's Rachel. She's in bad trouble, Hank. I need you bad . . ."

There was a long silence on the other end of the line. It gave Hunter the opportunity to think about his twin brother's words the day he and Rachel had married.

"She's the best thing about you, brother," Henry had said.

Last night he'd said it again, only in a much softer and kinder tone.

"She's the best thing about you, brother. Tell me what you need."

Hunter heard the rapping of knuckles on glass. He jumped up and looked at his watch. It was 9:47. He must have dozed off, but Rachel was his first thought and he was instantly awake and alert. He let Cook and his twin brother in the back door. Hunter stood like a zombie. Henry grabbed hold of him and hugged him hard, as though he'd saved all the strength from all the embraces he'd never given him over the years. Hunter held his brother tightly, too. Then Henry brought his hand up to the back of Hunter's head and stroked his hair.

"It'll be all right, brother," he said with emotion. "We'll get her back."

Hunter shut his eyes and tried to quell the pain. He inhaled one painful breath and then snapped himself out of it. There was business at hand. "How much has Cook told you?" he asked his brother.

"Pretty much everything."

Hunter nodded and went to the freezer and took out a large can of coffee. The rich smell hit him as soon as he removed the lid. "You'll have to shave off that beard," he said. "I brought my play book tonight and a press guide. You'll have to study both so you'll have at least an idea of who's who and what's going on. I starred the guys on the team I hang out with most. Of course you know Bert's my best friend, but he knows what's going on. I told him everything today after the team watched game film. He knew something was up anyway from last night, and I wanted him to be able to help you get through things if there's any questions or problems you have."

"Can't I just act like a total asshole?" Henry said with a smirk, trying to lighten the situation a little. "Then everyone will know I'm you."

"Funny, Hank," Hunter said, smiling. "I got treatment on my shoulder today, and I told everyone from Price to the trainers that I'm not planning on throwing this week in practice. And I told everyone in the media that I'd definitely be ready to go next Sunday. If anyone asks, make sure you go along with that. We don't want Rizzo getting nervous about me not being in there to toss his game. You won't have to really do anything but wince and pretend your shoulder hurts when they give you treatment. Just stand around in practice and act real solemn. Try not to talk to anyone more than saying yes or no. Bert's going to tell everyone that I'm just in a really shitty mood because of the injury and what happened with Blake Stevens a couple of weeks ago. You know what? If anybody asks, tell them you've got the flu. That stuff has been going around, and every guy I've seen with it has been miserable anyway. No one will bother you anyway. Everyone knows I hate it when I can't practice, so basically be a grump.

"That shouldn't be hard," Hunter added with a smile, getting in a jab of his own.

Cook was still nervous about the whole thing, so after they'd had the coffee, Hunter showed Henry to his bathroom where he removed his long, thick beard. To show him just how good it was, Hunter did a quick change with his brother, and they came back down to Cook with each other's clothes on.

"Damn, he does look like you, Hunter," Cook said.

"I'm Henry," Henry said.

Cook shook his head in disbelief. Except for their clothes and a three-day growth of beard on Hunter's face, the men were identical. Since quarterbacks aren't the type of athletes who have to do heavy weight training that would alter their physiques and since Henry had kept himself in good shape from working on what was left of the farm, their builds were the same, too.

"With your face clean-shaven like that," Cook said to Henry, "you look more like Hunter than he does."

Hunter put on an old, ugly pair of thick glasses that he'd found in a back drawer and pulled a Yankees hat on his head. Now there was no question as to who looked the most like Hunter Logan of the New York Titans.

"OK," Cook said, impressed. "Let's go."

Hunter had a small black canvas bag packed with some things, and he slung it over his shoulder.

"Wait a minute," Henry said, digging in an army duffel bag that sat where he'd dumped it on the kitchen floor. "I've got something for you, Hunt." Henry held out a Colt .45 automatic service revolver and said, "I thought with the kind of people you're dealing with that you might need something like this, brother."

Hunter took the weapon from Henry. He hadn't had much to do with guns since he was a kid, and then it had been mostly deer rifles. He nodded his head, though. Henry was right. A gun was a good idea with people like Tony Rizzo.

"Thanks," Hunter said. "I'll try to check in with you later in the week. Hopefully it won't take that long, but if we're not in the area, you'll be on your own. The phones aren't safe. If you have any questions about anything, just ask Bert when you see him at the complex. Remember, try not to talk unless you have to."

Hunter held out his hand, and his brother grasped it warmly and pulled him into another brief hug.

"Good luck," Henry said. "Bring her back."

Hunter nodded a final time. "I will, Hank. Thanks again."

Then he and Cook disappeared out the back and into the night.

"Listen," Cook said when they were in his car and heading back into Manhattan, "I know how anxious you are, Hunter, but it's important that you try to follow me in this as much as you can. I know how to do this kind of thing. I've done it before. To tell you the truth, I'm not in love with the idea of you toting that .45."

Hunter shrugged. "Yeah, well, I can't see myself going around with you and running into these guys and everyone having guns except me. Believe me, I don't want any shooting to be going on, but I don't want to be the guy without a gun if it does."

Cook nodded and said, "You're right, but do try to stick as close to me as you can."

"I can do that," Hunter said.

When they reached the city, Cook dropped Hunter at Avis to get them a new car. He didn't want to take any chances with his own car getting hot, so he dropped it in a garage and Hunter picked him up in a dark Le Sabre. It took them only a minute to transfer all of Cook's equipment to the new car, and they were off, headed uptown to Tony Rizzo's apartment on Fifth Avenue. Hunter drove while Cook fiddled with his homing equipment to change it back over to the first disc, which was still attached to Tony Rizzo's Mercedes. The signal was coming right from Rizzo's garage.

Cook cursed. "I knew it wasn't going to be easy," he muttered under his breath.

"What's up?" Hunter said.

"Rizzo's car is in the garage. I can call up to the apartment and see if anyone answers. If he's there, we can wait for him to come out. If he's gone, we'll have to wait until he comes back. That's most of what this business is, waiting."

They found a spot from where they could see the entrance to Tony's building. The street was quiet except for an occasional yellow cab racing by or an expensively dressed couple stepping from a limousine at the end of their night. This, after all, was the better side of town. Cook took his cellular phone out of his pocket. He dialed Tony Rizzo's apartment, got no answer, and returned to the car.

"He's not there," Cook said to Hunter, leaning his seat back and exhaling a big breath.

"You might as well get some sleep," he told Hunter. "I'll watch until I can't go anymore, and then I'll wake you."

Hunter tilted back his own seat. He tried to close his eyes, but his foot kept tapping uncontrollably and his mind kept racing.

"Cook?" he said, opening his eyes so he could see the entrance to

Rizzo's building but still remain tilted back in his seat. "Are you worried about your family?"

Cook was quiet a moment before he said, "Yeah, I am."

"How can you be here with me? I mean, I want you here. I could not even think about doing this if you weren't, but doesn't it get you?"

"The way I figure it," Cook said, "they're either hiding out someplace, in which case I won't find them because my Aunt Esther is a crafty old fox, or Rizzo has them or has done something with them. Either way on that one, I need to get to Rizzo just as bad as you do."

"So you're not doing this for me," Hunter said more to himself than anyone.

"I wouldn't quite say that," Cook said. "I feel responsible for Rachel. I want her back, too. I lost two people in this Rizzo business already, I don't want to lose another one."

"Cook?" Hunter said, closing his eyes. "Do you think I did something unforgivable?"

"No," Cook said. "You did something a lot of people do. Whether it's illegal or not, gambling is something that most people do at some time or other. The thing with a guy like you is, everyone's looking at you. You can't get away with things other people can. You're a big celebrity. People like to see you fall. People like to take advantage of you if they can. You're one of those people who has to be extra careful not to fuck up. You didn't do something so bad, same as me. Rizzo's the bad guy. Duncan Fellows was a bad guy. They're the reason we're here.

"Sure," Cook continued, "you wanted to keep playing this year to make all that money, but anyone would have. Same with me. I rushed into the Tommy Keel thing because I was anxious to get my little girl out of this city and be some big shot behind a desk down in Washington. But what you and I did wasn't bad. We just got caught up with the bad ones. It happens, man. It's called bad luck."

Cook looked over at Hunter Logan. The quarterback, the celebrity, the man so many people around the world wished so ardently they could be, was deep in a heavy sleep, his brow furrowed even then from the anguish and the pain he had inadvertently brought into his life. Cook reached back into the backseat and pulled a light blanket from one of his nylon duffel bags. He opened it and covered

Hunter, then took out a thermos they'd packed at the house and gulped down a cup of hot coffee before pouring a second that he would sip as the night went by.

When Henry woke up on Tuesday, he couldn't help exploring his brother's mansion. Henry had never been there before, and he marveled at the size and extravagance of the place. There were carpets as thick and soft as a sheep's coat in December, and brass and marble were everywhere. The woodwork was rich with color and texture, and little silver and crystal trinkets seemed to cover every surface without having the appearance of clutter. Henry spent twenty minutes in the bathroom trying to figure out what the bidet was before he settled on the idea that it was some weird drinking fountain for the kids.

Tuesday was his brother's only day off during the season, so Henry had all day to study his new teammates' faces and identities in the Titans' media guide. He made himself some eggs before he sat on the couch to familiarize himself with everyone. Each player had from one to five pages written about him, depending on how long he'd been with the team and how impressive his contributions had been. Some of the names Henry recognized from hearing them on the news or radio, even though he wasn't a sports fan. After two hours of players he cracked the thick three-ring binder that constituted the Titans' play book. After five minutes he decided he needed a break. He wondered how in hell anyone could make sense of all the Xs and Os interspersed between all the numbers and weird terminology. After lunch he went back at it again, but found himself rereading the same sentences over and over again. Finally he gave up on the play book and fished through some videotapes of Titans games, choosing a couple to watch and try to get a feel for the whole thing that way. After viewing the tapes and eating a pizza he had had delivered, Henry took one more run at the play book, reading it now only to try to get some of the terminology down and forgetting the complex strategy behind it all. He lay back on the couch, turned on the light, and crossed his legs to do some serious cramming.

The next morning, Henry awoke in the same position. When he first opened his eyes, he had no idea where he was. He hadn't spent many days off the farm where he'd grown up, and the surroundings he was in at present seemed much more like a dream than anything else. Henry made coffee but didn't eat. He was too nervous.

Bert met Henry outside the Titans' compound and walked in with him. After introducing himself quietly, Bert asked how Hunter was doing and if Henry had any word on Rachel. Henry said no. Bert led him into the locker room, talking in low tones without much formality. Basically Bert was trying to cram as much information about the team into Henry's head as he possibly could. The result was that Henry didn't remember a bit of it.

"So," Henry said, looking at his brother's Rolex, which now hung on his wrist, "where's the training room? I've got to be in there by eight-thirty. Hunter said those guys don't mess around, even for a big star like him."

Bert nodded knowingly and pointed out the door that led to the training room, where the players got treatment to help expedite the healing of their various injuries. Henry hung his shoulder down ever so slightly and rubbed it with the care of a newborn baby as he walked into the training room.

"Very funny," said Jerry, with a disgusted smile.

This hit Henry like a blast of cold air. He looked around to see if there was a clue to Jerry's words.

Then the trainer said, "How's the shoulder?"

Henry grimaced as best he could and rubbed it tenderly. "Sore," he murmured.

A couple of beefy linebackers in the hot tub snickered loudly at this. Jerry nodded his head angrily as if to say he could play that way too, and turned to prepare a table so that Henry could lie down while he applied ice and the high-voltage machine to the quarterback's shoulder.

"How's the throwing action?" Jerry said without looking up from the machine he was so carefully bent over.

"Huh?" Henry said, not having a clue as to what he was talking about. There were more snickers from the hot tub.

Jerry turned and said sarcastically, "Do we think we'll be well enough to throw the football today?"

"Oh, uh . . ." Henry instinctively started rolling the arm connected to his throwing shoulder and realized all at once his mistake. He had been babying his left shoulder, and it was his right that was supposed to be hurt. He grinned foolishly at Jerry and looked as contrite as possible.

"No, I, uh . . . it's too sore for me to do anything. I better just give it a rest so I'll be ready Sunday."

Jerry twisted his lips thoughtfully and said, "Get up on the table."

After treatment, Bert guided Henry through the different meeting rooms he would be in during the day and told him how the schedule went. When they got out onto the practice field, Henry spotted the black Town Car that he'd seen following him to the compound. He couldn't make out the person sitting in the front seat. He was parked in an obvious spot, lengthwise in the parking lot adjacent to the practice field, as if to make a statement. It was where everyone could see it, but only Henry seemed to notice.

During practice, Henry felt silly and self-conscious. He just stood around in a sweatsuit and tried to nod as knowingly as he could at all the instructional asides he got from the offensive coordinator during practice. At one point the coach stopped and said, "Hunter, what's wrong? Are you getting all of this?"

"Yeah," Henry said, "I'm just a little sick . . . flu."

The coach nodded knowingly and went on.

Finally the day ended. Henry could remember few other times he had been so relieved. He was tired of looking down at the ground and telling people he didn't feel well, tired of being on edge and wondering every moment if someone would find him out.

He said good-bye quietly to Bert, who talked loudly to him about going out for dinner with the wives and said Hunter's name in what Henry thought was a slightly overdone way.

Henry was almost out of the building when Dozer, the equipment man, tapped him on the shoulder and said above the noise of the locker room, "Hey, Hunter, they want you upstairs!"

"Who?" Henry asked. "Who wants me?"

Dozer shrugged and said, "Carter's office, but I don't know, he isn't supposed to be around today. Hey, Hunter, are you OK?"

Henry looked down at the floor, rubbed his shoulder, and mumbled, "Yeah, I just got that flu. I'm not myself."

Dozer looked at him oddly, shrugged, and walked away.

Henry made his way back to Bert's locker. He got Bert's attention and motioned him out in the hallway. "The equipment guy just said they want me up in the owner's office!" Henry whispered loudly when they were alone.

"Look," Bert said, "it's no big deal. The big guy probably wants to find out how your shoulder's feeling. It's nothing."

"Yeah, but the equipment guy said the owner's not here today."

"Aw, he don't know," Bert said, dismissing Dozer with a wave. "Carter could've come in unexpectedly. Just go up there and if anyone asks you if there's something wrong, tell them you're feeling sick like you've been doing all day. They'll want you to get out of their face fast if you say that."

"OK, so where do I go?"

Henry followed Bert's directions carefully up stairways and through a maze of corridors until he came to a secretary at a large desk outside what looked to be an impressive office, if the doorway and the outer sitting area were any indications.

"Go right in, Hunter," the secretary said, smiling warmly at him.

Henry tried to swallow, but he ended up by almost choking himself, his mouth was so dry. He looked back at the secretary as if she might give him some final advice, then opened the heavy office door, and went in. What he saw was not what he'd expected.

It had taken Camille only two days to get everything in order. She was surprised that she hadn't heard from Tony during that time. Usually he didn't go more than a day or two without checking up on her, even when he was off on business. But when she considered the magnitude of what he was doing, it didn't surprise her at all. Camille was tortured with what to do about Hunter Logan's wife during her entire drive back to the city. Something horrible was going on, of that she had no doubt. She knew Tony well enough to know that he was capable of anything, but she had never imagined that he would actually do something as heinous as kidnapping.

Then she wondered to herself if that's what it was. Maybe she should stay out of it. That was bullshit, she concluded angrily. At least if she was going to do what was best for herself, she could be honest about it. It wasn't all that hard really. She didn't owe anyone anything, and there was no love lost between her and Hunter's wife. They'd only met on rare occasions, and Camille remembered her as being a perfect bitch. There was also Tony to consider. She might be able to hide from him if he was only searching for her half-heartedly, but if she crossed Tony and hurt him in any way, she hated to imagine what he'd do to her. She did know this: If she caused him trouble, he wouldn't stop looking until he found her.

That night she stayed in her own apartment overlooking the East River. It was a lonely place, especially after the hustle and bustle that always seemed to be going on at Tony's. It was noon when she finally got into bed. She slept through the afternoon and into Monday night.

The next morning, Camille was up early. She turned on the radio and listened for some news about the quarterback's wife. There was nothing. On her way to the travel agency, she picked up a *New York Times*. There was nothing suspicious about Hunter Logan, only something about his bad shoulder probably keeping him out of practice for the week. This puzzled Camille and gave her further reason to fend for herself. Obviously Hunter Logan would know if his wife was gone and do something about it. People would know. Hunter Logan wasn't exactly a guy people didn't talk about. And then, maybe she'd been mistaken about the whole thing. Maybe the woman was just someone who looked like Hunter's wife.

Camille got a flight out to Zurich for the next day. Her father was away at an NFL owners' meeting, and she fretted a little about not saying good-bye, but she knew she could get him to come visit her after the season. Besides, he had his life, she had hers. At least she would have hers after she put an ocean between her and Tony Rizzo.

It did take some time to get her money wired, and she had to wait until Wednesday to sign some papers that would send more money over when her trust fund made its next disbursement. She didn't know for sure how long she was going to lie low, but she knew it would be long after this whole mess blew over. She spent Tuesday night in her apartment packing. Most of her favorite clothes were at Tony's, but she didn't dare take a chance of showing up around there. She did her best and finished a couple of bottles of late-harvest Riesling while she worked.

By eleven she was drunk and unconcerned about Hunter Logan, his wife, or Tony Rizzo, for that matter. Her thoughts were focused on Europe and the kind of man she wanted to get first. She thought a tall, handsome blonde with a big smile and a genial manner would be her first conquest, the exact opposite of Tony and an easy type to find in Zurich. That night Camille slept the peaceful sleep of a woman whose already limited conscience was completely quelled by alcohol.

She was at the gate in Kennedy International Airport when she changed her mind. She checked when the next flight was, changed her ticket, and flagged down a passing limousine. She waved a hundred-dollar bill at the driver and told him to take her to the Titans' facility in Merrick.

Her father's secretary told her that the team had finished practice a half hour ago.

"Get me Hunter Logan," Camille said as she let herself into her father's office.

Because of the incredible beauty of the girl and the way she was looking at him, Henry briefly wondered if his brother had been pulling some double duty. She looked as though she had come straight out of a Coors commercial. He didn't have much time to enjoy her, though. After only a few seconds of that radiant smile, the blonde's mouth dropped into a tough, angry line.

"Hunter?" she said.

"Y-yes," Henry replied in a subdued voice, his eyes still roving.

Camille stood staring at him for several moments before saying, "Who are you?"

"I—I'm Hunter," Henry said, completely off balance.

"Of course," said Camille sarcastically. "Don't tell me, you're his twin brother."

Henry was floored. His mouth hung slightly ajar.

Camille smiled ever so slightly. "Tell me what's going on. I want to know."

Henry hesitated.

"Look," Camille said abruptly, "I came here to help. I want to know what the hell's going on before I lay my life on the line for some woman I don't even know and don't want to know, for that matter."

"How—how'd you know," Henry said, shaken by the forceful determination of the girl. "How'd you know I was Hunter's twin?"

Camille shrugged. "I got the file on him from the team. I read everything they had. I remember reading about a twin brother. I knew right away you weren't him. Not by the way you look. You look just like him. It's the way you looked at me. You looked surprised, knocked off your feet. If I didn't do that to Hunter Logan in a bathing suit, I certainly wouldn't be able to do it in jeans and a blouse. I don't think there's any woman that knocks Hunter Logan off his feet—except maybe his wife. She's why I'm here. I know where she is."

"You know?" Henry said, bringing his thumb and forefinger up to his chin, feeling for the beard that wasn't there.

Camille nodded, then looked impatiently at her watch. "Look, I don't know why you're here, but I'm going to tell you how to get to the cabin where Rachel is. I'm not going to write it down or say it twice. I don't want anyone to know that I told you. I don't want any part of this shit. I just want to help Hunter. Any guy that sticks to his wife like he does deserves to keep her if he can."

Camille held up her hand and said, "I don't want to know anything from you except if you'll pass the message on to Hunter. You better tell him to get to her quick. I'm no expert, but I didn't think she looked too good."

Henry nodded. "I'll tell him. I don't know when I'll see him, but it should be soon."

He listened carefully to what Camille told him. Then she was gone. She didn't say good-bye or wait for a thank-you, she just left. Henry stood there for a few moments, taking everything in, then turned and left himself. He could only hope now that Hunter would contact him soon.

In the large cobblestone fireplace the fire crackled. Carl and Tony sat in large chairs facing the blaze. Carl shifted nervously in his chair and ran his eyes around the interior of the log structure. Even though it was a cabin, it was nicer than the home in which he'd grown up on Long Island. The thick wood beams were adorned with Native American rugs and paintings. To Carl the place was more like a museum than a hunting cabin, but that wasn't why he was nervous.

He had never been alone with Tony before, and Tony wasn't saying anything. He was just sitting there staring at the fire. He heard Mike Cometti banging around in the kitchen. Even though Carl wasn't particularly fond of Mikey, he wished Mikey was there. Anything would be better than being alone with Tony and having nothing to say.

To make matters worse, the woman had been rattling her handcuffs loudly against the headboard of her bed with increasing intensity. This didn't seem to faze Tony at all. Carl, however, wished he could go in there and club her over the head to shut her up.

Finally Tony spoke, "Go in there and see what she wants."

Carl got up. He was the only one who had had contact with Rachel since they'd taken her from her home last Saturday night.

He hated it, watching her while she peed and then locking her back up to the bed, taking in her food, but he did what Tony said. He opened the door to the bedroom where she was being kept and carefully avoided her eyes. He had only looked at her eyes once. They had been alive with hatred and disgust, and he was afraid if he looked at her again he would have to hurt her, and Tony had said specifically that he wasn't to hurt her. Most of the time she was drugged anyway. He put some drops that Tony had given him in her food, but there was always one time during the day when she came out of her drugged state. Angelo told him it was so the drug didn't kill her. That was when he usually had to go in and take her to the bathroom, like now.

When Carl returned to his chair by the fire, he sat down with a heavy sigh. He stole a glance at Tony, who remained unmoved. He looked at his watch and wondered when Angelo would be back. Tony had sent him into the city for something. He wished it would be soon. Carl loved being around Angelo. He never made Carl nervous.

"Carl," Tony said, making Carl jump in his seat, "I have something very important for you to do."

Tony let the words hang in the air like the thin trail of smoke from the fire. Carl felt his heart race. His senses were heightened and he was almost nauseated by the pungent smell of burning hardwood. His mind spun with the gravity of what was happening. Angelo had warned him of this moment, and Carl had awaited it as a child awaits Christmas. Angelo had told him how it would be.

"You'll be alone with Tony," he'd said. "He'll tell you he has something for you to do. It will be something important."

Carl had been worried.

"Don't worry," Angelo had said, "you'll know it when it happens. Then you'll do whatever it is he wants."

Carl had wondered what that would be. He'd thought of a million things that it could be, but now, with the moment at hand, his mind drew a blank.

"There's going to be a new order of things inside the family," Tony was saying. "I am going to be running things, Carl. You may have already guessed it."

Tony now stared at Carl as though he expected Carl to say

something intelligent. Carl tried to swallow. He gave a feeble nod and did his best to look like he had already guessed it.

"What I'm telling you must be between you and me. I'm giving you what will be the most important job anyone's ever done in this family—and, of course, when you're done, you'll be a part of the family.

"I'm going to make you one of my soldiers, Carl. You'll be under Angelo, but you'll have interests of your own."

Carl looked at the floor. He was numb, like a robot whose joints were frozen with rust. Carl lurched to the floor on one knee and bowed his head. No one had told him to do this, but he wanted to do something, show some sign of how great he considered Tony Rizzo to be. He might have ended up prostrate on the floor if Tony hadn't told him to get up and sit down.

"Like I said," Tony continued, "just as important as you doing the job is you keeping absolutely quiet about it. If you say anything, even to Angelo, especially to him, he won't have any respect for you, Carl. Silence is very important in our business. That's part of the test.

"In fact, this job is so important, I'd do it myself if I could, but I can't. See, Carl, I'm going to be taking over the Mondolffi family. My mother was a Mondolffi, and my father was the one who got this family through the tough times in the sixties when all that Kennedy shit hit the fan. So now it's my turn. It's time for me to take charge of things."

Carl felt the thrill any novice feels when he's taken into the confidence of the master. He was at the center of things, big things.

"The heads of the other families have asked me to take things over," Tony said importantly. "Part of that is doing something with my uncle.

"I can't do it myself. If I were to kill my uncle with my own hands, the other families would never recognize me as the head of the family. That's something that goes back hundreds of years. No godfather can ever kill another godfather. That's what your job is, Carl. You're going to kill my Uncle Vinny."

Tony chose to refer to his uncle that way to reduce his importance in Carl's mind. He didn't want him fully cognizant of the magnitude of the act or its possible consequences.

Carl's jaw hung loosely from his face, and he looked at Tony with amazement. Tony wondered if he'd made a mistake.

"I am honored, Tony," Carl said, removing all doubt not only with his words but with the awe in which they were delivered. "I've waited all my life for this chance. I won't disappoint you."

"Good," Tony said with an unusually warm and sincere smile. "I knew you were the one, Carl."

Carl nodded, this time assertively. He was the one. He believed that.

"It has to happen on Sunday morning, Carl," Tony said. "My uncle thinks Sunday is like a fucking holiday or something, like everyone's safe on Sunday. Every Sunday morning he gets up at six and walks out to the curb himself to get the paper."

Tony's eyes wandered to the fire and seemed to lose their focus.

"He says that's how he stays in touch with reality, my uncle," he said in a distracted tone, "getting the fucking paper. Walking out in his neighborhood just like any regular schmuck would do. Since I was a kid I knew that would be the way to get him . . . fucking Sunday morning."

Now Tony's gaze returned to Carl and fixed on him. His eyes were dark and his handsome face burned with intensity. He spoke in abrupt sentences that were both businesslike and precise.

"My uncle will come out about five after six. I want you to rent a car and park it down the street about five-thirty. Not too far, you need to be able to see when he comes out of the door. Ears will be sleeping in the car parked out front. When my uncle is almost to the street, you pull up, nice and slow. Get out of the car. Shoot Ears, then my uncle.

"I've got a machine pistol that I'm going to give you. You'll use it initially to waste Ears and drop my uncle. Then—and this is the most important part, Carl—after you empty the clip, I'll give you an unmarked .38 that you'll use to empty into my uncle's head. There'll be no fuck-ups on this. If I find out that there aren't five slugs in my uncle's brain, then you fucked up. Five bullets, Carl. The machine gun is just to take out Ears and keep my uncle from running into the house. There won't be anyone else around. You'll feel like you need to get out of there quick, but you won't. You'll have plenty of time. Do the job right, Carl. It's the beginning of everything for you, Carl.

"I want you to leave here tonight."

The sun had dropped behind the buildings that rose above the trees in Central Park, leaving a bloody swatch in the sky that Hunter would have considered beautiful under different circumstances. The night was quickly turning cool, a typical October evening in New York. Cook had dozed off in the driver's seat and left Hunter at the watch. Hunter sniffed the air. It was stale and stuffy. He felt like he had to get out of the car, but Cook had warned him to stay put, adding that they could never know when the moment for them to move would come.

Hunter's whole body ached, especially his shoulder. They'd done nothing but sit now for two days, leaving the confines of the car only to get food or use the bathroom in a little Greek diner two blocks away. Cook had also prevented Hunter from checking in with Henry during this time because he didn't trust the phone. The lack of activity allowed the aches to settle into Hunter's football-damaged body. Even though he could put the seat all the way back and stretch out his legs, he was still confined to the car.

His mind ached, too. For several hours he was alert and nervous, expecting Tony Rizzo to appear at any moment. Then he experienced a period of depression where he chastised himself for what had happened to Rachel and tortured himself with morbid thoughts of what might happen. He tried his best to keep cool about things, like Cook, but it wasn't happening.

"Cook," Hunter said, nudging the agent from his sleep. "Cook, come on. I'm telling you, we've got to do something. I can't stand this shit. I can't stand it. She's out there, Cook, and we're doing nothing. We're just sitting."

Cook reluctantly rubbed the sleep from his eyes and gave a heavy sigh. He hadn't worked with a rookie in a long time.

"OK," Cook said patiently, "I'll give it to you again. Finding someone isn't like in the movies. You don't just pick up a trail and start chasing someone in your car. A stake-out is about patience, and that's the only way they pay off, if you're patient."

"But there has to be something we can do!" Hunter said passionately. "I know what you're saying, but we have to do more!"

Cook shook his head wearily. "Look," he said, "I'll say it again. We're playing the best cards we have. We don't know where Rachel is because we don't know where Rizzo is. If we find Rizzo, I bet we'll find Rachel. So the best way to find Rizzo is to wait right here. He will come back here."

"But maybe not before Sunday," Hunter said.

"Right, maybe not," Cook replied, taking a coffee-stained styrofoam cup off the dash and slugging down a cold, bitter gulp, "but . . . this is the best thing we got right now. And if it doesn't pan out this week, it'll be next week. Like I said, a lot of this business is just waiting."

"Cook," Hunter said angrily, "you're talking about more than a fucking week! We've got to do something before that."

"Listen, man," Cook said, his nostrils flaring just a bit and his eyes narrowing at Hunter, "I hear what you're saying, but we're doing all we can. Hey, we're here, we're looking for your family, man. We're not even trying to find mine. How you think that makes me feel?"

Hunter was silent for a while thinking about this. "I'm sorry, Cook," he said, and then quietly "I'm going fucking crazy."

"Look!"

The word cut through two days of stale air like a blast of cold wind. Hunter followed Cook's finger across the street to the large, thick frame of a man he instantly recognized. It was Angelo Quatrini. He had popped suddenly from a cab that stopped at the corner. Walking up Fifth Avenue, he disappeared into Tony Rizzo's building.

While Angelo was inside, Hunter was afraid to say a word. He didn't want to hope too much.

"Maybe this is it," Cook mumbled, but more to himself than anything else.

When Angelo emerged, he crossed the street, then looked carefully up and down Fifth Avenue before he began to move.

"Shit!" Cook said, scrambling from the car as Angelo Quatrini hopped over the low stone wall that separated the park from the sidewalk. Without saying it, they had both assumed Angelo would get into another cab.

"You stay on channel two and keep as close as you can!" Cook barked to Hunter as he sped away on foot.

Hunter slammed the car in gear and pulled out onto Fifth. He crawled along. "Cook!" he whispered into the radio. "Cook! Are you there?"

There was a burst of static, and then Cook's voice came over the walkie-talkie in an out-of-breath whisper. "I've got him! Go down to that road that cuts through the park and get to the other side. He's headed that way."

Hunter cursed himself. He'd passed Seventy-second Street, which cut through the park. He checked his rearview mirror. There was a steady stream of yellow taxis heading toward him.

"Fuck it," he said and threw the car into reverse. In a blare of horns, Hunter edged backward up Fifth until he got to the cut-through. Then he threw it in drive and raced off. When he got to Central Park West on the other side, he pulled up onto the curb on the park side of the street and whispered frantically into the walkie-talkie.

"Cook! Cook! What's happening?"

"He's coming out of the park," Cook said. "Do you see him?"

Hunter peered up ahead in the gloom. He did see a big figure waving down a cab about three blocks up.

"Come get me! Come get me!" Cook shouted at the same time Angelo was climbing into a cab.

Hunter was already on his way and Angelo's cab was only a block ahead of them before Cook was back in his seat and they were racing up Central Park West.

"OK, OK," Cook said, "not too fast. Keep it back here. We're close enough, this is just right."

Hunter's hands trembled on the wheel, and his stomach was in a knot. They couldn't let him get away.

It was no trick at all to follow the taxi across the Triboro Bridge, down the BQE, and into the heart of Brooklyn. Angelo Quatrini got out at the curbside in front of what Cook knew was his house, a small light-green two-story with battered screens on its windows and doors and peeling paint on its siding.

"Keep driving," Cook said to Hunter as he slouched down in the seat. "I don't know what he's up to, but it's something. He was at Tony's for a reason. I'm guessing he was sent to get something. If he was, then he'll be going back to take whatever it is to Tony. Stop here."

Hunter parked the car at the curb, and they both looked back through the rear window at Angelo's house. The light went on in the upstairs and stayed on. Cook rubbed his eyes with his forefinger and thumb.

"OK," he said, "I know you don't want to hear this, but we've just got to wait."

CHAPTER 41

Angelo Quatrini holed up for a full day, and when he went, he went fast. Late Friday night a cab pulled up in front of his house. He emerged suddenly and got into the waiting car. It sped off and Hunter, who'd kept his place as the driver, pulled away from the curb in pursuit.

The cab wound its way slowly through Brooklyn and crossed the Fifty-ninth Street Bridge to Manhattan.

"I don't like this," Cook muttered.

"What's the problem?" Hunter said. "We're right behind him."

"I know," Cook said. "It's too easy, like he's lulling us to sleep."

The word was no sooner out of Cook's mouth than Angelo burst from the cab, which hadn't even come to a complete stop, and shot down a subway station and into the endless arteries of the city.

For almost an hour Cook was able to stay with Angelo, dodging up into the street for brief moments between train changes so that he could radio his position to Hunter. Cook knew from the start it was hopeless. The bad feeling had been with him before Angelo left his house, and once he got into the subway Cook knew that all else would be desperation. But Cook rode the trains for another hour after he'd lost him because that was how he was beginning to feel, desperate.

Hunter finally picked Cook up in front of Penn Station. Cook emerged from the big, ugly building with a pack of bums that were on their way home for the night. Cook's face looked as downtrodden and hopeless as his toothless companions. The only thing that separated him from them was his clothes. Hunter's chin sank slowly to his own chest and he let out a deep sigh. Cook got in beside him and they just sat.

"What do we do?" Hunter finally said to break the silence.

Cook thought for a few moments, then said, "Start over."

Hunter nodded and put the car in gear. He cut across town to Madison Avenue and headed uptown toward Tony Rizzo's place.

"Do you think he knew we were following him?" Hunter asked.

"Yeah," Cook said, "he knew. He knew someone was following him, but not necessarily us. But Angelo's used to being watched and followed. My team's been following him a lot lately, and I'm sure he's on the lookout. Fellows was obviously keeping the whole Mondolffi family very well informed. I'm sure he didn't know it was you. They still think you're going to work every day."

"We should check on Henry," Hunter said. "Don't you think?"

Cook said, "Yeah, we could do that. You could check on your brother and get a change of clothes. Then we'll head right back here and set up camp again."

Hunter turned the car down a side street and headed for the Midtown Tunnel. The smell of them both from the past four days and the excitement of the past four hours forced him to crack his window. The cold air whistled in as they raced along the Long Island Expressway. Hunter blinked his eyes to keep awake. There was a strange voice inside his head, though, that was lulling him to sleep. In a way, he wanted to. He would welcome the blackness, then the instant flash of light as the car careened off the road and smashed into a concrete embankment, then total darkness and nothing, forever. That was an attractive thought when on the other side was only the pain and anguish of having ruined a life of promise and happiness . . .

"Hunter!" Cook bellowed.

Hunter jerked the car back onto the road and snapped to life. Adrenaline rushed through his veins for what must have been the twentieth time that day, and he marveled at the limits of the human body.

"Why don't you let me drive," Cook said.

"I'm OK," Hunter replied. "Really, I am. That scared the shit out of me. I'll get us there."

They first drove past the end of the street to make sure Lonny's Town Car was where it was supposed to be. There was no sign of it, so they approached the house from the front. Hunter slowed as he passed the entrance to his house. In the driveway sat the long black car.

"Keep going," Cook said.

"What do you think it means?" Hunter asked.

"I don't know," Cook replied. "Maybe nothing. Maybe they're just reminding you that they're there."

Hunter wove the car around through the dark streets to where they could approach his house from the rear. He worried about the car in the driveway. The idea that they were on to his ruse gave him a sick feeling in the pit of his stomach. The place looked big and empty sitting there in the dark without either of the people that gave it life. Hunter stumbled through the backyard like a drunk, then let them quietly in the back door with a key.

Cautiously they moved through the house. Henry was sound asleep in Hunter's bedroom. Dull moonlight fell in from the window and Hunter paused for a moment over the form that looked like the man he used to be. Henry bolted up frantically when Hunter put a hand on his leg.

"It's me," Hunter said in a low tone. "Henry, it's Hunter. Is everything all right?"

Henry rubbed his eyes and grunted. Suddenly he raised his eyes to Hunter. "Where've you been? I know where she is," he said excitedly.

Hunter gave Cook a quick glance. He dropped down beside his brother and gripped the front of his T-shirt. "How?" he said. "Where?"

Henry related to them his conversation with Camille Carter down to the last detail. He'd repeated her directions to himself a thousand times during the week, fearful beyond words that he might forget. When he finished, the three of them remained still there, in the dark.

Hunter jumped to his feet, "Let's go!"

Cook caught him by the sleeve. "Hold up," he said. "You got to sleep, man."

Hunter looked at Cook like he was mad. "Are you fucking crazy? We've got to get her!"

Cook held firm. He spoke quietly but forcefully. "If you try to go there now, you'll get Rachel killed."

The word seemed almost to echo down the long hallway outside the bedroom.

Hunter eased back. "Why?"

"Look at you," Cook said. "You can barely stand up. You lie down. I'll lie down. We'll get a good sleep. Tomorrow Henry can go to work and get rid of that car out there."

"What's up with that?"

Henry shrugged and said, "I don't know. That guy just follows me wherever I go, and two nights ago he started pulling right into the driveway after me and sitting there."

"When Henry goes, we'll take some showers and get some new clothes. Then we'll do this thing right. You can't just go running off half-cocked and expect to go into that cabin with guns blazing and come out with your wife in one piece. We need to do it right."

"But we've got to get her by Sunday," Hunter screeched in the voice of a madman. "You said yourself we don't know what they'll do with her after the game. We should go now."

"Listen," Cook said. "I've done this kind of thing before. You have to do it right or people will get hurt. We've got time. We can stake it out tomorrow and get her tomorrow night or even Sunday morning if we have to."

"Hey," Henry interjected, "you've got to do something before Sunday about me, too. I can't play in that game. You've got to be there."

Hunter almost stumbled on his feet. "You're not tired, Cook," he said. "If you're not, then I'm not. I want to get my wife."

Cook led Hunter gently by the arm as he spoke and deposited him on his own bed. "I'm tired, too," he said. "Just close your eyes for a little and we'll go get her. Trust me."

Cook was certain that Hunter was asleep before his head hit the bed.

"It's been a long week," Cook said to Henry without looking at him, "and hard on him."

Together they got Hunter's head up on the pillows and stripped him down to his shorts before covering him up with a blanket. Cook found a guest room and lay himself down. He, too, fell asleep in an instant. No one was there to take his clothes off or cover him up, but Cook never knew the difference.

Saturday morning was chilly and gray. The sun was no more than a pale yellow orb that glowed weakly from time to time through the eastern bank of clouds. The foliage was at its peak colors. Bright oranges and burning reds lit most of the trees that covered the Catskill Mountains. The wind was steady from the west and promising some kind of autumn storm.

Tony slept until almost nine. Even Angelo, who hadn't gotten in until the early morning hours, was up before Tony. Mikey had attended to Rachel and packed his bag in the car already. Both his men were sitting at the rustic plank-topped kitchen table having coffee when Tony came in. All three were dressed in flannel shirts, jeans, and Timberland boots. Tony sat down and watched Mikey pour him a cup, then took a swig before he began to talk.

"Everything OK, Ang?" he said.

Angelo shrugged. "I got the tickets. I can't believe you sent me back there for fucking football tickets. I couldn't get back right away because the fucking FBI was following me again. I took my time to lose them. I wanted to be sure."

Tony nodded. "Good."

For almost anyone else, Tony would have had a barrage of nervous questions to ask to assure himself that they hadn't been followed. But Angelo, he knew, did not make those kinds of mistakes.

"Where's Carl?" Angelo said.

Tony paused for a moment and had another swig of the strong, hot coffee. "I had a job for him Ang, a big job."

Tony saw Angelo's eyes dart at him with interest before he looked away.

"You gonna make him, Tony?" Angelo said, his gaze directed out the window at the colorful trees that encircled the cabin.

"That's what you want, Ang," Tony said.

"I want him with me," Angelo said quietly.

Tony allowed himself a smirk. He wasn't worried because he

knew Angelo wouldn't look at him. He was pleased that Angelo was so invested in Carl. It would make his acceptance of what was to come much easier. Making Carl a member of the family was the bone Tony was tossing to Angelo to help him forget about his ultimate loyalty to Tony's uncle. He knew Angelo didn't need much more. Besides, once his uncle was gone, he was gone. Angelo would be a big problem only if he were to find out about Tony's plans before they had been enacted.

"I'll take care of it," Tony said to assure Angelo that he wasn't going to take Carl away from him.

Angelo did not smile, but his eyes narrowed ever so slightly and Tony knew he was pleased.

"I want you to take care of the bitch for a couple of days," Tony said. "Mikey and I have some business with Meeker in Atlantic City tonight, and then we'll be going to the game tomorrow."

"What am I gonna do with her?" Angelo asked.

"I don't know, Ang," Tony said. "It depends how Sunday goes. I'm assuming everything will go OK. If it does, I think I'll give the bitch back to him. That'll cause the least amount of trouble. We can make him happy to have her back and still keep him on a string with the idea that we might just take her again if he pisses us off. I don't know. If there's any kind of fuck-up, I'll probably have you just make her disappear. Either way, I'll be back Sunday night to discuss it with you."

This made the corner of Angelo's mouth pull back in what was almost a smile. Mikey jumped up and pulled a frittata that he had been baking out of the oven. The three of them greedily dug into the traditional Italian breakfast of eggs, sausage, tomatoes, potatoes, and various other vegetables and cheeses all set up in a deep dish pie. After Mikey cleaned up the kitchen, he and Tony loaded themselves into the car. Angelo came out before they pulled away, and Tony rolled down his window.

"This the stuff Carl's been feeding her?" Angelo said, holding up a small prescription bottle.

"Yeah," Tony said. "Just put a couple drops in her drink, but make sure it's only two. That stuff's strong, and I don't want you to kill her right now."

"Who, me?" Angelo said gleefully in a rare display of jest.

Tony chuckled, "Really, Ang, don't fuck around with her. Just keep her drugged and we'll be back."

Angelo nodded, yes, he would do that.

Hunter didn't know where he was. Reality rushed at him like an unexpected wave and he sprang from the bed in a panic. Gray daylight fell in through the window. Hunter saw that the clock read 9:35. He'd fallen asleep! He was worried that Cook had decided to leave him as a liability and gone after Rachel alone. Hunter believed in Cook, but he had no intention of letting anyone go get Rachel without him. He crashed down the stairs three at a time and bounded into the kitchen in just his shorts. Cook looked up at him from the kitchen table.

"What the hell's wrong?" Cook asked excitedly, bracing himself in his chair.

Hunter felt foolish. Of course Cook hadn't left without him. "N-nothing," he said, looking down at his undershorts. "I'm ready to go."

"Hunter," Cook said with a solemn and apologetic air, "I didn't think it was a good idea to go last night. You needed the rest, and so did I."

"No, I know," Hunter said. "You were right. Obviously I needed it. But I'm ready to go now. I want to get her."

"Of course," Cook said, getting up from the table.

"Want a piece of toast or something? I had some with Henry before he left for practice. By the way, I swore on my mother's grave I'd have you at the game tomorrow to step back into yourself. He's very nervous about that."

"Thank God for Hank. Did you tell him I'd be there?"

"Yes," Cook said, "I told him that."

Cook convinced Hunter to shower and change while he whipped up some breakfast for him. After he'd eaten, Hunter and Cook packed up some extra clothes and set out through the back door, this time not because of anyone watching the front, but because their car was that way.

"Where's 1212 Peninsula Boulevard?" Cook asked when they got into the car.

"Not too far," said Hunter, "Why?"

"I got the address from the phone book," Cook said. "I want to stop there for some things. It's an army-navy store."

Hunter looked at Cook briefly out of the corner of his eye. "Why's that?"

"You'll see," Cook said.

Cook found gray forest camouflage hunting gear that was weatherproof and warm. They outfitted themselves from boots to hats. Then Cook spoke into the store owner's ear, and the two of them disappeared into the back of the store, returning a few moments later, each carrying a Kevlar vest.

"I don't know what the hell you guys are doing," the store owner said, "and I don't want to know, but you got some damn good gear."

Cook only nodded impatiently and asked the man to ring everything up.

Before too long, Cook and Hunter crossed the Hudson at the Tappan Zee Bridge and were on their way upstate to find and rescue Rachel.

"Cook," Hunter said as they slowed down for a toll booth, "what are you going to do about the FBI? I mean, it probably doesn't look too good for you, being a suspect in this Fellows killing and on the run from everyone. What are you going to do?"

"Well, the first thing I'm going to do is help you get your wife back. I'll take care of the Bureau after that. It'll work out. I'm not guilty of anything."

"If—if you think I can help out, I don't know how, but if there's anything I can do . . ."

"I appreciate it," Cook said. "You can help me corroborate my story. The only other thing would be if you happened to be tight with any big political people, someone who might back me up in all this, before I go back. It would be nice to have them thinking about all this from my viewpoint. The problem is that the Bureau is pretty closed. They don't listen to too many outsiders."

"How about Senator Ward?" Hunter said.

"Yeah, like him."

"I mean, how about if I have him call someone for you?" Hunter asked.

"He would be the right guy. He's the chairman of the Senate Judiciary Committee, a powerful guy up there and certainly someone who could get the word to Zulaff. That's the assistant director over me and Fellows and all of New York."

"I'll do it," Hunter said.

"I would appreciate that," Cook replied.

The road thumped by as they wound their way into the mountains on Route 17.

"Cook?" Hunter said.

"Yeah?"

"What's the plan? I mean, how are we going to do this?"

"I don't know," Cook said. "We'll scout it out, see what's what, how many of them there are, where she is, and then figure out the best way to get her."

Hunter took this in and frowned at the seriousness of the situation. They continued to ride in silence for some time, each in his own thoughts.

"If we get her," Cook said, "you're not necessarily safe, you know. Unless you're both willing to testify and enter the witness-protection program. It's different now with this kidnapping."

"I know," Hunter said. "I've been thinking the same thing. If that's what it takes, that's what we'll do. It would be tough. Rachel's so close to her parents, Sara is too. We wouldn't be able to see them, would we?"

"No," Cook said.

"Even with all that," Hunter said, looking from the road to Cook, "there are no guarantees, are there?"

"No," Cook said and shook his head.

Hunter pursed his lips. "We'd probably always be wondering, wouldn't we? I mean, if Rizzo or his people were going to find us."

"It can be hard," Cook admitted. "But it's better than the way things are right now. There might be another option, though."

"What?" Hunter said. "What are you thinking?"

"Just this," Cook said. "The only way to really be sure that Tony Rizzo leaves you alone is to kill him."

Hunter stared at Cook in disbelief, unsure he'd heard him correctly.

"Are you saying if we get the chance up at this cabin that we should try to kill Rizzo?" Hunter said. "I could kill the son of a bitch without blinking."

"I don't know," Cook said. "I used to think that, too, but it's different when it comes down to really doing it. If you kill someone, it seems to me that you become part of what you hate the most, the violence.

"But I'm not talking about either of us killing him," Cook said. "I'm thinking that his own people, or one of the other families, might kill him."

"Why would they do that?" Hunter asked.

"The way I see it," Cook said, "these other families are going to be putting a big hunk of cash down on this game, just like the Mondolffis. Tony promised some pretty big people this game. Otherwise he wouldn't have done something as desperate as grabbing Rachel, believe me. He must have heavy pressure on him to deliver Sunday's game against the Giants. He's willing to kill for that game, and if he is, others are, too. So . . ."

"So I win the game on Sunday," Hunter said, seeing exactly where Cook was headed, "and the other families kill Tony as retribution for what looks to them like a double cross."

"If we can grab Rachel back, you could win that game," Cook said. "If we can't get her, you've got to throw it and we'll go from there. I think Rizzo would kill her in an instant if you won that game. But if we've got her, we could put her and your daughter someplace safe and wait things out. He's going to have some real problems of his own. If he doesn't deliver on that game, I think we might find Tony Rizzo floating somewhere in the East River."

"What about the other families with me?" Hunter asked. "Won't they want to get me, too?"

"No," Cook said, "that's not how they do things. The Ianuzzos and the Gamones wouldn't blame you. You didn't set up the deal, Tony did. He would get the blame and only him. The Italian families are still very traditional with their beliefs about revenge. He's playing a high-stakes game. Everyone knows what happens to him if he loses."

Hunter thought about all this. He noticed a new-looking black Chevy Blazer on the other side of the highway that had been pulled over by the state police. He let up on his own gas, then accelerated again when he saw that the cop was busy writing a ticket.

"I just hope I can win that game," he said. "I haven't even practiced this week. Hell, I don't even know the game plan, Cook."

Cook looked over at Hunter and said, "I thought you were the greatest quarterback in the game right now."

Hunter huffed, "Well, you gotta practice to play. I'm good, but I don't like the idea of having to win that game to take Rizzo out. I mean, if I lose, he's safe and—"

"Yeah," Cook said, "witness protection. But you don't have much choice, do you? I mean, right now, if you could have your wife back, wouldn't you trade that for your career?"

"Of course," Hunter said angrily.

"I know," Cook said. "So look at it that way, and if you lose the game, then you and Rachel can testify against Rizzo, and the government will protect you."

"Maybe," Hunter said.

"We do a pretty damn good job," Cook replied. "And if you win, well . . . then Rizzo ceases to exist and you get your life back."

Hunter scowled from the pressure of the situation. "Let's just get Rachel out of there," he said. "You're right. After she's safe, anything else is just gravy."

It was just after noon when they pulled off Route 17 into the tiny town of Roscoe. They stopped at a country grocer and got some provisions in case they had to spend the night in the car or the woods. The cashier was a cranky old woman with drooping skin and thick, heavy-rimmed glasses. She mumbled something about "damn city people" when Hunter politely asked her for a box of No-Doz behind her on a decrepit old shelf.

"I can see they don't like people of color," Cook said as they climbed back into their car.

"Nah," Hunter said. "I think that old coot was just a bitch."

Cook nodded as though he agreed and they set off down 206. The wind blew some heavier clouds over the western peaks, and the sky began to spill infrequent raindrops on the windshield. The closer they got to their destination, the more grim-faced both Cook and Hunter became.

Finally Hunter said, "That's it!"

"Don't slow down!" Cook said. "Keep going. We'll pull off at the next place we can hide the car."

Hunter continued for another quarter mile until he saw the same dirt road that Camille had taken. He, too, pulled into the old dump, but instead of parking out in the open, he slowly eased the car back into a clump of trees so that even if someone pulled into the abandoned dump, they wouldn't spot the car. After they killed the engine, Hunter sat rigidly with his fingers white-knuckled on the steering wheel and his eyes shut tight.

Cook put a hand on his shoulder and gave it a squeeze. "Don't worry," he said, "it'll be all right."

"Let's go," Hunter said, and he popped the trunk before they got out.

Cook pulled the Kevlar vests out first and put his on over the sweatsuit that Hunter had let him borrow.

"You think there's going to be shooting?" Hunter said, following suit with the other vest.

"I don't want there to be any," Cook said. "You never do. But if there is shooting, you're a hell of a lot better with one of these babies on than without one. Now, do you know how to use that thing?"

Hunter looked up from the Colt .45 that he had been examining. "Yeah," he said. "It's been awhile, but I used to shoot some when we were kids. I hope it's like riding a bike."

Cook said, "I hope you don't need it, period."

The camouflage gear went on right over their sweatsuits and bullet-proof vests. It was warm and waterproof. Last were the new pairs of Timberlands. Hunter felt like a fool and said so.

"You won't feel like a fool if one of them looks out from that cabin and blinks because he thinks he saw something in the woods. Know your environment and make it work to your advantage. That's one of the things you learn if you want to survive in my line of work."

They knew from Camille's description that the cabin was a straight shot up the mountainside from where its driveway met the road. They snuck through the trees back toward the driveway, and once it was just in sight, they followed it uphill until they could make out the outline of the cabin.

Hunter reached into the pocket of his jacket and felt the cold, smooth shape of the .45. He had the irrational urge to run, run straight at the cabin with his gun out, kick the front door in, and just start shooting the hell out of Rizzo and his men. He started to tremble with nervous energy as this idea took form in his mind and acquired a life of its own.

"Easy," Cook whispered in his ear, "just take it easy. I know what's going through your mind, but just relax. We got a lot of looking to do before we go doing anything crazy. We don't even know if she's there for sure, so just get a hold and do what I do."

Cook got down on his stomach and crept closer to the cabin. Slowly and quietly they made their way around the perimeter of trees that surrounded the cabin. They saw no signs of life, and the only thing that made them suspect that someone was even there was the shiny black Cadillac that sat in the gravel out front. After the circuit was complete, Cook motioned Hunter to follow him deeper into the woods. When the cabin was no longer visible through the trees, Cook pulled off his hat and wiped his face.

"Did you see anything?" he said.

"No," Hunter said.

"No, neither did I," Cook said.

"So what are we going to do?" Hunter asked.

"We'll go back and watch. We'll wait until it's dark," Cook said, "before we approach the cabin. It'll be a hell of a lot easier then. We'll know where they are by the lights, and we'll be able to look in without them seeing out. This way, I think we'll find out if there are three of them in there or thirty. Plus, hopefully we can locate Rachel and protect her when things start to go down."

The dripping sky let up and the rain didn't come. The wind, however, continued to howl through the trees and tear at the colorful, dying leaves. The waiting was torturous for Hunter. As he lay staring at the lifeless cabin, his thoughts were sunk in despair and self-pity. Finally it was dark and the lights in the cabin came on.

"Now," Cook whispered, "I want you to stay right here and train your gun on that front door. If anything bad goes down, you start shooting at them as they pile out after me. I'm going to get a closer look at things."

Hunter tried to follow Cook's progress, but once he was ten feet away he completely lost sight of him. Once Hunter thought he saw Cook's shadow pass through the flat square of light that shone from the front left side of the cabin. Suddenly the front door opened, spilling light out of the cabin. Hunter's blood raced. He got to his feet and pulled the .45 from his pocket, raising it as he closed the distance between him and the large figure of Angelo Quatrini, who moved with amazing stealth out onto the front porch.

W

hen they got to Scott Meeker's Star casino in Atlantic City, Tony picked up the phone immediately. He had a lot of calls to make that he'd neglected over the past few days. He knew it wasn't likely that the FBI could have traced a call he made from the cabin, but they were so thorough these days, and taking Rachel Logan was such a risky venture, that he'd simply decided to lay low for the week. So, now that he was at the hotel, he had a lot of catching up to do. The first call was to Aaron to check on the numbers for the week. They had shifted the line from five to three and taken in twelve million on the Titans compared to four million on the Giants. The family's take would be more than nine million tax-free dollars on this one game.

"You know Mark Ianuzzo stopped by here on Wednesday, right?" Aaron said.

"No," Tony said, "I didn't."

"Well, he said you would say it was all right and to call you if I had a problem. I couldn't get you, of course, but he wasn't taking no for an answer. The workers all got kind of nervous. He had a couple of guys with him waving submachine guns around. He also had an accountant who wanted to take a look at our operation. I'm sorry, Tony, I didn't know what to do. They saw the imbalance in our books."

"That's OK," Tony said. "I should have told you it was OK, but who could have guessed the son of a bitch would want to see the fucking books."

Tony's next call was to Lonny in his car. Lonny reported that except for the fact that Hunter hadn't practiced all week, everything else was normal. The papers, Lonny told him, were assuring the fans that Hunter would be ready for the game on Sunday. Not wanting to take any chances, Tony called Grant Carter at his home. The owner was less than pleased to hear from Tony, but that didn't matter. Carter was appropriately cooperative. What did matter was that Tony emphasized the importance of Hunter Logan being on the field for the entirety of Sunday's game and that Grant Carter understood the implications if for some reason that failed to happen.

Tony plunked the phone down and stretched his legs out on the coffee table. Scott Meeker had given him and Mikey a luxurious suite, and it was spacious enough so that he had to raise his voice for Mikey to hear him from his room.

"Mikey!" he yelled. "Come in here. You want something to eat?"

"Yeah," Mikey said, emerging from his room like a dog happy to be called from its kennel.

"OK," Tony said and called room service. When he was through, he dialed his apartment in Manhattan. There was no answer, so he called Camille's apartment. There was no answer there either.

"That bitch," Tony mumbled. He dialed the Palladium and asked the manager if he'd seen Camille. The manager said he hadn't seen her since they had been in together the week before.

"Where the hell could she be?" Tony said, slamming the phone down and glaring at Mikey.

Mikey shrugged. "I dunno. Maybe she just went out for dinner?"

"That bitch," Tony mumbled again. "I told her to stay put."

After they'd eaten in their room, Tony and Mikey dressed themselves in jackets and went down to the tables. Scott Meeker met them and gave them each ten thousand dollars in chips to play for the night. Meeker was obviously jittery. He couldn't keep his hands still or his mouth shut.

"So," he said as the three of them sat at a blackjack table, "is everything set? It's set, isn't it?"

Tony looked blandly at Meeker. "What the fuck do you think?"

Meeker frowned and said, "I put a lot of money down on this one, Tony. Don't get mad at me for asking. The deal with Hunter Logan not practicing makes me nervous. Ianuzzo and Gamone both called me all week and wondered why you couldn't be reached. I think they're a little uptight about Logan's injury, too. I kept putting them off, telling them you were out of town, working on insuring that the deal came out OK. They were talking about calling the deal off until Wednesday."

"Yeah," Tony said, "that's when Ianuzzo showed up at my warehouse and put a gun in my accountant's face to see the books."

"But everything's OK?" Meeker said.

Tony frowned at the fat man. With his bright orange jacket, he looked like a gaudy human pumpkin with sparkling diamond rings.

"You think I'm worried about your money on this deal?" Tony growled, calling for another card and busting. "You think that's important here? I got the Gamones and the Ianuzzos putting millions on this game. I got my life on this game. You think your money's not safe? Fuck you."

"Hey, Tony," Meeker said apologetically, "I didn't mean anything. You know that. I'm just the nervous type." Here he gave a high-pitched little laugh as if to prove his point.

"Sometimes," Tony said, pushing his entire stack of chips out onto the table, "sometimes you just gotta take big chances."

The dealer hesitated and looked at the casino owner. A small group gathered around the table as people going by noticed the three tall stacks of black hundred-dollar chips.

"What are you looking at?" Meeker demanded. "Deal the cards!"

The dealer snapped the cards down on the table. Tony got an ace and flipped over a jack. The small group of onlookers gave a cheer.

Tony smiled, "See what I mean, Scotty?"

"Yeah," Meeker said, thinking that it was easy when you weren't playing with your own money but saying nothing.

They played for a while in silence, and Tony decreased his bets to drive away the people before he said, "Are the two big guys here yet?"

"No," Meeker said. "They're coming in tomorrow morning. They want to see you at nine."

"Yeah," Tony said. "OK. When I think about it, I wonder why in hell these guys want this meeting. I don't see the reason for it."

"Maybe they just like your company," Meeker said, throwing down his card.

TIM GREEN

Tony looked long and hard at him, saying nothing until Meeker couldn't stand it anymore and said, "What?"

"Sometimes I like your sense of humor, Scotty," he said. "But this is one of those times when I'm not fucking laughing."

"I'm sorry, Tony," Meeker said casually, thinking to himself that it would almost be worth it to lose his half-million dollars on the game just to watch Ianuzzo and Gamone tear Tony up into little pieces.

Hunter saw the muzzle of Angelo Quatrini's gun flash a bright orange flame in the night before the explosion rang in his ears. He rushed forward as fast as he could. He heard Cook's body crashing through some chairs to the floor of the porch and then saw him roll under the railing and over the edge to the ground below. Angelo Quatrini fired three more quick shots at Cook's form, then paused to assess the damage. He looked around instinctively, and it was then that he saw Hunter's shape moving toward him from the darkness. Angelo spun and crouched, leveling his gun. Hunter pulled up and began firing shots at Angelo. Hunter heard a bullet whiz by his head, and without thinking he dived to the ground. Angelo continued to fire at him, and Hunter rolled madly away, stopping only when he'd gotten himself behind the wheel of the Cadillac, parked directly in front of the cabin.

Hunter heard Angelo scramble off the porch and then there was silence. He froze where he was. His mind was churning with the possibilities. Was Cook dead? Where was Angelo? Where was Rachel?

It was that thought that spurred Hunter into action. Instantly he jumped to his feet and raced for the open doorway, expecting any minute for a bullet to strike him in the head and instantly kill him. He got to the door and into the cabin without anything happening. He flattened himself against the open door and listened for some kind of noise from without. Besides the moaning wind there was nothing. Hunter searched the interior of the cabin with a sweeping gaze. Nothing moved and there was no noise. It made Hunter think that Angelo Quatrini was alone. He brought his trembling hand up to his face and wiped the sweat out of his eyes. He tried to think.

A loud crash from within the cabin made him jump, and he raised his pistol in the direction from which it came. He heard it

428

again, coming through the thick log wall. It was the clanging, rattling noise of metal on metal. Then he heard the muffled noise of a woman's voice. He rushed across the great room and into a small hallway. Seeing a bedroom door on the left, he burst into the room. Rachel lay handcuffed to a brass headboard. Her skin was sickly pale, and her hair was tangled and matted. The large band of tape across her mouth was the most disturbing thing of all. Hot tears welled up in Hunter's eyes.

"My God," he moaned and threw himself down beside Rachel on the bed, holding her tightly and rocking her fragile figure back and forth like a child. The tears spilled down his face and into Rachel's greasy hair. She, too, was crying. Hunter heard a low laugh behind him and spun his head around.

Angelo Quatrini stood in the doorway of the bedroom with a big automatic pistol leveled at Hunter's head. His large, heavy frame shook ever so slightly as he chuckled quietly to himself. The gun was pointed almost casually at Hunter.

"Now," Angelo growled, "what am I supposed to do with you?"

The room exploded with the noise of gunfire, and Angelo's neck burst open like the stalk of an overripe milkweed. Another shot blew his elbow into jagged mess of bone and meat, and his gun clattered to the floor. Still two more bullets thudded into his torso, leaving holes that spouted more blood. Angelo looked confusedly at his elbow and reached up with his other hand to try to plug the leak in his neck. The effect was like putting his thumb over the end of a hose, and the blood sprayed about wildly out of control. He lurched sideways and then went over in a heap of blood and gore.

In the remnants of the shattered window that looked out onto the cabin's porch stood Ellis Cook, with his gun raised and smoking and his eyes glassed over in pain. His free hand was clamped over one side of his head, which appeared to be half blown off. Cook looked in the direction of Hunter and Rachel. His mouth dropped open as if he was about to speak. Then he staggered forward and fell over the jagged window and into the room, smashing the glass left from his barrage of bullets.

A pathetic sob escaped Rachel, and Hunter realized he hadn't yet taken the tape off of her mouth. Gently he pulled it away, cringing to himself at the oozing red patch of skin that remained. Then he held her. He held her close in a way that seemed like it would last forever.

When the smoke cleared and the ringing in his ears began to subside, Hunter could hear the silence through the moaning wind. He knew they were alone, and he knew he had to do two things. First, he had to get Cook to a hospital. Next, he had to get Rachel out to the Hamptons with her parents and Sara and then get all of them to a place they could hide until everything was over. Hunter fished through the pockets of Angelo Quatrini's corpse and found a large key chain and what he believed to be the keys to Rachel's handcuffs.

"Come on, Rachel," he said. "We've got to go."

Rachel had a hard time getting up and could barely walk. Hunter scooped her up and carried her out to the Cadillac. He opened the front door and gently set her down on the seat. Next Hunter draped Cook over his good shoulder and brought his limp body out to the car. He lay Cook across the backseat. He thought Cook was alive but wasn't sure. The man's head continued to bleed profusely, creating a sticky pool on the seat. Hunter climbed into the front seat and raced down the hill.

At the bottom he had to stop and find which of Angelo's keys opened the lock on the pipe gate. It only took a minute, and before long they were back on Route 17, racing toward New York. Hunter had seen a sign for a hospital nearby on their way in. He followed that same blue sign now. It was the third exit up, but the hospital was not far from the highway.

Hunter carried Cook into the emergency room and laid him as carefully as he could on an unoccupied gurney. A young round-faced doctor burst into the hall. He checked Cook over quickly and immediately began to administer CPR while at the same time barking orders to a couple of nurses who fluttered about wildly.

He thought he heard one of them murmer, "He's dead."

Hunter stood for a moment and watched the young doctor. He was smooth and quick and every movement seemed important. Hunter felt completely useless, and the trauma team carried on as if he wasn't there. Then he remembered Rachel in the car. He thought about Cook's words: If he won the game, Rizzo would be taken out by his own kind. On the other hand, his instincts told him to run, to go get Sara and make sure the three of them disappeared forever. He knew that when confrontation occurred, the human reaction was flight or fight. Right now he felt like he'd used up all the fight he had. Hunter clenched his fists and said a brief prayer for Cook, then jogged out into the night.

Henry woke up in the Meadowlands Marriott. It was only six o'clock, but that was when Henry got up. Bert snored soundly in the next bed, and Henry wondered how his wife ever got any rest. Henry pulled the telephone out from underneath the pair of jeans Bert had slung over the night table between the two beds. Bert's belt jingled loudly, and some change fell out of the pockets and clattered down onto the night table. The message light was not blinking. Henry knew from Bert that no calls were allowed into the players' rooms after eleven. He thought that Hunter might have tried to call sometime during the night and leave a message that he would be there by game time.

Henry got up and used the bathroom. He paced back into the bedroom and sat on his bed in the weak light that leaked through the curtains. Henry crossed his arms and rocked nervously back and forth. He had expected Hunter to be back by now. Instead of becoming more comfortable with his role as his brother as the week went on, Henry had become less and less comfortable. Right now he felt like pulling on his clothes and just sneaking out. He wanted to leave, to just go home and get back to his life. Sad as it was, it was his, and he was tired of worrying and pretending. But this was nothing more than wishing. He wouldn't let Hunter down. Most of all, he wouldn't let Rachel down. He had never had much to say to her, but he'd always admired her from a distance. He knew she was in danger, and that was why it was so important that he continue to play his role.

He got up and paced the floor between the TV and the beds. He wanted at least to get out of the room, into some light and away from Bert's awful noise. But he felt safer in these dark confines than he did wandering around the hotel. Out there he was likely to run into a coach or someone else who couldn't sleep late, and they would want to talk with him about the game or how his shoulder felt.

Henry lay back down on the bed to wait for the day to begin. If Hunter didn't show up, he had no idea in the world what he could do. He certainly couldn't go out there and play, but then again, he couldn't run either. The whole thing made him sweat. He couldn't wait to get back to West Virginia, where he was comfortable and where he belonged. As much as he hoped for that, though, he hoped even more that Hunter would get Rachel back and the two of them with Sara could be safe.

Bert finally woke up. They got ready and went down for the pre-game meal. Bert ate heartily but wasn't much of a comfort to Henry. Bert was getting on his game face, and he dealt with Henry's concerns about Hunter's showing up by saying, "Don't worry, it'll work out."

To Henry that could mean a lot of things. It could mean Bert thought Hunter would return in time. It could also mean that he wouldn't but that something else acceptable would happen. Henry couldn't think of another welcome solution, and Bert had nothing more to say. So instead of eating, Henry played with a pile of eggs and spaghetti while Bert cleaned up three full plates of food.

Because Henry was anxiously awaiting his brother, the time crawled by. Every minute he looked expectantly at the doorway for Hunter to wave him out so that they could switch places. On the bus ride to the stadium, Henry consoled himself with the idea that of course Hunter was waiting there for them. It was the logical place to make the switch. When the bus dropped them off in the stadium tunnel, Henry's eyes roamed the immediate area for a sign of his delinquent brother. In the locker room Henry checked the training room, the shower, and even the toilets, each place fully expecting to find Hunter. After he had checked the area thoroughly, he reported to Bert that something was wrong.

"Just hang tight," Bert said under his breath as he tightly wrapped a roll of wide white tape around his wrists for the contest. "He'll be here."

Henry looked around him. The locker room was filling up with Titans players. Each one was intent in his own game preparation. Henry tried to do something of the kind. He pulled some pads from the top shelf and began stuffing them into Hunter's game pants. His hands were beginning to tremble now. He cursed under his breath. What the hell had he gotten himself into? And where the hell was Hunter?

Henry, unable to keep still, got up and walked back out into the tunnel. There were all kinds of people milling through the dark gray passage: janitors, concessionaires, police, referees, and cheerleaders. Already the stadium above hummed with life. Henry felt a tap on his shoulder. He spun around with a relieved grin and found himself face to face with a sharply dressed, handsome young man with angry dark eyes. Beside him was a clone, a little shorter and not quite as tough-looking, but dressed in the same type of hand-knit sweater and leather coat and wearing the same long hair pulled back into a tight ponytail. Henry almost chuckled at the second guy, but the realization of who these two must be hit him first.

"The fuck you smiling at?" Tony Rizzo snarled, grabbing Henry tightly by the biceps.

Henry didn't know what to say.

"That's better," Rizzo said with a malignant grin. "Now you look scared. That's what I'm used to. I almost didn't recognize you without that fucking terrified shit-in-your-pants look.

"Yeah," Tony continued, "I just came by to make sure you were doing all right."

He pulled Henry close and hissed into his ear, "You fucking better be out there on that field, and you better lose this fucking game in a big way! If this fucking thing is even close, I'm gonna cut that little bitch of yours open from her cunt to her fucking chin!"

Rizzo separated himself from the pale and shaky form of Henry Logan. "Yeah," Rizzo said loudly, "It was great seeing you, Hunter. Good luck!"

Tony led Mikey up through a concrete stairwell to the concession area, where there was also a bank of pay phones. He pulled a piece of paper from his wallet and punched a Connecticut number into the phone.

"Motel 8" came the slow, lazy voice of a woman Tony just knew was ugly.

"Yes," Tony said, "I'm looking for a Mr. Burke, Carl Burke."

"Hang on . . ."

The phone rang seven times. Tony fidgeted and frowned at Mikey, who was looking on anxiously.

On the eighth ring, Carl picked up and said, "Tony?"

"Yeah."

"I—I did it. You should've seen it! There was fucking brains every-where. It was a fucking mess! I did it, Tony . . ."

"You emptied the .38 like I said?"

"Fucking A! Brains everywhere! Everything went fucking right! I did it, Tony!"

"Good, Carl. Very good. You stay right there where you are until I call you. I'll let you know when the dust settles and we'll bring you back. In the meantime, you don't go anywhere, got it?"

"I got it, Tony. I did it."

"Good, Carl. I'll talk with you soon."

Tony hung up the phone and turned to Mikey. His upper lip quivered uncontrollably.

"He did it?" Mikey asked.

Tony wanted to grab Mikey and spin him around, but he remem-bered himself. "Four hours from now," he said with quiet certainty, "I will be the head of the Mondolffi family."

Henry couldn't control a shudder after he watched the two of them go. His stomach turned and sank. Hunter was nowhere, and he was going to have to play. It was a nightmare. He did have to go out there or Rizzo would do what he said, of that Henry had no doubts. But how could he go when he didn't really have a clue about what to do? The coach would pull him out after the first play. Henry had no idea what he was doing. He didn't even know the hand signals that were used to send the play in from the sideline.

Henry made his way back into the locker room like a zombie. He found Bert by his locker, a storm of anger with bugged-out eyes.

"I don't know," Bert said, his eyes rolling half-crazy in his head, "you gotta just do it. I don't know what to say."

Henry sat on the stool in front of Hunter's locker and stared at the uniform that hung there. It was the uniform of the man people were calling one of the greatest ever to play the game. It would be frightening to put on that uniform even under normal circum-stances. Bert's mad words rang out clearly in his head. Henry was suddenly struck with a surge of resolve. If he had to do it, he would. He might fail, but he would try. He had to at least try, he absolutely had to.

TITANS

The day was warm for early October in New Jersey, and a steady breeze from the south carried with it the foul smells of industry combined with decaying wetlands. The crowd seemed not to notice, though. The contest today took on vast proportions as the die-hard fans for both the Titans and the Giants came to see their team claim the bragging rights to New York City. When the Titans jogged out onto the field for their pre-game warm-ups, half the crowd cheered ecstatically while the other half booed their lungs out.

Many of the eyes from both sides were on number thirteen, Hunter Logan. Every football fan in the nation knew that the great quarterback was having problems with his shoulder and that he had not taken a single snap in practice all week. Such a handicap would preclude most quarterbacks from seeing the field on Sunday, but Hunter Logan was not most quarterbacks. He was the man who had taken his team to the top, a Super Bowl victory, and the man who had only last week outgunned one of the game's legends, Joe Montana.

Again, when the eager crowd saw Hunter Logan's first pass, half cheered madly, but the other half, instead of booing, were conspicuously silent. The ball was a lame duck. It had wobbled through the air and fallen despicably short of its intended target. The next one was not much better. The Giants fans were given life. As the underdogs in this contest, they had been abuzz all week at the prospect of a wounded Hunter Logan. It could be the element they needed to put it in the face of their counterparts who had bragged so unabashedly for the entire off-season. A win for the Giants fans today would make the season a success no matter what happened later on. It didn't get much better, but on his final throw before the Titans retreated to their locker room before the start of the game, Logan did throw a short pass that resembled a spiral. The Titans fans were encouraged and cheered wildly in the hopes that he had only needed to get the kinks out after a week of inactivity and that by the end of the contest Hunter Logan would again be his brilliant self.

Henry jogged back into the locker room with the rest of the team, but he felt as if he was completely alone. Immersed in the fog of his own dream, he didn't notice Coach Price until he was on top of him.

"You better turn it up a notch, Logan!" Price said angrily with his face only about an inch from Henry's. "I know you got the man upstairs buffaloed with your heroics last weekend. Yeah, you got the job, you got the man, but if I have to play you this whole game and you dump a load of shit like you just did out there, I swear I'll make your life miserable. You may be a superstar right now, but you're getting old, Logan, and I just got here."

Price walked away without another word.

Five minutes later, the entire team was kneeling in a circle and holding each other's hands. A voice rose up from their midst and prayed for no injuries. It prayed for glory to give back to the creator. It prayed for courage and toughness and strength.

Henry Logan prayed on his own. He prayed for a miracle.

The Titans players were milling toward the doors of the locker room that led to the stadium when some scruffy-looking guy who resembled Hunter Logan burst in from the tunnel. Only about a third of the team even saw him, and they all kept pushing forward, not having time to indulge themselves in curiosities only minutes before the kickoff of a big game. The one man who was obviously affected to the point of distraction was Hunter Logan, or rather, the man the Titans believed was Hunter Logan.

"Damnation!" Henry cried, unconcerned now about who was there or who wasn't.

Hunter grabbed his brother with a quick, affectionate hug and then started to strip down right there in the middle of the locker room floor. Henry wasted no time but did the same.

"What the hell happened?" Henry said as they worked.

"I got Rachel!" Hunter said excitedly. "I had to hide her and Sara. I came back to win this game."

"You can't win this game," Henry said. "Those guys were here. They . . ."

It hit Henry." Are they safe for sure?" he said, working himself out of Hunter's uniform.

"Yeah," Hunter said. "They are, and winning this game is the only way I can make sure they stay that way for good. That's why I came back."

"You mean you came back to save my ass from having to go out there and shit all over myself," Henry said excitedly.

"That, too," Hunter said.

"That, too," Henry repeated in disgust. "You son of a bitch, I can't believe you would've left me!"

Henry got the rest of the uniform off, and Hunter worked fast to get it on.

"I don't know who's a bigger prick," Henry said, "that Mafia guy or Price."

Hunter grinned, "That's a tough call. No, not really. Rizzo is an animal."

He could hear "The Star Spangled Banner" from beyond the door that led out onto the field. He pulled on his turf shoes and laced them tightly.

"Hank," he said, standing up and gripping his brother's hand firmly, "I'll never forget this. I love you, Hank. I haven't said that for a lot of years, and I should have. I couldn't have saved Rachel without you. I may not see you again. You need to just get the hell out of here as fast and as far away as you can."

Henry pulled Hunter close and gave him a quick hug, then pushed him away, saying, "Good luck, little brother. Good luck."

Hunter smiled at their old joke of him being the younger one. He picked his helmet up from the floor and tucked it under his arm before he turned and dashed out through the locker-room doors and into the stadium.

Hunter went right to the Titans' sideline and found Bert.

"Bert . . ." he said.

"Hunt?" Bert said. "Is that you? Did you get her?"

"Yeah, she's safe . . . thanks. I'll tell you about it later."

"Damn," Bert said and nodded with relief.

"How'd you know it was me?" Hunter asked.

"Well," Bert said, "I knew Henry was nervous as hell, but not nervous enough to grow a full beard in five minutes. You need a shave."

"Yeah," Hunter said, "now tell me what the hell's going on. Is everything OK?"

"Yeah," Bert said. "Everyone's expecting you to play. Henry did a hell of a job. I don't know what would've happened if you didn't show. I didn't know what the hell to say to him."

The two of them stopped talking and turned their attention to the field, where the Titans were about to receive the kickoff. When Hunter trotted out onto the field with the Titans first-team offense, the place erupted with boos.

"What the hell are they booing at?" Hunter asked his center, Murphy, in the huddle.

"They didn't like those ducks you were throwing during warm-ups," said Weaver, who was one not to pull any punches, "and frankly neither did I."

"Warm-ups?" said Hunter.

"Yeah, if you call that shit you did out here a half hour ago warming up," Weaver said.

"OK," Hunter said, "forget that and let's win this. Two Twenty-Seven Strike Right on two. Ready . . . break!"

The first quarter, Hunter played like a guy who hadn't practiced all week. His passes were erratic and he under-threw his receivers. The Giants got a 7–0 lead and sat on it.

"Just hang with me," Hunter implored his teammates after each bad play. "I'm gonna get this one."

Steadily, as Hunter got warmer and warmer, his passes became more and more accurate. With a minute fifty-five to go in the half, the Titans defense got the ball back on their own three-yard-line. Hunter got into a groove and, using his team's two-minute offense, drove the entire ninety-seven yards for a touchdown to tie the game up at the half.

The Titans stormed into the locker room on the crest of the emotional wave Hunter had generated with his last-second touchdown pass. They would no doubt have the emotional edge coming out after the half. They knew from what they'd just seen that their quarterback was back in form. Enthusiasm and confidence spread like a drop of ink in a glass of water. Helmets were crashing about and war cries resounded through the thick, pungent air of the locker room, giving it the feel of some kind of prison riot.

No one seemed to notice Tony Rizzo and Mike Cometti as they wove through the team and stopped in front of Hunter Logan, who was downing a Gatorade on the stool in front of his locker. Tony stood calmly above him and then, with one quick movement, grabbed Hunter by the front of his jersey and yanked him to his feet before slamming him backward into his own locker.

"You son of a bitch!" Rizzo screamed. "You think I'm fucking kidding with you? You think I'm playing?"

"Hey!" Murphy, whose locker was two down from Hunter's, was on his feet in a blink.

"Hey, fuck you!" said Tony, pointing at the master pass he wore around his belt loop.

"I don't give a fuck if you're the owner's fucking son!" Murphy bellowed, grabbing a handful of Rizzo's leather coat and jerking him away from Hunter. "That's my fucking QB, you asshole! No one touches my QB."

"You . . ." Tony drew his fist back to punch Murphy in the chin, but before he could connect, Murphy swung his free hand in a wide, swift arc like a club that landed on the side of Tony Rizzo's head and knocked him off his feet. Mike Cometti threw a cheap shot at Murphy and hit him in the back of the head. Murphy reached up and rubbed the spot as if it were a gnat, then turned, and with a smile, grabbed Cometti and threw his body across the locker room and into a Coke machine, where he fell in a useless heap.

Before Rizzo could get to his feet, security guards and police were everywhere, dragging him and Mike Cometti out by their hair.

"You better fucking remember, Logan!" Rizzo screamed as they dragged him outside. "You better fucking remember what I'll do!"

The thrill of watching Rizzo take a thumping was like a drug for Hunter—it got him up fast, but soberly. Rizzo's bold appearance reminded Hunter of the kind of desperate, angry, and powerful force he was working against. He hoped Cook was right. If he was not, Hunter would have to run fast and pray hard.

In another way, though, Rizzo's appearance solidified Hunter's commitment. Rizzo would never leave him alone. Cook was right about that. He was the type that would never go away, a parasite that did not desist until its host was completely dry of blood. He could beat Rizzo by winning this game. He regretted that he wouldn't be there to watch what the vermin's own kind were going to do to him. He was sure it would not be pleasant.

Hunter left no doubts at all about his abilities in the second half. He put on a show. His throws were like rifle shots, fast and accurate. His leadership was evident on both sides of the ball. When the defense was out on the field, Hunter was right there beside the coaches, cheering, encouraging, and celebrating with his defensive teammates. By the middle of the fourth quarter the score was 28–7, and Hunter relaxed about the game. He wondered what Rizzo would try to do, and how much time he had to get his family to safety. He knew he would have at least a couple of hours after the game. It would be that long before Rizzo got back to his cabin and found Rachel gone.

After the final gun, Hunter ran off the field and into the locker room, where he quickly changed and left before the media was able to get in to interview him. He knew that would raise a ruckus. The quarterback was always the most interviewed player, and he would be expected to give the press their quotes after such a spectacular stomping of New York's other NFL team.

Hunter used his face and name to get one of the state troopers to give him an escort past the jammed-up traffic that snaked all the way to the Lincoln Tunnel. From there Hunter raced across Manhattan to the Midtown Tunnel and then took the Long Island Expressway until it turned into 27, which took him to the end of the island and Montauk. He had left his family out here at a small oceanside motel. He was afraid if anything went wrong and Rizzo found out Rachel had been rescued, that he might have his people go to Rachel's parents' place in Quogue. It seemed unlikely, but now that Hunter had her back, he was taking no chances. Rachel's parents were with her and Sara.

Hunter had had Morty go to the bank in West Hampton on Saturday morning and withdraw fifty thousand dollars in cash. Hunter didn't know what was going to happen with Rizzo for sure, and he wanted to be able to lie low for a long time if necessary.

When he pulled into the motel lot, the sun was beginning to set. He got out of his car and tasted the ocean air. It smelled pungent but clean, and the breeze was warm. Hunter still had an edge of adrenaline, but it was wearing off fast. He'd gotten a few hours' sleep last night at this very hotel—once he'd reunited Rachel and Sara and her parents and gotten them all moved out here. Now the long evening shadows made the warm light coming through the window of their room even more inviting. Hunter could already feel how good it was going to be to lie down and collapse with Rachel and Sara snugly tucked in beside him in the same soft, cozy bed. The image made Hunter yawn. His father-in-law appeared from his room, adjoining theirs, and carefully closed the door.

"How is she?" Hunter asked.

"She's fine," Morty replied. "I have a good friend who's a doctor. Don't worry, he wouldn't say a word to anyone. He came and looked at her today. He told her to rest as much as she could and eat. Her mother's seen to that end of it."

Hunter nodded and started to move toward his own door.

"Well," Morty said quietly, "you did good. Do you think that will be it?"

"I don't know," Hunter said, stopping and turning toward his father-in-law. "That's what Cook seemed to think, but I can't be sure. Tony Rizzo isn't going to go down easy, I know that. And if he has the chance, and he can find us . . ."

"So, will we go?" Morty asked.

"Yes," Hunter said. "I think we should."

"We'll have to wait until morning," Morty said. "The last ferry left at seven-thirty. It's the off-season."

"I think we'll be all right here tonight. You didn't say anything to anyone when you went to town today?"

"Of course not."

"I know," Hunter said, "I'm just tired . . . and worried."

"I am, too," Morty said. "But you've done well. Don't worry. They won't get to any of us again."

Hunter held out a hand and Morty took it before giving his son-in-law a hug. "You did good," he said in a low voice. "You did very good."

Hunter let himself into their room and Sara jumped up and into his arms. Rachel smiled warmly from the bed. Hunter was surprised at how much better she looked already. The blood was back in her face, and her hair was a glossy black.

"You look . . . You look beautiful, honey," Hunter said, carrying his little girl in his arms and bending down to give Rachel a long, warm kiss.

"Thank you," she said. "You played great, Hunter. You did it."

"I hope so," he fretted, stroking her soft cheek gently, "but let's not even talk about it anymore. Let's just be together, and know that we won't be apart again, ever."

Tony Rizzo went rigid at about the same time in the fourth quarter that Hunter Logan relaxed.

"Let's go," he told Mikey, and the two of them left their seats and the stadium.

Mikey knew better than to say anything right now, but he was having a hard time holding it in.

The silence was too much. "You want me to go back in there and kill that fucking Logan?" he said when they finally reached their car.

"What the fuck's your problem?" Tony said with a glare. "You know as well as I do that you ain't going back there to kill anybody, let alone a guy who's surrounded by cops and security guards.

"Besides," Tony said, starting the engine, "payback for that son of a bitch is gonna be with his little wife. I said I was gonna fuck her before I snuffed her, and now I'm gonna do it. I may be fucked in this, but that fucker is gonna wish this day never came. He thinks the FBI can protect him? Ha!"

The traffic was already thick with people trying to beat the rush, and Mikey was surprised at Tony's patience. He had imagined Tony would be bouncing off the walls.

"Tony?" he began again, unable to help himself and emboldened by fear. "Aren't we in a little trouble with all this?"

Tony snorted half a laugh. "Trouble is not the word."

Tony got on 95 and stopped at Fort Lee, which was the last town in Jersey before the George Washington Bridge. He found a Hertz and rented Mikey a car.

"Now," he said to his protégé, "you take this car and go back to my apartment. Drive right into the garage and wear this fucking Hertz cap pulled down low over your head in case the feds are still sniffing around there. Go into my closet, and behind my shoes is a wall safe. Here, I'll write down the combination.

"Take all the cash that's in there, Mikey. It's a half million," Tony said. "We're gonna have to lay low for a long time. We might even have to leave the fucking country. With my uncle dead, Vincent, Jr.'s gonna be looking for us. Without Ianuzzo and Gamone, I'm done. They'll probably want a piece of me themselves for all this."

Mikey looked down at his shoes—they were Ballys, just like Tony's. "You're pretty calm about all this," Mikey said. "You OK?"

"Hey," Tony said with a grim smile, "this business isn't easy. Now is when I need to keep cool. I can get us through this, Mikey. Just get me that money and come right up to the cabin."

"OK, Tony."

Mikey watched as Tony Rizzo made his way through the Hertz lot to the black Blazer. He felt a surge of pride. Tony was so cool, even now.

Mikey raced into the garage just like Tony had said, with the goofy Hertz hat pulled low like some minimum-wage worker with half his senses. Old Willie, the attendant, waved nonchalantly when he saw Mikey crouched low in the driver's seat. Willie was used to it all.

Mikey got out of the rental car and looked around. There was no sign of anyone or anything unusual. He made his way up to Tony's apartment and let himself in with a key. Sitting in the two big chairs in Tony's living room were Sal Gamone and Mark Ianuzzo. Mikey was flanked by two of their henchmen, men the equivalent size and meanness of Angelo Quatrini. Two more stood directly behind their bosses.

Sal Gamone spoke. "Where's Tony?"

Mikey's mouth hung open. "I . . ."

Sal blinked slowly, as if he was disappointed that a quicker, better answer was not forthcoming.

Mikey heard the spit of a silencer and felt his legs go out from under him. Blood was sprayed everywhere and it showed up in gruesome scarlet spatters all over the white marble foyer. Screaming in pain, Mikey writhed on the floor.

"Where's Tony?" Sal said in the same quiet voice from the living room, without bothering to look and see if Mikey had heard him.

"He's at his cabin!" Mikey cried. "I can show you! It's in the mountains . . . please . . ."

"Why are you here?" Sal asked.

"Tony sent me to get his money from the safe," Mikey bawled.

"Where is the safe?"

"In the closet, behind his shoes. My God! My knee! Please don't hurt me!"

"What is the combination?"

"It's here! It's in my pocket, written down."

Sal took the time to clear the money out of Tony's safe and split it with Mark Ianuzzo before the two of them left and got into a long, dark limousine. They followed their men, who rode with Mike Cometti between them in a crimson Buick Electra. For almost two hours they rode upstate. Neither of them spoke a word. Both were disappointed with the whole business and intent on cleaning things up as quickly as possible. They'd both been around long enough to know that Tony would try to run. But they had known from Meeker that Tony had a safe where he kept his cash. They knew Tony, or someone, would have to come back for it, so they had waited like patient spiders.

The young doctor whom everyone called Cappy got up from his cot and stretched, scratching his hairy belly which hung out from under his T-shirt and spilled over the waist of his sky-blue scrubs. He was overweight from all the junk food he ate—no time for real meals. He looked at his watch and hurriedly threw on his white coat, pushing his feet into a worn-out pair of Docksiders at the same time. He loved what he did, saving people's lives, and the thought of beating death made him hurry down the hall. He did not even bother to grab a doughnut from the half-empty box that lay askew on the counter of the empty nurses' station.

He knew if the patient was still alive, he was going to make it. It was one of those cases where the damage was either going to kill the guy or make him stronger.

Cappy liked the idea of making someone better than they were before. It was like the six-million-dollar-man. Their ICU had only four beds, but it was better than nothing. Fortunately for Cappy's mystery patient, there had been a vacancy last night. Without intensive care, the man wouldn't have had a chance. As he covered the last four paces of the hallway to ICU, Cappy wondered who this man was and what he did. He suspected it had something to do with drugs, but he really had no idea. It didn't matter anyway. A win was a win.

Cappy smiled broadly when he entered the room. The heart monitor was beeping along merrily. He moved in and started giving the patient a once-over of sorts, just to make sure there was nothing he'd missed. It was possible. He had operated for fourteen hours and done some procedures he'd hitherto performed only on cadavers. But everything looked good.

When the man opened his eye, Cappy jumped. It scared the hell out of him.

"You're one tough son of a gun," Cappy said to the man admiringly. With a smile he added, "But then again, you had one hell of a surgeon."

Tony suspected what had happened the moment he saw the gate hanging open off the driveway below the cabin. It would certainly explain Hunter Logan's refusal to heed his warnings. Tony knew for sure what had happened the instant he saw the front door to the cabin hanging ajar. He walked quietly into the cabin and stood over Angelo Quatrini's body. A thick pool of coagulated black blood lay in a sticky mess around the body, and Tony's shoes left distinct prints into the room. He moved to the window, and broken glass crunched under his feet. He wondered for a few moments how it had happened. There was blood all over the sill, and out on the porch as well. It didn't surprise Tony that Angelo may have taken other lives with him. The only surprise was that Angelo himself was dead. That was something that Tony had never been able to envision, and he half expected Angelo to get up from the floor where he lay like the stiffened carcass of some oversize road kill.

Tony gazed at Angelo's face. A few greedy flies scurried and buzzed about his lips. His eyes were wide open but foggy and lifeless. Tony shook his head and went back into the living room to sit down and wait. Mikey would be back soon, he knew that. Of all the things in the world he didn't know, he did know that the next person to come through that door would be Mikey.

Tony sat for an hour and a half without moving. He was thinking, planning just what they were going to do, where they were going to go, and how they would start things all over again. He smiled from time to time, thinking that he'd drop Hunter Logan a little line, just to let him know that for the rest of his life he would have to worry about when it would come. It would come. Tony promised himself that. It would come to his wife, and his little girl, and finally, after he'd seen his life torn to pieces and everything he loved destroyed, then and only then would Tony Rizzo gleefully plant three slugs in the back of his head.

Tony heard a car coming up the drive. Moving his head back against the chair, he looked up into the heavy beams of the cabin. He started from his seat when he realized there was a ruckus. Mikey came through the door like a shot and fell splayed out on his face on the wood-plank floor. As if from nowhere, two big, heavy-set men appeared and trained their jet-black automatic weapons on him. Frozen with his arms half raised in the air, Tony heard another car pull up outside and feet crunching on gravel as the newcomers approached the front porch.

When he saw Sal Gamone and Mark Ianuzzo, he smiled warmly and said, "Sal! Mark! I'm glad you came yourselves! This is something that I needed to explain to you myself. Everything will be fine. Don't worry, I'm going to get all your money back. It will be easy for me. I know—"

Sal held his hand up for silence. He glanced at Mike Cometti, who was groveling and crying like a child on the floor. He gave one of his men a puzzled look, and the man ripped off a burst of automatic fire that shook the floor and silenced Mike Cometti for good.

Tony's mouth hung open for a moment, but he quickly regained his composure and held up his hands as if to fend off a friendly blow. "Now, wait—" he began.

"Where's your phone, Tony?" Sal asked politely.

"Here," Tony said, lifting the phone anxiously.

"You dial," Sal said. "I want you to call your uncle."

"My uncle . . ." Tony dialed the number and then held the phone out once again.

"No. You talk," Sal said.

"Hello" came the sad, quiet voice at the other end.

Tony didn't know what to do, but Sal was looking at him expectantly. "Vinny? Vinny, it's me, Tony. Vinny, I just heard . . . I'm sorry . . ."

There was a long silence, then Vincent Mondolffi, Jr., spoke, "Tony, my father treated you like a son for your whole life. You—you'll rot in hell."

"Hey, fuck you!" Tony bellowed, sounding as insulted as he could. He was still hanging on, still trying to squirm and snake his way out. There was always a way out. Tony believed that.

But Sal Gamone snatched the phone from his hand before he could continue his act. "Vinny?" he said gently. "I'm sorry what happened, Vinny. We all loved and respected your father. Mark Ianuzzo and I are here because we want to see justice done. You know as well as anyone that we can't have people doing things like this. This is why we have the council, and we want you to know, as the one who will be taking over your family, that this is how we do things. Now, did you find the guy that did it? Your neighbor got the plate? You already paid him a visit? It was Tony's man? You're sure?"

Sal looked at Tony in disgust as if he actually believed this was the first he'd heard of it. "We didn't want to make a mistake, Vinny, but if you're sure, we're going to make a gift out of this for you. Yes . . . we'll gift-wrap it in the East River."

Sal stepped back as he said those words, and automatic fire hit Tony's lower legs from different angles at the same time, dropping him in his tracks. The rest of his body was riddled with hot lead as he lay there in a spasm of gore.

The shooting stopped, and Tony looked up defiantly at Sal Gamone and Mark Ianuzzo. He focused on them because in his mind they were his equals. From the corner of his eye he saw one of their nameless thugs bend down over his broken body. It wasn't right! Tony's eyes clouded with anger, and he willed these men to acknowledge his greatness. They would have to dirty their own hands if they wanted to put an end to him!

Tony felt a cold barrel of steel pushed up behind his ear, and he screamed in rage as he watched the passive faces of the godfathers for some kind of sign. The gun exploded and his mind spun wildly downward into the blackened depths of an empty soul.

EPILOGUE

Hunter walked alone on the dark beach. Night had only just come, and he could make out a figure in white running toward him. It was Rachel, and she was beautiful, but terror was cut into her face as if it were a permanent part of her moment-to-moment existence.

She was crying. "Hunter! Hunter!"

Her moans came to him through the steady surge of the waves and gave it a surreal quality. He froze in his tracks, knowing without her saying that they had come, that they had finally found his family. He looked past Rachel at their house, which sat like an old ghost, pale and white among a cluster of twisted pines, enclosed in the darkening night. It wasn't a house that he thought of as his own anymore, although inside he knew it was his, and he knew that it was where Sara was . . . with them.

"Where's Sara!" he screamed at the top of his lungs. "Where is Sara!"

The sound of Rachel's voice told him what words could not.

"Hunter! Hunnnt-errrrr!"

It was a death wail.

His insides turned to lead and he began to vomit the viscera of his inner being out onto the wet sand. The sound was itself sickening.

"Hunter!"

"Nooooooo!" he screamed, tearing himself away.

"Hunter!"

Hunter could smell the ocean. A warm breeze wafted in from the open window. Outside, he could see the big trees swaying heavily in the morning breeze. Rachel stood at the bedside with her hand on his arm and a look of concern on her face.

"Hunter?" she said lovingly. "Are you all right?"

He reached up and pulled her close, feeling her warm flesh as if for the first time. "Kiss me," he said softly as he pulled her close to him.

"Is everything OK, Hunter?"

Hunter put his chin on her head and gazed out the window again. "Yes," he said. "I had a dream . . .

"I want to go," he said. "I want to tell him myself."

"OK," Rachel said, gently pulling away and getting to her feet. "Sara's all set. All you have to do is get dressed."

Hunter propped himself up on one elbow. "God, I love you, Rachel," he said.

"I love you, too."

"I'm so sorry . . . you know that," he said.

"I know that, but you don't have to be. It happened, but it wasn't your fault, Hunter. It wasn't."

Hunter nodded, but she knew it would still be some time before he believed her.

"It doesn't matter now anyway," she said with a warm smile. "I'm here. You're here, and Sara. We're all together. That's what matters."

Hunter nodded and almost smiled. "OK," he said, rising from the bed. "I'll throw on some jeans and we'll go."

Sara chattered the entire way. Rachel and Hunter were relieved at how quickly she had recovered from the trauma of the past few weeks. It was as though none of it had ever happened. She had already met once with a psychologist; they all were doing it. Rachel wanted to make sure that everything that was buried would stay buried, a precaution Hunter had readily agreed to. Already the doctor had assured them that Sara would be fine. Hunter didn't worry about Rachel—she was a rock. And himself? He shook his head as he pulled off the highway. He didn't think he deserved to bury it. He wanted to keep it with him, not to torment him, but to remind him. Hunter didn't like making the same kind of mistake twice.

In the daylight he didn't recognize anything, but, as before, he simply followed the blue signs with the large white Hs, and within minutes they were pulling into the parking lot of a brick, single-story building that looked too simple to be a hospital. They were able to park close to the entrance. Not that it mattered, the sun shone brightly and the air was unseasonably warm. Inside, an elderly volunteer in a candy striper's uniform gave them directions. They walked down a long corridor, then another. Outside the door to Cook's room stood two rigid-faced agents in dark suits. They looked at Hunter and his family and stepped aside so they could pass.

A young but overweight doctor was listening to Cook's lungs as they walked in. Natasha and Aunt Esther sat beside each other in chairs backed up against the window on the far side of the room. Natasha smiled shyly and Esther gave a curt nod. Hunter already knew the story of how the old aunt had taken Natasha and disappeared for weeks, making her way slowly and cautiously down to Georgia, where there were people she knew and trusted, the same people whom she knew Cook would contact as soon as he could. He gave the old woman a respectful smile.

The doctor finished his exam and turned to greet his patient's guests. "Well, damn!" Cappy exclaimed, sticking his stethoscope haphazardly into his coat pocket and extending his hand to Hunter. "I'm Dr. Capman, Cappy, really. Cook told me you were coming," he said, his fat red face beaming with true admiration. "Told me that it must have been you who brought him in, but I don't know. It wasn't you, was it?"

Hunter nodded. "Yes, it was me."

"Damn, I could've met you twice," Cappy said, rubbing his nose and stepping aside so that they could see Cook. "Well, it was a pleasure. I have some other patients to see, but I'll try to stop back before you leave. I love to talk to anyone who'll listen about how I saved Agent Cook. He'll be like new in a few weeks. Well, I don't know about new, but all his moving parts will work, and that's a lot considering the shape he was in when you delivered him. He's my Lazarus, back from the dead . . ." Cappy left the room with a wave and a parting salvo of chuckles.

Cook lifted his right hand as much as he could, and Hunter reached out and shook it gently before he introduced his family to

Natasha and Esther. Then he turned to Cook. "My God, Cook," he said. "You made it."

Cook nodded his swollen head slightly and in a soft, raspy voice he said, "Thank you."

Hunter shrugged it off and said, "I should be the one thanking you. Here," he said, taking a folded newspaper that Rachel had been holding for him in her pocketbook.

It was a copy of the *New York Times* metro section from a week ago.

"I know you know about it," Hunter said, "but I didn't know if you had seen the picture. I did. I wouldn't believe it until I did."

The caption above the picture read MAFIA KILLING ESCALATES, BODY FOUND IN EAST RIVER. The picture below was clearly the mangled form that had once been Tony Rizzo. The media had had a field day when Vincent Mondolffi and Tony Rizzo turned up dead within a day of each other. The article also mentioned that the bodies of Angelo Quatrini, William Vantressa, Michael Cometti, and Carl Lutz had been found and were presumed to be victims of the same mob war. There was no mention made of Hunter or Cook or Duncan Fellows. As far as the world was concerned, none of it had ever happened.

"So . . ." Hunter said, "you were right."

Cook nodded slowly and said, "I'm glad for you. You deserve to have your life back."

"So do you," Hunter said, smiling. "In fact, that's one of the reasons I'm here. Remember that senator I told you about? The one I know?"

Cook furrowed his swollen brow, then said, "Yeah, I do."

"Well, I called him as soon as I found out Rizzo was dead. I told him everything, and I told him about you. Well, I'll let you hear it from them, but I wanted to be here when you did."

Hunter picked up the phone on the table next to Cook's bed and began dialing. "Miles Zulaff, please . . . This is Hunter Logan. Thank you . . . Miles? I've got Cook here. No, Senator Ward and I thought it would be better if you told him."

Hunter put the phone up to Cook's ear. Cook slowly raised his hand and held the receiver gently against the good side of his head.

"Hello, sir."

"Cook?" said the FBI assistant director. "They tell me you're going to be all right. I'm glad to hear it. We've cleared everything up, Cook. I'm sorry about the guards that have been there, but, well, we just didn't know what the hell was going on. But let's not talk about all that," Zulaff continued. "We'll have plenty of time for that when you get to Washington. We're going ahead with our special task forces around the country, and the director wants someone who knows the practical difficulties of the field to coordinate our efforts from here. That's you . . . if you want it."

"Yes," Cook said. "Thank you, sir. I look forward to it."

"Great! Well, when you're better and you get back, we've got a lot of work to do . . . Oh, Cook. There is one thing . . ."

"Yes?"

"I got a call this morning from Agent Duffy. He asked if he could be reassigned to your staff here in Washington. I didn't know how you felt about that."

"That would be fine," Cook said.

"Good, well, get well Cook. We need you back."

Cook held out the phone, and Hunter put it back on the hook. Cook's good eye searched out his little Natasha, and they smiled at each other. Then he looked at Hunter. His friend was standing there, also smiling at him, with one arm around Rachel and the other around Sara. Cook thought then that Hunter Logan was a man who had everything. He was right.

ACKNOWLEDGMENTS

Thanks to Syracuse Police Sergeant Michael Kerwin and former Chief of Police Frank Sardino for their insight into the world of gambling and their wonderful stories about the mob. And thanks to FBI Special Agent Art Nearbhaus for his guidance on the inner workings of the FBI and organized crime in New York. I would also like to thank all the people at Turner Publishing for giving so much of themselves to this project, especially my editor, Kevin Mulroy, for his tireless work and unending patience, and my publisher, Michael Reagan, for his guidance, friendship, and belief in me as a writer. And finally, a special thanks to Stu Lisson for his generous support from the beginning.

About the Author

Tim Green, a former defensive end for the Atlanta Falcons, is currently an NFL color analyst for Fox Broadcasting and a weekly commentator on life in the NFL for National Public Radio. He is a recent graduate of Syracuse University Law School and the author of *Ruffians*. Tim Green lives with his wife and three children in upstate New York.